THE PHANTASM CHRONICLES: THE CALL OF THE CARDINAL

Maclellan Moorwood

Cover design by: Klaus Woods

*For Nicholas and Luca, without whose support
this adventure would not be possible.*

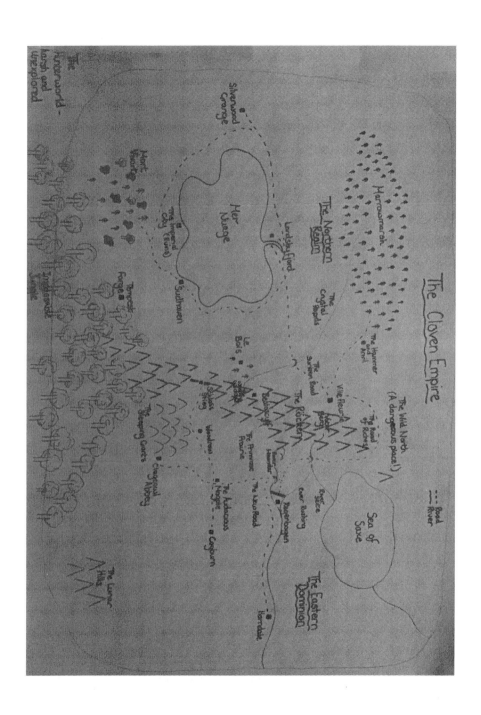

The Cloven Empire

CHAPTER ONE

T he first rays of dawn were still several hours away as the silent figures on horseback rode swiftly away from the sleeping city – retreating shadows, barely noticed save for the muffled, hollow gallop of hooves on the compacted dirt road and the ghostly whipping of their cloaks in the chilling gale.

The night air was unseasonably harsh as it stung the faces of the five riders and tugged persistently at their dark, woollen hoods. It roared incessantly in their ears and was fast becoming the beginnings of a storm: the first uncertain drops of rain were falling from the inky sky and the ominous, iron-grey clouds were promising more.

They kept riding. At length, the small party reached a portion of the road where the land on either side of it rose slightly to create a shallow channel, down which it twisted and turned out of sight. The shelter protected them slightly from the bitter gust and they took a moment to pause for thought.

Alene reached up and lowered her thick hood to better observe her companions. As she did so, she shook a tumbling cascade of tousled, ebony hair out of her rather extraordinary face. Beautiful would be the immediately obvious word to describe her features, but she did not quite meet the necessary criteria for this description: her dark, upturned eyes were tinged around the iris with a crimson glow and they had an intense, shrewd quality to them as if she was never truly at ease; her undeniably long yet elegant nose curved upwards slightly and her usually graceful, pleasant mouth – which was quick to smile and reveal white, perfectly positioned teeth –

was presently set in a worried grimace, a thousand different thoughts and uncertainties racing through her mind as she surveyed the scene before her. Her skin, upon closer inspection, was a muted grey and was mottled with fern-green, one of the few truly obvious indications of her less than ordinary beginnings. The heavy travelling cloak within which she now wrapped herself was hiding ordinary woollen clothing, a stark contrast to the finery she had found herself in of late but a surprisingly comforting reminder of her life before: an affectionate embrace in this tempestuous situation which Alene Idir, Queen Consort of Regenbogen and her Serene Highness of the Eastern Dominion, now found herself.

By now, the rain had begun in earnest. Lightning forks pierced the gloom, allowing Alene brief, momentary glimpses of her friend's taught faces, turned towards her for guidance as thunder rumbled in the distance like colossal drums of war. The young queen raised her face to the heavens; she had the uncomfortably eerie feeling that this did not bode well for the task ahead, not when so much was at stake.

The temporary shelter of the road bank was keeping the worst of the rain from them, which was now blowing almost horizontally and threatened to worsen before the night was over. As another flash of light illuminated the scene around her, Roan came alongside Alene on his mount and lowered his own hood. His youthful face, framed by dripping curtains of sodden, auburn hair, was creased in agitation and clearly betrayed him to be well beyond the border of his comfort zone.

'So, might I be asking what we have in the manner of a plan?' he asked, his trademark cocky and laidback attitude shining through despite being what may as well have been a world away from his fine and luxurious apartments in the castle which they had left behind. Alene had to admire his determination: as courageous, loyal and proficient in combat as Roan undoubtedly was – being the only son of the captain of the castle guard had rubbed off on him in many ways – he was and always had been a creature of comfort. To leave all of that behind, Alene knew, was a monumental step - one which she had to be careful not to understate. Roan was one of her most trusted allies in court life and a true, dedicated friend. She smiled faintly at him and raised her eyebrows; she had not the faintest idea what their plan was to be.

At length, and after careful consideration, she eventually replied. 'We head for the Schloss Stieg,' she announced to the small assembly. 'That's the only safe passage through the mountains which I know of and, since time is of the essence, we can't risk any ill-considered acts of bravery or stupidity by attempting a riskier route. It is absolutely *imperative* that our purpose remain unknown for as long as possible, so discretion is key!' She paused for a moment and then added, 'They *must* be stopped. Too much now depends on us.'

She averted her eyes to the west and could see in the distance the jagged peaks and spires of the Rücken mountain range, imposing silhouettes against the night sky which still lit up suddenly from time to time with every flash of lightning and accompanying crash of thunder. They seemed so distant, and yet their journey would take them even further. Alene took a long, steadying breath as the magnitude of their task washed over her for the first time. Everything up until now had been adrenaline!

She felt a reassuring pressure on her frigid hand as Roan reached over and took it within his own. It was warm – much warmer than hers – and a hint of comfort flickered through her in spite of everything. She found the strength to turn back to him and smiled. He truly was her closest and most trusted friend.

The other riders came forward and removed their hoods. Nox and Griffin were looking grim but determined, whereas Lionel was clearly terrified beneath his shock of thick, sandy hair. Alene had never asked him his age, but she would have guessed that he was of around twelve years. A child. She pitied him and owed him a debt of gratitude: an unusual mixture of emotions that left her quite unsure how to feel. He remained silent and shivering, and it was Nox who spoke.

'We need to leave the road,' she announced. 'Our friend here
–' she gestured to the young Lionel, '– is proof that there are
spies everywhere, and we cannot rule out being followed. I
know this land well; we should make camp in one of the caves
in the foothills of the mountains and formulate a true plan
with the benefit of sleep and breakfast on our side.'

She looked to Alene for approval. Nobody spoke. This was
the way it was to be, she realised. What made her fit to lead?
A crown did not equal the right to be followed, merely the obligation, and Alene had little experience of inspiring others,
regardless of her rank. She took another steadying gasp of cold
night air which was howling its way into their temporary
sanctuary by now and was like daggers of ice on her exposed
face. She made the decision to trust Nox's words. She, after all,
knew these lands better than anyone else she knew.

'Very well,' she spoke to the group, her voice rising over the
wail of the storm. She reached up and replaced her hood, resumed her grip on the reins of her faithful steed, Thane, and
urged him into a gentle trot.

At length, the land levelled and they were robbed of their
shelter. The storm raged around them and tore mercilessly at
their robes and cloaks. Thick rain fell in sheets and the whole
party was soon soaked to the skin, streaming hair clinging to
doused faces and hands numb from the ice-cold deluge, fumbling to pull their sodden cloaks closer around them to fend
off the bite as they hurried on, as fast as they dared in the black
of night. The road was becoming a quagmire and the horses
were slipping dangerously in the vast quantities of mud beneath their hooves. Even so, it was important that they leave
the road behind them as Nox had advised and head into open
country, uphill into the foothills of the mammoth mountain
range to their right. Alene shuddered to think of how the
horses would cope with the change in terrain in this weather,
and how the higher altitude would surely mean harsher conditions to endure. Eventually, Nox led the way off of the

streaming highway and onto the craggy terrain of the road-side.

For an hour or so, they rode on in silence. After a short while, the rain mercifully began to ease and the wind was less deafening than it had been. Alene's eyes, despite being exceptionally sharp, were finding it difficult to negotiate the crevices and hollows in the uneven ground. Too often did she hear the mount of a companion stumble and slip or feel Thane almost lose his footing beneath her.

At length, the sky began to lighten in the south and the weary party was able to use this newfound visibility to traverse a particularly steep incline which led to a rocky plateau. They were now truly in the base of the great range: the Rücken, which ran almost the full length of the lands known to Alene; known to anybody who inhabited the Eastern Dominion. Even Nox had little knowledge of what lay to the south or much further north of either end of the Rücken, and her knowledge of this land was unparalleled.

This plateau was not too large – some of the great shelves of granite and slate higher up were immense! Alene could see the shadowy entrance to a cave across the flat, rugged stretch and it was towards this sanctuary in the cliffside that Nox and Roan headed, dismounting and leading their exhausted horses behind them. Lionel took one, uncertain glance at Alene and then followed, practically swaying with exhaustion as he dismounted and walked slowly away. There was little in the way of vegetation on their lonely outcrop but some sparse wisps of yellow grass and willowing poppies were bravely pushing their way through the cracks in the rocks, glistening in the light of the rising sun with beads of bright raindrops. It was to the grass growing around the cave entrance that the horses flocked as they were loosely tethered beside it: Roan gently nuzzled his own horse and scratched his ears affectionately. They had all earned a rest, and he left them to their meagre feast as he joined Nox and Lionel in the shelter of the cave.

Alene leaned forward and gently whispered words of thanks

and gratitude into Thane's ear. He was her steed, her confidant, a gift of love from her husband, treasured and adored. He pawed the ground restlessly as Griffin rode over and together they turned, looking out over the lowlands through which they had just travelled.

The stars overhead were fading into the dark blue sky as the horizon in the south blazed with pinks, reds and gold. A light breeze had replaced last night's storm and the scents of pine and snow were drifting down from the peaks high above. Distant howls floated down to them from the north as the savage Rücken wolves returned to their domain high in the mountain passes. The River Meander and the River Rushing shone brilliantly in the morning rays as they twisted and turned towards the far-off city of Regenbogen: the City of Rainbows.

Regenbogen castle was a beautiful yet imposing spectacle of colour and majesty. High on a granite spire surrounded by immeasurable expanses of flatlands, the many turrets and towers of the grand fortress commanded a spectacular view over its domain. The cliff sides of the high point upon which it was built were so densely forested with lush, golden-green foliage that they were completely hidden from view to Alene, but she had leisurely strolled and ridden along the steep woodland paths so many times that they were as familiar to her as her husband's face. From the portcullis of the Rainbow Gate at the summit, the spiderweb of trails weaved and wandered in countless directions through peaceful beauty: past gentle, elegant waterfalls and secluded benches carved from the cliff face itself until it reached the town far below. From Alene's vantage point, many uncomfortable miles away on her gusty perch, she could see the small town coming alive in the dawn's first light; see the smoke rising like floating corkscrews from the thatched forges and bakers beginning their morning trade. And although she was in reality much too far away to see, Alene imagined that she was watching the good and kind people of Regenbogen taking to the streets for water from the river to make their breakfasts, tiny ants moving through a toy town in the far-off haven.

Alene was not worried about leaving her home: the town was protected on two sides by the two rivers, one raging and foaming and the other wide, freezing, yet merciful. Regenbogen had been built many hundreds of years before – maybe more, for all Alene knew – on the land where the two rivers joined and the mountainside where the castle resides protected the town below from the east. The only safe entrance to this, the capital city of the Eastern Dominion, was through the Painted Wall, a long stretch of bricks and mortar which ran from river to river, enclosing the town on its only vulnerable side.

It had been through the main gate in this impressive structure that Alene and her company had left, fleeing like spectres into the black of night, only hours before. Looking down on all of this now, the familiar comfort of home, Alene felt an aching longing in her heart. She could almost smell the scent of the morning dew on the leaves as she took her morning stroll down the mountain, the deliciously tempting aroma of bread and pies being prepared in the inns and bakeries. She could see in her mind's eye the intricate, breathtakingly beautiful and awe-inspiring murals and frescos which adorned every outer wall of the castle, from their bases hidden by the canopy of leaves to the battlements high above and blue-tiled roofs of the soaring, circular towers. This vibrant yet imposing artwork also featured on the Painted Wall and was what gave Regenbogen its name.

At this thought, Alene felt another sharp stab of loss: the frescos of Regenbogen were of particular delight to her husband the king, his family being the line to begin this decades-lasting endeavour more than five hundred years before. Recalling his smile when he gazed upon them during their sunset strolls brought a lump to her throat and she desired more than anything to reach out across the gulf between them to wherever he was at this moment, maybe only now waking from a peaceful night's sleep in some far-off palace, oblivious and ignorant to the terrible weight of the events which had been set in motion. She wanted to tell him how much she loved him, to squeeze his hand and brush his cheek with her lips, to whisper in his ear that she would be back, and not to let her absence upon his return from his trip distress him too much, that she would be back by his side, hopefully before too much time had passed.

The iron storm clouds which were still rumbling and flashing with anger were finally disappearing behind the Vater Berg to the north – the tallest and most imposing peak in the entire range. With a deep sigh of acceptance, Alene tore her eyes away from the life she had known for the last ten years, since King Gerecht, her love, had changed her life. She instead turned to the task ahead: a task for which she would require the assistance of her most trusted friends and allies. She dismounted and, with Griffin by her side, led Thane towards the entrance to the chilly cave.

Griffin had remained silent for much of the night. He was the only one of the party who carried no weapons: he was the only person Alene knew who did not need them. His entire self was as deliberate and proficient as any sword, and this was often a comforting reassurance to the calm, contemplative Griffin. As they walked wearily towards their temporary refuge, he finally spoke.

'How do we know he's telling us the whole truth?' His voice was placid, but Alene could tell that this had been playing on his mind, perhaps since before they had fled Regenbogen the previous night. She thought about this. Lionel had brought them world-shattering news, had passed through treacherous terrain and braved hellish creatures of the mountains to reach them. After deliberation, she replied.

'He's not telling us the whole truth – he doesn't know the whole truth, maybe nobody does. The whole truth would terrify him.' She took a steadying breath, then continued. 'However, he told us what we needed to know and we can find out more along the way. The world will one day sing songs of his bravery, maybe even ours if our mission is a success. The Schloss Stieg is a gambit: if we can use it to gain an early lead then we may well be successful yet.' A wry smile crossed her lips and she turned her mottled face, meeting Griffin's golden eyes as she brushed a stray strand of ebony hair from her dark ones. 'The bandits will make for an interesting challenge – they've controlled the castle and the pass for as far back as I can remember, but strategy meetings will wait until after breakfast. And sleep.'

Alene, feeling less like a queen now than she had in many years, tethered Thane with the other horses and, stooping low to avoid the low cave roof, followed Griffin to join the others around the welcoming glow and delicious warmth of the campfire.

CHAPTER TWO

E arly morning slowly gave way to midday as the company of travellers dozed fitfully in their makeshift camp. The serene and calming birdsong of sunrise was steadily replaced by an unsettling sense of quiet and unnerving calm which stretched in all directions and threatened to creep through the opening in the side of the mountain and engulf the sleeping allies. As the sun rose, its rays fell upon the weathered yet radiant face of Nox, crouching just within the safety of the cave's mouth and absent-mindedly prodding the remains of the campfire which she had constructed hastily yet expertly earlier that morning.

Keeping watch. That was her excuse for being awake and away from the safety of her companions, but the truth was that she could barely lie down and force herself to shut her eyes without a bubbling, molten inferno of uncertainty and anxiety erupting inside her. It had threatened to consume her and so here she sat, tracing lines and patterns in the lingering embers and ashes of the fire with a short stick of kindling, acutely aware that she was exhausted and would love nothing more than to drift into a refreshing, dreamless sleep.

The silence bothered her. It was unnatural for this time of day when the mountains usually resonated with the whispers of wind through the long grass and the gentle murmur of snowmelt cascading and tumbling elegantly in silver streams from the high peaks.

Yes, the silence definitely bothered her.

She had spent most of her life, these last twenty years since she was 9 years old, living in the wilderness of The Empire: Northern Realm or Eastern Dominion, it hardly mattered to her. She ranged and she hunted, she spent winters in the towns and sometimes on remote homesteads to avoid the worst of the blizzards. She was more prepared for this journey than any of her fellow travellers, even Alene, and yet she was terrified. She planned to keep that to herself.

Of all those present in this chilly, inconspicuous cave – carpeted with damp moss and swathed with a thick, pearlescent canopy of spiderwebs – Alene was the only one who Nox could even consider a friend. In truth, she had only met Roan once prior to the night before and Griffin and the young Lionel were practical strangers to her. Alene and Nox's friendship stretched back many years, all the way back to when Alene Idir was simply a wandering child, unwanted by her own people, and to when Nox was still known as Jardinia, of the noble house O'Hare.

Nox shook herself mentally. She had cast aside her old life, and it was most certainly the right choice. To think about that now would not help matters, not with a swarm of half-formed ideas and disjointed thoughts already seething in her head. This had however been what led Nox to Alene, a lost and lonely girl, shunned by her family in the elven kingdom of Marrowmarsh for being an abomination, a product of her mother's foolish infatuation with a human high lord. They had been partners for a time, living off the land and working hard in the winters to pay their way in whatever haven they found themselves. In this way, Nox and Alene had forged an unbreakable bond, one which had undeniably been tested when Alene had found herself as Iontach of Regenbogen and Her Serene Highness of the Eastern Dominion, but which had weathered the change and had survived to this day, as Nox knew it would.

Because of this unexpected twist of fate for her friend,

Nox had only seen Alene periodically over the last eleven years, and then only for hours at a time at the most. She simply did not suit the life at court or bustling towns such as Regenbogen, and for these reasons she had repeatedly refused Alene's offers of a more stable life in her new world. That would have been too much like what she had left behind all those years ago in the halls of her father. Nowadays, she only made the journey to the rainbow city to replace her nets which she used for fishing (this being the best place to source the fine silk necessary for this without travelling to Ville Fleurie in the Northern Realm) and to deliver pertinent information to her old friend on the affairs and matters of the wild countryside. It had been just this which had brought Nox to Alene's grand hall the previous night. She had been informing her of some worrying rumours regarding the Rücken wolves when Lionel had been ushered in by Griffin, and the whole night had been thrown into chaos.

Nox thought on that for a moment. She had heard that the wolves of the Rücken mountains had been pressing further and further down the River Meander towards Regenbogen in recent weeks and indeed had heard their haunting howls herself during their flight from the city last night. She had no immediate worries: the wolves would not venture this far down into the feet of the mountains by daylight. Even so, she found her hands searching for reassurance at her belt, where her short sword and axe were carefully secured. She heard stirring behind her and turned to see Griffin sitting up and staring around in groggy confusion, possibly forgetting for one blissful moment where he was and what task he had agreed to undertake. He saw her hunched silhouette in the mouth of the dark cave and rose to join her.

'I'll take over, you sleep,' were his only words to her as he crouched beside her. Short and to the point. Nox studied him for a brief spell, not wanting to be caught looking but curious nonetheless. He had no visible weapons at all, and this unnerved her. Was this wiry, short individual a mage? Could that explain why he appeared unarmed? A master of the arcane would have no need of physical weaponry or protection. Instinctively, Nox shuffled uncomfortably and her insides burned with anxiety. She held a long, deep-rooted mistrust for sorcery of all styles and hoped strongly that she was wrong.

Griffin looked her way and his hard face softened slightly. Had he seen her staring? She thought she had better answer him.

'I don't feel much like sleeping,' she replied, having to simultaneously fight the urge to let out a quaking yawn of exhaustion. 'Besides, the others will be up soon and we really ought to be on the move before long.' This was true enough: the sun had by now passed its highest point and would soon begin its long descent to the horizon in the far-off north. He continued to look at her, almost quizzically, and Nox was inexplicably annoyed. What was his problem? But then she suddenly realised that she had been looking at him mere moments before in the same manner and looked away in embarrassment.

He appeared not to notice. He did not reply either and Nox found the curiosity welling up within. She had always been a solitary person, relying on nobody but herself, but the curiosity welled up regardless. Eventually, she spoke again.

'So, what's your story?' She cringed inwardly: she sounded completely pathetic! She had always prided herself for being tough, brave and self-reliant, and for the most part that was still true. When it came to this stranger sitting beside her though, she felt an unease which she was desperate to rid herself of. He turned back to face her and she saw a flicker of surprise in his eyes. He turned back to look out over the stunning landscape before them. She did the same. At length, he spoke.

'There really isn't much to tell. I'm the stable master

at the palace of Regenbogen and that's how I know Queen Alene and Sir Roan.' He turned back suddenly and fixed her with a penetrating stare, 'Do I bother you?' he asked, rather sharply.

'No, no,' Nox spluttered, thoroughly taken by surprise. 'I'm sorry, I'm not used to being around people. I just wondered what you brought to the table, so to speak. I mean, you have no weapons or...*anything* at all like that which could help in a fight, what use are you to us for the task at hand?' She was aware that the last part was incredibly rude, but it slipped out in a rush of words before she could stem them.

Surprisingly, he smiled his first real smile at her and rose to walk out of the cave. Nox took this smile as a strange invitation and followed him to where the five horses were tethered nearby, pulling long threads of grass from between rocks and drinking icy water from shallow puddles, the only reminder that the previous night had been dank, torrential and downright miserable. He began gently stroking the neck of his own horse in a loving, sentimental way. He turned to her as he did this and smiled again.

'I can tell you don't spend much time with other people,' he said, laughing gently: Nox found that she quite liked the sound and smiled herself. 'I'm quite the same, to be honest with you. Oh, I'm around people plenty enough, but it's the horses who I love. They understand me, and I understand them. You could say that that is one of the things which I, er, '*bring to the table*',' he looked up at her and raised his eyebrows good-naturedly. 'But don't worry, that's not all I'm good for, I have other skills which may prove useful.'

Nox found herself liking this stranger (no, she must begin thinking of him as Griffin! That is his name, after all!) more and more. He was more than what he initially appeared, much like herself, and not at all concerned with what others' views of him might be. She admired that: it was one more thing that they had in common.

'But don't worry,' he suddenly added, still looking at her, 'I am no mage. My path is not the one of sorcery.'

Despite being strong-willed, capable and not caring what others thought of her, Nox could not help but blush a fierce and deep crimson in her usually pale cheeks. Had he read her mind? Was he lying? How else could he know? Or was he just *that* good at reading her, like an open book? He was smirking shrewdly to himself now as he began checking the hooves of each horse in turn, including her own Emmet. She brushed a strand of chestnut-coloured hair out of her emerald eyes and cleared her throat nervously.

'I...why would you...I never mentioned...good,' she finished awkwardly. 'I'm glad.' She decided, against her usually solitary attitude, to trust him and added, 'I don't really talk about it, you see, but I'm not really particularly trusting of...magic.'

Griffin looked at her directly, neither smiling nor frowning, simply an earnest look of friendship and said, 'I can keep a secret.'

He walked back into the mouth of the cave and disappeared in the gloom within. Nox smiled faintly and followed.

The others were rousing, so Nox went to Alene's side and bent low over her, whispering in her ear, 'We need to talk. All of us.'

Alene was still groggy from sleep but nodded in agreement, and so when all were up, stretched and as alert as they could be, they strolled out into the sunlight and towards the edge of their rocky outcrop. Once there, they sat in a row on the edge, legs dangling limply into the nothingness of open air.

Despite being relatively low down in the great range of mountains which completely bisected The Empire, the known world to all present, they were still high enough up to command a stunningly breathtaking view of the land below for miles around. The only civilisation within sight was the far-off city from which they had slipped, like thieves in the night, under cover of darkness hours before: Regenbogen. It was a far cry from a shadowy fortress now, however. The many bright and beautiful frescos and murals which embellished every surface of the palace and city wall were shining like beacons across the expanse between them. Nox glanced sideways at Alene. The splendour of her home, so near and yet so very far away, must surely be causing her great pain: a siren call and a cold dagger of self-refusal all in one. She herself was glad, as she often was, that she called no permanent dwelling home, so as never to be torn from it. She could not deny the beauty of the rainbow city though: its effect was mesmerising.

Nox wondered if she regretted visiting the city with her news of wolf pack behaviour. If she had not, she would not be in this sorry situation and would be free to pursue her own ends. However, that would then leave Alene without her support in the coming hardships, and Nox was under no uncertainty that Alene would always do what was right, with help from her friends or without. So no, she was not sad she had been present in the Grand Hall last night. She would be there for her friend, until the very end.

This view also meant one very important thing and was a key factor in her suggesting this location for a camp the previous night during that horrific storm: they could easily look out over the edge and see any living things below: specifically, anybody on horseback who may be out looking for them or, even worse, following them. Nox was paranoid by nature but had yet to find herself in any situation where this could be considered a disadvantage. She had the distinct impression that Alene's absence at court would be noticed, possibly by the wrong people, and she wanted to be prepared for this eventuality. She was not knowledgeable enough of the comings and goings of the various nobles and gentry in the palace, let alone those of the hundreds of servants, cooks, gardeners, maids and guards who worked there, to even begin to suspect any wrongdoings or treachery, but she suspected nonetheless.

'So,' began Roan hesitantly with a valiant attempt of casual airiness, but not quite managing the effect in his languid and dazed state. 'If I'm going to be completely honest with you all, I'm still not entirely certain what our plan actually is. I mean, I get it, I was there last night just like you all were. I heard what he had to say,' he said, gesturing at Lionel, who was sitting nervously at the end of the line-up, staring blankly out into the void and shifting uncomfortably at the mention of him. Roan continued, 'I felt the tension in that room, I get that this is a big deal – goodness knows I wouldn't be here if I didn't know that. But what we're actually going to do about it…that's what I'd like to know.'

Roan let the question hang in the uncertain silence as Nox's mind's eye transported her back to the Grand Hall in the royal palace, shadows of the midnight hour melding spectrally with flickering torchlight to create an illusionary effect. It had been as though every dark corner and under every bench in the vast, yawning expanse of space within the colossal hall, as well as the impenetrable blackness of the distant, vaulted ceiling, was crawling with menace and teeming with unseen dangers. The atmosphere had certainly supported this – Roan was right: the tension had been electric as Griffin came dashing through the painted oak double doors, the newly arrived Lionel at his heels.

Their new arrival was shivering uncontrollably, flushed a blotchy red from the frigid howl of the night gale outside and the hem of his travelling cloak and doeskin breeches soaked through from deep snow. Nox had known then that something serious was afoot: why would a young, terrified-looking boy arrive in the dead of night, and where had he travelled from in order to have trudged through such snow-drifts? He must, she knew, have been on one of the higher mountain passes, where snow remained all year round, but then that would suggest he had travelled from the Northern Realm. And that, more than anything else, spelled trouble!

The Northern Realm, where Queen Rowena reigned from her chateau of Ville Fleurie, had been engaged in an uneasy and tense alliance with the Eastern Dominion for many hundreds of years. This truce dated all the way back to the fracturing of The Empire, when the two kingdoms had risen from its ashes.

The Rücken acted as a natural, formidable boundary between them and was almost impassable without traversing certain high passes, little known to most and beyond the capabilities of many. Traders and travellers almost universally moved between kingdoms by riding into the distant north and along the chilly beaches of Saxe, the vast inland sea. Via this route, they could loop around the farthest reaches of the range and enter the Realm on relatively low land. This had one key danger, however: by travelling along the coasts of Saxe, these travellers put themselves at the mercy of the Goblin Hordes who camped along the shores. Yet people still made the journey. That was a testament to the terrifying reputation of the Rücken.

This young, freezing boy had braved the heights, though. Nox was immediately interested and moved forwards from the shadows to join the small group huddled around the firepit where the boy was desperately attempting to warm his numb hands, holding them as close to the flames as he could without burning them. She had been close to departure, not wishing to linger after delivering her news, but resolved to stay until her curiosity had been satisfied.

Alene was stood opposite her on the other side of the fire. Her form was obscured by smoke and she appeared to be dancing in the flames as they flickered and licked higher in the gloom. She was anxious for news of her husband, King Gerecht, who had been travelling now with his chief minister, Saggion, and a host of other high-ranking lords for nearly three months. The entirety of the Eastern Dominion was his kingdom, and it was the responsibility of Gerecht, of the royal house Künstler, to rule it all personally by visiting every town, city and temple on a grand tour. Alene had not heard from him for two weeks now, and the worry was clear on her face.

Nox, Roan, Alene and Griffin had listened to Lionel as he delivered his chilling message, apparently from the depths of Ville Fleurie itself: Queen Rowena had discovered the identity of the new Cardinal Phantasm, and that stunning revelation sent a shock of dawning dread through all those present. From there, a whirlwind of panic had erupted and the five had ridden out within the hour. Each one had been exhausted, Lionel most of all, but Alene had insisted that all who knew the news must accompany her. Nox felt that this was probably a wise decision – any and every one of them would be a target, knowing what they knew. Nox also, true to her untrusting nature, worried that one of the others may betray this knowledge to another party if left behind, and they could not allow that.

Back on their rocky overlook, in the pleasant warmth of the afternoon sun, Nox finally answered Roan's question.

'The new Cardinal Phantasm has emerged,' she reminded him ominously. 'There really is only one avenue open to us if we wish to avoid catastrophe!'

'Indeed,' interjected Alene, sighing with exhaustion and agitation. 'Gerecht has always insisted that the discovery of the new Cardinal would set the scene for a chaotic scramble for power. He has often told me that, in such a situation, somebody would need to take drastic steps, and I believe that he always intended to be the one to make such a play – to acquire the Cardinal Phantasm himself in order to keep it from those who would use it for evil. But now... it's finally happened...and Gerecht is nowhere to be found, off on his royal tour with Saggion and much of the court... and we've got to do it instead...'

Her voice trailed off, the uncertainty and worry as clear as the bluebell sky above their heads – and yet a plainer juxtaposition was not possible for how they each were feeling in their hearts. In truth, a dark shadow was passing over them all and they were each waiting to hold their breaths, waiting until the last possible second, before the ice-cold wave of pandemonium crashed over and engulfed them, washing away the lives they knew forever.

Nox knew that Alene was right. She turned to look at her but caught Griffin's eye instead. He nodded grimly as he met her gaze and she knew he agreed too.

'But that...' began Roan, evidently attempting to process what he had just heard, 'that's going to be close to impossible! Granted, we know where the new phantasm is. I suppose we could *theoretically* get there before Rowena's forces and spirit it away to safety. But that's a big 'theoretically', and we are many, many day's ride away from even entering the Northern Realm. They're sure to get there first.' Nox could not help but roll her eyes; was he always this pessimistic? He made her own demeanour seem positively radiant with positivity.

Alene suddenly scowled at Roan. 'We can't make assumptions. Queen Rowena might have no interest whatsoever in misusing the power of the Cardinal, we need to approach this with facts, not prejudice.'

'Oh, come on,' Roan shot back sceptically. 'She's an enemy of Regenbogen and everybody who calls the Dominion their home. There may be an alliance officially, but she still sits on her throne in Ville Fleurie and acts in the best interests of *her* kingdom, at the exclusion of all others. Why *wouldn't* she want the power which the phantasm would give her? Besides, *he* has already told us that the queen wants it and will do what she needs to get it.' He was gesturing at Lionel, apparently expecting this to justify his view.

Nobody seemed to have an answer to this, and so the

uncertain silence stretched on for a while longer. Then, as quiet as a mouse and as unexpected as anything which had happened so far that day, Lionel apprehensively cleared his throat at the end of the line and spoke timidly. It was the first time Nox had heard him speak since last night, and his voice was meek and shy.

'Ville Fleurie is definitely moving against Regenbogen and the Dominion, possibly against more than that. A team was dispatched to secure the cardinal phantasm, hours before I set off on my mission to reach you. I know all of this…it's all true, but…why is it so important? Why was it so important that I risk my life to reach you in time with my message? What is a phantasm anyway?' His voice grew in confidence as he spoke, as though his worries were being drawn out of him like poison from an infected injury. His conviction shone through: he was absolutely resolute in his statement about Ville Fleurie, the City of Blossoms and the capital of the Northern Realm, that forces within were making plays for the phantasm. Alene was looking less certain, and so Nox stood and began pacing, considering what to say before answering.

'In truth, no living being can be a phantasm, they can merely play host to one. A phantasm is a creature of pure power and wisdom unknown and misunderstood by most scholars and mages of this world. They hail from another plain, no one knows where specifically. Each phantasm is infinite and everlasting, transferring to another newborn mortal being upon the death of its host and lying dormant until the new vessel reaches adolescence. Upon the onset of puberty, certain tell-tale signs emerge which expose it for what it is – the host of a mighty and complex spirit that benefits from increased vitality, reflexes, senses and other properties as a reward for allowing a parasitic creature to live within it. In truth, of course, they have no choice, but they never really mind. Who would?'

She realised that she had been studying the uneven rock

beneath her feet as she paced. She looked up and saw Griffin twisted around where he sat, blinking at her in amazement. Even Roan seemed mildly impressed with the extent of her knowledge. Lionel was silent once more, yet stared intently at her with rapt amazement. Only Alene remained unmoved, continuing her sad lookout over their deserted vista.

'Alright, colour me impressed,' said Roan, standing up also and wandering leisurely over to where the horses stood. He continued, raising his voice slightly to be heard as he walked further away, and removed his weapon and oilcloth from the small pile within the entrance to their cave. Nox was astounded that any man in such a situation as theirs could leave his weapon in any other place but by his side at all times. Her own weapons, *Near* the short sword and *Far* the woodcutter's axe, were secured safely at her hip and remained there at all times. This was a man, Nox knew, who had never been truly in the wild in his life and had no true idea what the meaning of a weapon was. She highly doubted he could even shoot. He returned to the cliffside and sat back down, unwrapping his weapon from the brown suede cloth it was wrapped in.

Nox was stunned by what lay within the folds of the cloth: it was a bow, but unlike any she had ever seen before. The limbs appeared to be made of razor-sharp, elegantly curved iron and the string appeared to be simply hooked into the notch at either end – almost in a temporary fashion. Nox was surprised that such a design could function effectively but was snapped back into the situation at hand by the realisation that each of her companions were staring directly at her. Roan himself was smirking knowingly, no doubt noticing her glances of sceptical awe towards his beautifully crafted weapon, gleaming in the afternoon sun. She realised that she had completely missed what must have been another question, and merely smiled apologetically as her gaze returned to the ground.

She heard Roan ask, for what was evidently the second time, 'As I said, I'm sufficiently impressed with your encyclopaedic knowledge of phantasms, but how do you know all of this, and why is this case any different from any other phantasm? What's so special?'

Nox chose to answer his second question first. 'This case is different than any other because this is no ordinary phantasm, it is the re-emergence of the Cardinal Phantasm, the strongest of its kind and revered by all of the other phantasms as their leader. The Cardinal has been unaccounted for since the death of its prior host, almost fourteen years ago, but marks of this grand and empiric creature have recently, if our sources are to be believed,' (a sideways glance at Lionel confirmed that he had returned to avoiding everyone's gaze, his newfound confidence burning out as quickly as it had ignited), 'been reported on an adolescent boy living in the Northern Realm, in its most southern reaches in the swamps of Mort Vivant. This we all know, but what you do not know is that this boy has just unwittingly revealed himself to be one of the most uniquely powerful and supremely prophetic individuals in The Empire, perhaps even beyond our known world. His mastery over the fabric of matter and the mysteries of what has not yet occurred is without bound, and this almost limitless power is in the hands of an impressionable young boy, scared witless by what he is suddenly capable of and yet incapable of stopping those who would use his power for their own ends. Gerecht was correct when he told Alene that this discovery of the new vessel of the Cardinal Phantasm would result in a scramble for power, a mad rush to reach him before anybody else and manipulate him into bringing about their desires and fulfilling their wishes.'

She paused for a moment, then continued, addressing Roan's initial question. 'I know all of this,' she said with a weary sigh, 'because I have had the dubious pleasure of meeting two phantasms before now. Only regular ones, mind you, or as regular as an otherworldly spirit occupying a person can be. One of them was an old travelling companion of mine, before I met Alene. He taught me everything I know about the hidden corners and forgotten valleys of The Empire, but he was killed by bandits. Ironically, for all of his vitality and wisdom, he still died in the mud, sprawled across the road with his throat slit. Because that's important!' she suddenly added, looking back up at them, 'A phantasm host is just as mortal as any man or woman, even that of the Cardinal. This boy can be killed, and many people would be of the opinion that this would be a necessary, even preferential approach to thwart others in their quest to acquire him.'

Roan had finally grown silent, choosing instead to oil the sharp, iron limbs of his bow with a black cloth. Griffin stood and announced that he was going to ready the horses for a departure within the hour, taking Lionel with him to clear the cave of belongings and evidence of their stay. Alene made towards the gentler decline below them, apparently to scout for a safer way down than what they had used the previous night to ascend, but Nox grabbed her arm and pulled her quietly aside.

'What I don't understand,' she whispered urgently, before the others returned, 'is why *specifically* anyone covets the power of the Cardinal. Yes, yes – the power and the potential devastation that this could mean in a possible war between the Realm and the Dominion, I understand that, but something tells me that the stakes are much higher than that, if King Gerecht has been expecting this for years. War can happen any time, and probably will one day, but this is more…and you know it, don't you?'

She looked Alene straight in the eye, shrewdly searching for a flash of truth. Alene looked directly back, breathed deep, and answered.

'Gerecht told me the legacy of the Old Phantasm, the mortal who held the Cardinal until his death fourteen years ago. He was older than any other individual had been known to have lived since the time of The Empire, and he achieved this age by officially refusing to ever allow his powers to be used for the gain of others, even on threat of death. Because of this, he was confined in Ville Fleurie and left to live out his life in captivity.' Alene paused to brush her long, raven hair out of her face and continued in a more hurried rush, 'There was one thing he refused to do above everything else, and that was to alter a certain prophecy, made centuries before, which he believed the editing of would lead to certain death, to the destruction of all and the wasting of the very fabric which holds our world together. Gerecht believed that the arrival of a new Cardinal on the scene would lead to many wishing to coerce this prophecy from him, persuading him to rewrite it and allowing them to gain immense power. I promise, Nox, that this is everything I know, everything Gerecht told me and I regret not telling you sooner. Despite that, this is something which we must, for now, keep strictly to ourselves. The stakes cannot be so high for the others, the pressure would overwhelm them.'

She turned suddenly and stalked away. Nox took a few moments to absorb this new information. It was patchy at best, and if their mission were to be a success, they would need more solid facts, and soon!

As she mounted Emmet a few minutes later and began the slow, treacherous descent down the mountainside, she found herself feeling slightly ashamed for her friend: as much as she loved and trusted Alene, and could not begin to appreciate the burden which ruling as queen must have placed on her shoulders, she believed her to be inherently wrong about not divulging this knowledge to the other travellers. They had made the decision to accompany her at a mere moment's notice, and Nox felt that this spoke of strong morals – surely they had earned her respect and trust enough to be told the whole story? But then, Nox reflected somewhat gratefully, that was not her responsibility to decide. Heavy must indeed be a head that wears a crown.

CHAPTER THREE

The descent into the lower, rolling plains went much smoother than expected, Alene reflected, as they galloped in single file across lush grassland towards the distant sight of the Primrose Bridge, an ancient stone structure which spanned the River Meander and was, crucially for Alene's party, little used by most inhabitants of the Dominion. As welcoming as the sight of a friendly face would surely be to Alene, they could little afford to be recognised at a time like this. A complex concoction of feelings swelled in Alene's heart: she was travelling further away from where her heart lay in Regenbogen and yet she desperately wished to be as far away from her city as possible, for only then would she be able to truly blend in and disappear into the common folk.

Alene blinked in surprise at her own thoughts. In truth, it was not for Regenbogen that she felt pain in departing: that was undeniably for the familiarity of somewhere, anywhere, where she felt she belonged. And she had never let herself think of others as 'common folk' before. She herself was from the very fringes of society, shunned by her true people because of the folly of her mother, and she must not let herself forget that! But, regardless of all of this, she was still one of the most widely recognised faces within the Dominion and she could not risk being recognised.

She wondered if she would feel such sadness at having to leave her old home, if her life had gone differently and she had received a traditional elven upbringing in the depths of the forested realm of Marrowmarsh. She would have been well versed in the magic of her race and would have never even glimpsed the majesty of Regenbogen. As it was, her only heir-loom from her past life was her mottled slate and fern skin which merely served to make her even more distinctive and she had precious few memories of Marrowmarsh. She seemed to recall its outer edges where she had been abandoned, a mere child, scared and alone. She remembered a putrid and foul swamp with thin, twisted trees, bare and pale white, growing from the dank water. They had looked like finger bones, grasp-ing and clawing at the tangled overgrowth of vines above. She learned later that it was from these trees which humans derived their name for this realm: the marsh of bones, or Mar-rowmarsh.

Regardless of how she might have felt, she would never truly know. She had no inclination whatsoever to return to her ancestral home and what memories she did possess were poisoned by pain and betrayal. That stagnant and gloomy air of decay which she remembered could not be in any sharper contrast to Alene's current surroundings, and that filled her surprisingly with delight. The afternoon air was cool and re-freshing and she could hear the gentle, lazy journey of the River Meander ahead of them.

For once, she was not leading the way and was grateful for the respite in command. Roan and Griffin rode ahead, the former's long, auburn hair streaming brilliantly behind him and contrasting sharply with the cropped, dark-haired head of the latter. They both reached the bridge up ahead and slowed to a stop, turning and waiting for their slower companions.

Lionel caught up with them first, decidedly having taken a central position in the proceedings. This was the safest place for him, Alene knew. She herself came next, and Nox brought up the rear, perpetually guarding and on the alert for signs that they were being followed.

The river was slow and gentle, yet wide and deep. As such, the old, narrow bridge spanned a great distance and was in re-markably good condition, considering its age. Nevertheless, Griffin dismounted and began to lead his horse across on foot, looking her straight in the eye and walking slowly backwards whilst stroking her mane reassuringly. Alene considered this to be slightly melodramatic: it was a risky crossing, assuredly, but perfectly attainable with a degree of caution. Alene also stopped herself from contemplating the further dangers which undoubtedly awaited them on their journey, and what situations the poor steeds may still find themselves. Despite this, Alene was touched that Griffin took such care for the feelings and wellbeing of other animals. It was, of course, for this reason that he was an amazing stable master at Regenbogen.

Alene and the others followed his lead, albeit without the same doubtfully necessary caution. Alene stopped midway across as her gaze passed over the great central stone that made up part of the walkway which the others had just crossed over. In it, weathered and worn with age and the hundreds of feet which had passed over it for centuries, was a short inscription. Part of it was unintelligible, lost to the infinite mysteries of time. Other parts were obscured by dark green moss, and this more than anything revealed to Alene how little this bridge was actually used. Seized by a sudden curiosity, she stooped low and brushed the moss aside, the stone surface of the bridge slimy and damp underneath where it had been. She used her fingernail to scrape the mud out of the last few etched letters and could finally read most of the inscription. The top half, presumably a dedication to the builder, was gone forever, but the part which had remained covered for all of these years was readable in its entirety:

The Primrose Bridge is hereby dedicated to the life and vitality of our beloved Emperor, Peter II, and that of his line. Long may their Imperial Majesties reign over us.

Alene was stunned. She could feel Nox's impatience behind her, so she straightened up and continued to the other side. So, the Primrose bridge had been built in the time of The Empire. She had never had any reason to cross it before, yet had not supposed it to hold such a secret, a window into a history almost forgotten and rarely spoken of in the Eastern Dominion nor, as far as she could tell, in the Northern Realm either.

The Cloven Empire, as the history books referred to it, was once the dominant power in the known world, to such an extent that people still used 'Empire' to refer to the traversable world as a whole today. It had been created by uniting two culturally diverse lands over two thousand years ago and had flourished for more than a millennium before war caused it to fracture back into those original two kingdoms again, slightly less than six hundred years ago. These two kingdoms were the Eastern Dominion and the Northern Realm, and a tentative alliance had maintained peace and trade ever since, constantly threatening to spill over into conflict should the right conditions emerge.

Alene was not surprised that The Empire had ultimately been unsuccessful. The presence of the formidable and impenetrable Rücken range between its two main lands, hence the name 'Cloven Empire', effectively split it in two. A common language was shared between the Dominion and the Realm, but little else was able to be shared efficiently and proved too great of a barrier for The Empire to overcome in times of war. Since then, in the centuries between the fall of the last emperor and today, both the Dominion and the Realm had undergone extensive work to their cultures and infrastructures, almost with the goal in mind of eradicating any memory of their shameful beginnings as the ashes of a great regime. This forgotten gem in the wilds of the world reminded Alene that, despite the severity of the situation which they were in, and despite the Realm being on the opposite side of a potentially catastrophic race for the Cardinal Phantasm, the Dominion and the Realm had a lot in common and that maybe there could still be a peaceful solution to everything. She hoped with every breath that this was possible.

The Primrose Bridge was situated much further upriver on the Meander than the bridge commonly used by the people of Regenbogen: the 'new' bridge, as it was colloquially known, and was in much wilder and uncertain terrain. Despite this, it was still used infrequently by rangers and travellers who sought a more solitary path. They were still in the shadows of the Rücken and, with twilight approaching within the next few hours, this was a concern.

Nox appeared to be having similar thoughts. She was cautious by nature, Alene knew, but she seemed to be casting a wary eye to the craggy slopes more than ever. Alene followed her gaze: past green, lush lower foothills; over harsh, iron-grey cliffs and sheer drops and finally coming to rest – high, high above their position and dwarfing the world around them – atop snow-capped peaks and treacherous, hellish passes through the range which only the most foolhardy or desperate would ever attempt. Alene lowered her gaze to her companions, remounting their horses and restless to continue, and reflected with a resolute shake of her head that, even in their unenviable situation as potential saviours of the entire world, she would never gamble with their lives by making such a rash and reckless crossing.

As they continued, Nox rode alongside her and they both slowed to a gentle trot. Her old friend spoke quickly and to the point, 'We need to be away from the mountains before nightfall, I'm sure the wolves'll be descending soon and, if their recent activity can be used as any indicator, they're coming further and further down every night. We won't be safe here, so what's our next move?'

This assumption that she would immediately have a plan at her fingertips annoyed Alene slightly and she frowned. Why must it be her? She was a queen, not a ranger. Not anymore, at any rate. Regardless, it fell to her to rule and so she divulged the plan which she had indeed been working on feverishly in her head since the previous night, a veritable hornet's nest of activity buzzing beneath her temple and causing her severe anxiety and self-doubt.

'We need to head further into the Primrose Prairie,' she replied to Nox, referring to the expansive, rippling sea of grasslands which stretched out before them as far as one could see, hugging the feet of the mountains to the north-west and their right side and retreating eternally over the horizon to their left until it reached the New Road. This road was often travelled by traders, casual travellers and, most dangerously of all to the small party, Dominion soldiers and guards who patrolled and enforced law across the kingdom. These elite units would be sure to stop a band of hooded travellers roaming the kingdom in the dead of night and, upon inspection, would certainly recognise her as the wife and love of their sovereign king.

The New Road stretched all the way from Regenbogen, across the New Bridge, and continued south until it split: one branch took the traveller east to Cogburn, the largest city of the Dominion and the industrial epicentre of the kingdom. Another route led directly south and terminated in the chilly and misty ruins of Clagcowl Abbey. Yet another path led south-west across the Primrose Prairie and twisted through small farming villages and ranches until it reached the Schloss Stieg, a formidable shell of an ancient and imposing fortress, dark and rotten at its core and ravaged mercilessly for centuries by the ruthless weather which results from its location in a narrow, natural gap in the vast Rücken range.

The Schloss had been built by The Empire at the height of its power and was originally designed to provide luxurious respite for the emperors who would often make grand tours of the entire Empire, this location being the only safe passage without travelling many miles to the north. When the last emperor fell and his Empire split in two along the mountains, however, the treaty forged between the newly created Northern Realm and the Eastern Dominion forbade either kingdom from garrisoning the Schloss Stieg, as this would provide a clear dominance over the pass. As such, the castle was left to fall into ruin and in recent years had been seized by a strong coalition of bandit clans. This had, so far, gone unchallenged by either kingdom due to the sad truth that, with the pass guarded by an unsavoury yet neutral party, all involved felt more separated and therefore more protected from their uneasy allies. The only negative ramification of this was that it greatly complicated the role which traders played in The Empire, having to make the arduous and risky journey north along the shores of Saxe and contend with the goblins residing there in order to reach Ville Fleurie and return. This they did; after all, their trade made them richer than lords, and goblins were preferable to bandits when ferrying your weight in diamonds, spices and urns of precious oil on the back of a horse-drawn cart!

These traders would no doubt also be travelling like an army of ants up and down the New Road – this, of course, being the primary purpose for it being constructed at the formation of the Dominion. Alene was determined to avoid it, even if it did provide her with a direct path to the Schloss Stieg. They would, therefore, need to travel immediately south from their current position, across the Primrose Prairie, keeping the Rücken and the wolves at a safe distance to their right and the New Road, with the very real threat of discovery and exposure, at an even safer distance to their left, out of sight over the eastern horizon. Besides, Alene reflected, remaining off the beaten track would make it more difficult for them to be followed. She smirked to herself: Nox's cautiousness was rubbing off on her. She had a feeling that she would be glad of it before too long.

Roan, Griffin and Lionel had noticed that they had slowed down and made a wide, looping turn and returned to hear the plan. Roan's response was predictable. 'Let's go then!' he replied with ridiculous enthusiasm. 'We can make good progress by dusk and make even more if we keep travelling through the night.'

'I'm not so sure of that,' replied Griffin with a sigh. 'The prairies are known to be extremely fertile lands and are set-tled by farmers scattered across the plains. They often bring their wares to Regenbogen to make a sale and always pass through the town stables. I've heard them say many times that the rich, fertile land can sometimes be boggy and danger-ous to those who don't know their way. Men have sunk and drowned before, apparently. Cover of darkness might be more of a curse than a blessing.'

'But,' shot back Roan, still smiling with child-like roguish-ness, 'even I, pampered and unaccustomed as I am to the ways of the wild, have heard tales and myths of the strange and wonderful beasts which occupy the wider world beyond the Painted Wall. I also know that many of these beasts, particu-larly the, ahem, *larger* variety, call these serene and beautiful grasslands their home. Surely, given this rather crucial infor-mation, travelling at night would be safer so as to avoid these terrifying creatures.' He spoke the last part with ill-disguised amusement and mock fear, evidently wishing to leave it in no uncertain terms to the gathering that he was more than pre-pared to face off against any creatures which may cross his path on their perilous journey. He did, however, make a good point.

Roan was one of the most well-read and informed people who Alene had ever met. He had spent his childhood before she knew him training with his rather unique weapon, *Reaper*, all day with Captain Felix, his father and captain of the palace guard, spent his evenings in the castle library reading every available tome on every possible topic and spent every night after dark roaming the deserted corridors, slinking and prowl-ing like a black cat between the shadows and listening at key-holes of bedchambers and skulking just out of sight. By the age of fifteen, he could move so silently and swiftly that he could, almost leisurely, pick the pocket of one of his father's men and they would never know about it. Only Alene knew this secret, of course, but this detailed depiction of her best friend allowed her an insider's certainty: if Roan spoke of dangerous beasts on the prairies, it was sure to be true. She had to hide a smile, however, as she sat astride Thane, watching the familiar, fun-loving nature of Roan Felix re-emerge: he was a capable, smart and sensible man, a good friend who was strong of muscle and of heart, even if his often flippant and facetious attitude belied this.

The group turned to Nox for more context. She, after all, was the expert. However, they were all disappointed when she replied, eyes still flicking from the bridge behind them to the mountains towering above, 'My knowledge will be of little value if we choose to directly cross the Primrose Prairie. I know the farm road well, the road which leaves the New Road and leads west to the Schloss, but I wouldn't recommend that path if we wish to remain inconspicuous. I've always avoided the prairies themselves: nobody has ever given me a kind word in their favour. Dangerous and already well-populated – they hold no allure for my exploratory tendencies.

'However,' she continued, 'this is definitely the most direct route and the safest if we wish to avoid being seen. I would vote for a daytime crossing – we would have better chances of countering any dangers we may encounter if we can see it well.'

They all agreed, some begrudgingly, that this was sage advice. And so, with mere hours of sunlight remaining to them that day, they continued at top speed, making haste while they could. Alene's feelings of apprehension were beginning to ebb away now that they had a clear plan for the next couple of days. If they continued at this rate, Alene estimated they would approach the Schloss Stieg in a little under four days. She only hoped that this would be fast enough.

These musings were punctuated by thoughts of Gerecht, her beloved husband. Where would he be now? Somewhere on his royal tour, she supposed, but she would have given anything for more detail, a scrap of information which would allow her to picture him, safe and sound, possibly in a palace or castle belonging to one of the high lords or ladies whom he visited when undertaking his tours. It was an important part of his responsibility as king, his royal duty to maintain strong links with every portion of his kingdom and to ensure that all of the regional rulers followed his rule. At least there was one thing which Alene could be grateful for in this respect: Gerecht travelled with Saggion, his chief minister and trusted advisor, and there was no other man whom Alene trusted to keep her husband safe and in a politically stable situation. This was his job, after all, and she knew that he would risk his life to ensure that his king remained strong, in control and, above all else, informed of the comings and goings of his wider kingdom. She would have loved to imagine him, even now, approaching Gerecht and telling him of the perilous yet necessary journey which his wife and queen had undertaken in his name, and the name of the whole Dominion, possibly even the whole world, yet she knew that this was foolish. If Saggion were able to inform Gerecht of this, it would mean that they had been unsuccessful in their mission to remain inconspicuous and undetected. She had considered sending a message to Gerecht to inform him herself, but the thought was ludicrously reckless. No, she could not risk it, even for her love.

Saggion was definitely better for knowing well. He was the classic aged advisor, old and cantankerous, yet impossible not to warm to when he began to tell his stories of exploits long ago and offer wise counsel when you were in need of comfort. He was like a father to Gerecht and had become similarly so to her, since that fateful day many years ago when she had met her future husband...

Gerecht was altogether different: tall, strong and bold in her mind's eye with a cloth-of-gold cape and flowing robes of rainbow silk velvet, embroidered with gold and, often when the weather turned colder, lined with ermine. In reality, however, Alene knew that this was her image of the man she loved in imagination only: he was actually rather small and frail, sickly from a young age but with a sense of duty and loyalty to his kingdom unparalleled by any other within living memory.

The common people, when using his full title, called him 'His Resplendent Majesty', a clear sign of the love which they held for him, and he for them. This was just one of the faces which Alene loved: there was Gerecht the king, Gerecht the philanthropist who ensured poverty remained low and cared for his people, and Gerecht the husband. Her true love, whom Alene would walk through hellish flames to reach and save from war and destruction.

Before long, the sun had begun to set behind them in the north and the sky came alive with a glory of brilliant yellows, fiery oranges mixed with bronze and, eventually, a passionate scarlet which cast the rolling grasslands before them into shadow, forcing them to make camp. By now, they were far away from the mountains, yet they remained an ever-present behemoth crouched over them in the west. As such, there was no natural cover with which to set a camp. Reassuringly though, Nox announced that the night was to be a dry one, and so they were not too worried about sleeping without cover. Alene's mind did flicker occasionally whilst building a fire to the beasts and creatures roaming the prairie which Roan had spoken of, but she trusted her friends and their judgements. Better to remain and defend together than wander blindly into further danger.

She looked around her in the dying light of the sunset and the flickering first breaths of her small fire to see what everybody else was doing. Roan was nowhere to be seen, supposedly stalking some poor, unsuspecting beast with *Reaper* for their evening meal. Griffin was tending lovingly to the horses, including Thane who was clearly relishing the attention and was tossing his fiery mane in delight as Griffin brushed the tangles out of his auburn tail and stroked his gleaming, rose-grey flank and shoulders with a tender hand. Alene knew that Griffin would do this for all of the horses, before coming back to brush the dry mud from their legs later.

Nox had settled some distance away and was tending to her axe, apparently designating herself as the first to go on watch.

Alene was sorry that Nox had become embroiled in this situation: she knew that she had a deep mistrust, and even fear, of anything relating to sorcery or the arcane. That included any mention of phantasms, and Alene knew only too well that her past life as a member of the prosperous and respected O'Hare family of Sudhaven in the Northern Realm was largely to blame for this. Even so, Alene was glad for her companionship. Her expertise was beyond value when in the wild.

Lionel was sitting close by, continuing to look exhausted and uncomfortable. He had not spoken since that afternoon and appeared to have nothing more to say. Alene made the decision to help him, to relieve his tension and hopefully lift his spirits slightly. There was no way they could survive this journey without some positivity: she gained comfort by being with her friends and making this terrifying journey, this mad dash to the prize, together. He was alone in the world, no friends nearby and so young. She picked up her bow, which she usually wore over her back but which was currently lying beside her, and her twin swords, worn on each hip, and shuffled closer to the young boy.

Upon closer inspection, she was reassured in her initial judgement of him as being roughly twelve years old. He was the colour of rich, creamy milk and this, combined with his pale sandy hair, gave him the appearance of a fading spectre. He was also rather slight, Alene noticed, with little in the way of muscle and approximately five foot tall. She was again shocked at what this weak, frail-looking boy had been capable of: of escaping Ville Fleurie and crossing the frigid lower pass of the Vater Berg, the tallest mountain in the Rücken, of evading wolves and frostbite and fleeing down the eastern slopes, following the path of the River Rushing, through the Painted Wall and, finally, to his goal in the Grand Hall of Regenbogen Castle, the message he had been tasked to deliver tattooed on his heart, never allowing himself to think of anything else should he accidentally forget a key detail. This, if nothing else, must command a certain respect. And Alene could not also forget that, should they all survive this, they may owe this boy their lives.

'I'm sorry you've been dragged into all of this,' she said softly to him. He murmured a vague, noncommittal reply and avoided her gaze. Once again, she felt a stab of pity and – shockingly – guilt at his pathetic state of events. She rallied her thoughts and tried again. 'I mean, there really is no safer place for you in the world, considering what you know and who you've betrayed to bring us your story. The entire Dominion is forever in your debt, and I'll see to it you're well rewarded, but until then you must stay with us for your own protection.' She was also thinking of her own safety, of how one careless word from the wrong person could upset the entire affair, and how she was best suited to keep all who knew of her mission close by her side, but she remained silent on this point.

Lionel suddenly looked her directly in the eye and scowled darkly. Alene was shocked: she was not aware that this young boy's face could contort into such an aggrieved form. His eyes flashed in anger and he practically spat his reply: 'If I were doing this for the reward, would I not be making it plain? Would you not be able to see it in my manner? My voice? My way of carrying myself? Would you not be able to sense it in my very fibre? What little must you think of me, to think that I would use the fate of our world, the lives of countless countrymen of both yours and mine, to abuse them all for petty gain? I am here because I was tasked to be, by people higher and more authoritative than I will ever be, who are cursed with the responsibility of guarding the light from the shadows and forever trying to catch them both within their outstretched grasps. My mother warned me that the structure and integrity of the heavens and earth were at risk. That is not something to cower away in fear from – that is something to push against with all your might! I am terrified, ill-equipped, young, weak of body and lacking in tactics or great intellect. But I have courage. I will fight for what is right and good and just in the world. I am here.'

He was breathing heavily and a pale pink was beginning to creep up his neck and into his bony cheeks as he finished speaking. He did, however, hold her gaze with a steely determination and Alene was ashamed of herself for underestimating this young man.

'I'm very sorry,' she said after a moment. 'I realise now that I was wrong. I looked at you and saw a scared boy. I should have realised that, really, we are all scared children deep down. You just get better at hiding it with age. You are, however, absolutely right: you are here. And, if it pleases you, here you shall stay, by my side. It's alright to be scared, I have no idea what will come next, but I will be glad to have you here, on our quest to save the world.' She smiled at him at this, and he smiled back, somewhat reluctantly but genuinely all the same. She continued, 'At the next available chance, I will arm you with a sword. Can you fight?' She realised that she knew very little about him.

'Thank you, but swords are a bit heavy for me,' he said, patting his hip to draw her attention to a short, curved knife at his belt. 'I hope I will be brave enough to use it when you need me.' With this, he stood and bowed to her, somewhat clumsily, before rushing hastily away into the gathering gloom.

Alene stood as well, walking a little way away from the rest of the party and the pool of warm, flickering light around their makeshift camp. She had not lied: she was petrified of what lay ahead and, when she thought on it too intently, the magnitude of what came next, the enormity of their task, threatened to engulf her entirely. In the wrong hands, the power of the Cardinal Phantasm would be devastating, and if it were used to alter this unknown prophecy, the world was at stake. All would fall into ruin and Alene could not see how anybody could benefit from this. Roan was probably right: Queen Rowena was just the type of vain, cruel woman to embark on such an act of mindless destruction and to disregard the lives of the many for her own gain. But still, why would she want to?

Alene had only met Rowena once, many summers before on a diplomatic visit to Ville Fleurie, and her first impression was not a flattering one. She was known as 'the Rose Queen', and Alene had never been able to tell if it was meant satirically or affectionately. Certainly, Ville Fleurie was famous for its flowers and hanging gardens, yet the Queen of Regenbogen had never before met a ruler more able to mask a prickly and dangerous interior with such a fragrant perfume of beauty and deceit. Truly, the name was fitting. Rowena had welcomed Alene and Gerecht to her court in the City of Blossoms with smiles and hospitality, demonstrating her opulence by catering to their every whim, but the glamour could never quite thaw out her eyes, which watched her royal guests with obvious contempt and loathing. Alene had heard that Ville Fleurie shared a dangerously frosty relationship with the elves of Marrowmarsh, close by to the west, and had wondered if her own elvish blood and obviously non-human features had soured their budding relationship. Did Rowena harbour anti-elven sentiments, and was that why she craved the power of the Cardinal?

Suddenly, Alene was shaken from her reverie by a sound which pierced the still night air like the blast of a war horn and turned her blood to ice: somebody screamed shrilly nearby, an instinctive and harrowing cry of utter desperation and terror which plunged the night into chaos.

CHAPTER FOUR

The golden glow of the day's last rays was shining brightly on the crystal panes of the tall, grand windows of Ville Fleurie as Simeon walked at a brisk pace along the lavishly decorated corridor. The decadence of his surroundings appealed to Simeon, and he was pained to have to rush by without his usual thorough inspection of each piece. He would have to suffice with a cursory glance and a knowing nod of approval: knowing because, as he bitterly lamented after every visit to or journey down the Hall of Artefacts, he knew that they would never be his. Look, but never touch. These treasures appealed to his adventurous tendencies, to his appreciation of beautiful, glittering objects, but mostly they appealed to his greed.

Despite the haste of his errand, a small porcelain vase caught his eye and he slowed to a somewhat involuntary halt. Simeon's eyes flashed hungrily as he studied the intricate gold inlay of the base and the delicate brushstrokes of the long-dead master of art clearly evident within the subtle, elegant colours used to portray three minimalist wildflowers: a snow-drop, a bluebell and a poppy. That was all. That was enough.

A new piece for the queen's collection, Simeon enviously thought to himself as he tore his eyes away and marched onwards towards his destination. Queen Rowena, or the Rose Queen as she was often known, would want her final report before the day was out and Simeon was fast coming to the realisation that this would not be possible. She had asked for haste and discretion: Captain Simeon Castello of the palace guard could only give her one of these things.

Since the previous evening, he had discretely tracked down several important men at court and sent summons with trusted messengers to others further afield. He knew that it may be necessary to meet these individuals on the road, that it may be impossible to wait for them to join him at Ville Fleurie for the council. This, however, was the least of his problems: two key members of his elite team were proving incredibly difficult to track down. One was his best friend. The other was his wife.

The clandestine and secretive nature of his orders had immediately tantalised his curiosity when he was summoned to the queen's royal chambers the previous night. He had awoken to a gentle yet insistent knocking on the oak doors of his personal apartments, a little after midnight. It was his night off duty, but this apparently did not phase the queen. His eyes still itching with tiredness, he had made himself decent and advanced to the rapping sound with a candle held high to light his way. Upon opening the door, he had found Lorraine, the head of the household, fully dressed and with an anxious quality upon her doughy features. She had bidden him to proceed at once to the queen, who awaited his presence and so he had gone, not even pausing to wake his beloved Rita before quietly closing the door and hurrying away.

The private chambers of Queen Rowena were designed for comfort and splendour, lit at this hour by large candles on pedestals. These candles were made from fragrant bee's wax from the queen's own hives in the palace gardens and perfumed the room with a sweet aroma. Thick, richly-dyed rugs carpeted the waxed wooden floorboards which reflected the candlelight like the glassy surface of a lake and, sitting centrally astride an ornately-carved throne of black ebony, was Queen Rowena herself, nestled amongst many cushions and pillows to make her royal seat more comfortable.

She looked rather weak and frail in her gargantuan throne, its polished surface appearing to absorb much of the candlelight and thereby shrouding her in gloom. She had evidently been roused herself only recently, for although she was fully dressed in her usual royal regalia, what Simeon could perceive of her face was pale and wrinkled. Her eyes, however, were a different matter: they gleamed in the darkness and the fog of sleep had been successfully banished. She had been deep in conversation with her lady-in-waiting, Lady Sandrine, when Simeon had entered, but now she turned his way and spoke clearly and meaningfully across the shadows of the chamber. 'Captain Castello, I am glad you could be here so soon. I hope it was no inconvenience.'

Her voice was cold and hard. It could have been no clearer that Rowena cared very little that Simeon had been fast asleep on his night off, that he would rather be entwining his love in his warm embrace as the night passed outside like an unseen spectre. She rose from her throne, sure and steady, and paced the lavish suite. She appeared now to be gliding across the surface of the dark, shining floorboards which reflected her form back up at her, a form which was haggard and in the autumn of its existence despite her only being around the age of forty. Widowhood had hit her unexpectedly hard, mostly because many people were surprised to find that she had a heart capable of breaking. Despite this decline of body and health, her acid tongue and harsh words continued to poison and burn with thoughtless ferocity and she had continued to wear expensive, vibrant clothing throughout the expected mourning period following the king's unexpected death years prior. It appeared that even a broken heart would not encroach on her personal vanity.

Lorraine, the servant who had roused him, waited by the door and then escorted him back to his chambers when he had been given his orders, lit taper held high and illuminating the barren passageways which led back to the barracks located in the northern wing of the palace. They made the journey in silence. Once back in bed beside Rita, however, Simeon found that he had far too much information racing through his head and could not possibly settle down and sleep. He instead rose again and had worked tirelessly through the remainder of the night, writing lists and notes in a vain attempt to organise his chaotic thoughts. His quill scratched noisily in the silence of the bedchamber but still Rita did not stir and, as the first golden rays of dawn penetrated the glass panes of the window and lit up the room around him with warm, gentle light, he rose and walked silently from the room and into the palace beyond.

He held, tightly in his hand, a list. A list of those people in his employ, and a few who were not, whom he trusted implicitly. This would be key for the task ahead, and he had spent the following day sending letters, engaging in hushed conversations and traversing the vast estate of Ville Fleurie, including its sprawling grounds which sat nestled in the rolling foothills of the Vater Berg, the Father Mountain, in an attempt to track down any remaining individuals. It was this errand which found him, many tiring hours later in the light of the setting sun, reluctantly leaving the Hall of Artefacts and resuming his search.

Simeon descended the sweeping staircase – mahogany with a long, crimson carpet running down its centre – at a jog and exited the palace into an outer courtyard. The breeze of the evening was pleasant on his face and carried the scent of roses and other flowers from nearby fields. Closer at hand, a beautifully arranged sculpture of marble took centre-stage in the courtyard, bedecked with honeysuckle, trumpet vines and morning glory to such an extent that they became the art themselves, the original intention of the sculptor lost to history. A trickling fountain of clear spring water surrounded its base, feeding the flowers and emanating a soothing melody to the evening air.

This fountain was very much at home in Ville Fleurie: almost every wall and balcony was alive with hanging gardens, a festival of colour and beauty which Simeon was sure not only rivalled but positively outshone the garishly painted walls of Regenbogen in the east, which was reportedly daubed with primitive paint from base to battlements. Simeon had never seen, nor wished to see, the supposed City of Rainbows, but how could mere paint compare to the sheer majesty of living colour?

He turned left down a narrow tunnel and came out into another courtyard, this time slightly larger with several people dotted here and there, sitting together on carved benches or leaning against the balustrade which gave way to a stunning vista to the north. He saw noble lords and ladies engaging in the games of courtly love, saw handmaidens hurrying about on their last errands of the day and, dotted here and there, he saw hooded figures looking lost and uncertain in a world unfamiliar to them. On any other day of the year, this mysterious behaviour would have immediately aroused Simeon's suspicions, but today there was a perfectly innocent explanation. Tomorrow was the beginning of a week-long festival known as *Empire's End*, where people from both Realm and Dominion celebrated the fracturing of the old Empire and the rising of two new kingdoms from its ashes. This began every year with a grand market within the very walls of Ville Fleurie, where traders would unveil their most exotic and enrapturing wares to the excited public, already giddy with excitement from their annual admittance to the city's inner grounds.

Indeed, as Simeon looked, he noticed that these hooded individuals had small and shabby carts covered with grimy cloths and appeared to be scouting for a place to pitch their market stalls. The more lavish and prosperous merchants would already be well-settled into one of the many comfortable inns in the outer town, dining on roast mutton with creamy saffron sauce – a local delicacy – and would send their servants to set up before sunrise the next day but, regardless of rank, Simeon knew that all visitors to the City of Blossoms would have been thoroughly searched at the city gates already, and that was good enough for him.

Still, however, he saw no sign of Matteus or Rita. He was beginning to feel desperate now, and roughly pushed aside one of the hooded traders as he made his way across the courtyard and towards another avenue, down which he could see more people. He heard a sharp intake of breath and a thud behind him and he turned in spite of himself: the one he had shoved had fallen hard on the mosaic tiles at their feet and a bulging sack of apples lay strewn around. Several other merchants rushed to their aid but stopped short when they caught sight of Simeon's uniform. The trader community was notoriously tight-knit and would always defend one another, but picking a fight with the captain of the guard would not be a wise decision on the eve of Empire's End.

Simeon turned with a smirk and continued on his way. He loved the power which came with his rank. He also enjoyed the fear. To him, wandering merchants were just as bad as the gypsies of Regenbogen and Simeon could never understand why Rowena allowed them to besmirch their city. He often noted, however, that Rowena herself never descended from her private chambers and into the sunlight whilst the market was within the walls. She would not lower herself to that.

Another balcony revealed another sweeping vista to the north, and Simeon saw the famed Great Aqueduct of Ville Fleurie rising up and away from the city, climbing higher and higher towards the source: a spring of water in the highest reaches of the Vater Berg which provided the flowers and crops of the city with such nourishment that they truly had no match in either Realm or Dominion. Ville Fleurie owed its prosperity to the construction of the aqueduct and it was a symbol of pride for all who lived there.

There were fewer crowds here, mainly actors, jugglers, dancers and other street performers who had travelled to the festival in search of an adoring audience. They would receive a warm reception from the people of this city, Simeon thought to himself as he wandered further through the maze of airy courtyards and tight alleyways connecting them, but once the festival is over they will be shunned again and compelled to leave, returning to the fringes of society where they belonged. This hypocrisy of the festival – the infatuation with the otherwise contemptible – mirrored both the Realm's and the Dominion's obsession with The Empire, Simeon reflected. Each were predisposed to discourage slander and negativity in regards to the old Cloven Empire – in many respects they were both direct successors of it and were very much cut from the same cloth – and simultaneously desired to celebrate its downfall as the birth of their own kingdoms when they rose from the ashes of the once-mighty behemoth. The result of this was a wilful ignorance of the existence of The Empire for the majority of the year. Not this week though.

Dazzling sunset met Simeon as he strolled down a set of worn stone steps and rounded another corner to find himself in the outer courtyards of the palace. This section of the grounds was much more open and felt more alive and natural as a result. Instead of tight walled avenues between court-yards, a visitor to these much-celebrated gardens found gravel paths with short, knee-height hedges lining them, or some-times expertly tended rose bushes. These paths connected round, paved patios which were semi-obscured from view by larger hedges and trellises of honeysuckle, but from within which could be heard the murmur of cascading water which betrayed the presence of a hidden fountain. The remainder of this space was given to lawns which glowed emerald-green in the last light of the day and Simeon could not help but feel content and at ease as he strolled down an avenue lined with yellow roses, their fragrant perfume mixing with the gentle lighting and the soft crunch of the gravel beneath his boots to almost drive his urgent errand from his frantic mind.

Most of the visitors to court on the eve of Empire's End were either within the upper courtyards or had not yet entered the outer walls of the chateau, opting instead for the com-fort of the inns. The result was that this area of the grounds, where one could enjoy panoramic views of the early evening sky and marvel at the majestic Vater Berg as it towered over them to the north-east (from its treacherous faces of sheer black stone and shining ribbon of river which met the end of the aqueduct to the incomprehensible height and distance of its snowy peak), was largely deserted. Even so, some scattered newcomers were present in the gardens and were congregating around the various fountains.

Simeon felt sure that he would find his wife here. He walked beneath an archway of vines, heavy with crimson grapes, to find a crowd of around twenty highborn men and ladies gazing up in adoration at the sculpted figure in the centre of the fountain. Water streamed in airborne jets, over the statue's head in an elegant arch, landing back in the fountain with a delicate splash. Some ladies were kneeling at the edge of the water, hands clasped tightly and whispering to themselves, eyes never leaving those of the statue as they did so. Others reached over the water to touch its sculpted toes in stone sandals. The men were being more reserved, opting instead to scatter coins into the water. One well-dressed man even removed a large ruby from a chain around his neck and tossed it into the depths of the fountain before turning and leaving. Simeon knew why – this was the statue of Consilii, one of the divine children of Unus the One God.

Consilii had reached down from between the worlds and created men and therefore was revered by all humans. Or, as it seemed nowadays, that used to be the case. Unus and his children had been worshipped fervently in the time of The Empire and, like so many things dating from that most conflicting of eras, was often neglected in more recent times. However, greed had a way of bringing out the piety in people, and an offering to the god who created humans and the patron of riches – the pursuit of which is the most basic human yearning – would definitely be worthwhile on the night before the biggest market of the year. Still, however, no Rita.

Simeon walked on. He passed along another path and found himself this time beside a fountain which was entirely lonely. Again, Simeon was not surprised. This patio had been kept neat and manicured to uphold appearances, but nobody in

Ville Fleurie would be caught dead worshipping here, for selfish gain or otherwise. This was the statue of Cobalus, the daughter of Unus who had seen it fit to plague the world with goblins. Trade often necessitated contact between the chateau with the goblins who camped along the Sea of Saxe, but they were not welcomed within the palace walls and Simeon had to bite back a bitter curse as he glowered up at the ridiculous female above him. After all, it would be foolish to insult a god.

He hurried on. He knew the direction in which he was walking: each path naturally converged in the same place, and so he eventually found himself entering a small glade in the very centre of the park. Inside this secluded spot, there stood a statue more impressive than either which had preceded it. This was Unus, the One God who had created the world and the animals. As he knew he would from the moment he entered the palace grounds, he found Rita sat motionless on the stone rim of the fountain. She was deep in thought, absentmindedly running the tips of her fingers across the surface of the glassy water and creating ripples that fanned out and distorted the reflection of the sunset sky above. A light breeze passed through the serene clearing and Rita appeared to sense his presence, for she turned suddenly and looked up. Their eyes met. One beat. Then two.

'You're going to ask me to come with you, aren't you?' Her voice was slight but steady and full of a conviction that spoke plainly of many contemplative hours on the subject. Simeon weighed up his responses before replying.

'You want to come,' he said finally. 'You need to be by my side, that's clear. You always do. To ask you to stay would be a cruelty. Besides, you are the most gifted fighter in Ville Fleurie. I need you.'

This was perfectly true. Rita was without rival in battle and was seasoned in multiple disciplines. He would need the likes of her on his team in the coming weeks. He also knew his wife better than anyone, and she would not be able to remain behind whilst he placed himself and others in danger – to force her to do so would be a terrible sentence, despite what she might say. She was conflicted, that much was obvious from where she was sitting. She had come to Unus, who amongst other things was the patron of long journeys and free will. Some even said that it was he who first brought the phantasms into the world, but Simeon doubted that.

Rita slowly stood, her eyes remaining on his. She wore a long dress of claret silk which hung loosely down to her ankles and her blonde wavy hair hung over her shoulders in rippling sheets. Simeon crossed the space between them and enveloped her in a passionate embrace. His breath came in short sobs as his lips brushed her dark cheek and he reflected that, no matter what he chose, he would lose. If he asked her to accompany his group, he would be placing her in danger. If he ordered her to remain in Ville Fleurie, he would be condemning her to an agonising wait until he returned...or did not. She would feel useless, humiliated and powerless to help.

'The Cardinal Phantasm has emerged,' he whispered urgently in her ear, making up his mind. 'The queen wants him, alive and back here as soon as possible. I believe she plans to finally make a move on Regenbogen!'

She drew away from him, shock dawning on her face. She had evidently guessed that he was planning a long, dangerous journey – only that would have drawn her to consult the gods – but she luckily had no idea of the particulars. This was good, Simeon reflected with a sigh of relief. If she had known, then others may also have.

Finally, she spoke. 'You've known about this since last night. Why have you not left yet? If Rowena seeks to make her long-awaited move against our enemy, surely time is the most important factor?'

'No – the Queen is certain that we are the only ones who know of the Cardinal's awakening, her spies made sure that we knew immediately. Because of that, secrecy is far more important than speed. I've been gathering the old crowd all day, those who can be trusted to keep a secret and who will fight for the honour of our Northern Realm. We leave at dawn, with the opening of the gates for the market, and pass ourselves for queen's men on festival-related business. We are to meet other loyalists on the road who will join us. We may be in need of as many fighters as we can get!'

'Would disguises not be wise?' Rita questioned. 'To maintain the secrecy. Then we could leave immediately without arousing suspicion.'

Simeon noted the change in pronoun. *We.* She had made the choice to accompany him, as he knew she would. Despite the danger, Simeon was pleased: he loved his wife deeply and would be comforted by her presence. He smiled and answered her, pulling her into a sitting position on the edge of the fountain. 'We will encounter less opposition in our uniforms, as the Captain of Ville Fleurie on official business in the Realm. Besides, if we simply disappear then that will be noted within the palace, and that could prove our downfall before we even begin. No, we hide in plain sight.'

Rita pursed her lips and glanced up at the statue in the centre of the fountain. She was unconvinced, but he knew she was set on her decision. Without a further word, they rose together and walked briskly from the glade and down the canopied pathway opposite. As they walked, Simeon noted the uneasy silence between them. She definitely had misgivings. This annoyed Simeon slightly – should she not trust his judgement? Was he not the captain of the palace guard?

As they walked, they passed without observation through yet another shady courtyard with yet another ornate fountain. This time, however, the sculptor had depicted two figures: Arcano and his twin sister, Eclaire. These were Unus's youngest children who had brought magic into the world, followed shortly by the elves, the race most adept at utilising it. Elves entered Ville Fleurie occasionally but were not really welcome here, and magic was also discouraged strongly by the queen within the palace walls. With this in mind, Simeon was not surprised to find the courtyard deserted tonight.

They came to a halt at the grand double doors to the inner palace. This was the official ceremonial entrance to the main hub of the palace and featured a sweeping marble staircase that led up to the doors themselves, which were crafted from fragrant rosewood and inlaid with mother-of-Pearl motifs which prominently featured the rose of Ville Fleurie. The foot of the steps was flanked by severe-looking soldiers in pumpkin-coloured uniforms. They looked ridiculous, but Simeon and Rita both knew that these were not men to be crossed. These were members of the elite Saffron Guard, Queen Rowena's personal and formidable army who accompanied her at all times. Members of the Saffron Guard were beyond Simeon's command, answering only to the queen herself. Their presence here must mean that Rowena was nearby, possibly within the chambers immediately through the doors. Simeon was not prepared yet for a face-to-face meeting with the Rose Queen: she was sure to ask him for a full account of his team, and he still had not found Matteus.

He suggested that Rita continue to their chambers and prepare for an early departure, and he instead turned and followed the path around and past the doors and into another ornate garden which hugged the palace walls.

He had barely walked for five minutes when his attention was drawn to a small door of hard, black wood, nestled in the shadows of the palace walls and lower down than the level on which Simeon walked. A steep, irregular flight of stone steps led down to it and the top of these steps featured two captivating lanterns fashioned from rose gold which each contained a flickering black flame. In the gathering gloom of the post-sunset gardens, this dark fire gave off very little light, and yet the lamps themselves appeared to glow ethereally. A plaque made from the same material was set into the wall above the door, about eye-level with Simeon.

Simeon knew what was stamped upon it without needing to read it. This was the mysterious Shadow Archives. Many years ago, before the fall of The Empire, Ville Fleurie had been known as the Fief Nord, or Northern Stronghold, and often acted as the permanent home of lesser members of the imperial family over the years. Brothers and uncles of emperors would rule here with their family, or possibly dowager empresses with little remaining in the realms of real power. Ville Fleurie was a much more tolerant, and even curious, city in those days and enjoyed a prosperous relationship with the elves of Marrowmarsh. The fountains in the gardens dated from these times, as did the Shadow Archives, a repository of information gathered from this time of friendship with the elves, masters of sorcery and deceit. Simeon had never set foot in this strange and foreboding library, had no desire to, and knew nobody who had. He turned to resume his search but was startled to see the small black door begin to open.

With no place to hide, Simeon did the only other thing which he could think of doing in such a situation: he drew the knife at his belt and held it ready. He could think of no good reason why anybody would be entering the Shadow Archives – that kind of information was not welcome here!

He peered through the gathering gloom and sighed in relief, replacing his knife at his waist: it was Matteus.

'I hope you have a good reason for avoiding me all day,' he called through the darkness to his best friend, relief and success flooding through him at finally finding him. This feeling was so pronounced, in fact, that it initially eclipsed his confusion at *where* he found him. Matteus jumped slightly and turned his way.

'Of course, Sim,' he called back, making his way over. He fell into step beside him and they made their way back towards the main gates. 'I've been doing my research, delving into the deepest, darkest depths of the arcane in order to find the solution to your problem.' Simeon could hear the smirk in his voice, even though the light had now fully gone from the sky and all he could see in his friend's face was two pinpricks of light, his bright eyes which eternally danced with gentle mocking and mirth. Matteus was clearly loving this, dangling the thread of the unknown in front of him, hinting at some tantalising solution that Simeon was still unsure he even needed. After a few more drawn out seconds, Matteus continued.

'You need to contain the Cardinal Phantasm, naturally, and I have found a way.'

'How do you…?'

'Thomas,' came the immediate and simple reply. Of course, Simeon thought to himself. Of course Thomas would immediately tell Matteus about the Cardinal. Simeon had recruited Thomas earlier that day and was both furious and admittedly unsurprised that he would be so lax with the information entrusted to him. With a sigh though, Simeon reflected that Thomas would have known that Matteus would ultimately be a part of the mission, so his indiscretion was not meant maliciously. Despite this, he made a note to have words with him at a later date.

'Don't be cross, Sim,' Matteus said, serious all of a sudden. 'He meant well. Besides, he gave me the chance to consider the finer details of our mission, details which I am sure you haven't thought of. The Cardinal Phantasm is an almighty being, imbued with the powers of a god. There is only one way to successfully restrict the power of a being without using magic, and that is to utilise the unique properties of *inhibitite*, a metal that can be fashioned into bars and used to craft a cage. Rowena wants the Cardinal alive, I take it? Then according to the old records, this is the safest way. Otherwise, transport from Mort Vivant to Ville Fleurie will be nigh-on impossible without him either escaping or causing himself suicidal harm – both undesirable outcomes.'

Simeon was silent throughout this speech. It was true: he had only thought of the mission up to the acquisition of the Cardinal Phantasm. He had given no thought whatsoever to the return journey and how this would be achieved.

'Fine, Matt, fine. You win, you're the smartest. Okay, I'll ask:

where does one acquire inhibitite?'

'Luckily for us, not too far from here. With your permission, I'll send a messenger to The Hammer and Anvil immediately and we can collect our commission as soon as we arrive there'.

Simeon thought on this. The Hammer and Anvil was an inn to the west of here, possibly a full day's ride if they made haste, albeit in the wrong direction. It was close by the southern reaches of Marrowmarsh and its landlord was known for crafting rare artefacts with unusual qualities in his forge. Thought would have to be given as to how to conceal such a contraption – a portable cage would almost certainly draw unwanted attention on the road. Even so, this appeared to be a necessary amendment to his plan.

'Permission granted,' he replied with a sigh. 'Make preparations for a dawn departure, we rendezvous at the city gates.' With that, he turned and rushed away. He had a meeting with the queen to attend now that he had a full team – not to mention a plan! If he hurried, he may even have time for a much-needed rest before their mission began. Simeon found that he had little in the way of misgivings when it came to the task at hand. When the Künstlers of Regenbogen fell, and House Croître of Ville Fleurie sat on the thrones of both Realm and Dominion as a reunified Empire, there would be no need for the festival of Empire's End and that, he thought to himself as he climbed the marble steps and pushed open the rosewood double doors, would make his job an awful lot easier.

CHAPTER FIVE

Alene stumbled, momentarily uncertain of what she was experiencing, towards the source of the screaming which continued to pierce the night with terror and panic. She did not have far to go and she could hear her various companions converging on the scene from all directions. She knew whose scream she had heard, and this certainty was confirmed as she arrived to witness a shocking sight.

Lionel was sinking.

At least, he appeared to be sinking. Alene rushed forward, drawing her swords *Dawn* and *Dusk* from her belt as she ran, to a sight which swam out of the darkness before her and became more clear as the shadows gave way to the light of Roan's torch who appeared beside her.

Everything below the boy's knees had completely disappeared. The thick, rippling grass which carpeted the vast lands around them was still waving merrily in the gentle night breeze, and yet at the same time it was sucking the youngest member of their group down into its depths at an alarmingly fast rate. Pure horror was sculpted on Lionel's face and his eyes bulged with fear as he struggled frantically to wriggle himself free from the earth's merciless grasp. This appeared to be the wrong choice, however, as his entire body, rigid with shock, slipped further still into the hungry ground beneath him.

Alene turned desperately to Roan, hoping he would know what to do and that he would immediately spring into action. He was not looking at her though and was instead raising his torch higher, apparently to cast more light on the scene before them. His eyes darted every way across the situation, his features thick with concentration as he searched for a solution, a weakness he could manipulate to turn this twist of fortunes to their advantage.

He appeared to find none, however. Alene looked again, but it was no use. In this light, the ground before them was simply a living shadow which flicked this way and that as a chilly gust passed through and each patch of earth beneath may as well have been hidden by a deep ocean. Even her elven eyes, sharp and insightful, could not determine which areas were safe to tread and which were not. She hastily prodded the ground before her with the blade of her sword: nothing. There were no discerning differences to suggest that one area was any different from another. Did that mean that it was safe to walk on? Or was all of it dangerous, waiting to ensnare her? Panic began to rise in her chest as she frantically looked to the others, who had arrived behind her. Nobody said a word.

Lionel was whimpering quietly as he sank further down, now submerged to his hips. 'Help,' was all he said, his voice shaking and the plea for aid accompanied by large tears which streamed down his terrified face and shone brightly in the torchlight. Suddenly, he began to shake uncontrollably and screamed a loud cry of despair as he started to fight fiercely against the boggy earth, completely unaware that this was causing him to sink faster.

Alene made her move. She took two bounding leaps forward and seized both of Lionel's hands, tugging as hard and as fast as she could. A move of pure desperation, she knew, but what other choice did she have? She heard Roan gasp and swear in surprise behind her as he held his torch higher still to illuminate her struggle, and even heard Griffin shout out, most uncharacteristically, some jumbled plea for her to return to the safety of hard ground. None of them, however, made to follow and assist her. Alene knew, somewhere in the recesses of her mind, that this was not due to cowardice or lack of loyalty – this was because they were not stupid enough to engage themselves in such a fool-hardy plan. All of this was racing through her head when she felt her left foot begin to sink.

She turned her body, preparing to jump to safety, before realising that she was already ensnared in the powerful suction of the prairie. Cold terror surged in her stomach as she pulled harder, and harder again, at her sinking leg which had already disappeared far beyond the top of her boots. A thousand thoughts began cascading through her frozen consciousness, unable to move, yet unable to settle her hyperactive heart. What would happen to the mission if she died here tonight?

Griffin's voice cracked through her foggy panic like a whip and brought her back to the situation completely. She had let her fear take over, she realised, and instead craned her top half around, twisting at the waist, to look at Griffin who looked her directly in the eye and spoke clearly and forcefully.

'Alene, you need to stop moving,' he said slowly, never breaking eye contact and smiling reassuringly at her. 'You will sink faster if you resist. Hold Lionel's hand and stay as still as you can. Help is on the way!'

Alene looked sideways at Lionel, who had heard what Griffin had said and, with great difficulty, had stopped struggling. He held out a shaking hand to Alene and she took it, taking great, deep breaths as she did. The long moments stretched out, seeming infinite but only in truth a few seconds. They both felt their descent into the ground slowing down and seeming to stop. They looked at each other and smiled with relief. Lionel's tears had stopped but he was paler than ever and smeared in thick dirt. Despite this, his smile was genuine and Alene realised with shock that this was the first time she had seen him smile at all.

'It's going to be alright,' she whispered to him so that

only he could hear. 'The prairie won't win tonight - you'll see! Soon we'll be safely back in our beds, resting for a new day.'

Lionel looked back at her and smiled again, his blue eyes shining with hope and relief. 'If we survive this, I'm going to give all my silver to the fountain of Unus,' he declared. 'The will of Unus stopped us from sinking, I know it!'

Alene had no chance to answer, for as she was thinking of a reply, she heard hooves approaching and saw Nox rushing back into the torchlight with Thane and Emmet beside her. She was holding their reins tightly and stopped just before the line of torches which Roan had been spearing into the earth to create a perimeter between safe land and deadly bog. She and Griffin each took a long rope and tossed them expertly, one each for Alene and Lionel. The sinking pair each took a deep breath and let go of each other's hand and instead took a firm hold of their rope.

Griffin and Nox each leapt into action, pulling at the reins of one horse each, talking to them and encouraging them to pull harder. As they did, Alene felt the mud beneath her begin to mercifully relinquish its grip on her legs and she found that she could lean forwards and lay on the surface, allowing herself to be dragged across the long grass and to safety. It took a little longer to work Lionel free, as he had sunk so deep that he was in nearly to the armpits. At last, however, both he and Alene lay in the torchlight, gasping cool night air and wiping thick smears of foul-smelling mud from their clothes.

It was agreed, once everyone was sufficiently recovered, that nobody would venture far tonight. All would eat and sleep in the vicinity of the fire and, as the time had long since passed to safely hunt for supper, Roan produced rations of thick white bread, not yet stale from the kitchens at Regenbogen, and a wheel of creamy goat's cheese. Alene did not ask how he had been able to spirit these items away from the kitchen in the middle of the night – Roan's stealth and skills at traversing the castle unseen were well-known to her – but she also knew that Backen the cook and his servants were notoriously vigilant when it came to thieves in the storerooms. He truly was amazingly talented.

Soon after, they were all lying beneath their blankets and thinking of sleep. Of course, the party's unexpected drama tonight would add extra complication to their travel propositions, but Alene would give that no more thought until the morning, when they could talk together in the chilly light of dawn and her still-erratic heartbeat had had sufficient time to recover. Her roll and blankets were set up immediately beside Roan's, and a little way away from the others. Consequently, just as she was beginning to drift off to sleep, she heard Roan whisper tentatively to her right.

'Alene?'

She glanced over and saw his silhouette against the flickering embers of the fire: he was lying down but looking her way. She slowly sat up and glanced around; everybody else appeared to be sound asleep. She lay back down and replied, 'You okay?'

There was silence for a full minute, then she heard a dry, rattling sigh sound deeply from within Roan's blankets.

'I'm so sorry,' he gasped, and Alene was shocked and dismayed to hear his voice crack with anguish. 'I'm sorry I couldn't save you! Nox and Griffin knew what to do, they saved you and Lionel from the bog. I stood by and watched. I froze, I stayed silent. Even Griffin calmed you down and spoke to you, and he never speaks! I'm supposed to be your best friend, and I failed you completely. I'm sorry.'

Alene reached out a hand into the long grass rippling between them in the night breeze and he did the same. Their fingers entwined and Alene gave him a firm squeeze and a reassuring smile which he could not see in the dark. She hoped that the pressure of her grip in his was enough to convey how she felt, but she took a deep breath herself and answered him as well.

'You *are* my best friend,' she whispered. 'You are here, not from obligation or service but from friendship. I was an idiot to jump into the middle of that quagmire and I don't blame any of you for not following me. You froze once, that does not erase a near-lifetime of loyalty and friendship! Please, try and get some rest before tomorrow - we've got some difficult decisions to make and I need your mind at its sharpest.' She gave his hand one last squeeze and withdrew her own, back into the warmth of her blankets. Dusk and Dawn were lying by her side, ready if needed, and Alene was sure that Roan had Reaper beside him similarly. Only Griffin would sleep with no weapon, and Alene knew why.

'Oh, and just so you know,' Roan whispered at her sleepily, appearing to be falling asleep at last, 'that young lad's growing fond of you. Think he sees you as his saviour, since you rescued him and everything. He couldn't keep his eyes off you during supper.' He was teasing her – that was a good sign that he was returning to his usual self.

Alene rolled over and considered Roan's worries. Beneath his bravado and jesting exterior, Alene knew him to be a deeply insecure and conflicted man. Throughout his childhood, Roan had been torn between both sides of his warring family, never quite sure which decision was the right one and constantly feeling that he was being unfaithful to somebody. Finally, at ten years old, Roan had opted to join his father, Captain Felix, as a member of the household at Regenbogen. Yet he had never, in the many years in which he and Alene had been friends, felt that he could be true and faithful to himself, to allow himself to be happy. Instead, a life of blending into the shadows to avoid the scorn and prejudice of others had led to a retinue of skills which often proved handy, and his solitary discipline of endless training had made him deadly with the most unique weapon which Alene had ever known.

At some point within her reverie, sleep must have taken

her from the Primrose Prairie and transported her to dreams, for she saw the far-off edge of Marrowmarsh, the place of her birth to the elven clans. She had been abandoned, alone and scared, nearby these outer trees which looked and smelled of decaying death when she was still young. She often visited this place in her sleep but had no remaining memory of what lay within the interior of the forest. She was shocked and curious, therefore, to find her dream-self penetrating the fringe of the forest and glimpsing the hidden wonder and otherworldly glory of what lay beyond. She noted that there was a strange, ethereal quality to the golden light which filtered through the autumn-tinted leaves in the canopy above and illuminated a towering carving of pale wood. It depicted Arcano and Eclaire, the gods most revered by the elves of this kingdom, but she had only the briefest moment to admire the craftsmanship, for her dreamscape became foggy and detached; she could feel her roll beneath her and the weight of her blankets enveloping her. With a start, she sat up – returned to the fire, which was now little more than dying embers. It was still a few hours before dawn, and after a cursory glance at her surroundings to check that they were indeed still safe and that somebody was on watch to ensure this (at this hour it was Griffin, his back to her and surveying the darkness from his nest of blankets), she slumped back into a, this time, dreamless sleep.

Breakfast the next morning was a quiet and subdued affair: more bread and cheese, with fresh, crystal-clear water from a nearby brook which they could thankfully use to refill their water skins before continuing. Before that was possible, however, there was the matter of how to progress, and it was this topic that was weighing heavily on all minds present as they ate in silence.

Finally, Roan spoke. He was very much back on his usual form after a night's rest, but even he recognised that this was a serious and potentially contentious subject of discussion.

'Well, there's only one option left open to us,' he announced to the group. 'I proposed a journey by night: we now know that the dangers of that are too severe to seriously consider. I also advised us against the *scary* and *bloodthirsty* creatures of the prairies, if you rightly remember. We democratically decided that we were willing to risk these dangers. Do we still feel this way?'

Alene had something to say in answer to that, but Griffin answered and she waited her turn.

'Roan's right,' he said. 'Last night showed us just how insanely lucky we have been throughout our crossing yesterday to not fall victim to the marshy patches present on the prairie. If we stumbled into one whilst mounted then we would surely be unable to rescue the horses. We may have a slight chance of picking out these bogs in daylight, but I would call that marginal at best.'

'So, we continue to travel by day, being cautious to scout ahead for any sign of danger,' Alene summarised. 'And of course, we need to be aware that we share this prairie with wild animals more dangerous than we are used to. What choice do we have?'

'Queen Alene is right!' suddenly interjected Lionel, looking intensely in her direction. Alene blushed and avoided his gaze. Roan was right: she had a young admirer.

'I'm not so sure of that,' said Nox, who until now had remained silent and deep in thought. Lionel scowled at her but she ignored him and addressed Alene. 'We have another option. Up until now, we haven't considered the possibility that the road may be our safest, if not the most discreet, option. It would certainly be the one with the least physical dangers, as well as the fastest if one considers how long it will take us to negotiate countless camouflaged marshes and swamps which could be our downfall at any time. I *know* you wanted to avoid being seen,' she added, seeing Alene begin to argue, 'but I truly feel that, should we find it necessary, we can make our way down the Prairie Road which leads from the New Road towards the Schloss Stieg in relative secrecy, passing through villages and farms by night and avoiding travellers on the road.'

Alene sighed deeply and looked around at her companions: Nox looked directly at her, waiting for an answer; Griffin appeared to be thinking over this new information, whilst Roan was quietly nodding to himself, apparently in agreement. Lionel, on the other hand, was vehemently shaking his head in sycophantic defiance. She wished he would stop.

Was she risking all of their lives, for the sake of some added protection from prying eyes? Was she capable of putting her own desires ahead of the safety of others? No, of course not! It was the mission she was thinking of, that they all must think of. Nevertheless, she could not argue with Nox's logic. Had she been considering this from as early as yesterday in the cave? Earlier?

'Very well,' she said at last with a tinge of reluctance. 'We'll turn east and head for the New Road. But we must remain cautious! Nox, I want you and Griffin to do the talking, should we be stopped – your voices are less likely to be noted as highborn. The rest of us must keep our hoods up at all times! If we make the road by dusk, then travel through the night, we should be able to make our way onto the Prairie Road by tomorrow's daybreak. We should then be able to find somewhere off the track to take a rest.'

It could not have been clearer that certain members of the group were not thrilled at the prospect of a full day and night's ride ahead of them, but everybody packed up their small camp in silence and mounted their steeds. Lionel, in particular, appeared horrified at the idea – a far cry from his incessant and whole-hearted agreement of everything she had said all morning. This made Alene smirk wryly to herself.

As they set off at a gentle trot, Nox taking the lead this time and scanning the ground carefully before proceeding, Alene began to work out how many days it had been since Rowena and their competition at Ville Fleurie had found out about the new Cardinal Phantasm. Lionel had arrived in Regenbogen the night before the great feast of Empire's End began, so considering how long it would take him to make the journey up the aqueduct and down the mountain – a ridiculously risky manoeuvre she still thought – Rowena had known about the Cardinal for a full day beforehand. That was nearly three days. How far could they get in three days? Were Alene and her friends woefully behind? Was this a fool's errand, to attempt to claim back so much time against an enemy who was better equipped for such an undertaking? No, they must continue. She knew that, and kept telling herself whenever she felt a momentary pang of doubt.

As they rode, and as the sun climbed higher in the sky, the prairie seemed to come to life around them. This was evidently the most active time of the day for life in the grasslands, for Alene saw many different varieties of animals which she had previously only encountered in books. This truly was, as Nox had said, a strange place with an eclectic mix of the wondrous, the colossal and – as Alene saw once or twice in the thankfully far-off distance – the completely and utterly terrifying!

Some of these animals, such as the large herds of bison which roamed the plains and the small, fat grouse which occasionally ran across their paths, were more familiar to the group, but others were less so. Large hares – at least the size of a small pony – darted past at alarming speeds, often stopping to put their long, grey ears to the ground and listen, sometimes for whole minutes, before continuing. They appeared to have no fear of the travellers until Roan decided to raise his bow with the intention of shooting one for their dinner. At once, every hare in sight scattered and had disappeared within a few seconds into the long grass.

Every so often, Alene would hear the foreboding warning of a nearby rattlesnake. These prairie rattlesnakes were brightly coloured with blood-red shades and bright yellow diamonds, and the sight or sound of these was more than enough to make the whole party thankful that they were leaving the open grasslands soon.

Even more fear-inducing were the gargantuan imperial sloths – monolithic beasts which Roan had read about in the Regenbogen library and which appeared to roam mostly around the small copses which dotted the landscape. Alene only saw them from a distance, but even from this relative safety she could make out long, sabre-like claws and enormous, flat teeth which could be seen whenever they opened their mouths. Once, the group was passing dangerously close to a small clump of trees when, suddenly, two of these towering behemoths crashed out from within them and began clawing and biting at each other with vicious ferocity. Nox immediately led the group away to a safe distance.

'They have small links of bone, like chain mail, beneath their skin and fur', Roan told Alene as he rode beside her. They could get hit by a troll's war hammer and not even feel it!'

Alene simply smiled across at him. She had no desire to get any closer to the imperial sloths, especially if a troll with a war hammer was involved!

Roan seemed to read her mind. 'You're lucky we didn't meet Argentavis!'

'Who?' she asked, curious in spite of herself.

'Definitely not 'who', but 'what',' he replied, his usual knowing smirk on his face. 'Argentavis is the largest bird known to live in The Empire today, a colossal monster with razor talons and a long, slender beak with a hook on the end for disembowelling its prey while still alive. It is said to have a wingspan of twenty-six feet, if the copy of 'The Bestiary of Clagcowl Abbey' by Father Ambrosius Volvere in the Regenbogen library is to be believed. This tome also told me that it is jet-black, like a crow, although in the distant past it was much larger and had silver plumage. The only remaining examples in the wild are said to hunt these prairies.'

The look of disgust and revulsion on Alene's face must have been clearly evident, for Roan laughed again and added, 'Don't worry, they live on the very top of sheer cliff faces in the mountains and glide on their massive wings to ambush unsuspecting prey down here on the prairie. They're close to extinction and would never be able to glide this far away from the mountains – I think that's why they're much smaller nowadays, as they struggle to return to the high shelves of rock once they're down here. Big isn't always best.'

With this fresh horror of the Primrose Prairie safely stored in her head, threatening to work her imagination to hyperactivity, Alene continued to ride at a steady pace after her friends as Nox continued to scan the ground ahead for danger. Alene could not shake the creeping feeling in the corner of her eye that an enormous shadow was descending upon her from the periwinkle-blue sky to crush her beneath shining talons and rip out her guts with a hook-like beak, and she shot the retreating mountain tops behind them a cautious glance over her shoulder. She saw no sign of Argentavis, but what she did see turned her blood to ice.

Somebody was watching them.

'Stop!' she shouted urgently to the rest of the group, desperately trying to turn Thane around to get a better look without taking her eyes off the figure she had seen, far off in the distance and slightly to the north. As she watched, it turned and retreated over the far side of the ridge it had been watching them from.

She knew what she had seen: a large, hooded figure on a white horse and in a black cloak. The most distinctive feature of this rider had been a gleaming silver chest plate that reflected the late afternoon sun like a mirror. All of this, Alene could see with frantic clarity through her blessed elven eyes but she was unable to identify if the rider had been male or female.

'What did you see?' asked Nox sharply, riding back to come alongside Alene.

'A figure,' she answered slowly, straining to see any further activity on the rolling ridge to their right. She explained to the others what she had seen.

'I didn't see anything,' admitted Roan.

'Nor me,' said Griffin slowly, 'although Queen Alene's eyes are much more perceptive than ours. It is possible that we would have been unable to see anything, even if we had turned in time.'

'It couldn't have been spies from Ville Fleurie, could it?' asked Lionel, a shudder of fear betrayed in his high voice.

'Possibly,' added Nox, 'although that is not to rule out other parties. There must be other interested individuals and groups who would wish to possess the Cardinal. There are numerous small towns and villages from which such a people may operate, and Cogburn is not too far away. Either way, we must continue to make way before sunset. If we're being followed, then staying in the wilderness is now a fruitless venture – we will be seen, regardless.'

She turned in her saddle to continue on their way but was interrupted by Roan.

'Are we definitely sure that we *are* being followed?' he asked, with an apologetic glance sideways at Alene. 'I mean, a shining silver breastplate is not the kind of thing to wear if you want to remain inconspicuous, is it? Might it just be a ranger, or a farmhand tending to the bison herds?'

Alene did not begrudge him this scepticism, but her reply was curt and impatient: 'How many rangers or farm-hands do you know of who wear silver armour?' She raised her eyebrows at him and nodded at Nox, who turned and led the way, resuming their flight to the now relative safety of the New Road.

They arrived at the roadside just before nightfall, using the last light of day to lead their horses down the shallow gully which separated the road from open grassland and as-cend the other side. The road was made of dry, compacted earth and was quite deserted.

Without a word to each other, the five companions began to ride south with full haste, finally able to return to maximum speed and all thankful to be leaving the dangers of the Primrose Prairie behind them – at least for now.

CHAPTER SIX

A s the Queen of Regenbogen and her unconventional travelling party joined the New Road and proceeded southward away from the setting sun, Simeon and his team were making their way back towards Ville Fleurie on the other side of the Rücken, where the sun had not yet set but the sky was alive with the hues of approaching twilight. Two full days had elapsed since they had last seen the round towers and blossoming parapets of their capital city, but this was to be the closest they would get to home in a long time: this was merely a passing glance as they rejoined the main road leading south and onwards to their main goal.

Simeon sighed with frustration as he gazed across the fields of tulips and sunflowers. The retreating summer sunshine was reflecting off the distant greenhouses outside the palace walls and making them glimmer majestically. Two days. It had taken two entire days to make the round trip westward, along the old elven road to The Hammer and Anvil. There, they had found that their message had indeed arrived in good time ahead of them and that a solid carriage had been constructed, ready for them to take away immediately. This, of course, had been no ordinary carriage, but a rolling cage with dark – almost black – bars made of dense and foreboding inhibitite.

Simply being close to the odd metal made Simeon uneasy, yet Matteus assured him that this prison would render the powers of the Cardinal Phantasm completely inert. They had taken advantage of the hospitalities of the landlord for a few hours only and then left before the new day had even begun. Being the Captain of Ville Fleurie, and being on official business for Her Royal Majesty, ensured that Simeon was always served the best food and afforded the most comfortable rooms when on the road, but he was anxious to get on his way on this occasion and the return journey had been a lot slower, having to escort the cumbersome carriage and travelling at the appropriately slower pace. Two days, and back where they started. Again, Simeon sighed with frustration.

As usual, Simeon was leading the way: the place of a captain was at the head of a party. It was crucial that his authority be established immediately, especially since many in this particular team were personal friends and acquaintances. He needed to be confident that they saw him as a leader and would respond appropriately to commands in any situation. Any insubordination would be dealt with severely, no matter who it came from. Immediately behind him, he could hear the rhythmic creaking of the prison carriage as its large wooden wheels bounced in potholes and splashed in puddles from the recent rain shower. This was being pulled by Rita, who sat astride an enormous shire horse called Betty. A gentle giant by all accounts, Betty had been provided begrudgingly by the stables of The Hammer and Anvil to pull their new acquisition. The power of Simeon's station and badge were quite extraordinary.

Betty's chestnut flank gleamed and Rita had taken to stroking her long mane as they proceeded, whispering words of encouragement in her ear. Simeon rolled his eyes whenever he heard her doing this. His wife may be a formidable warrioress, but her emotions betrayed the typical female weakness which lay beneath. Despite this, she was currently clad for battle, with a long tunic over trousers and bronze armour lined with bear fur over her chest and shoulders. Her white-blonde hair was pulled back in a braid and her travelling cloak of thick wool was hanging loosely down her back.

Behind Rita and the carriage, the rest of the team rode in single file, Thomas bringing up the far rear. Simeon wished he could slow down and draw level with his love, to ask her how she was coping with the road, if the sight of their home across the fields was upsetting her, but he knew that that would appear unprofessional. On this mission, Rita was a soldier first, and his wife second. Technically, Rita had never served in a company but her skills in combat spoke for themselves. They were what had attracted him to her in the first place.

Some years before, Simeon had happened upon his wife, then a young woman, in the far north of the Realm. She had grown up in a very distinct culture, on the frontier of the Realm and the Dominion. The main visitors to her remote village were the occasional merchants travelling along the Road of Riches between Regenbogen and Ville Fleurie, but it was the ever-present threat of attack from the goblins from the northern shores of Saxe which necessitated the practice of having all children battle-ready by their fifteenth birthday. Gender was not considered a hindrance on these inhospitable plains, and so a young woman was able to rise to become the most celebrated warrioress in the region. Rita had largely given up this aspect of her life since she had joined him as his wife in Ville Fleurie – it would not do for a lady of court to be stronger than a husband! He had continued her training however, almost as if he knew that the day would come when her skills would prove useful. He loved his wife – more than the moon and the stars in the sky – and he made sure that she had everything she could want. Even a highborn noblewoman could not boast the power she held as the wife of Captain Simeon Castello.

Simeon could see the crossroads ahead of him. To turn left would lead them home to the capital, but their journey was to take them right and south, through rolling fields of wheat and barley along a route known as the Sunken

Road. As he squinted ahead, slightly blinded by the setting sun in the north to his left, he noticed that the crossroads were not deserted. A tall figure on a black horse was sitting stately beside the wooden signpost and appeared to be looking their way. Simeon had a moment of panic as he contemplated how to hide the inhibitite cage, sure it would attract the curiosity of any stranger on the road, but relaxed when he realised that he recognised the black-haired, olive-skinned woman waiting for them ahead.

As they drew near, Lady Sandrine Bosque, chief lady-in-waiting and trusted advisor of Queen Rowena, rode forward slightly to meet them.

'Captain Castello, I am so glad to have caught you as you passed by.'

Her voice was rich and smooth, and she spoke with no sense of urgency or haste. In fact, one could have been forgiven for mistaking this for nothing more than a warm greeting from an old friend. Lady Sandrine's smiles were generous and her eyes shone when they looked his way. She apparently recalled who Simeon was travelling with, for she raised her gaze slightly and saw Rita just behind him. Her smile, if possible, became even warmer and she called out affectionately, 'Lady Castello, it's a pleasure to see you so well. Travel plainly agrees with you!'

Simeon stole himself a look back at Rita. Lady Sandrine was quite right: the country air and exertion of the day had radiated his wife's natural beauty and she appeared in her element. Simeon knew that Lady Sandrine was using Rita's official title as a courtesy in front of the other soldiers – the two of them were actually very close friends.

Rita smiled back in response but did not return the compliment: she was playing the part of soldier expertly, affording her captain the respect he deserved and allowing him to control the direction of the conversation with their palace liaison.

'The pleasure is ours, my lady. I trust that this evening

finds you well and that our beloved capital city is enjoying a prosperous and orderly Empire's End. I must confess, however, to be quite surprised to encounter you here at the crossroads, and alone. May I enquire the reason for such an honour?' He spoke clearly and professionally; to speak to Lady Sandrine Bosque was to speak to the queen.

This manner of his address prompted another warm – and somewhat teasing – smile. Sandrine had an uncanny awareness of the effect her position had on people and often found it amusing. Simeon was all too aware of this but was also acutely aware that he had a somewhat similar disposition to his own underlings.

'Business, I'm afraid, brings me to the crossroads tonight,' she answered him, in the same formal tone as he had used. Was she toying with him? 'Fitting, how we should meet here, when the fate of our kingdom is currently sitting at a crossroad, entirely at the mercy of the success or failure of your mission. As such, Her Majesty has asked me to add another member to your party – a personal appointment by the queen herself. Your newest addition is to meet you further down the Sunken Road at the old mill belonging to House Thresh. Please welcome them and treat them as a member of your own team. This is the queen's express wish.'

This last sentence was more serious and with significantly less warmth than their previous exchanges. Had she noticed the shadow which crossed his features at her mention of a new party member? He had certainly attempted to keep a neutral expression but was quite shocked at what was an unprecedented move by Queen Rowena to interfere with his company. Did she not trust him?

'You need not worry,' came his reply after a few charged seconds. 'The queen will not be disappointed with our performance, or our hospitality. We must, regrettably, make our departure, I fear. We wish to arrive at the crossing as soon as we are able, and you must be sure to make your safe return to the palace before night truly falls. With your permission, we will part ways – please pass our unending loyalty on to Her Majesty and wish us well on our journey.'

In the end, they parted on good terms. After all, Simeon reflected later that night, it was not Sandrine's fault that her mistress was a known conniver and manipulator. Simeon obeyed and respected Rowena, but it was not for no reason that she was known as the Rose Queen, with the sharpest thorns imaginable, as well as the most poisonous. Many times prior to tonight, Simeon had found himself glad that he was fighting for her side in the silent war for victory against the Eastern Dominion – a war which, with her at the helm – they were certain to win!

After they had watched Lady Sandrine's black horse galloping back towards Ville Fleurie, her positioned side-saddle with more grace and elegance than Simeon would have thought possible, the team turned in the direction of the Sunken Road. The stars began to blink into existence above them in a perfectly clear sky and the still night was punctuated only by the song of a distant nightingale and the incessant creaking of the absurd prison cell behind him.

As the sun rose in the south on a new day, the third day of Empire's End, the weary team of soldiers from Ville Fleurie slowed to a halt by the side of the old farm track which made up a large part of their route south. They had travelled all through the night, Simeon wishing to place as much distance as possible between them and their starting position at the crossroads – he was still bitter that they had taken two days to make a positively ludicrous trip for a pointless contraption which continued to slow them down even now.

He knew that this was possibly irrational and foolish, and was aware that they required the carriage for their future success, but he did not care for the cage at all: it had an unnerving quality which he could not quite put his finger on. He mistrusted it, like it was threatening him. He reminded himself that Rita was in charge of it, and that he trusted her judgement and ability more than many of the other members of the team. He was being silly.

As a result of the continuous journeying throughout the night, the entire team was ensnared by fatigue and Simeon had reluctantly called a halt when the terrain allowed it. The slow, crawling pace of their progress was causing him severe annoyance.

Rita was occupied with tending to the horses. She paid particular attention to his own stallion, Titan, but also afforded a lot of time and affection to Betty, whom she had unaccountably grown fond of. Again, Simeon rolled his eyes as he watched her attaching the feed bag to her muzzle and lovingly smoothing out her mane. Women, even his formidable wife, were incredibly sentimental creatures!

Matteus and Thomas busied themselves with creating a fire and cooking something which, in spite of himself, Simeon found overwhelmingly compelling. He moved over and sat beside them, looking around him with interest as he began to relax somewhat, and suddenly let out a deep yawn of exhaustion: perhaps taking a rest was not such a bad idea after all.

His party numbered eight in total, and the remaining men of the company were laying out rolls and blankets for a morning rest. Their newest addition would bring their total to nine, Simeon reflected as he watched their work. These men were hand-picked by him personally. How would a newcomer with no previous ties of loyalty to him fit into the team? Could he trust them?

Their southward journey so far had brought them down the Sunken Road – a long, winding track used most often by farmers or the occasional trader or diplomat. Travellers between Ville Fleurie in the north of the Realm and the southern extent of the kingdom were not as common as they once had been, as the capital boasted little of practical value which could not be found in the more urban and commercial centres in the central region which had grown out of obscurity in the last century.

The Sunken Road got its name from the fact that it was bordered on both sides by steep, grassy banks, about eight feet high. These banks led up to fields filled with wheat and barley, swaying golden in the morning breeze. They had arrived at a short portion of the road which ran up and level with the fields, allowing them to set up their camp on the edge of one of them, but the track would soon sink again into the narrow gully and they would be forced to journey without a chance of resting until they reached the end of the road at the river crossing.

The field in which Simeon and the team found themselves resting had been harvested, and hundreds of pyramid-shaped bales populated the landscape like a city of tents. Further down the road, Simeon could see a mill in the distance. This was the land of House Thresh, a wealthy farming family that provided the capital with grain, crops and hay for livestock. The mill ahead was where they were to rendezvous with their latest recruit, and Simeon ordered two of his men to ride ahead and bring them to him.

They returned within the hour. Simeon was dozing lazily in the morning sunshine, a gentle breeze playing across his face as he closed his eyes and listened to the playful birdsong above him. The sun warmed his face delicately and his hand was enclosed within Rita's, who lay beside him on her own makeshift bed. He breathed deeply and wished he could allow himself to have a few more moments of peace, but he must remain vigilant and ready for his new arrival. He also had his professionalism as captain to maintain: he could not be seen to show affection for any of his team – even his wife.

He stirred and rose as he heard them approach. His men dismounted immediately and, with his leave, left to steal themselves a few hours' sleep before they resumed their journey. Simeon, on the other hand, had immediately lost any interest in sleep and was staring incredulously at the queen's personal appointment to his mission. He had expected a queen's man, sycophantic and slimy, reporting anything and everything back to Rowena and creating nothing but ill-will and discontent amongst his loyalists. He was prepared to have to justify every decision he made as captain and to walk on proverbial eggshells, the ever-present threat that he may be overruled by executive power from the queen herself. He had resigned himself to this misery, ever since he had departed Sandrine's company the previous night.

Yes, he had expected a queen's man.

He had not expected a queen's woman.

'Captain Castello, it is an honour to serve in your personal guard on this most sensitive of missions. Allow me to report to you in the professional manner: I am Adelaide, a personal representative of Her Majesty, Queen Rowena, on previous missions which have required discretion of the highest order.'

She paused, eyeing him hesitantly, but it could not be argued that she conducted herself with the utmost professionalism. This did not, however, excuse the fact that he had been laboured with a woman, one who would undoubtedly cause distraction amongst his men – she was certainly conventionally attractive – and slow them down in times of combat or peril. It had not escaped him that this female held no title of office: she had no military background of note, nor was she highborn.

He supposed he had better offer her a reply and greeting, so he cleared his throat, dispelling his disbelief. 'Welcome,' he replied stiffly, 'as you know, I am Captain Castello and I am the commander of this mission. All decisions are to be made by me personally, and I expect all soldiers in my company to follow orders. We are currently taking a short break for recuperation but I expect us ready by midday to continue on to the crossing at the Crystal Rapids.'

Adelaide nodded in response and, without a further word to Simeon, led her grey mare away towards the remainder of the team and began to introduce herself.

Simeon retired to his own bed, where Rita continued to sleep nearby, undisturbed by the events of the previous minutes. He was not impressed by this overconfident, bold woman and, as he settled down for what he highly doubted would be the refreshing and calming rest which he had hoped for, he reflected that he would be affording significant attention to her actions in the coming days. He was not sure how to feel, but he knew that he was not satisfied with this situation. And with that, he drifted into a restless sleep.

Later that day, as the various members of the team bustled around, strapping blankets to the backs of horses and generally erasing all evidence of their short stay at the roadside, Simeon helped Rita recouple Betty with the rolling prison carriage. This was mainly an opportunity to seek her opinion on Adelaide, but could not deny that he was also desperate for a brief moment with his love, to gaze upon her dark bronze beauty and shining halo of blonde hair which was still tied back in a tight braid. He had been trying so hard to think of her as a soldier, as an indiscriminate member of the team, and as a result he had almost tricked himself into forgetting that she was here with him.

As he finished buckling the straps on Betty's saddle, he wondered what his purpose was in doing this. Was it not what he wanted, to have her here? Then why was he torturing himself? All men, even a captain, deserved to be with the person they loved, did they not?

'I won't lie, it will be a relief having another woman on the journey,' admitted Rita, smirking across at Simeon with knowing amusement. She knew him well, better than any other, and she knew that commanding an unknown woman was not his ideal situation. 'I say you should wait to see her in combat and judge her on her merits.'

'I'm still hoping that there won't be much need for combat,' grunted Simeon begrudgingly. He would not let the men know it, but he would much prefer a boring, straightforward journey there, arrest the Cardinal Phantasm, and return without ever having to draw a sword or spill blood. He had no moral problems with doing so, and securing the Cardinal was necessary for the Realm to move forward with its plan against the Dominion, but he was not looking for adventure or a mission any more complicated than this one already was.

'Even so,' persisted Rita, following him and lowering her voice to a whisper as Thomas passed close by carrying a bedroll, 'you're worried that she's an agent of Rowena. And really, does that matter? We're all on the same side! Anything you do or order us to do on the mission will be in the service of Ville Fleurie and the Northern Realm as a whole. How can that be threatened by having a spy of the queen in our midst? Just accept her, and let's get on with our day.'

She put her hand on his shoulder to stop him, turned him around to face her and enveloped him in a loving, comforting embrace. He felt himself relax and melt into her. To know that she supported him and was there for him was what he needed at that moment. The smell of her hair was familiar, his heart skipped and he felt an overwhelming surge of love. The kiss between them as they pulled apart was passionate and full of love, and Simeon made his mind up there and then that he did not care if it discredited him in the eyes of his men – Captain Castello was travelling with his wife, the Lady Rita Castello, and she happened to be the most incredible fighter he had ever met. If they were bothered by that, he did not care.

As they made their way along the track an hour later and the banks of the Sunken Road rose again to obscure them from the outside world, Simeon wondered if he was being weak-willed. He had resumed his eye-rolling as he heard her chatting with Betty behind him, but Adelaide was riding at the back with Matteus and Thomas. This worried him slightly: would they maintain their dignity, their control, or would they embarrass him by bringing their company into disrepute in front of an agent of the queen? Matteus was his best friend, but he knew him too well to know what he was like with beautiful women, and the idea of him endangering the mission and Simeon's reputation by liaising romantically with Adelaide was making Simeon more anxious than was perhaps necessary.

Simeon's attention was brought back to the road ahead of him with a jolt of lightning. He sensed movement around the next corner, obscured by the overgrown banks which twisted and turned out of sight. No individual or animal emerged however, and Simeon's suspicions were immediately aroused. He held his hand up for those behind him to halt and dismounted tentatively. As determined as he was to avoid unnecessary bloodshed, in this situation he felt more in control with a drawn weapon, and his weapon of choice really required that he use both hands.

As he moved forward, he reached over his shoulder and removed this weapon from its sheath. The two-handed claymore which emerged was nearly five feet of smoky white metal, like stormy mist rolling down the distant mountains. This was Cumulonimbus, the harbinger of the approaching storm, and Simeon wielded her with brutal elegance.

The corner approached and Simeon made to turn around it, prepared for what he might find, his heart beating like a drum, but was surprised to see a short, slightly older man stroll leisurely into sight, his hands behind his back and an easy smile on his heavily stubbled face. His clothes were worn and frayed but also showed clear signs that they had once been finely tailored and he appeared to be unarmed. He had no visible mount or supplies, and that made little sense out here on open farmland. Simeon raised his voice and addressed the newcomer clearly and directly.

'Greetings. What business sees you travelling on the Sunken Road?' he asked. 'Are you farmer, merchant or pilgrim?'

'I am none of these fine professions,' came the reply from the man as he continued strolling towards them. On closer inspection, his shoulder-length hair was grizzled and matted and his face was pockmarked with scars. His eyes, however, were glinting with shrewdness and cunning as he finally stopped walking, stopping a distance far enough away to avoid direct contact but close enough to make a point. Every alarm bell in Simeon's head was sounding with suspicion, but the unusual character continued, 'Nor am I cleric, ranger or weary traveller. My name is Pyre, and I am a proud representative of the Republic of Caterva. But I am not here to talk about that...yet. You see, I'm curious about something. What reason might a retinue of guards – guards from the City of Blossoms, no less – have for travelling this far away from their beloved home? I am familiar with the soldiers who keep the queen's peace on these roads, and you are not they. And what is more, you are accompanied by the most curious contraption I have ever had the fortune of laying my eyes on.'

Simeon did not need to follow this individual's gaze to know he was referring to their cell for the eventual incarceration of the Cardinal. And what did he mean, *the Republic of Caterva*? Simeon had studied maps of the known world for his entire career and he felt sure that no such place existed.

Pyre continued, his gracious smile transforming before Simeon's eyes into a mocking smirk as his voice dripped with sarcasm. 'What could you possibly need such a secure cage for? I wonder, are you after a particularly *phan*-tastic prize? Please do tell me, I'm dying to know!'

Simeon had not missed the obvious emphasis in that last sentence and immediately calculated the risk in his head. This man was claiming to be from another country and knew of their plan for the Cardinal Phantasm. He was a danger to their mission, and the peace of the Realm.

'Sir,' he shouted, raising his sword in preparation and stepping forward, 'I believe you to be a threat to the Realm. I am placing you under arrest, in the name of Queen Rowena of Ville Fleurie and the Northern Realm. Until we can escort you to a jail in the next town, you will travel as our prisoner. Surrender yourself by raising both hands high above your head and turning around.'

He was expecting the smug smirk to slide off his face and it to be replaced by panic, but instead there came a low, threatening chuckle, wheezy and dry like reeds on stone.

'I think not,' he whispered, barely audible above the breeze which whipped the wheat in the fields above them. The day turned cold in that moment, as Simeon suddenly realised that he was not at all in control of the situation. Despite his team behind him, despite Cumulonimbus gripped tightly in both hands and despite the power he carried as a man of the queen, this strange, sinister man had complete control over what was occurring, and what was about to occur.

He whistled. High and clear, two short bursts.

At once, the high banks on either side of them erupted with activity. Simeon looked up in alarm and saw men, all carrying rusty swords and wearing long, woollen robes, glaring down at them. Simeon guessed around ten. Then, he heard the rumble of loose earth as three men slid expertly down into the sunken track between himself and Rita, completely cutting him off from the rest of the team. He saw Rita and Betty stumble back in shock. At the rear of the party, yet more men were sliding down to cut off their retreat. They were entirely surrounded.

Simeon could see only one way out of this: fight. Their attackers had the high ground advantage, and they could close in, restricting the manoeuvres which Simeon could put into action. Most of his team were very familiar with working together, surely he could work that to his advantage. He needed to think, he needed to concentrate. But only one thing kept racing through his head: Rita. He was responsible for leading her into this trap. If she died, that would be on his head and conscience. He would not allow that, though. He needed to think.

He knew they could get out of this, but how many casualties they would suffer was impossible to predict. Certainly some.

He gripped his claymore with sweating palms and stared their leader, the mysterious and conniving Pyre, directly in the eye. His eyes continued to dance with a flickering flame of mocking victory. Simeon gritted his teeth, bent his knees and prepared to pounce.

But then something unexpected happened. A whirling blur of steel and black swooped like a magnificent bird of prey from the fields above and descended on the attackers behind Simeon like a shadowy spectre. The three men fell to the ground in different directions, completely taken by surprise. Simeon whipped around to see what had happened, and what he saw made his jaw drop.

Adelaide was standing amongst the three scattered men, a long, slightly curved and impossibly sharp blade held expertly in both hands. A quick glance above his head surprised Simeon further, for all of the men who had stood above them were now lying, dead, in the long grass of the bank.

Matteus and Thomas sprang into action at the rear of the group, taking on the three aggressors who would have cut off their retreat. Closer by, Adelaide was searing the air with deadly razor sweeps from her thin, gleaming sword which were barely parried by her targets: the shallow trench was ringing with the deafening cries of metal on metal.

Her footwork made Simeon dizzy: she used the steep banks as another surface, running up and along them, slicing at her enemies as she moved. She caught one across the chest and he staggered, slumping to the ground as blood pumped through the openings in his veins and blossomed out onto the harvest grass.

Rita sprang into action, leaping off Betty in one great bound and piercing the back of another's skull with her war spear. It penetrated the front of his face, and she yanked it out with grim satisfaction as the now lifeless body crumpled in a heap.

Simeon suddenly realised, with genuine dismay, that he had forgotten Pyre. He hurtled back around, intending to arrest him for questioning, and saw that he was escaping, striding purposefully yet calmly away from them in the direction he had first appeared. Simeon wasted no time and sprang after him, Cumulonimbus held ready. He soon caught up with the retreating criminal – who made no indication of fear or haste – and swung his mighty greatsword, aiming for a glancing blow to his back which would injure and incapacitate but not mortally wound.

This never happened.

A wall of black flame erupted, as if from nowhere, inches from his nose which forced him back, falling to the ground and clutching at his scorched face in both hands. His eyes streamed and his skin blistered under his fingers. Blinking through the pain and the tears, he saw that Pyre was nowhere to be seen.

He fumbled for his sword, which he had dropped in the grass, and staggered forwards, around the corner and out of sight of his team. No sign. It was as if he had simply disappeared.

Simeon hurried back to find that the battle had been won. Miraculously, they had suffered no casualties, but all of their attackers were dead and beyond interrogation. He saw Rita above him, scanning the crop fields for further threats, and climbed the bank to reach her. She was still holding her bloody spear, battle-ready, but upon seeing Simeon she rushed to him and cried out in anguish at his burned face.

'What happened?' she uttered, 'What foul sorcery has done this to your poor face?' Simeon tried to answer, but he was too thankful to be alive and to still have a full team with which to continue his mission. He simply drew her close and held her.

As Matteus, Thomas and a younger member of the team called Rolf piled the bodies of the deceased into the cage – they would properly bury them once they cleared the farmland – Simeon and Rita sat at the top of the bank, looking down on the activity.

'What happened?' he asked her.

She knew what he meant. 'Matteus said that she disappeared up the bank and into the wheat the second the leader appeared in the lane. When the others came out of hiding and surrounded us, she must have made her way around them, killing them all above. That's the only explanation I can come up with – they were all dead, the next time I looked. But I definitely saw her jump down from up high and take on the ones near me! She killed two of them on her own!'

Yes, Simeon had seen that part, too. He looked down, scanning the track below him for Adelaide, whom they all owed their lives. She was not there. He raised his eyes and his heart skipped a beat in surprise: there she was, sitting on the top of the bank opposite, quietly watching the events unfold below as well.

She had not seen him looking, so Simeon took the opportunity to examine her further, perhaps properly for the first time, and certainly in a very different light. Her long, black cloak reached from neck to ankles and fastened at the front, obscuring the clothes she wore beneath. Perhaps armour, although Simeon doubted it judging by the agility and manoeuvrability she had displayed earlier. She had curious hair which she wore loose and flowing and which appeared mostly black. At certain angles, however, and when the sun shone on it in a certain way, Simeon could see streaks of a silvery blonde mixed in with the jet. Her face was pale with a slight rose to her cheeks and she had brown, almond-shaped eyes. She looked very different from anybody Simeon had met before, and he wondered where she was from, where she called home.

Suddenly, from across the road, Adelaide's gaze rose and her eyes met his. She smiled, quick and fleeting, before she rose, jumped agilely down into the track and began to help her teammates.

CHAPTER SEVEN

Riding through the night on good road had resulted in significant progress being made by Alene and her companions. The night air was warm and dry, and the five friends travelled in single file without speaking, as fast as their dear horses could carry them. Alene knew that they would need to stop soon, if only to allow their faithful mounts a well-deserved rest, and intended to ask Nox if she knew of a safe place where they might briefly leave the road to do so. Nox was still leading the way, followed closely by Griffin, and so she postponed the stop for now. They would do best to travel as far as possible under cover of night.

Alene had begun to notice that Nox and Griffin often travelled nearby each other; this made her smile whenever it caught her attention. Was there something new there, some growing affection? Or had they merely bonded over their numerous similarities which, Alene had to admit, she had never realised were so many.

She had known Nox for many years – it was Nox in fact who had saved her and helped her to adjust to life in the wild. She had worked alongside Griffin for a number of years also, him working in the castle stables and her fulfilling her duties as queen. From the beginning, from the moment she had been brought back by Gerecht to live in the unfathomably large castle as his bride, she had felt alone. Gerecht loved her and spent as much time with her as he could – and even Saggion made an effort to make her feel at home – but she had never truly felt in the early days that Regenbogen had been her home. Was it her desire for the wild mountains and moorlands which made her feel trapped, or was it that she was still mourning the loss of her old life as a whole? The freedom, the company of Nox wherever she went. Despite her coming in later years to love Regenbogen with all her heart, as much as she loved her husband and it feeling more of a home to her than any other place in the world, she doubted she would ever have come to feel like that without Roan and Griffin.

She had met Griffin on her very first day in Regenbogen – in fact, he was the first person she met, aside from Gerecht, Saggion and her ladies-in-waiting. The whole ordeal had threatened to overwhelm her, and her beloved was needed for a council meeting. She had set out on a long, meandering walk through the woods which clung to the cliff faces, down the secluded, sloped paths and felt her heart begin to slow and calm as she slipped back into nature. Those paths felt so serene and isolated: the sounds of the town below a million miles away. She had eventually found herself wandering into the stables, lost to distraction. Griffin had been sitting beside a bench of tools, not yet stable master but merely a servant boy. He had barely spoken to her, and she had barely spoken to him, but that had been, to her very great surprise, exactly what she had needed on that first day. Everybody else had bustled around and fussed over her, but he simply sat and provided company. She had returned to him every morning after that for a month; they had eventually spoken more and swapped stories. A loyal and loving friendship had grown from that first encounter, and Alene was forever grateful.

She squinted ahead in the darkness. She could only see him from behind but she knew that he looked exactly the same, remaining unchanged by the years. He was a short, slim man in his late twenties with short, cropped dark hair. He had loyally agreed to accompany her on this mission at a moment's notice, and she knew that he would always be there for her. Yes, she reflected as the sun began to rise, he and Nox had a great many things in common.

Nox must have been thinking of the horses as well, for she

slowed down and allowed the others to catch up. When they did, she stopped completely and turned Emmet so that she was facing them all.

'We've exhausted the night,' she announced. 'The sun is rising and soon the road will be busy with travellers. There's bound to be even more than usual, with so many people making their way north to Regenbogen for the feast of Empire's End.'

This concerned Alene. She knew that her face, as distinctive and memorable as it was with her mottled-grey-and-green skin and red eyes, would be instantly recognised as that of the queen. Elves were not a common sight in the Dominion. She once again considered the merits of their plan: of travelling to the Schloss Stieg and slipping through the Vale of Screams to the other side of the Rücken. Would it not be faster to attempt a route over the mountain tops? It would certainly mean avoiding the main roads, but Alene knew that her plan was truly the only option: Nox knew of no high passage which would get them safely to the other side, and to attempt it regardless would pose a risk to each life on the journey as well as the failure of the mission. Nox spoke again, bringing Alene back to practicality.

'There is an inn, a little further up the road at the crossroads. We will need to turn west there and take the Prairie Road to the Schloss Stieg. I would strongly suggest resting at the inn, staying off the road and resuming our journey tonight. Three night's travel should see us safely to the villages nearby the ruins of the Schloss and we can plan our covert approach in finer detail.'

Alene was immediately concerned. 'I don't think we should stay at the inn,' she said at once, trying to put as much authority as she could muster into her voice, but spoiling the effect slightly with a nervous quaver. 'We'll be seen! The inns on the main road are too busy. If I'm recognised, word will reach our enemies – wherever they might be. Ville Fleurie, the Schloss, elsewhere in the Realm...'

'My Queen,' began Griffin tentatively, looking her in the eye in an attempt to appeal to her rational side, 'the horses need rest – more than a stop by the side of the highway! They've got us this far; they deserve a break.'

'Besides,' added Nox, 'It's going to rain soon, and it's going to be a big one. There's nowhere to shelter on the roadside.' She too looked Alene straight in the eye with a steely determination. 'We'll be safe,' she assured her, 'We'll keep two of us on watch in the stable at all times to watch for approaching travellers – we can rest in shifts. If the rider with the gleaming chest plate arrives, we'll know about it.'

Alene swallowed hard, wanting to argue back. They had been ready to follow her lead before, so why should now be any different? She looked at Roan, who looked back and nodded his head once. So that was that: she was outnumbered.

Lionel looked as though he was about to speak, probably in favour of Alene, which was something she did not feel would be of any help in this situation, so she nodded back at Nox and looked away. She reached up and raised her woollen hood, tucking her long, ebony hair inside of it. In the half-light of sunrise, the shadow within the hood masked her features and all that could be seen was the crimson glow of two anxious and slightly nettled eyes.

They rode on in silence and reached the crossroads as the stars finally went out above them and the sun rose fully over the horizon. It was not becoming too bright, however, as menacing black storm clouds were fast dominating the sky and the distant rumble of thunder heralded the approaching storm. Alene could not help reaching up constantly to readjust and secure her hood. Being recognised now would spell disaster!

They slowed to a stop and Alene's eyes were drawn first to a large wooden signpost, pointing the way in four directions. To ride directly through the crossroads would eventually take them to the ruins of Clagcowl Abbey on the edge of the Sleeping Giants: chilly moorland with thick, rolling fog which was seldom visited save for the occasional ranger. This route was poorly maintained and long tufts of grass and weeds had been allowed to crack the surface of the road.

The left turn would eventually lead the follower to Cogburn, the largest city in the Eastern Dominion and the industrial epicentre of the entire kingdom. It was the right turn which they would eventually take, a well-traversed highway which twisted and turned over the Primrose Prairie and led through various ranches and farmland before reaching the dilapidated castle which was their destination. It would be the only way to pass through the gap in the Rücken and to the Vale of Screams on the other side. This was the road that would eventually lead them to the Northern Realm if everything went according to plan.

The inn itself was a large, two-storey building which was quite impressive for a roadside tavern. The painted wooden sign which hung above the door was swaying in the warm, pre-storm breeze with loud creaks of protest on its rusty hinges. This sign announced the inn to be called The Audacious Magpie and the party dismounted, one by one, leading their horses into the cobbled inn-yard. A stable door stood open to their left as they entered the enclosed courtyard and they stopped, looking at each other.

'I'll take the first shift,' Griffin told the group. 'I can get the horses settled and soothed before I switch for a rest.'

'Perfect,' said Roan, smiling tiredly and rubbing his eyes. 'I'll stay out too. I can sit at the stable door and keep a watch on the yard.' Nox raised her eyebrows at him as he yawned and he hastily added, 'Don't worry! I'm tired, but I'm used to all-nighters, I can manage another few hours before I stagger to bed.' He flashed them his roguish grin and led his horse through the open door.

At present, the yard was deserted, but the clatter of horse-shoes on the cobbled yard was sure to have alerted someone within to their presence. Sure enough, as she, Nox and Lionel made their way from the stable and crossed the yard, the heavy wooden door swung open and they were greeted by a tall young man in a grubby white apron. His short blond hair was stuck up at odd ends and his face was smudged with soot and flour. He smiled broadly as they approached.

'Welcome,' he called in greeting, throwing wide his tanned, muscular arms, 'to The Audacious Magpie. Please come in, make yourselves comfortable. My name is Mykel and I will be honoured to take care of you this morning. Will it be food and ale for you or is it a bed you desire?'

Alene once again checked her hood surreptitiously. Nox answered.

'Thank you for your hospitality,' she said with a warm, easy smile, perfected over years of ingratiating herself to others. She could turn it on instantly, and Alene had seen it many times in their shared past. It came in handy when they needed a bed for the winter.

'We appreciate that we are very early and have taken you away from your work,' she continued, eyeing the evidence of early-morning baking smeared on his smooth face. 'My companions and I have travelled a long way and would appreciate being shown to a room straight away. We are happy to share but would be extremely grateful to have some food served to our room, when you are not too busy.' She smiled again as he stepped aside and ushered them in.

The paved room was dimly lit by a flickering fire under a wide stone hearth at the far end. A high bar with rickety stools dominated the long wall and the rest of the space was populated by scrubbed wooden tables and benches. The stubs of candles sat in dishes on each table, burned down from the night before and twisted into molten shards and pools of wax.

The party walked through the deserted room and climbed the groaning wooden staircase beyond. Mykel followed them up and, once on the landing above, slid past them and opened another door into a small room. Inside were two beds and an empty basin, which Mykel returned and filled with warm water a few moments later. They let Lionel wash first – he had been travelling longer than them, after all – and by the time Alene and Nox had washed as well, Mykel had yet again returned, this time with a tray bearing hot stew and freshly-made rye bread.

They ate in silence. One of the benefits of arriving so early was freshly prepared food, and Alene felt true warmth filling her from within as she swallowed spoonfuls of diced pheasant and potatoes, using large chunks of bread to soak up the broth. Once they had finished, the bowls piled back on the tray in the corner, Lionel took some clean blankets and a straw-filled cushion to the floor at the foot of the beds and curled up, falling asleep almost immediately. Alene and Nox took the beds, but neither were as quick to relax. Only now did Alene dare to remove her hood, sure that Mykel would not return whilst they were sleeping. Lionel's soft snores sounded from the floor at their feet for a long time before Alene finally felt sleep take her.

Seconds later, or so it seemed to her, Alene's eyes shot open and bright sunlight was shining through the glass panes in the window. For a moment, she thought that it was this that had woken her from her sleep, except that Nox had sat up in bed as well. Something had startled them, but what was it?

Then they heard it: a ringing clatter of horseshoes on the cobbles in the courtyard below. Alene's heart plummeted like a rock and her stomach churned with fear – somebody had found them!

It took a moment for her to realise that she was being irrational. The inn must have received several patrons that morning since they had fallen asleep; this was merely one more who would escort their horse to the stable, enter the establishment for food and drink and then leave, never the wiser that Queen Alene Idir had ever been present at The Audacious Magpie.

And yet her anxiety persisted. She rose from her bed and slipped silently across the room, not wishing to wake Lionel who continued to snooze, and peeked around the window frame to survey the scene below.

And what she saw made her blood freeze in her veins.

A pale horse stood below in the yard, and astride it was a tall, hooded individual with a long, black cloak hung loosely over their shoulders in the morning sun. Blazing brilliantly in the dazzling rays, a shining silver breastplate was visible beneath it and Alene knew immediately that this was the person who had been following them, who had spied on them from the ridge and retreated when they had been spotted.

She gasped in shock and Nox darted across the chamber to join her. She took one look and ducked down, out of sight. Alene followed suit.

'What do we do?' asked Alene, her voice hurried and hushed, yet remarkably calm compared to how she was feeling on the inside.

'We wait,' was the ranger's immediate reply. Nox was cool and collected, and this was an immense relief to Alene. Nox would know what to do. 'We wait until we observe more. They may yet leave; in which case we're safe. If not, then we need to consider fleeing the scene. Either way, we need to be prepared.' She crossed the room again and returned with Alene's cloak and boots, donning her own in the process. She then bent down next to Lionel and shook him gently by the shoulder to rouse him, pushing a finger to his lips as he stirred to instil silence.

All of this was done in a matter of seconds. As this occurred, the mysterious spy outside swung their leg over and dismounted the white horse. It tossed its head in impatience and its pale mane shone brilliantly as it was led towards the stable door. Alene gasped again as she remembered that Roan and Griffin were concealed within the stable, possibly just out of sight. What was going through their heads at this moment? Were they having the same hushed, hurried conversation as they were?

The seconds stretched on like hours as the ominous new arrival crossed the cobbles and the three friends crouched at the window above, holding their collective breath, their hearts beating fiercely against their ribs.

Suddenly, the figure stopped. It seemed to tense and its head turned sharply beneath the black hood and it looked up, directly at their window. They all instinctively ducked down beneath the windowsill and looked wide-eyed at each other. Had they been seen?

'Did you see its face?' mouthed Nox in the silence.

Alene shook her head slightly, hardly daring to move. Despite this, they slowly peered over the sill again and saw that the figure's gaze had returned to the stable door.

Except that the doorway was no longer empty.

Roan was stood, tall and resolute, with Reaper held steady in his arms and a long, black arrow notched.

'What is your business here?' he called, loudly and clearly, across the yard.

Alene watched, transfixed, her sharp elven eyes darting from Roan, to Reaper, to their black-cloaked pursuer and back again. A minute passed, and Alene wondered if any answer would come at all. Nox was tense beside her; Lionel kept letting out short, tremulous gasps of panic.

Then, quite suddenly, the unknown individual reached beneath its cloak and drew a shining silver sword, completely unlike anything Alene had seen before. Nox rose and ran towards the door to their chamber, motioning silently that Alene was to stay, so she and Lionel continued to watch, Alene wishing more than anything that she did not need to stay out of sight. She knew one thing, however, and that was that she would not hesitate to make her presence known if any of her friends were in danger. For now though, she must remain hidden.

One step. The gleaming figure with the silver sword took one step towards Roan, raising its weapon as it did so. Alene noticed that they wore red gloves made of leather. As quick as a flash of lightning, Roan drew his bow and loosed his arrow; Alene heard it hit the silver breastplate of its target and glance off, snapped in half.

The unknown assailant was still for a second, momentarily stunned.

Then it let out a roar of rage and anger – a terrifying bellow like a wounded boar – and charged towards the stable door, raising its dazzling sword high in both hands.

Except they never reached the stable, for down from the roof above descended Griffin, crouched and ready to pounce like a wildcat. The figure paused again, assessing their target, and in that split second, Griffin whirled like a tornado, pivoting on his hands to swing his outstretched legs out and around with such force that he caught his attacker around the knees and brought them clattering to the ground in a heap, the silver sword scuttling across the cobbles and out of reach.

If they were stunned, they did not show it, for they instantly rolled and regained their footing. Another split second passed, wherein the situation was assessed. The cloaked figure sprang, but this was no attack: they mounted the white horse and wheeled around, tearing at full speed out of the yard and through the archway onto the highway, sparks flying from the cobbles as it went.

The inn door flew open and Nox sprinted out, breathing heavily and both weapons held high, only to see the back of the retreating figure as it fled onto the road. Alene flung open the window and leaned out as far as she could, hood drawn tightly over her features again.

'Upstairs, now!' was her only instruction and sure enough, they entered the room barely a minute later. All appeared unharmed, yet Roan had a look of deep, bitter resentment on his usually laughing face.

'We could have finished it, here and now!' he almost shouted at Griffin. His teeth were gritted and his fists were clenched tight, white and shaking. The usually quiet and calm Griffin bristled and went brick-red in the face.

'We didn't need to kill him, Roan – we wanted to drive him off. I will not spill unnecessary blood! It worked, didn't it? We can make our move now, begin immediately and escape his gaze. He'll think twice before confronting us again, that's for sure.'

'You're so naïve!' retorted Roan, still shaking and his voice unnaturally high. 'If he's alive, he's a danger to the mission. He's a danger to Alene. He's a danger to all of us. If he kills us now, it'll be your fault!'

Griffin opened his mouth, but no words came out. He appeared stunned into silence, but Nox suddenly stepped into the fray.

'Back off, Roan!' she whispered, quiet yet poisonous. Her eyes sparked with deadly flame and she had them set squarely on Roan. 'Griffin did what he thought was right. It would do us no good to kill him or take him captive. We need to remain inconspicuous – what could be more of a statement than taking a prisoner in a roadside tavern?'

Alene suspected that she knew why Nox was taking Griffin's side, and it had nothing to do with the situation at hand. However, she had to agree with her logic. She looked at Roan, who was now looking her way, eyes pleading for support. She could not give him that: to kill their attacker would have been a huge mistake. Indeed, confronting him in the first place was a reckless act, and yet Alene would not turn against her best friend. She would not tear the group asunder when they needed more than ever to act as a unified team.

Lionel said nothing, sitting on the bed and gazing wide-eyed from one person to another as each spoke. He was whiter than normal beneath his shining blond hair but appeared to be taking it in his stride.

Something unlocked in Alene's memory and she suddenly remembered. 'Did you get his sword?' she asked, remembering that it had been knocked to the ground.

Griffin grunted and tossed it on the vacant bed. It was long and, as it had appeared, was made from polished silver. Nox picked it up and surveyed it carefully, running her fingers down its blade and holding it up to the light from the window.

Eventually she sighed and put it back on the bed.

'No marks to show us the bladesmith' she told them. 'It's intricately made, but I'm afraid that's as far as my knowledge on the subject goes.'

Alene turned to Griffin. 'You keep saying 'he'. Are you sure it's a man?'

'Definitely,' he replied without hesitation. 'He was strong – begging your pardon, he was much stronger than any woman I have ever met or heard of.'

'He wailed, also,' added Roan, still looking bitter. 'The noise he made when he charged sent shivers down my spine. It was either a man, or a beast.'

'Did you see his face?' asked Nox.

They both shook their heads. Griffin's face creased in confusion as he said, 'I ought to have done, I looked down at him as he fell. His hood remained secure, and yet I looked down into his face and saw what was beneath. It's strange – I should have seen everything, and yet I remember none of it. It's as though my memory has been wiped clean and I can't seem to recollect his features.'

'Magic,' muttered Nox darkly. 'Some form of glamour, I would bet.'

Alene was troubled by this news as well. She had little in the experience of magic, and the prospect of an adversary with arcane skills made her uncomfortable.

'Either way, we must continue on,' she said instead, choosing not to display her true emotions at the previous revelation. 'The horses are not yet ready, what can we do, Griffin?'

'Your Majesty, I fear we must escape on foot. Our current friends cannot travel another day without sleep and rest. We will come back for them, one day. With your permission, I will arrange with Mykel to keep them here and we can pick up new mounts at the next village.'

Alene was torn: she knew that there was wisdom in Griffin's words, knew that to force the horses to continue would be a death sentence for them, and yet was heartbroken at the thought of abandoning Thane. He was her last connection to her love, Gerecht, out here in the wilderness of the Dominion, but she sighed and nodded once. Griffin left the room and they heard him descend the creaking wooden stairs.

Roan gripped her shoulder affectionately. 'Don't worry,' he whispered. 'We'll come back for them one day.'

It was with a heavy heart that Alene left the chamber a few minutes later, hood pulled up over her ebony hair. Roan led the way, Alene followed with Lionel close behind and Nox brought up the rear. She was deep in thought: who was their attacker? Why was he interested in their mission? Did he know of the Cardinal? As they began to descend the stairs however, she was brought sharply back to reality as she realised that a conversation was occurring down in the bar. Roan stopped ahead of her and words floated up to them from downstairs.

'I beg your leave, I know not to what you are referring,' came Griffin's voice, calm and level, completely at ease. Alene, however, could hear the merest tinge of uncertainty in his skilful subterfuge. He was clearly unsure of who he was talking to.

'I will say it again then,' came the reply: a man's voice, cold and sneering. 'I represent the Republic of Caterva, and I have reason to believe that you travel with none other than the Iontach of Regenbogen, her Serene Highness Queen Alene Idir.'

Alene had to hold herself up on the bannister. Her knees buckled below her in shock; how had she been recognised? She had been so careful!

'What's more,' the voice continued, 'I know that you head for the Schloss Stieg, and intend to pass through the Vale of Screams. You seek the most valued of prizes – the sovereign of the phantasms, the Cardinal, and you see we simply cannot allow that to happen. The Republic will rise, and her type will become extinct. You, however, could be a valuable asset to our cause: we seek communion with the common people of this land.' The sentence hung in the air for a second only before Griffin replied. His voice was far less composed than it had been a moment before.

'I tell you all, I know nothing of which you speak. I travel alone on a pilgrimage to Clagcowl Abbey in the south.'

There was a ripple of cruel laughter at this from around the room: Griffin was outnumbered. Alene was desperate to come to his aid, but Roan held up a hand authoritatively. She knew he was right – Griffin had just said that he was alone. To descend into the bar would prove him to be a liar. Besides, she would then be recognised for certain.

'We can soon solve this problem,' came the cold voice again. They heard heavy footsteps on the stone floor as he walked away, across the room. Then he spoke again. 'Was this man alone?'

Alene heard Mykel stammer in fear from behind the bar, 'Erm…I don't…erm…you see…I didn't see…yes, I believe he was alone.'

Alene felt a rush of gratitude for Mykel; he was keeping their secret, for no other reason than to protect them. He did not sound convincing however, and another cackle of cruel mirth erupted from the mass below.

'I have no wish to spill blood of the people,' came the cold voice again in a mocking tone, 'but if I find that you are both lying to me, I will kill you personally. I am Ignitus, a servant of Caterva – remember that!'

Footsteps again, but this time they were approaching the staircase, where Alene and her party were crouched in hiding. It was now or never, Alene knew. They would have to fight their way out of this!

At that moment, a muffled thud came from across the room, the unmistakable sound of a body falling to the ground. The footsteps stopped, just away from the foot of the steps.

'That was a very poor choice of action,' Ignitus said from just below them. His voice was no longer mocking, but victorious and full of malice. He had turned around and was walking back the way he had come, back towards the bar. Alene knew that Griffin was in trouble, however it was Roan who sprang into action, leaping the last few steps and drawing Reaper in one fluid motion. He let loose a black-fletched arrow and the whole room heard a sharp intake of breath, a strangled cry of pain and, finally, a crash as another body hit the paved floor.

One heartbeat. Then two. Then thunder erupted from the room below as what sounded like twenty people charged as one towards Roan. He smirked as he loosed one more arrow and then ran out of sight, into the fray. Alene was immediately behind him, and the sight that greeted her took her breath away.

Twenty was about right. Twenty men and women, all wearing green woollen robes and carrying ancient-looking swords. Roan had jumped high over the heads of those nearest him and made his way to Griffin and Mykel beside the bar. Whilst Mykel ducked to safety, Griffin spun gracefully into the air and delivered a perfectly aimed kick to the neck of the nearest thug, who let out a grunt and crumpled. Griffin needed no weapons: his entire body was a weapon!

Roan charged and, as he did, he turned Reaper expertly in his hands. The handle split: each shining, razor-sharp limb of the bow was now a deadly, curved sickle that flashed menacingly in the firelight, one in each hand. This weapon was one-of-a-kind, and Roan was the only person alive who was skilled enough to wield it. It was these sickles which gave it its name: Reaper.

He spun through the onslaught, bodies dropping to the floor around him. Nearby, Griffin's fingertips were masterfully finding pressure points, reducing the enemy attack one by one.

Alene shook herself into action and drew her own weapons. She had not used Dawn and Dusk for some time but found that the muscles in her arms and body remembered well how to twist and turn in a deadly dance. Both falchions were curved and tapered into a vicious tip, and she held Dawn in front of her to attack and Dusk behind her in a backhand grip, primarily for defence and backward attacks.

As she cut down her first aggressor, her hood slipped and her grey-green skin and red eyes were exposed for all to see. One woman saw and opened her mouth to shout. Alene dove towards her, intent on silencing her, but a heavy axe flew through the air and embedded itself deep in the woman's face. Blood spurted from the deep gorge across her previously pretty features and she fell. Nox appeared and retrieved Far from her victim, wrenching it out with a sickening squelch as she raised Near and disappeared from view.

Even Lionel was in the fray. He was proving efficient at using his size to his advantage, ducking under thrusts and sweeps to deliver a knife puncture to the gut of his would-be killer. His luck only got him so far though, and he soon found himself dizzy and sprawled on the dusty floor, blood gushing from his nose after a brutal kick to the face.

Alene was beginning to feel that they may, in fact, win – that they might be able to escape and continue on their mission. She stooped to help Lionel as Roan and Nox dispatched the final two attackers and was helping him to his feet when the door to the inn crashed open and the room was flooded by green-cloaked men and women. They fanned around the perimeter of the room, surrounding them.

Alene saw Nox and Roan overpowered as strong men the size of ogres wrenched their weapons from their hands and held their arms tight, forcing them into a kneeling position. They had been completely taken by surprise, and now they looked up at Alene in shock and defeat. Nox had a deep cut across her cheek which was bleeding and Roan had a bloodied lip with the beginnings of a black eye forming. Alene looked frantically for Griffin before locating him, unconscious yet clearly alive, beside the bar.

'Your Majesty, we have been expecting you,' called a short woman from across the room. She sneered as she prowled the circle of her followers, Alene in the centre. 'That incident in the yard told us everything we needed to know: the queen is here, and she is on her way to get the Cardinal. Your silver-plated enemy escaped our clutches, whomever he may be, but you, Your Majesty, will not.'

The way she said 'Your Majesty' was full of sarcasm and irony, and Alene did not understand why. Were these forces of the Northern Realm? No, she reminded herself. They were from the Republic of Caterva, wherever that may be. One thing was clear: they were not affiliated with their adversary with the silver chest plate.

Alene needed a way out of this. There must be a way.

She counted twenty more.

She saw Griffin, motionless.

She saw Nox and Roan, wide-eyed and defeated.

She felt Lionel beside her, mopping his nose yet standing defiantly.

The fear washed over her. Threatened to engulf her. Cold panic. This was her fault, her responsibility!

She must do something.

There must be a way!

A perishing cold flickered deep in her core. Icicles pierced her gut and lungs as she felt an iron grip squeezing her heart and forcing her to her knees. Her hands shook uncontrollably as burning tears streamed down her cheeks and she coughed and spluttered as she fought for consciousness. Then, from deep inside of her, words that she recognised as her own burst free from her lips in a violent scream.

'You have not won! You have no idea who you are dealing with!'

With that, Alene arched her back and screamed as black flame erupted from her body. It wreathed her, spinning faster and faster, licking the floor on which she stood and scorching it black. Dense fireballs of coal-black flames formed in her outstretched palms and tongues of flame emanated from her open mouth. As one, the magical fire rushed the onlookers, engulfing them in searing flame as they writhed on the ground in pain and agony.

Only Roan, Nox, Griffin, Lionel and Mykel were spared,

and they rushed through the licking flames without injury as the building began to collapse around them. Roan carried the unconscious Griffin over his shoulder and Nox and Mykel worked together to support Alene, who had now slumped into a deep and magically-induced sleep. Lionel retrieved Alene's weapons from the floor and hurried after them as they fled the burning remains of The Audacious Magpie and disappeared out, once again, into the wild.

CHAPTER EIGHT

I t was not until later that day, as the sun was setting, that Alene began to awaken. She stirred groggily, slowly becoming aware of her surroundings: of the cool, damp grass beneath her; of the light breeze playing against her face and the scent of earth after a storm; of the frantic whispers of people nearby. Her head was throbbing and every joint felt as though it was swelling in agony. She kept her eyes closed for a few moments more, sensitive to the light of the setting sun which she could see through her eyelids, and listened to the voices.

'Do you think she's always been able to do that?' asked one of them quietly.

'She never has before,' replied another in a hushed voice. 'My bet is she did it spontaneously, heat of the moment. It'll be her elven blood probably. Either way, we're lucky she did, or we'd all be dead right now!'

Alene did not know what the voices were talking about, but as she racked her brain, trying to recall memories from her last waking moments, she found herself reliving half-memories of black flames and flickering darkness. She gasped in horror and sat up, almost hitting her head on the underside of a large hedge. She disentangled herself from the shrubs above her and lay back down, looking around her to get her bearings. She appeared to be lying on the edge of a field, immediately beside and slightly underneath a hedgerow which bordered the road on its other side. From her position here, she could see and hear everything and everyone who may pass by on the road whilst remaining completely obscured from view. She rolled over, feeling the throb in her head pound painfully as she did so, to see Griffin and Roan lying a short distance away in quiet conversation. They stopped when they saw her awake and shuffled close.

'Queen Alene, are you quite alright?' asked Griffin, concern in his voice as he looked her over. He appeared unharmed but groggy. Alene recalled that he had been knocked unconscious and was immediately concerned.

'I'm fine, but what about you? You were hurt, were you not?'

'Never mind me, My Queen,' he answered with a smile. She looked at Roan also, whose lip and left eye had swelled and coloured in the recent hours.

Her attention turned to the state of their situation. 'Where are we? What happened to our supplies? And the horses?'

Roan answered. 'We managed to save some supplies – mostly blankets and food – and all of our weapons are accounted for, but we lost some of our provisions in the fire.'

Flashes of the past returned to her as she saw the black flames engulfing the bar, licking up walls and devouring the wooden building.

Roan continued. 'The horses are fine. Mykel got them all out before the fire spread to the stable and has taken them on the road to Cogburn. The hope is that we will be able to return one day, reclaim our devoted friends and repay Mykel for his hospitality, his loyalty and his inn which you destroyed.' He smiled playfully at Alene, which surprisingly made the latter part of this information slightly easier to take in.

Alene sat up further and looked around again. She could see no sign of Nox or Lionel and feared the worst. Griffin seemed to read her mind.

'Nox and the boy are scouting ahead,' he told her. 'Once you are strong enough to travel, we must press on. The road will be longer on foot.'

Alene was more than ready to make progress yet swayed alarmingly as she stood up. A few minutes later, and with many deep breaths of cool evening air, they were ready to move and she retrieved her weapons from the ground beside her. She secured Dawn and Dusk at her belt, whereas her bow was normally slung over her back. It was made of wood from Marrowmarsh, and as such was bone-white and extremely supple. She had acquired it in her youth, shortly after her expulsion from the elven kingdom and it was inscribed with runes and symbols which she did not fully understand but appreciated for what they were: they were intended to fortify strength and patience for the wielder, to make them a more effective bowman. Her twin falchions had a different origin story, but Alene could not bring herself to think of it now.

Further up the road, they encountered Lionel, who had been lying hidden amongst more foliage and reported that he had seen nobody pass on the road since earlier in the afternoon. From this, they inferred that no more representatives of the Republic of Caterva were in the immediate vicinity and that it was safe for them to make progress. As they walked, Alene asked questions, attempting to fill the gaps in her memory.

'What is the Republic of Caterva?' she asked. She had never heard of it before but was sure that Roan would have. She was surprised then to hear that he had not seen it mentioned before in any books. He was not completely ignorant on the subject though and gave his opinion on the matter.

'I think it's an anti-monarchy movement,' he said slowly, looking sideways at Alene as he did so. 'The way they spoke, the manner of their agenda, the fact that they seemed to hate you specifically, Alene, and yet did not want to hurt 'the people', I think that they're planning to overthrow the central government.'

'But Gerecht *is* the central government!' insisted Alene.

'Gerecht and his ministers, especially Chief Minister Saggion, govern the Eastern Dominion effectively and justly. Why would anybody want to jeopardise that? To end that would be to allow anarchy to rule!'

'Hmm,' muttered Roan. Alene knew that he was not overly fond of Saggion, that Saggion had never been particularly fond of him, but surely he must see that no good could come from an end to centuries of ruling protocol.

He chose to change the subject instead of pursuing this topic. 'We know that our friend, the silver swordsman, is not with the Republic, so that's still a mystery for another day.' He paused and looked sideways at Alene again, then glanced at Griffin who merely shrugged. Roan took a deep breath and ploughed on. 'And there's also the matter of how we escaped...'

Alene looked at him sharply. Lionel's head perked up and he stared at Alene, waiting for some response. She did not know what to say though. She could remember the tsunami of black fire devouring the legions of the enemy and had the uncomfortable suspicion that it had been her that had caused it. Was it sorcery?

She took a long time to answer. Finally, she confessed, 'I don't know what happened. I felt like I was dying – that my entire life force and essence was being drawn from me and projected outwards. I felt freezing cold and empty on the inside, it was terrible. And yet also exhilarating. I don't know what it was though. It couldn't be...magic. Could it?' She looked at Roan, pleadingly, begging him for a logical, well-researched answer. Lionel gawped at her; mouth hung slightly open. Roan reached out and held her hand in his before answering.

'It is entirely possible that it was magic,' he said softly and gently. She noticed the change in his demeanour: no jokes now. This was the Roan who cared fiercely for his best friend, who placed caring for her at the very top of his priorities. She was terrified of what she was becoming, and

Roan knew that.

'You have elven blood, so the magic is there inside you,' he continued. 'That's not normally enough though. According to my readings on elven culture, the ability to harness magic only manifests once an elf has been trained to locate it inside them and release it in small bursts, manipulating it for their own ends. My hypothesis is that you released your magic accidentally in a moment of desperation – but you released all of it, causing your body to shut down in order to stop you from killing yourself.' He squeezed her fingers and drew her gaze back to his. 'Does that sound plausible?'

Alene thought for a moment. She had felt that her very essence, her life force, was being sucked from her. She had felt cold and decay inside her soul. It was perfectly plausible that Roan was correct, that she had desperately expelled all of her magic – magic she did not even know she had – at once and had begun to suffer a heightened type of malnourishment as a result. She looked at him and nodded, letting go of his hand and walking ahead.

Further up the deserted road – which, Alene realised, was the Prairie Road leading west towards the mountains – Nox sat on the grassy verge waiting for them. She was slowly chewing on a chunk of stale bread and Alene suddenly realised how hungry she was; the pheasant stew seemed an age ago!

As they neared Nox, she rose and walked towards them. She put one hand on Griffin's shoulder and told him that there was a small ranch by the roadside a few miles ahead. She glanced around at Roan and Lionel, but pointedly did not meet Alene's gaze. She turned and walked ahead, alone and with purpose. Roan trotted ahead to walk alongside her, intent on discovering more about what lay ahead, and left Alene to walk with Griffin and Lionel.

'Don't be upset, My Queen,' Griffin whispered gently to her. Alene looked at him, shocked and slightly embarrassed that he had noticed. Then she realised with horror that tears were welling in her black and red eyes. She had suspected that this would happen, ever since she had woken up and discovered that she had performed magic, but was saddened deeply by it all the same.

'Has she said anything?' she asked.

'No, but she has suffered an immense shock, that's for certain,' he replied. 'You know Nox better than anybody, so I daresay you could shed more light on this behaviour than anyone else, but I have come to realise that she has a deep mistrust, and even fear, of anything magical. On our first day, she asked me if I was a mage; the relief when I told her 'no' was palpable. I begin to feel a strange affinity, even a fondness, for Nox and yet I know so little about her.'

Alene sighed. 'Her story really is not mine to tell,' she told him heavily, 'but her dislike of magic is because of her mother. I won't say any more – it is her business and not mine – but I hope with all my heart that she can see past this and remember that I would never hurt her like she did'.

'It will come with time,' he answered. Then he did something very uncharacteristic for Griffin: he draped his arm around her shoulder and pulled her close into a hug. He released her rather quickly, but the gesture was there. This journey was bringing them all closer together, in ways which the previous decade had not even been able to do.

The next day was long and arduous. Without horses, and with dwindling rations of stale bread and cheese, they trudged on in silence. The ranch which Nox had spoken of turned out to be abandoned, with no trace of food or animals, so they had no choice but to continue on foot.

And then, as the sun began to set again and the weary party was dreaming longingly of their roadside beds, they heard activity behind them.

Alene turned hastily and looked down the road, the way they had come. In the far distance, over the rolling hills which they had just traversed, a long, snaking train of horse-drawn caravans was slowly catching up with them. Alene immediately looked to Nox for guidance, but she persisted in avoiding her gaze. Alene bit her lip. Gypsies.

Griffin motioned for his companions to descend the roadside and they gathered together beneath the hedgerow. This section of the road was completely obscured from the fields to the south by this thick hedge but overlooked the prairie to the north with an unobstructed view. They crouched in the gathering gloom of dusk, awaiting the passing of the caravans. Alene waited with bated breath and a beating heart. If they passed them by, they could continue their journey unseen and avoid detection. She also had her own selfish reasons for wanting to avoid gypsies, but only Nox knew this.

At length, they heard the rhythmic clip-clopping of horses' hooves on the dirt road and the gentle creaking of large, wooden wheels approaching. Then they saw them: huge, shaggy horses festooned with dangling brasses on leather straps. Their manes were much longer than Thane's had been, flowing and glossy in the dying light of the day. Chestnut, palomino, dun and dapple – Alene lost count of how many passed them by in their hidden hideaway – and each one was pulling an elaborately decorated gypsy wagon.

Some of these had rounded roofs, others were more box-like and rectangular. All of them though were beautifully painted with bright colours and floral designs that covered every available surface and transformed the caravans into a festival of beauty. Alene was surprised that they reminded her of the frescos of Regenbogen. Others had blooming boxes of trailing flowers that cascaded from the roofs in glorious sheets and swayed from side to side in the lull of the wagons as they made their way past. Each caravan was being commanded by one or two dark-skinned, dark-haired men or women who held the reins loosely and lazily, more content with gazing out across the prairie and taking long drinks from bottles of different coloured glass. From within the folds of the coverings, Alene could see more travellers – sometimes up to eight more – peeking out at the road ahead with carefree, content expressions.

Some gypsies walked alongside the wagons, strolling leisurely by, hand-in-hand. They wore long, flowing dresses of bright materials decorated with glittering jewellery and loose, flowing headscarves of smooth silk. The men were dressed similarly, except that they appeared to be wearing breeches beneath the draped fabric around their waist. Children wearing very little at all were chasing each other, weaving in and out of the wagons and shrieking with delight in the evening air as they caught each other, tackling them to the ground and rolling around in the dirt.

For all the mirth and contentment, Alene did not trust these gypsies. A run-in with one particular family had transformed the life of one close to her but left a bitter taste in her mouth and a deep mistrust for the gypsy people. If they were spotted, crouching at the side of the road under the hedge, Alene was under no doubt that they would be robbed for their worldly possessions and left dead in the ditch. There were at least a hundred of them – perhaps more – and there was little chance that they would be able to fight their way away this time, especially with Alene in her weakened state and after a full day's travel on foot.

At last, the final caravan groaned and swayed past them. Alene allowed herself to breathe a sigh of relief and glanced over at Griffin, who smiled reassuringly at her. Nox opened her mouth, presumably to whisper advice or instructions for their next move, when suddenly they heard a shout from the roadside.

'Whoa there, halt I say!' came the authoritative cry of a man's deep voice and, slowly and reluctantly, the train of wagons came to a stop.

Alene ducked down as low as she could so that she was

lying flat on her stomach in the damp leaves. The others followed suit and Alene saw Nox retrieve Far from her belt. On her other side, Lionel drew his dagger.

All was silent for a second more, then they heard a soft thud as somebody hopped down from the final wagon onto the road. It had been a little way ahead of them when it had stopped, so none of them could see who it was, but Alene's heart sank as she heard the soft crunch of footsteps strolling their way slowly towards their hiding spot.

And then, quite suddenly, they had been discovered. A large, round-bellied man with a thick, black beard was staring down at them from the road. There was no mistake that he was looking right at them: his shrewd eyes passed over each of them in turn, yet he remained silent. Then, he spoke.

'Weary travellers,' he began, his face emotionless, betraying nothing. 'The road is long; the night is to be tempestuous and inhospitable. You will find little in the way of shelter along the Prairie Road; might I suggest you climb aboard and offer us your company tonight? You could pay us back with a story, I'm sure you have a good one.'

Roan made to speak, but Alene's hand shot out and she squeezed his arm in an iron grip. He glanced her way in alarm, but she merely shook her head, eyes pleading.

The stranger above them seemed impatient, but not calculating. He descended the bank slowly, careful not to slip on the wet leaves and foliage. Nox drew her knees up beneath her, ready to spring with Far should she need to. When the gypsy had made his way down to the bottom of the shallow gully, he bent down on his haunches and looked Alene straight in the eye. Despite her hood, she knew immediately that he recognised her. He looked at her for a few moments more, then raised his hands, arms bent, over his head: a sign that he was unarmed and meant no harm to the party.

Then he said, in a quiet whisper, 'I believe I have the

honour of addressing Queen Alene Idir of Regenbogen, do I not?'

A flickering light of courage ignited in her heart, and she replied defiantly, 'You do. And what, may I ask, is your business with myself and my companions?' There was little use in denying her identity: one good look was enough to confirm it.

'I have an acquaintance at The Audacious Magpie called Mykel,' he whispered back, smiling slightly at her reply. 'We crossed paths earlier today on the road to Cogburn and he spoke to me of the queen of the rainbow city, making her way west across the Primrose Prairie. He swore me to discretion but implored me to offer you my assistance, should we encounter you on the road. Do not fear, Your Majesty, you can trust me'. He smiled down at her and she was suddenly conflicted. If this man were a trusted confidante of Mykel, could they trust him? She glanced sideways at her companions, only to see them already staring at her.

Alene swallowed hard, brain working feverishly. He knew who she was. If he meant them harm, he would do so, whether they believed him or not. On the other hand, if he truly was offering them passage across the prairie, safely away from prying eyes within the refuge of one of the horse-drawn wagons, then that could speed up their journey and have them at the Schloss Stieg in half the time. All of this raced through her head in a matter of moments, and she made her mind up, disentangling herself from the hedge bottom and standing tall to face their supposed benefactor. As she raised her hands to pull back her hood however, he suddenly glanced behind him and whispered, 'Beggin' your pardon, Your Majesty, but I would keep your face covered for now. Not all of my family are privy to your identity, and it would do best to keep it that way for now.'

Alene paused, then nodded once. She scurried up the bank and the gypsy followed her. Her friends were the last ones up and onto the road, Lionel still gripping his knife tightly and Griffin glancing around vigilantly. Nox, however, appeared to be taking the gypsy at his word and had replaced Far at her belt. They all walked the short distance to the wagon closest to them, the final one in the caravan, and used the short wooden steps to ascend into the interior.

The inside of the wagon was nowhere near as extravagant as the lavish exterior. Instead of bright, vibrant murals and riots of stunning blooms, the soft and plush furnishings spoke solely of simple comfort. Alene hesitated at the door, but Roan gently slid past her and entered, so she followed and took a seat on a thick carpet of comfortable pillows. Lionel sat beside her, knife in hand, but Nox and Griffin chose to remain standing.

The cabin began to rock and sway as the caravan resumed its journey. The party remained silent, listening for any sounds from outside. Everybody was thinking the same thing: had they made the correct decision? Could they trust these people?

Five minutes passed, then ten. Still, nobody said a word. Alene's eyes flicked in every direction, taking in her surroundings, her companions. Nox continued to avoid her gaze, looking resolutely ahead at the door; Roan had removed Reaper from his back and was oiling its razor limbs; Lionel sat, agitated and uncertain, absent-mindedly twirling his dagger in his fingers; Griffin leaned against the far wall, eyes closed, listening.

Eventually, they heard footsteps walking the length of the wagon outside and hop onto the ladder outside as it continued to move along. The door opened and the gypsy entered, accompanied by a younger woman of around eighteen. She had blonde, curly hair which was partially covered by a dark red headscarf and she smiled warmly and sincerely at them all as she entered.

'My father has informed me of who you are,' she said softly, moving to sit cross-legged on another cushion. She jingled and clinked slightly as the many stone beads which she wore around her skirt swung and clattered against each other. 'You have nothing to fear from me or my fathers, but I must implore you to remain vigilant around the rest of our family – not all of them are as loyal as us. My name is Constantina, and this is my father, Menowin.'

Alene found herself drawn to Constantina, in spite of herself. The man who had approached them by the roadside, Menowin, smiled also but remained standing.

'My husband and I are the heads of this family,' he said, 'and while you remain safely in our wagon, you will remain safe. However, you must not venture outside: I implore you to stay concealed. We can deliver you safely through the villages along the Prairie Road and into the very shadow of the Schloss Stieg, but only with discretion and vigilance.' He turned to leave, but as he put his hand on the door handle, he faced them again and his face split into an unexpected smile under his bushy black beard. 'Until then, I suggest you get some rest, it is nearly night and you have had a long day.'

Menowin opened the door and left. Constantina smiled and leant back against the wall on her cushion but made no show of leaving. Alene looked around at her friends and smiled.

'Get some sleep everyone,' she said to the group. 'I will take first watch tonight.'

It was a sign of how exhausted they all were that nobody argued. Roan and Lionel lay down and curled up on the cushions where they sat and were asleep almost instantly. Nox and Griffin took a few minutes to settle themselves, choosing a spot on the floor and arranging blankets before they too were sound asleep. Alene yawned and leant against the wall, Dawn laid over her lap, as she listened to the deep breathing and soft snoring around her.

The rocking of the wagon as it made its way along the road was calming – so calming, in fact, that she was soon fast asleep.

CHAPTER NINE

As sleep took over, and Alene's consciousness was whisked away to the far-off plains of dream, the gypsy wagon continued to sway around her. Alene was not there though. She was many years ago, a much younger woman on the wind-swept and frozen shores of Saxe.

She had only one friend in the entire Empire: her companion, Lady Jardinia of House O'Hare, known to most as Nox. They looked after one another, travelled to the furthest reaches of wilderness and known civilisation in search of adventure and a meaning to their shredded half-lives. They were all each other had, their whole worlds and their guiding light in an existence of darkness.

It was winter, the coldest for a decade. Alene and Nox had been caught by an approaching snowstorm whilst making their way back into the Dominion after a summer in the Northern Realm and had sought shelter in a goblin camp on the western shore. The Road of Riches was long and exposed, and the goblins of western Saxe were known to trade with Ville Fleurie from time to time – they were certainly more civilised than the savage northern and eastern goblins who populated the other shores. Nox had offered them venison and grouse in exchange for a winter refuge, and no goblin had ever been known to pass up venison or grouse!

The winter had passed without incident. She and Nox had fought alongside their hosts on the frozen surface of the sea against the rival tribes and had helped to harvest the precious and elusive diamond fish. These miraculous creatures are so treasured because, as well as bearing scales as strong and beautiful as diamonds, they are also one of the only animals alive to contain the vitamins and minerals essential to goblin life. And so, with packs full of diamond scales given in payment and gratitude, they had departed the shoreline at the onset of spring and had begun the admittedly pleasant journey into the heartland of the Dominion.

Only, they had not gotten very far.

One morning, as Alene and Nox sat atop the crest of a hill eating their breakfast – fried fish caught from the River Seite – they became aware of a certain amount of commotion below them on the road. They had stayed low, remaining out of sight, as they saw a retinue of guards riding ahead of and behind an opulent carriage of rainbow jewels and gold framework which glittered and shone brilliantly in the sun. As they watched from above, however, arrows rained down on the soldiers from a hidden position in a nearby copse and they fell to the ground one by one, their horses rearing and bolting into the open fields.

Before the carriage door could open, five men had darted from their cover and surrounded it.

Bandits.

One of them reached out and wrenched open the gilded door. From out of it stepped a young man, around the same age as Alene, wearing splendid robes of rainbow silk. Accompanying him was a much older man who hobbled pitifully as he walked.

Alene and Nox watched for a moment, wondering what to do. As a general rule, they did not interfere with the comings and goings of bandits on the road – that was a fast way to make enemies with the Union of Thieves and Outlaws – but when they saw the old man knocked mercilessly to the dusty surface of the road and kicked repeatedly as the men cackled mockingly, Alene made her mind up that she would not allow that to happen. That was not the kind of world which she wished to live in!

In the end, it had only taken three arrows in quick succession to subdue three of the thugs. The other two had fled like cowards, leaving their injured comrades to scramble away into the woods. By the time Alene had made her way down to the roadside, there was no sign of them.

Nox had swept the area, checking for any remaining dangers, as Alene approached the wealthy victims. The young man was bleeding from a head injury and his silk robes were torn, but he was already kneeling on the ground, checking on the old man and helping him up.

'Thank you, thank you so much!' he had positively gushed at Alene as she arrived by his side. They were both very shaken – the young one especially – but neither appeared seriously injured.

The older man now took her hand in both of his own and thanked her profusely. 'You shall be rewarded above all others!' he had promised her, but Alene had made it quite clear that she had not helped them for a reward. The young man had looked at her with adoration in his eyes, and he had loved her from that day onwards.

Back in the swaying gypsy wagon, Alene's eyes suddenly snapped open. She had fallen asleep; how could she have been so careless? She took a quick glance around the cabin and saw that her four friends slept on, perfectly safe. She also saw the gypsy girl, Constantina, sat on her cushion in the corner and reading a large book encased in red leather. She had not seen her stir, so she closed her eyes again, reflecting on her dream but careful not to drift off again.

That day, the day from her dream, had been the first day she had met Gerecht and Saggion. He had invited her and Nox back to Regenbogen in gratitude and their love had blossomed from that moment. Alene recalled that they had stayed up late one night in the great assembly hall, flickering torches and firepits lighting their midnight heart-to-heart. It had been then, in those early days of their budding romance, that Gerecht had first kissed her. It had been awkward, shy, his lips on her rough ranger hands...but it had been a kiss. He had asked her to marry him, to be his queen, and she had said yes.

She had been accepted, finally allowed to join a society in which she felt she could belong. Nox had left that night, and it had not been until much later that Alene realised what she had sacrificed in order to enter this new world of opulence. In some ways, she had traded her freedom for a gilded cage. She was in love, but was she still Alene? She was still unsure of the answer, especially since she was now apparently learning new secrets about herself – secrets which had managed to drive her friend away from her once again.

She sighed and rolled over. That night in the Grand Hall had also been the night when Gerecht had told her a harrowing story – a story which helped to explain why he had been so shaken up by the events which had unfolded on the roadside a few days earlier. He told her that he had been held-up by the side of the road once before, when he was much younger, and he had actually been taken captive for many days and nights.

As a young, helpless boy, already a king but unsure of how to be one, Gerecht had been kidnapped and held hostage – terrified, crying and humiliated.

By gypsies.

This had fostered a deep mistrust of these people which persisted to this day, and which had certainly coloured Alene's impression of them also. Gerecht had never, however, allowed this fear to affect how he ruled his kingdom. Gerecht was better than that, better than his aggressors.

Alene opened her eyes and stretched. This caught Constantina's attention and she smiled at her, offering a friendly wave across the small room. Alene smiled back, but the warmth was not quite there despite her finding the young woman slightly compelling. Constantina seemed to notice this, for she said, 'You know, you didn't need to stay awake on guard – or wake up again when you fell asleep for that matter. Father asked me to keep watch for you so you might get some rest.'

Alene blushed. Was her mistrust so plain? There had to be something in her misgivings – why, had they not been warned against exposing themselves to the rest of the 'family' who travelled alongside them? A chilling thought suddenly struck Alene, and she had opened her mouth before she had truly considered her words.

'Have you ever made the acquaintance of Madam Vadodara?' she asked, the question spilling from her lips and bursting into the silence of the room with the subtlety of a hammer. Alene was even more embarrassed than ever: she had not intended to be so blunt.

Constantina stared at her, blinking in surprise. To her, the question must have been unexpected and abrupt. Her forehead creased in thought and confusion.

'The name rings a bell in the fogs of my memory,' she said slowly, eyes out of focus as she thought carefully. 'But disjointed, abstract, as though I've merely heard the name, never met the woman herself. She is certainly not a member of our family, and we have had occasional contact with other families in recent years, so I might have heard of her there. Why do you ask of this woman?'

Alene hesitated. This had been the woman who had whisked away her husband when he was still a child, who had tortured him and tormented his nightmares, every evening ever since. Gerecht said that she was a witch, a demon who had read his soul through his eyes and incinerated his heart in searing agony with a touch of her fingertips. This had been many years ago and Alene was not surprised that Constantina had never met her, but she had needed to be sure. Alene may never have laid eyes on this despicable woman herself, but she still saw her pale, malicious face whenever she heard the ringing sounds of gypsy bells or the sickly-sweet scent of burning incense.

She felt her pulse steadying but decided that this was a story she was not ready to share with a virtual stranger. 'No reason, other than trivial curiosity. Think nothing of it.'

Alene got to her feet, shakily in the gloom and motion of the wagon, and made her way to the door. The caravan had continued on its journey through the dusk and twilight and it was now fully dark. She leaned against the bottom half of the door, gazing out at the road on which they had already progessed yet unable to see the road which they were still to travel. Clusters of lights were visible in the darkness: they had evidently already passed through some of the many small villages along the Prairie Road. She watched for a while longer, taking in the chilly evening air in deep, contemplative breaths.

After this, Alene found her eyelids growing heavier and itching with tiredness. Her joints were aching with a full day's travel and she was tempted, in spite of her initial misgivings, to trust Constantina and to sleep a short while longer. She was saved from this decision by Nox, who woke up suddenly, as if on cue. She saw that Alene was awake and began to smile at her, a comforting flicker of a past existence. The flicker had died away as suddenly as it had appeared however, for Nox suddenly seemed to recall their current situation and averted her gaze entirely.

Alene bit her lip; was this the moment to force a conversation about what had happened back at the inn? After a few moment's thought, she decided against it and returned to lie down on the cushions. At least if Nox was awake, Alene could get some more sleep.

It took her a lot longer to fall asleep this time. Thoughts of Gerecht, of phantasms and of Madam Vadodara raced through her mind.

And Nox.

Had she really lost her oldest friend? She could not believe that a friendship so strong and treasured could be shattered by one revelation, however unexpected.

The black tongues of flame raged mercilessly through her mind and she shuddered involuntarily. She had intentionally put off thinking about the events at The Audacious Magpie since her conversation with Roan and Griffin the previous day.

Magic. Could she do more? Did she want to? She was admittedly terrified of what else she might be capable of, as well as what it had the potential to do to her friendship. Similarly, she was not particularly keen to embrace even a sliver of the heritage which had pushed her away. Despite all of this though, Alene knew that she would need all of her strength to complete the mission, especially if they had even more enemies than they knew. Just who were the Republic of Caterva?

This time when she drifted into sleep, it was dreamless and deep, so that when Alene woke again, it was morning.

The next day passed without incident or noteworthy events. The party met Menowin's husband, Silvanus, that morning over breakfast when he entered the wagon after a night of being on patrol. He was like his husband in many ways: quick to smile and with a deep, booming laugh, but Silvanus was a lot thinner than Menowin and his head was covered with a great deal more hair, only greying instead of black.

Roan immediately established a comfortable back-and-forth with both men and, from listening to their easy chatting, Alene established that they co-ruled the family together. This seemed to consist of keeping the peace and maintaining law and order within their tribe, as well as negotiating contact with other gypsy families. Their life was one of constant change and fluidity, never staying in one place for long.

They had been in power for nearly five years now, having been voted for by their people, and hoped to pass leadership to their daughter one day. This was by no means set in stone however, as this was a true democracy and the family could choose their rulers to ensure that their way of life was protected and maintained. This, Silvanus assured them, was the most effective method of rule which they knew – one which had helped to ensure the survival of the gypsies for hundreds of years. Alene was not convinced: she shuddered to think what Gerecht – or even, indeed, Rowena of the Northern Realm – would think of kings and queens being voted for!

As the day progressed, they watched several more ranches pass them by on the road to the mountains. Muscular, tanned men and women raised their heads from their work in the stack yards to watch them pass with mistrust and fear and Alene could see even more people busy at work in the fields beyond, using strong horses to drag ploughs through rich soil. The fertile soil of the prairie made this the breadbasket of the Dominion and it pleased Alene to see her husband's subjects working together towards a better future for all.

It was a complicated mix of emotions however, as despite feeling warmth and pride at these people, she had to remain hidden from them and maintained a strong suspicion of anyone not in her immediate party. She found herself growing fonder of her gypsy hosts – especially of Constantina, who stayed up with her on watch that night and kept her company. She had even woven her a new bag from coloured wool on the old loom in the corner, Alene sitting beside her as she worked expertly by candlelight. The young gypsy girl was a wealth of information on this part of the world, of gypsy culture and of many other things besides.

'My fathers adopted me when I was still a baby,' she told her that night. 'A storm had been brewing one evening, just before sunset, or so I am told. My parents were only lesser members of the family in those days and were in charge of scouting ahead for food or provisions. They came across a farmhouse, evidently occupied but with no light at the window. As they drew near, they say that a forked bolt of lightning struck the windmill attached to the house and set the sails ablaze before spreading to the thatched roof of the house.'

Alene listened carefully as she watched her new friend weave the wool with precision. She was unbelievably talented and her sweet voice enraptured her, drawing her into the story so that she may as well have been stood there herself before the burning building.

She continued, 'It was then that they heard my crying from the upper floor. They rushed in and, according to my fathers, beheld a horrific sight: a man and woman, my birth parents I suppose, slain on the dusty floor in a fresh pool of blood.'

'Bandits,' said a voice behind her, making Alene jump in surprise – she had not heard Menowin enter the wagon. 'We searched far and wide for some family or relation of the babe, to ensure she was well cared for. Funnily enough, it took us a lot longer than you might expect to realise that we had become her family. She grew up as one of us, into the beautiful young woman you see before you now.'

Constantina blushed, and Alene asked her, 'Do you ever wonder about your parents? Your birth parents, I mean? Who they were, why they were killed?'

'Sometimes, maybe,' mused Constantina vaguely. 'I would like to know a little more about them, should there be anyone left in the world who knows anything to tell, but it doesn't make me overly sad. I'll always be thankful to them for bringing me into the world, for giving me life, but they are not my parents – my fathers have raised me and loved me and continue to show me the right path.'

Alene turned and smiled at Menowin, who smiled back. It was a content, loving smile of fatherly pride.

'But less of me,' Constantina suddenly said, looking up from her loom to consider Alene directly, 'what of you, Your Majesty? We have skirted around the purpose of your journey, and I am not fool enough to ask you for more detail. Your business belongs to you, and my fathers and I have made the decision to leave that be. However, there is one matter which I feel does need discussion: I sense a deep, loving friendship between you and Nox, one that has had a very recent knock. What, may I ask, is all that about? I would like to think I could help.'

Alene was immensely glad that her hosts were not pushing her for information on the mission. It was simply something she could not discuss with outsiders. She felt little better discussing something so personal as her relationship with Nox, but she was beginning to feel that she could open up to these people in ways she could not with others.

'I did something which she didn't like, or which shocked her greatly.' She was reluctant to say more, especially since she had not yet got her head around it herself. How would she say it?

Menowin shocked her by leaning forwards and taking hold of her hand. She looked at him and he stared back at her, compassionately and with something resembling love: the love of a father. Alene found this an unfamiliar feeling, having never had a loving parent, but immediately felt calmed.

'My child, I sense it inside of you,' he whispered reassuringly. 'It churns in you like a caged animal, a wolf howling for release. But this is something which you should not fear – the magic has been beneath your elven skin since the day you were born. Our people have very few dealings with the elves, but those times we have had contact have taught me that magic will often spill out in times of fear or anger, regardless of whether you have learned to harness it or not.'

Alene sat motionless and silent. Tears were beginning to form in the corners of her eyes, and as she blinked they began to flow freely down her cheeks and dripped into her lap. Nothing to fear.

'Your magic is part of who you are, just as much as the colour of your skin and your sharp eyes,' Constantina continued. 'I know first-hand that your heritage does not mean a thing about who your family is, that family is who loves you and sticks by you, but I also know that your heritage is still an important part of you. I am the only member of our large family with pale skin, and yet it matters very little to anybody. Your friend will be the same, I am sure. Given time.'

'I wish I could be of more use to you, Your Majesty,' Menowin added, 'but my knowledge of magic is very limited. I can sense it in you but have little practical advice for you on how to use it and control it. I would strongly suggest that you do find someone who can help you though, as this power will continue to burst out in moments of pressure now that the stopper has been removed.'

The door suddenly sprang open and Silvanus entered quickly and quietly. As he removed his hood, he extinguished the guttering candle with his thumb and forefinger, plunging the wagon into pitch blackness. From the darkness pressing in on her eyes, she heard him whisper urgently to the gathered travellers.

'We've spotted a rider on a white horse in the far distance,' he said hastily. 'The moon and stars have betrayed his coming by illuminating his pale mount and gleaming silver chest. We don't see men of this sort on the road in times of peace. Something is not right, so we're going on lockdown until he's passed.'

Alene recognised the description immediately, and as her friends woke up around her in the darkness, she quickly explained their past dealings with the mysterious rider with the silver breastplate.

'So we were right to be cautious,' Silvanus surmised quietly, almost to himself. Then he added, 'It is a precaution we take when there is a threat of bandits – we have found that by reducing visibility we pose less of a target. We have tried showing strength before, by posting armed guards along the train, but that only drew more unwanted attention. Don't worry though: I am sure he will pass through.'

Menowin disappeared through the door and Constantina bolted it behind him.

They waited in silence, sat cross-legged on the scattered cushions in total darkness with hearts beating violently in their chests. At length, they heard the pounding hooves of an approaching rider. He stopped, and for a while there was only silence. Then, quite suddenly, they heard voices ahead of them. They were muffled, unintelligible and still far-off, but appeared to be conversation. What was going on?

The voices got louder and clearer as each new person spoke until eventually they heard the voice of Menowin, driving their own wagon, speak up. 'I've seen you make your way along our train, asking questions and moving on. I tell you: we are simple gypsies on the highway and want no trouble from you. Ask your questions and be gone!'

More silence, but Menowin seemed to hear the rider's reply perfectly well, for he said, 'We have no outsiders travelling with our family, I am unsure what you have been told.'

More silence.

'No, you may not check any of the wagons in our caravan – we have sleeping women and children to think of, and our business belongs to us.'

There was only silence after that, and shortly after they heard hooves trotting into motion and then galloping off into the distance in the direction they had come. After another few minutes, Alene heard Silvanus get up beside her and light a new candle which he placed on the table beside the melted stub of the old one.

Alene let out a long, shaking breath which she had not realised she was holding, and over the next few minutes, the other occupants of the wagon seemed to return to a quiet calm. Constantina stretched out and closed her eyes and Nox, Griffin and Lionel returned to sleep as well. Roan shuffled over to where Silvanus was reseating himself beside Alene and they sat awhile in quiet company.

'I hope you don't think me impudent, Your Majesty,' Silvanus suddenly said, 'but my daughter informed me that you were enquiring after a gypsy named Madam Vadodara.'

Alene tensed at the name but nodded regardless.

'We very seldom speak of her,' Silvanus continued gravely. 'She was a notoriously brutal head of a family of gypsies who were known throughout The Empire around twenty years ago or so. She was a known kidnapper of children and a thief, bringing the name and reputation of all honest gypsy families into disrepute. They would mercilessly raid towns and villages and she would send her family members into battle with a blood-curdling shriek.'

Alene asked, rather unsure if she wanted to hear the answer or not, 'What happened to her?'

Silvanus looked away, and Alene noticed that tears were beginning to form in his own eyes. 'I am not proud of it, but the time eventually came when something needed to be done. I was only a young man at the time – Menowin and I had barely reached the age of maturity – but all men and women who were of age were invited to the Grand Council of Gypsies, an assembly of all the families in The Empire. We convened on the edge of the known map, the Hinterworld, for fear that Vadodara would perceive our threat, and there we made the decision that her family must be eliminated. I say again, I am not proud of that decision, for it resulted in the War of the Gypsy Families and the spilling of gypsy blood. At its conclusion, however, Madam

Vadodara was dead and her family extinct.'

Tears were falling freely now into his greying beard. 'I pray every evening to the gods for absolution of my part and the part of my family, but it will never be enough to cure my heart of the slaying of gypsy kin. Nevertheless, it was a necessary action to rid the world of a despicable evil.'

'I must say,' said Alene after a few minutes' silence, 'that I am relieved to hear that she will never again hurt or terrify the people of my kingdom. It lifts a weight off my heart.' She did not share Gerecht's experience with Vadodara – that was not her tale to tell.

There was more silence, which eventually stretched through the whole of the night. When Alene awoke in the morning light, she found that she and her four companions were alone in the room. Their gypsy hosts were nowhere to be seen, so the friends convened around the table for breakfast as the sun flooded in from a prairie alive with birdsong.

Roan was as chatty and apparently carefree as usual – perhaps more so. Nox continued to avoid Alene's gaze and Lionel smiled politely whenever he was addressed directly but otherwise remained silent. Griffin stood at the door in his usual reverie, so conversation consisted mainly of Roan discussing everything which came into his head and Alene sometimes inputting single word responses. Her heart was not fully in it, she was still considering how to bring up the somewhat awkward subject of her new talents with Nox. She was therefore slightly shocked when Nox looked up and addressed the room at large, cutting Roan off halfway through his animated chatter on the finer points of lock picking.

'Have we all remembered that we have a mission to complete?' she asked in what Alene considered to be an abrupt and rude manner. 'Do we actually have a plan, or are we going to stay in this wagon for the rest of our lives? What are we planning to do when we get to the end of the road?' She turned her head and looked at Alene, directly for the first time in days. Alene had thought she wanted Nox to look at her, but she was wrong. There was a mixture of emotions behind those eyes: anger, fear, betrayal, loss. The result was a sledgehammer to her chest. Was that how her oldest friend saw her? Was that how her oldest friendship was to end? She found that the predominant emotion to come from this was her own anger, and this came pouring out of her as she replied.

'Of course we have a plan! Do you think I would be sitting here, enjoying the ride, if I weren't completely sure of what we were to do next? We are to get within sight of the Schloss Stieg and stake it out, make our way through unseen and enter the Northern Realm through the Vale of Screams. After that, it should be only a matter of days before we arrive at Mort Vivant, where Lionel says the Cardinal's new host, this adolescent boy, is living. We get there, we explain the situation and we safely escort him back to Regenbogen to keep him out of Rowena's hands. Do you really think I would lead my best friends into danger without a plan?'

This all came out in a rush, humiliation and venom aimed squarely at Nox. How dare she insinuate that she had no idea what she was doing?

Nox was momentarily taken aback, but then her face contorted in hurt and spite, similar to how Alene imagined she looked herself, and positively shouted, 'And why is this so important, Alene? Why does Rowena want the power of the Cardinal Phantasm? You know, don't you? You told me, our very first day out of Regenbogen, and yet here we are, near to a week later and you still haven't seen it fit to inform the rest of your friends exactly why they are risking their lives!'

Alene blanched. She felt as though she had been slapped, hard, across the face. Instead of answering though, she hurled all the spite she could muster at Nox. All she wanted in that moment was to make her hurt, to show her how it felt for your oldest friend to suddenly treat you with such contempt that she would not even look at you. 'I could talk about that, Jardinia, couldn't I? Or possibly we could talk about you. You saw me use magic, an inheritance from my people, and you have completely refused to look at me ever since. I was scared, Nox! I still am, and yet you weren't there for me! Why was that, Nox? I know why, of course I do. But you know what, Nox? I'm not vindictive and spiteful enough to hurl that information across a crowded room. We all hold secrets, whether that be why I've chosen to keep certain elements of the mission to myself, elements which I myself don't fully understand, or whether it be you, keeping the dirty little secret of House O'Hare a closely guarded humiliation which you then use as an excuse to discriminate against others who were born with magic running through their veins. Yes, we've all got secrets, Nox! Mine are for the good of the world – are yours?

Alene was breathing heavily. Nox was looking at her, jaw set and brick-red. She did not look capable of speech. Griffin was watching from the door, evidently torn over whether to intervene. Roan looked so comically awkward, sat in between the two women that Alene might have laughed at him in any other situation. Lionel looked as though he would rather be anywhere else other than at the table but dared not move.

The tension in the room was heavy like an approaching storm, yet it disappeared immediately when Silvanus, Menowin and Constantina all entered the wagon, one after the other, looking grave.

'I'm sorry to interrupt, Your Majesty,' Silvanus hurriedly stammered as he began stuffing a canvas bag with loaves of bread, 'but I am sorry to say that you must leave immediately, you are no longer safe here!'

CHAPTER TEN

'**W**hat?' stuttered Alene as she struggled to comprehend what she had just heard. 'Is everything okay?'

'Not really, no,' said Menowin from beside the doorway, breathing heavily and looking very pale indeed. 'We've been overthrown as heads of the family.'

Constantina sank down into a chair and elaborated. 'After the rider travelled by last night and asked about who we were harbouring in our caravan, many members of the family are now of the opinion that my fathers made the wrong decision in aiding you. They think we put the family in danger for the sake of an outsider, so they voted us down this morning.'

'Yes,' said Silvanus, still dashing around but now wrapping several cured fish in cloth and adding it to the sack, 'and they are at this moment voting for a new head of the family. Once that has happened, they will pass a vote on whether to continue to aid you or whether to drop you off at the next village – I have little fear in betting that it will be the latter!'

'It would be disastrous for your mission if that were to happen,' interjected Menowin, still keeping watch at the door for any approaching gypsies. 'The villages around here owe little allegiance to you or to Regenbogen: their loyalty is to whoever poses the greatest threat to them and their families and, in the case of these villages, that loyalty lies with the bandits of the Schloss Stieg. If you are recognised passing through any of these on the road then word will reach the Schloss ahead of you and you will find the approach impossible.'

'Your only chance is to slip away unseen,' chimed in Constantina with a quaver in her voice. 'Do you have any friends in this part of the world?'

Alene began to shake her head, but was stopped by Roan who simply said, 'Yes'.

'Very good,' replied Constantina, 'then I suggest you make your way to them immediately.'

Alene wanted to say something, to apologise for their presence leading to such disaster for the two men and their daughter. They had wanted Constantina to follow in their footsteps one day, to become the new head of the family! Something in her eyes must have betrayed her thoughts though, for as Silvanus returned to the table with a sack full of food, he took her hands and earnestly said, 'Don't you worry, my child. It has been an honour to serve you and aid you in any small way we have been able. We would not have had it any other way, so save your worries and regrets! We were always good leaders, if I do say so myself, and we will find ourselves back in power before long, you mark my words! Our daughter will be head of the family one day, and when she is, she will tell tales of the time when this caravan played host to the queen of the Eastern Dominion!'

There was very little time for proper goodbyes. Alene managed a quick hug and words of sincerest thanks with each of the three before she was being dragged by Griffin out of the open door, down onto the road slipping by beneath them and into the gully. She was not unaware of the symmetry of their predicament: here they were, back underneath a thorn bush on the edge of the highway.

This was not for long though, for as soon as the train of wagons had disappeared around the corner, the party scrambled up to the roadside and began running in the opposite direction. For all of Alene's assurances that she had a plan, she now found herself completely at the mercy of the wild. Where would they go? They could not stick to the road, not on foot. It would take only one farmer to recognise her and their passage through the Vale of Screams would be barred. There was also the constant threat of the rider with the silver breastplate, who had last been seen heading in the direction which they were now travelling. On top of all of this, if they kept running as they were, they were going in completely the wrong direction. She stopped and turned to her companions, who stopped as well.

'What now?' she asked, almost pleadingly. She half-expected Nox to begin their argument again, and she would not have blamed her, but she seemed to have gone back to avoiding her gaze. Roan answered.

'Because we are in a certain degree of danger of being caught by unsavoury characters, and because being caught would apparently lead to an event which would affect the fate of the world...apparently,' he said, raising his eyebrows at Alene, who blushed, 'and because I do happen to know of a place where we might be somewhat safer than we are now, I feel it might be time for you all to meet my mother.'

By a fairly ridiculous coincidence, the entrance to the Woodrow estate was little more than half a day's walk away. They had passed it in the night, a hulking ruin which would once have inspired awe but which now mostly inspired pity.

When they arrived there in the mid-afternoon sunshine, the old gatehouse greeted them in silence. There were no gatekeepers or guards present to ask them for their intentions, nor any actual gates to creak open in tired protest. In fact, the gatehouse served no actual purpose, seeing as there were no walls surrounding the estate; it simply bordered open prairie land. Alene was considerably confused. What was this place? Did Roan's mother truly live here?

They made their way off the road and onto the wide avenue, passing under the gatehouse archway which seemed as though it could crumble and collapse at any moment. The avenue was bordered by tall, beautifully coloured maple trees and this created the impression that they were walking down a red-lit tunnel. As they walked, Roan spoke to them all, uncharacteristically serious and with an obvious degree of anxiety.

'Trust me,' he said to the group at large, 'I would have loved nothing more than to have quietly slipped by this place in the dead of night, to have seen little more than the distant glow of candles in the windows. This is not our destination by choice, but by obvious necessity. Woodrow is not my home – and never has been – but I have family here and I believe we can rely on them to offer us aid.'

Alene continued to look around her in amazement. The private avenue leading off the road and out of sight amongst the trees had an unmistakable air of pomp and arrogance, yet one which had been allowed to decay and stagnate. The trees were encroaching on each other, having been allowed to grow wild and unchecked, in places growing into the road and forcing the party to stoop or stumble over fallen branches that had failed to be removed. Alene highly doubted that a carriage would be able to traverse the avenue without considerable work to the approach. Thick tufts of weeds protruded in places from between the black basalt stones which paved their way and some of this paving had been pushed up and outwards from below, apparently by wayward roots.

All was calm. The five travellers walked on in a natural silence for nearly twenty minutes, only occasionally turning a grand, sweeping corner which resulted in them being completely hidden from the main road. Alene found herself growing less anxious as time went by: if Menowin and Silvanus' replacements did indeed wish to track them down and turn them in to the rider with the silver breast-plate then they would have no reason to believe that they would have made this turn off the road. Nevertheless, she was sure to keep her wits about her and a cautious ear ready for any approaching sounds from behind.

Eventually, the trees around them began to thin out and chinks of scattered sunlight shone through onto their path. The whole demeanour of the avenue began to change: it appeared well-loved, tired yet maintained. The paving was more even and the trees began to thin still further until they were spaced at measured intervals, as Alene suspected they all had been, once upon a time. Suddenly they walked out into dazzling sunlight and they blinked up at the most remarkable House Alene had ever seen.

For that was exactly what it was. This was no castle, no palace. This was definitely a house, one which sat at the end of the avenue with a grand atmosphere of opulence and pride. In contrast to the more distant aspects of the grounds through which they had just travelled, the main house was immaculately kept, crystal windows shining magnificently over three towering floors. Alene counted six chimneys and the building stretched out at either side to create two impressive wings. The whole edifice appeared to be made from pale sandstone, except for the sloping roof which was tiled with grey slate. A beautiful fountain was positioned centrally, a little way ahead of the front doors which were crafted from a glossy chestnut wood.

Roan paused, seemingly involuntarily. The rest of the group, walking ahead of them, did not notice but Alene hung back to offer him words of encouragement.

'Is she really as bad as you've told me?' she asked delicately. Roan had not spoken much of his mother, or indeed any family beyond his father, but what he had said was not particularly positive. Alene suspected a tense relationship, one which she hoped would not cause Roan too much pain to relive. This was, as far as she was aware, the first time he had seen his mother in many years and Alene suddenly realised that it was for her own benefit that he was putting himself through this difficult experience. She understood what it felt like to have a fraught relationship with a parent, and Alene was saddened yet grateful that he was doing it for her, for the good of the mission.

'Let's put it this way,' he said quietly as the others walked out of earshot, 'if I could go through the rest of my life and never set eyes on the woman again, I would be forever thankful. I have never heard a kind word out of my mother's mouth, but everything which means something to me – my dreams, my goals – is wrong. If it doesn't fit in with her incredibly narrow view of the world, it is wrong. Who I am...who I wish I could be...wrong.'

He paused, and Alene struggled for something to say but was saved from this as he continued in a much quieter voice. 'It's difficult, you know, to be told every day that you're worthless. To be told every day how what you believe is wrong, yet when you try to politely argue your case, told your opinion doesn't matter and that you should respect your elders. She drove my father away, all the way to Regenbogen, and my visits here after that were a dread. I haven't seen her for years...I wonder if she'll remember who I am...'

Alene was shocked. She had had no idea how much bitter resentment Roan had been carrying around all these years. What kind of an inconsiderate friend was she? She reached out and squeezed his hand but he did not look at her. They simply walked in silence.

The path crossed over a small humpbacked bridge which took them over a trickling stream before widening out to encompass the entire front of the house. It became gravel at this point and it crunched underfoot as they made their way passed the fountain and up to the imposing front door.

Nox, Griffin and Lionel had reached the porch ahead of them and were stood waiting. Everyone seemed to feel that it should be Roan who knocked, so Alene let go of his hand and raised her hood as he stepped forward. He stood for only a second, hand raised but hanging motionless in the air, before he took hold of the great pewter knocker and banged it three times. The loud raps echoed on the wood and then there was silence again. Alene noticed that the knocker was fashioned in the shape of a lion's head holding a large ring in its mouth.

The silence rang on for over a minute, to the point where Alene considered asking Roan to knock again. Then, quite suddenly and without any audible warning, the huge door began to swing inwardly open, slowly and heavily.

A young man stood inside, panting slightly and wiping his brow. He had evidently had to dash to answer the door but was dressed immaculately in a pale brown coat with shining brass buttons, complete with a richly inlaid waistcoat. His clothes were quite foreign to Alene, who had considered herself well-versed on the fashions of court, despite having no real interest in them herself.

The young servant raised one eyebrow at the assembly on the doorstep, evidently not considering them to be honoured visitors. His impatience was palpable, but Roan cleared his throat and the young man looked his way.

'Sir, my name is Roan, of the ancient House Thounshende. I am here to seek an audience with my mother, the Lady Daphne Thounshende. Please inform her that I have arrived.'

The shock dawning on the servant's face was almost comical, yet it was still mixed with what must have been enough doubt to give him pause, for he withdrew and shut the door, leaving them outside whilst he hurried off to report their presence. Roan turned and looked, somewhat pleadingly but with a trace of his usual playful nature, at

Alene and she smirked at him.

'The ancient House Thounshende?' she asked him in a mocking whisper. 'What would Captain Felix say about that – his own son throwing aside his family name for the sake of a flashy title?'

Roan rolled his eyes and smiled. 'Father's name would get me nowhere here,' he whispered back, aware that the doorman could return at any moment. 'Mother always placed more importance on the heritage and the past of her family name than she did on the present or the future of it. She's a snob, really, but we can play that to our advantage, can we not?'

It took a few minutes for anything to happen. Then, eventually, the door opened again and they were greeted by a stately woman of around fifty years of age with sleek auburn hair hanging freely over her shoulders. She was tall and wore a beautiful dress of grey velvet. Her shrewd green eyes raked their faces, one by one, before she finally settled on Roan. Alene felt that this must have been intentional – he was, after all, stood at the front of the group.

'Good afternoon,' she said to him after a moment. Her lips were thin and pursed, and she made no effort to smile or show any warmth. 'Do I have any particular pleasure for receiving this visit, or are you here for something?'

Roan's smile was gone – any warmth or affection which had been in his voice had utterly disappeared. The voice which replied was more unlike that of her best friend than Alene had ever heard it.

'Mother,' he began, formal and distant, yet resolute and unwavering, 'I approach you and your imperial kin in a time of great need and we beseech you to provide us with sanctuary. We have been on the road for many days now and are in need of a safe place to recover and regroup our plans.' He paused a moment, took a deep breath and continued. 'I am very aware that we have not spoken for some time, and did not part on friendly terms, but I would seek to change that. Please.'

That final word seemed to take Roan every ounce of strength to utter, for it brought him to silence and he waited, looking up into the face of his mother. Lady Daphne's features remained unmoved, a mask of indifference. When she spoke, she spoke clearly and confidently, the mask never faltering for an instant.

'Roan, you are a son of House Thounshende. You are descended from emperors; your blood is worth more than this estate. And yet you are not welcome here. You see, whereas your blood belongs to me and to history, your soul tore away and chose the path of your father long ago. He was a poor choice, the wrong choice – I know that now. Your father represents my folly, as all great ones bear. Unfortunately, you are part and parcel of that stain on my past. You represent the descent that my family can sink to. No, I believe I will not permit you entry to Woodrow.'

There was silence. Alene could not believe what she had just heard. This woman was turning away her own son, her blood, her child. And yet, was that not exactly what had become of her, years before when her family had forsaken her? She was overcome with a burning ball of anger in her stomach. Roan was simply staring up into the face of his mother, who was still standing on the steps with her arms folded. Daphne's face continued to betray not a hint to her true feelings, and Alene could only see the back of Roan's head. The seconds stretched on. It felt like minutes.

Lady Daphne sighed and turned. As she did, Alene would have sworn that she saw the mask-like visage she wore slipping slightly, only around the eyes. They flashed with a new emotion, but Alene could not make it out. As Daphne made to swing the large door shut, Alene seized what might be their last chance and flung back her woollen hood. This was not enough on its own to attract the woman's attention, so Alene took a steadying breath and announced loudly, 'You are in the presence of Alene Idir, Iontach of Regenbogen and

Queen of the Eastern Dominion. We request shelter and aid, in the name of King Gerecht of House Künstler, His Resplendent Majesty and the monarch of this kingdom.' Alene knew this was a gamble: revealing herself in this way would either gain them sanctuary or bring their mission to ruin. Despite this, she also knew that failure to leave the road – at least for now – was certain to bring them into contact with their enemies, be it the Republic of Caterva or their pursuer with the silver breastplate.

Lady Daphne stopped and turned slowly, her face showing true emotion for the first time. Shock was evident as she looked coldly at Alene, her grey and mossy-green face now revealed. She rallied herself remarkably quickly, however, and replied, 'Greetings, Lady Alene. You will find that those splendid titles will serve you very little at Woodrow – indeed, pretenders are rarely welcomed warmly to any court, as I am sure you would agree. However…your presence here *does* change the situation, to be sure.'

Alene could not believe her ears! She had been denied the respect of her royal title and had been called a pretender. Whether she was Roan's mother or not, Alene could not bring herself to see a single positive quality in this odious woman. Regardless, she held her gaze with her chin high and her back straight. Roan made motion beside her, perhaps to speak out in her defence, but she placed a hand on his upper arm without looking away from the face in front of her, silencing him for the moment. She would not be intimidated by this repulsive individual.

Finally, Lady Daphne spoke again. She sighed and stepped back, announcing to the group that they had better enter. The whole party climbed the steps, one after the other, and passed over the threshold into a grand entrance panelled with rich-coloured wood and with a floor tiled with black and white tessellated hexagons.

Common courtesy of being a guest in anyone's house – castle or cottage – dictated that they leave their weapons at the door, and so they disarmed silently and with no small degree of apprehension. Reaper, Near, Far, Dawn and Dusk were leant up against the wall opposite the main door and nearby a grand wooden staircase leading to the upper levels, whilst Alene hung her bone-white bow and quiver on a hook which looked as though it had been designed for just such a purpose. Alene noticed quietly that Lionel did not relinquish his short blade but kept it concealed beneath the waist of his tunic. Their travelling cloaks and bags were also deposited and, with that, Lady Daphne turned and led the way down a panelled hallway, the others following at a short distance.

Roan led the way, but Alene was only half a step behind him. She wanted him to know that she was there for him – she felt somewhat responsible still for placing him in this position. No wonder he had chosen to leave with Captain Felix when he had been given the choice, and Alene could quite plainly see why he had rarely returned to visit his mother in the intervening years.

They passed by many doors set into the wall. Some were open, offering them glimpses of lavishly decorated rooms beyond. Alene only had a chance to give each a cursory glance before being whisked onwards, but she could not shake the feeling that this place held an ancient quality, worn and tired like the outer reaches of the estate, faded with time yet meticulously manicured and dressed up with bygone grandeur.

Eventually, they reached the end of the hall and Lady Daphne touched the cut-glass doorknob with long, spindly fingers as if to turn it. She paused, however, turning to look at them all and lowering her voice, appearing to speak to them for the first time with something resembling respect.

'Woodrow is my home, but I am far removed from the true power of this house,' she said in a hushed tone, looking at each of them in turn. 'I am claiming responsibility for your presence, as family and because I suspect we can be mutually beneficial to each other's plights. But I warn you, if you place my position in this house in danger, you will be without my assistance. You remain silent unless spoken to, you remember your place.'

Alene bit her tongue and nodded curtly. *Her* place was considerably higher than some self-entitled landed squire, but she did as requested and seethed silently.

The door opened and Daphne entered, leaving the others to follow in her wake. After the gloom and shadows of the hall, the sunlight streaming in through the tall windows left them dazzled. Through these, Alene could see additional areas of the grounds which had been hidden to them on their approach to the house: rolling lawns with ornamental flowerbeds, small paths leading off into little copses where one could get lost on an afternoon's walk. Further afield, Alene could see the Primrose Prairie stretching towards and across the horizon – a return to true, unadulterated wilderness. This was certainly a strange place to find such purposeful and forced finery!

Returning her attention to the room itself, Alene's impression of antiquated opulence was reinforced: it was not that the furnishings or decorations looked shabby or unfit for purpose, just slightly tired, of a time long passed. She could not quite put her finger on it – the grandeur was there, proud and decadent, but with a veneer of fantasy and self-deception. The actual style of the room was quite unlike anything Alene had ever seen, with richly coloured wallpapers and floral chaises positioned around a low table housing a small potted plant. Fussy frills adorned every surface and small crystal ornaments sat on delicate tables dotted here and there. The overall effect was not pleasant to Alene's eyes or taste, seeming altogether strange.

The occupants of the room were similarly adorned. There were three in total: two men and a woman. The younger male was lounging amiably on the chaise with the woman, both drinking from long-stemmed glasses and sitting much too close together for them not to be a couple. They both appeared to be in their thirties and, as Daphne entered the room with the newcomers, they turned as one and looked quizzically from one to the next. Their faces betrayed no hint of their reaction, other than a mild curiosity. Then, in one fluid motion, both had risen and were standing before them, awaiting introduction.

The older male, however, did not rise. He merely glared coldly at them. Alene may have imagined it, but it seemed that he held particular contempt for her above the others. Did he resent them intruding into his home? Who was this man, to deny her the reverence she had come to expect from her husband's subjects?

Daphne appeared slightly flustered as she made formal introductions, attempting an air of superiority and elegance but not being quite successful. Alene knew that she was taking a risk, bringing them into her home, but who were these people to inspire such anxiety? She found herself feeling almost sympathetic towards Roan's vile mother.

'Your Grace, Grand Duke Maximilian; My Lady Lilliana; may I introduce Lady Alene Künstler, the wife of Lord Gerecht Künstler of Regenbogen. I also have the pleasure of reacquainting you with Lord Roan Thounshende, my son and heir.'

Alene could not believe her ears but forced her face to remain neutral. Not only had she been introduced first – she was more accustomed to having others introduced to her initially, then being introduced herself – but she had also been afforded a title that did not even exist! House Künstler had not been Lords for over half a millennium, since the fall of The Empire.

Daphne drew another breath, preparing to continue the formalities, but the man before them – Grand Duke Maximilian – interrupted and looked through the small crowd towards the back, where Nox was skulking, still in the doorway. He addressed her directly.

'If I am not mistaken, I have the sincerest pleasure of receiving a member of House O'Hare of Sudhaven,' he said, confidently and clearly. He had a surprisingly soft voice but it filled the room with a ring of authority and power. Nox was silent for only a moment, then replied.

'You do, Your Grace. I am Lady Jardinia O'Hare, the only daughter of Lord Drake and Lady Felicity. I am pleased that my family holds high regard at Woodrow.'

Alene could not help but smile, despite her own snub and her current uncertainty with her oldest friend. Nox had adapted to the situation almost immediately, slipping into her old life as a member of a noble house to best take advantage of the situation. Alene knew that this must be causing her discomfort, however: her history with her family was considerable and she mostly preferred to disown them entirely.

The grand duke appeared impressed as he spoke again. 'Sudhaven was always loyal to our family in the past. House O'Hare provided us with some of our most formidable fighters in the war, and you could never mistake them with their shining emerald eyes, or so the annals tell. As a member of that illustrious family, you are very welcome here.'

Alene continued to grow more and more perplexed by the second and, judging by the look on her face when she stole a glance back at her, Nox was no wiser than she was.

Daphne paused for a few seconds longer, waiting to see if the grand duke would say anything more. He did not though, and so she continued the introductions by turning to address Alene.

'You have the honour of being presented before The Grand Duke and Duchess of Woodrow, His Grace Maximilian, heir to the imperial House Cezaro, and Lady Lilliana. Lady Lilliana is also my sister.'

Lady Lilliana made her way forward and surprised everybody by warmly embracing her nephew Roan. Nobody could have been more surprised than Roan himself though, who tensed momentarily, shock on his face as he registered what was happening. Then he was hugging her back, eyes closed and smiling. Over their heads, Alene noticed that Daphne also appeared stunned by her sister's behaviour. As they parted and she crossed back over to stand beside her husband, Lilliana spoke for the first time.

'My nephew, my heart soars to see you again. I cannot help but remind myself that there is little in the way of age between us. Why, you are much more a brother to me than a nephew. You are indeed most welcome here, as are your companions.' Her voice was sweet and high, childlike but with a regal weight behind it. She had the same auburn hair as her sister, which she wore loose and over one shoulder.

Thus far, the whole room had virtually ignored Alene, save for the formalities. Griffin and Lionel had been completely excluded also but, as people of common birth, Alene was not surprised by this. Then, a dry cough sounded from across the room and every other person in the room swivelled immediately to face the only occupants still sitting, all falling silent as the older man began to speak.

'My son, my daughter-by-law, you speak too freely and with too much affection for these strangers! Have you not realised that we host the wife of the pretender here in our midst? And an elf too, no less! On two counts, this woman is responsible for six hundred years of misery for our family. She is not welcome here; she will leave immediately.'

Alene said nothing: shock had rendered her temporarily mute. The older man looked away from his son and locked eyes with her instead, and what she saw was pure hatred radiating across the room towards her.

Maximilian looked at her for the first time with a softer yet still untrusting expression. 'You have the honour of being in the presence of my father, Emperor Frederick IX,' he said.

Realisation dawned on Alene with the force of a lightning bolt. The emperor. House Cezaro. That name swam out of the recesses of her memory to meet her where she stood. She had heard it only a few times before, in her lessons on Empire history provided by Saggion when she became queen. She had been told in no uncertain terms that a good queen must know the history of her kingdom, and so Minister Saggion had taken her under his wing, teaching her everything he knew. She had not been the most enthusiastic student however – young and in love, with a castle and town to explore. Some facts did stick in her memory though, and this name was one of them.

Cezaro. The house of the last emperors before The Empire was split into the Northern Realm and Eastern Dominion. Alene could barely recollect the details, but she now knew who she was dealing with. What remained of the imperial family had withdrawn from public life immediately following the war, half a millennium ago, but they had never renounced their claim to the throne of The Empire. Alene had no idea that they lived in the Dominion. She was sure that Gerecht must know but was surprised all the same.

Frederick spoke again. 'I am the Emperor in Exile – let us not forget that, my son. A miscarriage of history led to our downfall, and we will contest that until the end of days or the extinction of our house. I say again, a Künstler and an elf is not welcome at Woodrow. Be gone now, woman. Do not darken our future as you have done so our past.'

'If it does please you, Your Majesty,' spoke up Daphne, a little timidly from beside one of the small tables, 'may we please discuss this in more privacy? I believe that I have further information which will persuade you to change your mind.'

Frederick turned on her with thunder in his eyes. He looked set to unleash an inferno of rage, but Maximilian stepped in and, announcing that he thought this a fine idea, ushered everyone else out of the room and back into the darkness of the hallway.

As they made their way back towards the grand entrance hall, the grand duke fell in step beside Alene and spoke properly to her for the first time.

'I will speak candidly,' he said. 'You would not be seeking shelter at Woodrow unless you were travelling covertly. Your clothes and companions back up my theory. I am very interested in what the nature of your journey may be, for I can think of only one enemy who would necessitate such discretion. You move against House Croître of Ville Fleurie if I am not mistaken.'

Alene said nothing. Maximilian continued.

'Daphne will convince my father that he should extend you permission to stay, you need not worry about that. He will see that aiding you is the sensible choice, given that your journey holds such critical importance to the future of The Empire.'

Alene could not argue with this but suspected that Maximilian was not completely on the same page as she was. The success or failure of their mission would indeed shape the future of the whole of existence, something which she still had not fully shared with her friends, and she felt sure that Frederick and his family would agree with her if they knew the full truth. Was this worth revealing her hand though? Who could she trust with the truth when she had so far trusted nobody at all?

'In the morning, after you have rested and recovered, we will convene in the Gilded Room. I would ask for complete honesty from your party, and in return we will provide you with what you need to continue. We at Woodrow are eager to form any alliance which could lead to a change in the map of The Empire. My father will be convinced of this, have no fear.'

Alene listened and considered what her host was saying. Roan was stood a short distance away, deep in reminiscence with Lilliana, and the others were standing by the door, clearly unsure what to do or where to go. Alene looked at Maximilian and spoke with a levelled tone.

'Whilst you are under the wrong assumption regarding my mission – I do not desire nor have I ever wished for war – you are correct that it could drastically change the map. The fate of the whole Empire, possibly the worlds beyond this one also, are at stake and that includes your lives here at Woodrow. We do require assistance...' she took one last deep breath and revealed their secret, '...the Cardinal Phantasm has re-emerged.'

The effect on the room was electric. Nox and Griffin whipped around and gaped at her, not quite believing their ears that she had revealed the true nature of their mission to a stranger. Roan and Lilliana stopped talking immediately but froze where they were, listening intently. Maximilian's stare seemed to bore into her soul as he considered her. Why had she trusted him with this? Had she made a mistake?

Finally, he spoke again. 'I see. We are aware of the awesome power of the Cardinal and I have an idea of what you speak. Despite this, we require a full congregation tomorrow to discuss this fully with all present. I am inclined to believe that you are right – that your mission may in fact transcend the importance of us all, even the emperor. After all, an emperor needs an empire. I have some magical ability myself, so I feel more able to understand the importance of this, if you understand my meaning.'

Alene thought that she did: the magic she had discovered inside her had given her yet another viewpoint on the life of a phantasm. What must it be like to live with an almighty being within you?

As they were ascending the waxed wooden staircase a few minutes later – bags and weapons in hand and heading for guest accommodation on the first floor – Alene was suddenly struck by an absurd yet brilliant thought. She allowed her friends to follow the same aloof servant who had answered the door to them that afternoon as he led them upstairs, as she descended back into the entranceway and smiled graciously at the grand duke.

'Begging your pardon for asking such a question, Your Grace, but do you have the same aversion to elven culture as your father, the emperor?' Alene thought that a little flattery might aid her now, and she was certainly not above that.

'I consider the interference of the elves of Marrowmarsh to be a key factor in the downfall of my family,' he replied stiffly, not meeting her gaze, 'and I believe with all my heart that a person's history and heritage is one of the most important badges of distinction they can bear. However, I also hold a deep desire for a brighter future. I happen to know that you have left your race in your past, and yet I can feel a strong power inside of you, fighting to crash out like a wave. This power scares me, but I do not detest it – I see it as hope for the future you fight for.'

Alene turned this over in her head. 'I need help,' she said at last. 'I need to harness and control my power. In return, I offer complete transparency of our journey and what we know.'

Maximilian smiled and Alene realised that she was growing rather fond of him. 'We will discuss this tomorrow. I think I may be able to help you, but we can talk more tomorrow.'

Lilliana smiled warmly at Alene, who smiled back and slowly made her way up the wide staircase and into the upper levels of Woodrow.

CHAPTER ELEVEN

Roan was not sure how to feel. He had visited Wood-row only four times before, all in the first few years following his parent's separation. Daphne's younger and more beautiful sister had recently made a very advantageous marriage to the heir of The Empire, and she had travelled to live with her and her new husband in their palace of exile. All of this was years ago now, and still Daphne remained at Woodrow, outdone and outshone by her more successful younger sister.

Roan knew that a certain degree of his mother's resentment towards him was because he had abandoned her to her pathetic leeching, having stopped visiting after a few occasions. The number of letters had dried up also in recent years, but Roan could not bring himself to feel guilty for this. He knew, in his heart, that his mother was a horrible person.

And yet, he could not say that he hated being at Woodrow as he thought he would. He had enjoyed a brief but animated reunion with his aunt Lilliana the previous day, and it had felt as though the years had melted away. It was true what she had said: they had always been more like siblings than aunt and nephew. She was only six years his senior and their childhoods had been shared. This, Roan suspected, was another source of bitterness for his mother. Daphne never could bear being left on the periphery, so to be condemned to live as a guest in her sister's home while her only son and heir preferred the company of his father and aunt to hers was a cruel punishment. She deserved it, Roan reflected. She should have been more tolerant of her son if she desired his affection so much!

As Roan made his way down for breakfast that morning, he met Nox on the staircase. He had dressed for the occasion, adorned in a doublet of dark green velvet with gold fastenings and a pair of well-fitted buckskin breeches. He had jumped at the chance to bathe and had spent a good deal of time cleaning himself and rinsing the grime and dirt from his long, auburn hair. Despite this, he had not for a moment considered that the others might take the same opportunity and was therefore stunned to see Nox wearing a flowing dress of blue silk adorned by silver and pearl. He had to admit, the look suited her figure immensely and her clean chestnut hair, which she wore loose and flowing, complemented the look nicely. He told her so as they made their way down the staircase. She rolled her eyes but smiled at the compliment all the same.

'I find myself playing a part,' she grimaced good-naturedly. 'If we wish to remain here – and we really must for now – then I am to be Lady Jardinia. I can be honest with you Roan: I did not think I would ever play this role again. We need rest, we need shelter. I can suffer a few days.'

Roan was stunned. He could not believe how Nox had seemed to describe his own plight as well as her own. They had more in common than he had thought!

When they entered the large, airy dining room for breakfast, it was to find it only half-attended. Emperor Frederick was there, as was Roan's mother and aunt. Roan had known that Griffin and Lionel were not welcome at formal gatherings due to their rank, but he was curious as to the whereabouts of Alene and Maximilian.

Daphne noticed their arrival and rose to greet them. Roan was shocked and slightly alarmed to see that she was smiling at him. What was wrong with her? She *never* smiled at him!

'Come and join us, please,' she insisted as they made

their way towards the table. Nox and Roan took two vacant seats and surveyed the spread. Fresh fruit and cured meats were on offer, as were a variety of cheeses and breads. Roan knew enough about Woodrow to know that it was entirely self-sufficient, wishing to owe nothing to the outside world which had shunned them.

'I hope that everybody had a restful night,' smiled Lilliana affectionately around the table. Then she addressed Roan and Nox specifically as she added, 'I am glad you found the clothes we left out for you. They may not be the current fashion, but they are clean and warm.'

'We know how to treat guests here at Woodrow,' added the emperor from the head of the table. 'When we ruled from the Imperial City, many years ago, we held balls and festivals like none seen in the world since!'

Roan had to fight the urge to roll his eyes. He was used to the imperial family's tendency to live in the past instead of the present – after all, his own house, Thounshende, was a junior branch of the family – but he still found it a complete bore when long reminisces were imminent. Nox, however, appeared curious.

'I have passed by the ruins of the Imperial City on more than one occasion,' she said, addressing the emperor with interest. 'I have always been struck by what an awe-inspiring place it must have been in its day.'

Again, Roan had to hide his scorn. Nox was playing her part expertly, much better than he was. He wondered again where Alene was and if this pantomime was really worth it for a few days of luxury. They would need to take to the road again soon, so why not now? They were all well-rested and he was sure that they could take on the mysterious rider with the silver breastplate in a fair fight. True, he had not the faintest idea of which way they should go, now that they knew the Prairie Road was unsafe and teeming with spies for the Schloss Stieg, but was that not a trivial detail?

The emperor was speaking, and so Roan listened, helping himself to an apple and some fresh bread.

'Our histories tell us that the Imperial City was the largest and most resplendent settlement in the entire Empire – greater than Fief Nord or even Ostbastei.' After seeing the puzzled look on Nox's face, he added, 'those being the true names for the cities of Ville Fleurie and Regenbogen. They were built as twin cities, in the time of The Empire, to facilitate trade with other races, namely the treacherous goblins and elves. A folly of our forebears, it must be admitted.'

A minute passed, and Roan began to think that Nox had let the subject pass. He was glad she had – nothing made a Cezaro more excitable than discussing the past. He began to butter another piece of bread, wanting nothing more than to have a peaceful breakfast, when he heard Nox speak again. What she said made him cringe.

'I would love to hear more about The Empire, if you were willing to talk to me about it.'

Roan knew what Nox was doing. Did she think she could ingratiate herself to Frederick by engaging in his favourite hobby? Evidently the answer was yes, for Roan strongly suspected that Nox was not at all interested in history. He met his mother's gaze across the table and she rose her eyebrows at him: apparently she found the whole affair slightly ridiculous as well.

The emperor, however, was entirely taken in by her supposed curiosity. He cleared his throat importantly and began.

'House Cezaro ruled over The Empire for a thousand years,' he told her, putting down his utensils and fixing her with a penetrating stare from his dark eyes. It was not an unfriendly face, now that Roan studied it further: he had the same short, black hair as his son and the same olive complexion as well, only his face was more careworn and his hair streaked liberally by more grey.

The eyes were definitely different though, as Maximilian's unusually bright blue eyes had caught Roan's attention at once during their introduction the previous day. He had been caught off guard and had needed to take a few deep breaths to steady his heart, which had fluttered to life like a caged butterfly. He felt no such inappropriate attraction for the senior Cezaro however, so he resigned himself to hearing his story – a story he had grown up hearing and felt he could recite in his sleep. His mother had raised her head proudly, as had his aunt Lilliana, although Roan noted that both seemed less enthusiastic than Frederick.

'At that time, our Empire stretched from sunrise to sunset: from the frozen wastelands of the northern nomads to the impossibly impenetrable jungles and the Lunar Hills in the south. We ruled the lands east of the Rücken, all the way to the famed diamond mines on the banks of the River Meander, and we ruled those lands to the west of the mountains, all the way to the rich farmlands along the western frontier and the outer borders of Marrowmarsh. Truly, the world was an empire that was ruled justly and with peace. It was Clovis, the first emperor, who united the smaller petty kingdoms and began the reforms which would change the world forever.' Frederick smiled genuinely as he recounted his family's history, then he added, 'He never encroached on the Hinterworld though...and neither did any of the succeeding emperors...we do not do well there...'

He paused, apparently lost in thought. Roan knew what he meant: he had read many accounts of people who had ventured into the Hinterworld, and none of them were pleasant.

The Hinterworld was a vast expanse of blistering hot desert as far as one could see, nigh-on impassable and with terrifying beasts roaming it constantly. It encircled the Empire, the known world, in all directions and was effectively the edge of existence. Roan had only read of one man who had travelled far into the Hinterworld and returned to report on it – an unnamed ranger who insisted that the

Hinterworld simply ended with an impenetrable but invisible wall. This had, as far as Roan could tell, effectively led to the end of exploration into the Hinterworld, as even the rangers could either see no point in risking their lives or else set off and never returned. Roan wondered if Nox had ever entered the Hinterworld. She was not forthcoming this time, however, and the emperor continued his story.

'Over the centuries, The Empire grew stronger and more resplendent. We built great fortresses, palaces and cities – the jewels of The Empire being the Schloss Stieg, not too far from here but overrun by bandits and thieves; Ostbastei, now held by the usurpers under the name 'Regenbogen'; Fief Nord, now Ville Fleurie and still beautiful by all accounts, and of course the Imperial City itself, far to the west across the mountains and lying in tattered ruins. It breaks my heart to think of my ancestors buried in the forgotten crypts and cemeteries beneath centuries of rubble.'

He paused again, blinking rapidly and sighing deep. At length, he spoke again. This time, however, there was a sharpness to his voice.

'There came a time of unrest on our borders. The elves from Marrowmarsh ignited a war with the goblins, who in those days were far more numerous but even then were concentrated around Saxe. I will never, for as long as I may be privileged to live, forgive those of elven or goblin blood for the part they played in the fracturing of our Empire!

'There were, or so history tells me, two families with considerable power who wished to take advantage of this precarious situation.' He looked at Nox, and also at Roan. 'You know their names, I am sure.'

Nox did not speak, so Roan said their names, surprised that his voice was hushed and croaking. 'House Künstler and House Croître.'

Frederick looked at him and nodded. True tears were now flowing down his wrinkled cheeks. Roan knew this part of the story well: the families who would one day become the rulers of the Dominion and the Realm, respectively. They spread the word that the emperor was incapable of protecting his lands from the skirmishes to the north between other races, and that the people must unite to take back power and place it in stronger hands. Whether this was true or not – whether The Empire had ever been in true danger from the elves or goblins – was lost to history, but Roan knew that the people had listened and united.

Frederick was speaking again, and Roan returned his attention to what he was saying.

'We knew that the end would soon be upon us,' he whispered, now looking down at his hands in his lap and shaking slightly. 'Lesser members of the imperial family had already fled to safer sanctuary – including here at Woodrow,' he gestured around them at the grand house they were situated in, 'but the emperor and his son refused to abandon the Imperial City. They would not allow it to fall.' He turned to Nox and asked her, 'Do you know how the Imperial City was defended?'

Nox shook her head politely, but Roan knew that she was lying. The walls of the Imperial City were legendary – how could she not know?

Frederick appeared content with her answer though, for he continued, 'The walls of the Imperial City were fifty feet high and constructed from granite. Now, I hear you thinking that they do not sound as impressive as one might think, but you would be very wrong indeed. There were actually six separate walls radiating from the central city, close together and each with gatehouses in different positions along their circumference. This created narrow alleys and passageways between and within each wall, each of which was split and blocked in places as well. The top of each wall would be alive with posted sentries, armed with bows, spears and boiling oil. The whole construction amounted to what was designed to be the world's most deadly labyrinth.'

Roan was always impressed at this feat of engineering. He had seen sketches of it in books, considered to be the greatest wonder of the known world. The people of the city were trusted with the great maze's secret, and in return were safe from the outside world in times of war. The walls were what allowed Clovis to unite the kingdoms and form The Empire in the first place.

'If Lord Croître, or even Lord Künstler, had laid siege to the city, the walls would have defeated their armies and we could have negotiated some form of peace, but alas it was not to be.' A full minute of silence followed this, whilst Frederick composed himself. Finally, he spoke again.

'Alas, it was not to be either pretender who rode up to our gates on the last day of The Empire, almost precisely six hundred and forty-four years ago. No, we could have negotiated with men...but the goblins got there first...'

Words seemed to completely fail Frederick at this point and he shook with silent sobs. Lilliana rose and made her way around the table to kneel beside him and grasp his hand affectionately. Daphne scowled at Nox, as though this was her fault, as if it had been she who had scaled the walls at the head of a goblin army and sacked the Imperial City. Tomorrow marked the culmination of the week-long feast of Empire's End and would signify the date on which this massacre occurred. Roan suspected that there would be no celebrations or feasts in this household come the morrow!

Roan had read of this event as well. He could see in his mind's eye, as clearly as if he were there himself, thousands upon thousands of goblins swarming the labyrinthine walls like ants on a carcass. They had overwhelmed the sentries on the parapets above, claiming the narrow tunnels and passageways of the labyrinth for themselves before turning their gaze to the centre of the maze – the city filled with citizens and refugees. There had been no escape from the Imperial City: the people were now prisoners within their own deadly trap. When the goblins had finally finished and satiated their bloodlust, a smoking ruin and cracked, charred walls were all that remained of the ancient wonder.

Nobody was speaking. Lilliana was still knelt beside the emperor but had let go of his hand; Daphne had returned to her breakfast plate; Nox was looking as though bringing up such a subject may have been a bad idea.

But then suddenly Frederick took a steadying gasp and looked up, eyes red and face shining but with a clear determination to finish his story. He was still addressing Nox, whom he seemed to have growing affection for.

'Your house, my dear, House O'Hare, were always good to us. You see, whilst Emperor Francis VI did indeed remain in his palace in the inner city, awaiting his fate with his faithful Golden Guard and eventually perished there – still sitting atop his imperial throne – his son and daughter were urged to flee, to protect the bloodline of The Empire. They used a series of secret passageways and emerged in the swamplands on the coasts of the Mer Nuage. From there, it was a difficult journey to Sudhaven, one which they were ill-prepared for and not accustomed to. Your family, Lady Jardinia, offered them shelter, protection and discretion. When the time came, they arranged for their safe passage over the Rücken and here to Woodrow. And so that, my dear, is why I have permitted your party to stay at my court. It may be six hundred and forty-four years late, but my family can finally repay our debt of gratitude.'

Nox was stunned. Roan could tell that she either knew only some of this information, or none of it. She said nothing, simply smiling and returning to her plate. Frederick followed her lead and, not too long later, they all parted ways and left the dining room.

Roan barely paid attention to where he was going. He made his way out of the main doors and around the side of the house, deep in thought as he absent-mindedly put one foot in front of the other. The family whom Frederick had been referring to, the subject of his whole story and the source of his great pride, was not only his family but Roan's as well. Whereas House Cezaro were descended from the last emperor's son, Leopold, and therefore inherited the imperial titles and rights, House Thounshende were descended from the last emperor's daughter, Augusta.

Both Leopold and Augusta had escaped the fall of The Empire and had made their way to Woodrow, and so the blood of the old Empire flowed through the veins of Lilliana, Daphne and Roan too. Augusta had eventually left Woodrow and married, but House Thounshende had never forgotten that their blood was worth more than that of others. And that thought was what made Roan sick. He did not buy into the idea that a person's blood or heritage made them special, and neither had his father.

Now, after many centuries, the families were united again and Roan knew that House Cezaro had waited for an opening to make their move ever since their power was taken from them. They were in a nest of vipers, regardless of what anyone else thought.

That afternoon, as Roan was returning to his room on the first floor, he found himself walking down a hallway – on a trajectory for a headlong collision with his mother, of all people, who was walking towards him in the opposite direction. He could see no way out of this one.

He studied the rich carpet beneath his feet, face lowered until he was almost upon her. Then, as naturally as he could, he raised his head and met her gaze, smiling thinly and almost apologetically.

'Good evening, mother,' he said, rather too cheerily, hoping she would let him pass without further comment. He was not in the mood to speak to this vile woman, whom he sometimes saw horrifying glimpses of himself in but had no inclination for anything other than the barest of relationships with for the rest of his days, or probably for the rest of *her* days.

He thought that she had a similar opinion of him – as he said, horrifying glimpses! – and was therefore quite taken aback when she called back to him after he had already passed.

'I really did fail you, didn't I?'

She had dropped the posh airs and graces. This was simply his mother. But Roan would have been heartbroken to imagine any other parent speaking to their child like Daphne Thounshende was speaking to hers now. Pure spite sculpted her face: she appeared to be sucking a particularly bitter lemon. Her words were spat out like venom and her hair appeared somewhat wild, shaken when she must have turned rather forcefully from its natural resting place down her back to give her a mildly crazed, lunatic appearance. The sudden transformation was inappropriately humorous to Roan, but he forced himself to appear only slightly interested, and not in the least bit amused. He had always received a strange feeling of warped power when baiting his mother – his little way of weathering the constant storm of her disappointment. Today though, the actual content of what she was saying did not marry up to her dramatic flair, and it was this which made him answer her sincerely.

'I haven't got the faintest idea what you're talking about, mother of mine,' he replied coolly. Ever since Frederick had made his declaration of honouring his debt to House O'Hare that morning at breakfast, Roan knew that it was not only his familial connections keeping them safe. He could afford to speak his mind and be his true self, something which he had done rather explosively in the past with his mother, and something which she only *ever* did when facing off against him – yet another thing they had in common, Roan reflected with bizarre and inopportune irony.

'You really hate me, and I am not ignorant as to why,' she continued with an attempt at returning to her usually reserved manner but not quite managing to hide the glint of malice in her eyes. 'I have been everything you despise, your entire life. Heritage and vintage are important to me, and regardless of whether that is 'right' in today's world – in *your* world – it is 'right' in mine. Of course, you mirrored your father from the beginning and that, I concede, was not always to your detriment. He was not a bad man, just the wrong one for me. Regardless, he never showed anything save for scorn and ridicule for my values, and you follow him in this respect like a doppelgänger.'

Roan had to think for a moment before he spoke again. He lowered his gaze, more so to avoid staring stupidly in her direction, and considered this. Was she truly painting herself as the victim? He had been subjected to a childhood of tears and an adolescence of burning inferiority, never feeling as though he was quite good enough, and she had the audacity to blame *him* for *her* woes?

He looked back up, intending to speak with what he hoped would be a detached and neutral air, but the look on her face caused him to come up short. Her eyes were brimming with unshed tears and, what was more alarming, she was making no attempt to hide them. Roan knew that this was no ploy on his emotions – Daphne had never been known to show him even a shadow of weakness in his many years since he left her womb, so this had to be genuine and involuntary.

She continued in little more than a whisper, and Roan found himself inching closer to hear her better. This whisper was not venomous or vindictive. It was cracked and hollow, with pure anguish echoing from within.

'You left me!' she gasped quietly, never breaking his gaze.

'Your father fled back to Regenbogen with his tail between his legs, content to abandon me. Still young. Still beautiful. I did not care. My family name and my fair grace would ensure that I would not be alone for long. No, I cared not for the loss of that man.

'But you followed him,' she continued, 'and that broke my heart. You always reminded me of the worst of him, and you have no idea how wrenching it is, to look upon a face you love and feel bile rising up in your throat. You hurt me by your mere presence, but I loved you as a son and heir. When you chose your father over your mother, you changed everything. I'm not sure I ever fully recovered.'

She finished speaking and breathed deep, more content, as though she had been drawing a poison from within by speaking with her heart, perhaps for the first time in many long years. Despite suddenly feeling as though he were looking upon his mother with clear eyes for the first time, and feeling as though he did not hate what he saw, he still had to fight the urge to roll his eyes.

You have no idea how wrenching it is, to look upon a face you love and feel bile rising up in your throat.

Was she being serious? Was it not plain that he knew *exactly* how this felt? As he prepared to speak, he found his heart beating wildly as he formed his next question – possibly the most important question he had ever asked her.

'So...I'm not a disappointment to you?' He had always thought she had never considered him a worthy successor to the family name, but now he did not know what to think.

'That depends. You hurt and disappointed me greatly when you chose *him* over me, over your family. But are you a disappointment? To me? Never! You are my blood, my heir.' She said all of this stiffly and with noticeable concentration, as though speaking what was in her heart was a foreign language to her, a new and unfamiliar sensation.

There was a full minute's silence following this declaration, and Roan found that he could have easily welled up as well. Indeed, his eyes did prick with emotion but he fortified his resolve, not fully daring to believe what he heard, not quite yet at least.

'But I will never provide you with a further generation,' he spoke quietly, echoing her whisper and averting his gaze again. He could feel her continue to look his way, only mere yards from him in the otherwise deserted corridor. If she had been inclined, she could have reached over and taken his hand, but perhaps that was too much to expect at present. A leopard may change their spots, but not so suddenly as that!

One fortifying breath, then he continued. 'I do not love as others love. My eye lingers elsewhere, more akin to your tastes than to my father's. To be myself, to find happiness and acceptance, I need to accept that, and I need others to accept it also. You have always known this; I know that is correct. It was one of the reasons you hated me, for denying you your descendants.' He looked up and locked eyes with his mother again. 'Or so I thought,' he finished.

As Roan had spoken, Daphne had mobilised her calm and by the time he looked up, she had almost returned to her stately self. Roan saw her jerk slightly, as though she had been tempted to move towards him but had reconsidered. Finally, she spoke.

'It is true, it was a blow to me when I realised that the Thounshende name dies with us. We are the sons and daughters of emperors and the extinction of an ancient line is always a sadness. However, your aunt has passed our blood back into the senior branch of the imperial family and I can live with that. Indeed, I have known for many years that the happiness you seek will not be as simple as that of most men, perhaps even beyond your grasp forever. However, I am truly and sincerely sorry if I ever gave you leave to assume I was in any way afflicted by whom you choose to love. Individuals with a pedigree as rich as ours do not bow to the prejudice of lesser men. You do, however, need to seek permission from yourself. You have deep conflict and that must be resolved before you can be happy with someone to love.'

Roan was truly shedding tears by this point, silent and reserved. 'Father never spoke to me of this,' was all he could mutter.

'Your father,' Daphne replied with a bitter edge, 'never knew you as I did. It's funny what we choose to remember, is it not? Now come, we had better join your companions and mine in the Gilded Room for the council. Let us consider this our apology to each other and see if time will heal the rest.' She then did something which took Roan fully by surprise: she hooked her arm around his and allowed him to escort her down the long hall.

'Besides,' said Lady Daphne Thounshende as they made their way down the main stairway and into the hall below, the barest hint of a smile flickering across her thawing features, 'I am sure I know of a good many lords whom would be more than agreeable for my son. And if you marry one of them, you would certainly be going down a different path from your father. Funnily enough, after all is said and done, I might see that as a small victory.'

CHAPTER TWELVE

D usk was steadily being ushered in by twilight as Simeon's travelling party arrived atop the cliffs overlooking the Mer Nuage. This inland sea was vast – larger even than Saxe in the north – and would take many precious weeks which they did not have to travel around its eastern shores and to their destination in the southern extents of the Realm. This was out of the question, and so they intended to make use of the famous Sudhaven Ferry to cross the sea in a little more than three days. The plan was a good one and would ensure that they avoided any more unnecessary detours or delays.

Adelaide sat astride Enchantress in the gathering gloom, a cool evening wind whipping her hair out in sheets as she squinted down at the glowing windows of each individual building on the cliffside opposite. The team stood at one side of a narrow fjord that twisted and turned out of sight ahead of them before the steep rock faces levelled out and joined the sea properly. It was to the town illuminated by oil lanterns opposite them that they headed, however, making the last mile or so of travel around the end of the fjord to the other side. This town was Landsbyfjord and, as unremarkable as it looked, was in actuality one of the richest centres of economy in the Northern Realm.

Beginning life as a fishing village, Landsbyfjord had discovered that the Mer Nuage held more than just fish when it found oil beneath the seabed along the northern coastline. The people of this small community were creative and resourceful, manipulating the oil in different ways to burn as fuel and embalm their dead. They also learned how to thicken it into a tar-like substance and waterproof their vessels, becoming unparalleled for sea travel save for the O'Hare's of Sudhaven, who had admittedly discovered a secret of their own.

Landsbyfjord grew fat and rich from trade facilitated by their abundance of oil, fish and salt. Their coffers grew heavier with gold and diamonds and the vast quantity of merchants which passed through – perhaps also increased by their role as the northern terminus of the Sudhaven Ferry – gave them access to spices and cloths which would otherwise be foreign and exotic to them.

It was true: Landsbyfjord and Sudhaven shared a friendly rivalry, but together they represented the economic centre of power for the entire realm. Rowena may hold power in name and command the military, Adelaide reflected, but the purse strings were controlled and tied securely by the Alliance of the Mer Nuage.

Pondering on the Rose Queen got Adelaide considering begrudgingly just how much Rowena had accomplished in her time as monarch. She had risen to power following the untimely death of her husband the king, who had succeeded his father before him. By right, Rowena had little real claim to the throne of Ville Fleurie and had made her play for power on the same evening as the king's passing, when most queens would be wild with grief and entering mourning. Some may consider this cutthroat or even despicable, but Adelaide saw it for what it was: a woman fighting tooth and nail to retain her home and livelihood in an absolute monarchy where women simply did not have the same standing as men.

She was all-powerful indeed, but she would be nothing without the Alliance of the Mer Nuage.

The cliffs above Landsbyfjord were adorned with a colossal lighthouse – towering into the dark blue sky, a needle of brickwork with a crown of dancing flame. It was the job of this majestic structure to guide vessels safely down the fjord and into the harbour at its end and it was now guiding the party of

Captain Simeon Castello safely into the cliffside village.

It had been many days since Adelaide had joined the company, and tonight was the culmination of Empire's End. As such, she had expected to find the village alive with festivities and revelry, perhaps with a market similar to that which would be coming to an end in Ville Fleurie tonight also. She was surprised, therefore, to find that the dusk-enshrouded streets were almost deserted: the day's labours over and only the occasional late-returner wandering lazily home, coming in and out of view as they proceeded through coronas of light from the oil street lamps.

The village itself consisted of a winding path down the cliffside with houses built into the stone. At its base, a harbour housed various docks and trade posts and at the top, where Adelaide and her companions now stood, a small number of wooden buildings were scattered around in the shadow of the great lighthouse. It was towards one of these that the party rode.

Simeon, leading the way as usual, arrived first at the village stables. He dismounted Titan and led him by the reins into one of the stalls. A tired-looking ostler came bustling around the corner, absent-mindedly stretching his arm out, palm raised, for payment. It was a few short seconds before he raised his gaze and, when he did, Simeon's uniform and fierce glare were enough to convince him that these particular customers would have no need to pay tonight.

Adelaide despised this about the captain. The now petrified ostler was scurrying to and fro, attempting to help all of the men at once. As he approached her, a needlessly apologetic look on his face, she smiled warmly at him and discretely pressed a golden coin into his fist as she passed him the reins of her own horse. If anything, he looked even more terrified but, with a further smile and nod of encouragement from Adelaide, he smiled nervously back and practically fled into the stables. She barely had time to reach out and stroke Enchantress' flank before she disappeared inside.

Simeon called his company together at this point, so Adelaide joined the small group of men huddled together outside the door of a small inn a little way away. She noticed that Rita remained astride Betty, the precious cargo of the inhibitite cage forever on her mind. She had taken her responsibility for this item seriously, and appeared to be unwilling to leave it now, even to rest.

'Right men,' Simeon announced in quiet yet clear tones to the assembled group. 'The ferry leaves the harbour just after dawn. We will stay tonight in the inn and make our way down to the foot of the cliffs before the sun rises.'

Adelaide glanced up at the sign above the inn door: '*The Maelstrom*'. She hoped this was not foreboding.

'I will not be joining you tonight, however,' he continued. 'I will be remaining with our cargo. Maintain dignity and discretion and remember – we are men of Ville Fleurie on business for Her Majesty the queen. What might reflect badly on you will reflect badly on her.' Simeon gave Adelaide a very knowing sideways glance at this mention of Queen Rowena, and Adelaide had to fight the amused smirk which threatened to give her away.

For Adelaide had not told her captain the whole truth.

Or, more accurately, had not told him any truth at all.

Adelaide had a secret. More than one, actually.

The truth was that Adelaide did not belong to Rowena. She never had, and certainly never would. It was true that Lady Sandrine Bosque had approached Simeon at the crossroads earlier that week and announced a new addition to his company. It was even true that this new addition had waited at the windmill of House Thresh on the Sunken Road, preparing to join the party as they passed. What was not true, however, was that this new addition was Adelaide.

The company was dispersing. Some lingered, momentarily uncertain of how to proceed, but most headed immediately into the unfortunately-named inn for a well-deserved meal and rest. Adelaide hoped that these would both be paid for fairly: she was not prepared to deprive the people of this village their living, no matter how successful they may be.

She readjusted her long, black cloak to ensure that it fully protected her. Adelaide was as eager as any of the men to reach her bed, but she had business to attend to before this could happen. She made to follow them through the open door but slipped around the shadowy corner of the building instead. Here there were no flickering torches to expose her and she melted into the darkness like a spectre.

Peering carefully around the corner, Adelaide observed Simeon with his lady wife. Away from the influence of his men, Simeon allowed his love to shine with its fullest strength and he touched Rita's face gently and kissed her passionately – a stolen moment whilst nobody was looking, or so he thought. This side of the captain intrigued Adelaide: she could understand this man so much more, as though this were the truth beneath the veneer. He clearly loved Rita very much but felt conflict with his duty to treat each in his company equally and without favour.

Suddenly, to her left on the far side of the inn, Adelaide heard movement and slunk deeper into the inky shadows to avoid detection. Squinting across towards the base of the stone lighthouse, she realised that its lower levels had barred windows – a prison of sorts, apparently. Armed guards were stationed at its oaken door and seemed to patrol the streets from time to time. These would be the guards of Lord Fischer, no doubt, who ruled Landsbyfjord fairly and justly and was renowned for his revolutionary method of law enforcement: simply put, he paid his officers generously and encouraged his senior guards to promote transparency and tolerance between the officials and the common people of his village. As such, guards under his employ were far less likely to fall to corruption or become power-hungry tyrants. Harmony existed in Landsbyfjord, but Adelaide found it difficult to believe that everything could be as perfect as it appeared to outsiders.

She needed to send a message, and the presence of so many guards was sure to make that more of a challenge than she had anticipated. Regardless of this, it was crucial that she achieve her task before boarding the ferry the next morning, as otherwise it would be a further three days before she could make contact with her mistress. That would be too long.

She slipped out of her hiding place in the gloom and raised her black hood. Simeon and Rita were nowhere to be seen, and so she ran.

It was almost other-worldly to see Adelaide move through the streets that night. She ducked and soared – sometimes through deserted alleyways, often over thatched or tiled rooftops, but never seen unless she chose to be seen. Tonight, Adelaide chose not to be seen.

She reached the cliff top and dropped expertly over its edge, falling with effortless control a short distance before landing on the cliffside path which snaked down towards the harbour. Adelaide's goal was the postal master's loft at the dockside. Some scholars may question the logic of housing delivery pigeons at the base, as opposed to the top, of a fjord, but those scholars would surely not be men of business. The postal master of Landsbyfjord knew very well that travellers were strongly motivated by the prospect of a long voyage over a cruel and tempestuous sea to send those they love one last message – very possibly their last ever. Conversely, he also knew that those disembarking from a long voyage over a cruel and tempestuous sea were sure to immediately send word home that they had survived the ordeal. For both of these reasons, he knew that the place for pigeons was as close to the water as possible. This man knew the sea well. He knew business equally well.

Adelaide was a stranger to Landsbyfjord but knew the location of her destination on good authority. By dropping down sheer edges of cliff, she was able to traverse the serpentine pathway quietly, quickly and clandestinely. As such, she arrived on the edge of the lower market square by the water's edge in a little less than five minutes. All was dark and deserted, and Adelaide was struck again by the noticeable absence of the expected revelries of the week's conclusion.

She walked quietly and purposefully around the perimeter of the square and vaulted a stone wall with fluid grace, landing in the postal office's rear yard. She remained crouched, assessing her location. She was surrounded by wire coops, each of which housed sleeping pigeons. Her presence had not disturbed them and they slept on, unaware that anything out of the ordinary was occurring beside them. Adelaide slowly straightened up. These were no good, she knew. Only birds of lesser value would be cooped outside, those bred and trained for local deliveries or for journeys to neighbouring farmsteads to request provisions. This was not what she was looking for.

She looked up at the building and saw an upper window, shutters closed and certainly bolted. Security was tight in Landsbyfjord.

This was no matter for Adelaide. Like a cat pouncing upon prey, she leaped up into the air and negotiated the building's many weathered cracks with her clever fingers, using them as leverage to hang beside the window and work the latch with her knife: perfect for just such an occasion as this.

With that, she was in. The room was dark and she quickly closed the shutters again to maintain this. All the better to avoid unwanted attention. Her eyes were used to the darkness, it would be of no consequence to her.

In the pitch-black room with her black cloak and black hair, she was practically invisible. Only her curious streaks of silver through this long hair could be seen, appearing to shine or glow in the darkness. Her hood remained in place however, so this was not too much of a problem. Adelaide reached into her cloak and withdrew a minuscule scroll of parchment. She knew what it said by heart, it having been written in her hand earlier that day and only consisting of three words:

Landsbyfjord
All well

It was sealed with a drop of colourless wax – this being the universal sign of post for servant classes – and bore the name of her mistress on the outside as a form of address.

Lorraine
Head of Household

She held it securely yet delicately between her dexterous fingers as she slinked along the rows of pigeon coops which were the only feature of this room. Looking closely, Adelaide could make out tiny circlets of dyed fabric around the ankles of each bird. One coop housed pigeons all bearing a blue marker. She knew these to be birds trained specifically for sending messages across the sea to Sudhaven. Another's inhabitants all sported a black band: pigeons reserved only for use by diplomats and merchants willing to pay enough gold to send a message to the Eastern Dominion. These brave specimens needed to be hardy enough to survive crossing the Rücken but seldom saw much service nowadays except for the rare message to Cogburn. As such, there were only three birds in this one.

Finally, she found them: the pigeons designated a dark, pumpkin-orange band. This was saffron, the colour of Ville Fleurie. She had to take care to make no noise whatsoever as she eased open the cage door and gently cupped the sleeping pigeon, so as not to disturb the others: the resulting cacophony would surely be enough to wake the whole village!

It was to the credit of the postal master that his pigeon was so well trained that it barely responded at all to being picked up. It cooed softly as she attached her minute scroll to its leg and carried it over to the window, which she reopened and allowed the clever bird to soar away into the night in a northerly direction where the sun had set half an hour before.

She watched it disappear briefly before making her silent retreat. She replaced everything as it was and re-latched the window as she exited. She knew that her message would reach Ville Fleurie soon enough and would be delivered without question to her mistress: the colourless wax would be overlooked immediately and draw no suspicions, she was sure, and no lower servants would dare to open the private mail of the head of the household.

In truth, Lorraine was not so much her mistress as she was her long-term client. Adelaide was sworn to serve her and the people she represented but knew very few of the many secrets she kept or whom she truly served. She was paid well though, and that was good enough for her.

She thought back on their last meeting, roughly one week ago on the eve of Empire's End. The afternoon sun had shone brightly down on the crystal panes of the great greenhouses of Ville Fleurie where many exotic and tropical plants grew. Adelaide had heard tales of a dense forest in the southern extremes of The Empire, even crossing into the Hinterworld, where these plants grew naturally, but she had never seen this with her own eyes. Lorraine had sent for her early that morning and she had left her lodgings in a nearby tavern known as *The Crossed Swords* to meet with her.

Jobs from Lorraine often paid well and were never too physically taxing but were always perplexing and shrouded in intrigue. That was why she liked Adelaide: she had little experience of certainty and had spent her entire life on the periphery of her own great mystery. She felt that Lorraine fancied herself as a spymaster, trading in secrets and pulling strings from the shadows. Who she was in actuality though, Adelaide did not know. That afternoon, however, she was to be given a full and detailed briefing.

'I have a dire and immediate use of your services,' she had begun as soon as Adelaide had arrived at the greenhouse: a secluded enough spot at this time of day with so many people arriving in the main courtyard at the opposite side of the palace. 'You are to assume the role of a member of Rowena's guard and join a secret expedition which will be leaving the palace first thing in the morning.'

Adelaide had learned from experience in the past that it was best to not ask questions of her clients, especially if no answers were forthcoming. However, on this occasion she was to be impersonating a royal guard, on a secret mission no less, so she felt that some answers were required.

'I will need to know the nature of the expedition, the additional members of it whom I will be expected to fool and the eventual goal I am to accomplish.' She remained professional. This was a job, after all – one she was very good at. She suspected that her eventual goal was sabotage, but she was unsure to what end.

Lorraine looked up at her, and Adelaide sensed an uncertainty and turmoil behind her eyes which she had never sensed before. This was altogether different, she realised. This was serious. Lives rested on this mission, she knew instinctively.

'I confess, I am not sure how to proceed. May I speak plainly, with no fear of this being repeated?' she suddenly asked. Adelaide nodded once. She was the one paying her, after all.

'I sent my only son away last night,' she whispered distractedly, suddenly nervous and agitated, looking around her despite nobody else being anywhere in sight. 'I sent him over the Vater Berg to Regenbogen with an urgent message for King Gerecht. I had to, there was no way I could risk the contents of that most important of messages being intercepted. I don't even know if he's alive!'

The professionalism was gone. This was simply a woman. Adelaide felt for her, but the mention of Regenbogen piqued her interest. Was that where she was to be going? The Eastern Dominion, being a constitutional monarchy and therefore run by a king with assistance from various advisors, was supposedly much more tolerant of minorities than the Northern Realm, where Rowena's whim was law. She could grow to like that kind of acceptance, although she was not well-travelled enough to have visited it often, and never to Regenbogen itself.

Her attention returned to Lorraine as she continued. 'Ever since I was a young woman, a simple chambermaid in a palace as grand and as awe-inspiring as Ville Fleurie, I have been in the service of someone far more powerful than Rowena. It has been my duty to wait and listen and last night my wait was over: there is a new Cardinal Phantasm, and Rowena aims to seize it!'

If Lorraine had been expecting some form of explosive reaction to this revelation, she was to be disappointed. Adelaide knew very little of phantasms and cared even less. Lorraine filled her in, the best she could with what little information she could afford to divulge. The general summary though was that she was to travel with the party of Captain Simeon Castello and sabotage the mission, as close to its conclusion as possible so as not to allow Rowena time to respond. Under no circumstances must the new Cardinal be allowed to return to Ville Fleurie. This would, so she was informed multiple times and with increasing emphasis and melodrama, threaten the very future of our world.

Adelaide had been paid half in advance for this. However, there was a condition to receiving the rest of her reward and it was not one which she was willing to follow. Once she had secured the phantasm, she was expected to spirit it away to an undisclosed location and care for it herself. No, this was not something she would be doing.

She would stop Rowena from securing this most coveted of prizes, as she had been paid to do. But she would go no further than that. She thought it best to not sour the agreement with Lorraine however and said nothing.

She had not been able to resist the temptation of surveying her new captain before leaving to ready herself for the mission though. She had entered the city disguised as a poor trader and watched him from a distance, her almond eyes observing him from beneath her black hood. As she had passed him, she had purposefully walked into him, making it seem as though he had barged into her and knocked her painfully to the ground. She had wanted to see what he would do, and she was not disappointed: he completely ignored her and continued to walk, as self-entitled, arrogant and cruel as she had expected.

The first part of her mission had been simply standard. She had ridden for the old mill on the Sunken Road and eliminated Rowena's appointment to the team, taking his place. She had then waited to meet her new captain officially for the first time.

Since then, Adelaide's impression of Simeon had not changed at all.

Concentration securely back in the present – the darkened streets of Landsbyfjord – Adelaide slipped around another corner and back into the square.

And straight into Captain Simeon Castello.

He stared at her, dumbfounded.

She stared back, momentarily stunned into silence, mind working feverishly behind a placidly calm expression to think of an explanation as to why she would be down here by the docks instead of up at the inn with the others.

Simeon appeared to be having an internal struggle. His face twitched uncertainly as he evidently fought with himself over what to say. Eventually, he said, 'I have a good feeling I know what you're doing here.'

Adelaide was confident enough that he had no true idea why she was really there and could not even begin to imagine where her true loyalties lay. She therefore let him continue uninterrupted.

'If you're anything like me,' he began, and Adelaide was intrigued to hear a note of hesitation in his voice, 'you have maybe come down to where the water starts to get a good look at it before tomorrow's crossing. I can't say it's made me feel any better though. The surface is so calm this far into the fjord that it's a poor reflection of what it will actually be like on the open waves.'

Adelaide realised approximately halfway through Simeon's speech what he was talking about: he was nervous about the crossing tomorrow. Adelaide almost smiled: the rude and arrogant captain was showing some humanity at last!

She decided that the safest move was to play along. 'I give very little thought or fear to fighting and killing men twice my size, and yet the prospect of tomorrow has caused me to feel utterly powerless,' she said. 'But I know that we will all be perfectly fine, Captain. After all, the Sudhaven Ferry is famous!'

She smiled at him in the darkness, lowering her hood as she did so. With a leap of her heart, she was shocked to realise that her smile was genuine and heartfelt.

Simeon began to walk back up the hill, twisting up the cliff, and Adelaide fell in beside him. She watched him out of the corner of her eye, seeing him almost for the first time. She had been right when she had thought of him as hiding behind a veneer, as she seemed to be gleaning her first true peek at the man beneath. She was not sure what she was seeing yet, not sure if she liked it, but at least it seemed true.

'I must say,' he suddenly said with an air of somebody desperately attempting to fill an awkward silence, 'you are exceptionally gifted with your sword, and such a strangely-styled one too!'

Adelaide had never actually minded awkward silences but found that she did not mind continuing her conversation with the captain either, so she replied, 'Yes, Captain. I have had it since my childhood. It is designed more for slashing than cutting or hacking, which heavier swords are often used for. It complements my speed as well, to be sure.'

She glanced at his back and added, 'Your sword is truly astounding also, Captain. I'm surprised you can even lift it, never mind raise and swing it!'

They were engaging in a very professional conversation, which Adelaide found herself to be enjoying and it certainly seemed to be taking Simeon's mind off his nerves. She wondered why he had decided to confide in her. She imagined he had told Rita as well, but why was he not talking to her about this now?

Simeon seemed to be keen on continuing the conversation. 'It's called Cumulonimbus. It's a claymore really, a great sword which I need two hands to wield. It's not truly mine though, it belongs to the office of the captain.' He seemed to be relaxing a bit now and was speaking less formally. 'What is your sword called? All good weapons need a name!'

Adelaide paused, only briefly, before answering. 'It's called Father.'

'Why?'

'Well, it's a bit silly I suppose, but I have no memory – none at all – of my life before I was eight years old. It's strange, I know. But, you see, that also means that I have no recollection of ever having parents, or anyone really, to look after me and love me. I've always had Father, and it kept me safe when I was scared and stayed with me, no matter what. So really, if you look at it like that, it really is the perfect name for my sword.' Adelaide was shocked: it had all rushed out of her without a second thought to whether she should say it or not. Why had she chosen to trust him?

There was silence for a full five minutes as they continued their uphill climb, both panting slightly with the steep incline. Eventually, Simeon spoke again.

'You know, we actually have that in common.' She looked at him quizzically and he clarified, 'I never knew my parents either. Growing up, I lived amongst the poorest of the poor and worked my fingers to the bone every day for enough food to survive. But I had high aspirations: I set my sights on the grandest and most beautiful palace in The Empire and told myself I would one day live there. I sometimes forget where I came from, sometimes yearn for grandeur a little too strongly, but I never forget that the only reason I am who I am today is that I worked my hardest every day and never stopped. If I don't give my all, even for one day, I could lose everything. It gives me motivation to be the best. It gives me duty.'

Adelaide suddenly realised why she was finding it so easy to talk to Simeon, and why he seemed to be telling her some very personal truths as well. They were the same. Their lives had gone in very different directions, but they had both had the same beginnings, suffered the same hardships and made the same sacrifices to claw themselves up to where they were. She realised that this evening walk up the cliffside had taught her more about her captain than four days on the road. She also realised that she had suddenly begun to think of him as a friend, although she was sure that this was not a mutual feeling.

She searched around for something else to say, less personal. 'They don't seem to be celebrating Empire's End,' she said, hopefully in a conversational manner.

'No,' he answered. 'This part of the Realm has always been more tolerant when it comes to The Empire. Of course, the ruins of the Imperial City are not too far from the southern shores of the Mer Nuage, and Sudhaven in particular was a big supporter of the emperor in the war. As a result, the cultures of those towns and villages in The Alliance of the Mer Nuage are decidedly anti-Empire's End.'

Adelaide thought she noted a certain tone in his voice. 'Not a fan either, are you?'

'Not at all, actually. Too much change. Too much uncertainty.'

They reached the top of the cliff and Simeon bade her goodnight, making his way towards the stables, where she assumed Rita would be waiting for him, possibly brushing down Betty after a long day. She understood why they were remaining out here: the inhibitite cage was worth more than any of their lives at this moment. His mission depended on it.

Adelaide turned towards The Maelstrom in the suddenly dazzling brightness of the lighthouse and reflected on this.

His mission might depend on the inhibitite cage.

Hers, however, most certainly did not.

Adelaide was different. The inhibitite sensed it and gnawed at her hungrily when she stood too close. That was definitely something she would not be sharing in an evening stroll with Captain Castello. She shifted her long, black cloak uncomfortably as she thought about this.

And anyway, the cage was only useful for returning the Cardinal Phantasm to Ville Fleurie. Which would not be happening.

Not because she was going to be taking it into hiding, to babysit it for the ransom of half of her wage, as requested.

No, the way Adelaide saw it, she had been paid upfront for a job: stop the team from acquiring the Cardinal Phantasm.

She would do that, the best and most certain way she knew how.

She will meet this strange creature. She will look into its eyes. And she will spill its blood. Every drop.

For the good of the future of our world. Apparently.

CHAPTER THIRTEEN

A s Alene left the Gilded Room with her companions, eyes itching with tiredness, she could not help but let out a tremendous yawn of exhaustion. She would have the luxury of only a few more precious hours of sleep in her grand lodgings at Woodrow before they were to slip off again on their seemingly impossible quest. Even with a plan now firmly under their belts, the information they had gleaned from their hosts added monumental gravitas to their already feverish endeavour.

As she settled into bed mere minutes later for what she hoped would be a restful night, Alene reflected that she remembered little in the way of small details from their assembly with the emperor. She supposed that there must have been pleasantries passed around the table, a mixture of sincere from some and forced from others. She could vaguely recall being in receipt of more than one mistrusting glare from Frederick, but she had given it little thought when it was accompanied almost immediately by a reassuring smile and wink from Max.

She had grown remarkably fond of the Grand Duke of Woodrow over the course of the day. It was his fault she was so tired and removed from the conversation. They had convened in the ballroom before sunrise, as per Max's instructions which had arrived at her door moments before. He had been waiting for her when she had arrived. It was fortunate that she had dressed in her travelling clothes rather than the elaborate dress which had been laid out for her, as when she entered the ballroom through the intricately carved double doors it was to see him stood in its centre, a far cry from the bedecked duke she had met the previous day. His breeches and shirt were tight-fitting but simple, devoid of finery or embellishment. She had smiled: it appeared they were not so different from one another.

The similarities continued. Max dispensed with the formalities immediately by conjuring a small, perfectly spherical ball of blue lightning in his outstretched palm. He demonstrated how effortlessly he could control this by allowing it to flow from one hand to the other, crackling slightly as it did so. He then sent it inwards, his skin flickering like dying embers in a grate and the hairs on his arms standing on end. Alene had looked deep into his eyes, and they sparked and danced with energy. Then, in one fluid motion, he channelled it outwards forcefully through both outstretched palms and practically obliterated an alabaster vase situated at the far end of the room – a clear thirty feet away!

'Magic works differently for different races, and there are always rules to be obeyed,' Max had told her with only the merest hint of pride in what he had just accomplished.

'Most humans must train their entire lives if they wish to master the art, and only then if they are born with the talent. Magic can, theoretically, be absorbed and channelled by anybody – but it would be foolhardy in the extreme to attempt it without proper training and discipline! Doing so would be an incredibly infallible way of combusting oneself in an explosion of pure energy. For that is what magic is: raw and wild energy, present in the earth itself. A human who possesses the skill could draw in this magic and sculpt it to their desire and whim, and they are whom the wider world refers to as mages. They will tire quickly however, as the act of drawing in this external force and maintaining its stability whilst it is within them demands total and complete concentration. A life's dedication to grasp and a lifetime to perfect – if ever!

'My magic, however, has more in common with your own, with that of the elves: most magical of mortal beings. The imperial family were blessed long ago with a gift, to be passed down strictly through the male line and only then to the eldest in each generation. It is said that this gift came directly from Arcano and Eclaire, although I doubt that. If the gods ever existed, they would surely set their sights higher for a source of amusement – like bringing shining empires to ruin and tearing the lives of innocent people asunder.' His voice was bitter and jaded, but he shook his head absent-mindedly and continued. 'Wherever the gift came from, it is my responsibility to bear at present, as it was my father's before me. One day I will pass it to my son, and the power of magic will leave me forever. How will I feel when that time comes? Only then will I know. I do not dread it: I will have a son and heir to entrust it to.

Elven magic comes from within. Their own bodies produce a source, and therefore they require less concentration and training to wield it. It is much more instinctive and driven by the emotions of the individual in question. This apparent ease, however, comes with a cost – whereas a regular human will eventually tire and find it impossible to perform magic until they have rested, an elf will find they are able to continue indefinitely. The problem with this is simple. When forced into extreme emotions or situation necessitates such a reckless act, an elf can exhaust their entire life force, draining their essence until nothing remains.'

Alene had given this a good deal of thought. This sounded suspiciously similar to what had happened to her after their encounter in The Audacious Magpie. She had been overcome by her need to protect her friends and had, as a result, spent the rest of the day in a magic-induced coma. What could have happened, had she used even a fraction more of her inner magic? She shuddered to think.

'Of course, ancient magic is also present in the ways of

the phantasms, but I confess to knowing very little in this subject. But do not worry – my father the emperor will be able to help you in this regard later.'

The rest of the day had been spent in intense training. Max had first taught her that her emotions must be controlled and released with purpose. He had clear pride in his gift and wanted to demonstrate it further. Alene, on the other hand, barely managed to produce a dancing black spark on the tip of one finger and this resulted in her having to rest for some time before continuing. No matter how strongly she believed in herself and wished to show her potential, this was all she was able to accomplish. She wondered vaguely if her half-elven blood was to blame for her weakness. Did her power work differently? Throughout these exercises, she thought she could sense a flickering warmth deep inside of her, but only fleetingly and only on the very edges of exhaustion. She reached inward for it, but it continued to elude her in all but the merest of grazes with her fingertips.

By late afternoon, Alene's reserves were entirely depleted and she had been forced to accept that she had learned very little of real value. She had wandered wearily through the empty corridors of Woodrow with Maximilian on their way to the assembly in the Gilded Room and had passed around the cloister of an ancient-feeling courtyard on their way. The air in this forgotten corner of the house had felt heavy, unnatural. She had been tempted to ask Max what this place was, why it appeared so neglected and ethereal, overgrown with moss, gnarled trees twisting upwards towards the afternoon sunlight and the remains of ancient sculptures scattered here and there when something more mysterious caught her attention.

On first inspection, it was simply a door. A rough, wooden door of unimpressive craftsmanship and without any discerning features. Despite all of this, however, this modest door drew her in, as a moth is often drawn to a flame. She had taken two shaking, uncertain steps towards it when a dry cough beside her cracked through the fog in her head and broke the spell. Max was looking at her, no longer smiling but looking sheepish, as though he had revealed a secret he had no right to tell.

'What is that?' she had asked shakily, pointing hesitantly towards the door.

Maximilian had sighed regrettably and shaken his head. 'I am afraid that this is a secret for the imperial family only,' he had told her apologetically. It is known as the Sanctum Praeterita, and it is our repository of history, a library if you will. Unfortunately, that is all I am at liberty to divulge. Shall we continue?'

With great, albeit somewhat inexplicable, reluctance, Alene tore her gaze from the fascinating door and had continued.

As she lay there in bed, hours later and in much need of sleep before their early departure, Alene's wandering thoughts again came to the Sanctum Praeterita, and she considered for one crazed moment what she would find if she were to slip from her room in the night and try that wooden door. It was sure to be locked, but she could try. She would never be sure if she did not try, would she? It took an alarmingly long time on this track of thought before she became aware of how ridiculous she was being. She rolled over with a deep desire for sleep to take her away and, after a few more moments, it did.

The next morning was a whirlwind of rushed activity and hurried farewells in the pale, pre-dawn light. Old family ties had been renewed and some unlikely friendships had been struck during their brief stay at Woodrow, and Alene would never have bet that they would be parting on such good terms.

Nox – back in her ranger attire – bowed to Emperor Frederick, who kissed her hand in return. Roan hugged Lilliana farewell and even allowed his mother an unprecedented show of affection by taking her hand. Alene had missed much of what had occurred in this forgotten bastion of a bygone era, but she knew that she had forged a lasting friendship with Maximilian through his – admittedly futile – support of her through her struggles to harness her wild power. She was unsure how such a bond could survive once life returned to normal: she was after all a 'pretender' to his crown. Despite this, Alene was glad to have met him and sincerely hoped that their paths would cross again. Her only regret was that she was still no closer to controlling the power which was her birthright.

It had been decided that they would leave the estate via an underground tunnel, the better to leave the vicinity of the Prairie Road undetected and put some untraceable distance between them and their silver-plated hunter, whom they could not forget was still out there searching for them with an unknown agenda.

This tunnel was to take them a significant amount of time to traverse. Two full days would see them take a direct route beneath the southern extent of the prairie and emerge in the shadow of Clagcowl Abbey. Alene remembered from her sleep-fogged memories of the previous evening that this tunnel dated from when the abbey had been fully funcional, when monks would travel to and from Woodrow regularly and needed a safe and direct route to avoid the dangers of the open road. It had not been used for many years but Alene had come to suspect that Woodrow was protected from time by more than just good maintenance. Magic played a part, she was sure, and she hypothesised that this preservation extended to this tunnel also. They would see.

Nox continued to avoid Alene and, as their paths had not naturally passed since the afternoon of their arrival at the estate, she had not yet had an opportunity to push the matter. Nox now travelled at the rear of the party with Griffin, who did not seem to mind at all that he had been essentially ignored by their hosts for the previous two days. Rank meant something at Woodrow, whether Alene liked it or not.

Lionel had taken his familiar position in the middle of the group. He also did not seem to mind his time away from the centre of attention. Indeed, he had taken the opportunity to clean himself up and get some much-needed sleep, as well as a few decent meals. He looked all the better for it and appeared to be in higher spirits than Alene had ever seen him. He was smiling to himself and she slowed down to allow him to draw beside her.

'How are you feeling?' she asked him warmly. Seeing him look so well was like a tonic to her, so early in the morning.

'Really very well, thank you, Your Majesty,' he replied with another smile. He must have felt at ease with her, more so than he had before their brief stay at Woodrow, because he continued, 'I have enjoyed the opportunity to recover somewhat from our journey so far, although I am glad to be on the road again. It was almost too easy to forget how little time we have for our mission to be a success, but now it's back to the task at hand!' Alene smiled to herself. *Our* mission. He was beginning to consider himself a real member of the team, and so was she.

'I was just thinking of mother,' he said, a tinge of uncertainty edging his voice now. 'My hope is that I can return to her when all is said and done. She has remained a spy for many years within the walls of Ville Fleurie without arousing suspicion and I am sure she will be safe now. I only wish I could be sure that my presence beside you on the mission will not expose her. It would be my fault.'

He paused, apparently deep in thought. Alene thought

before speaking. She had inadvertently offended this brave young man when she had spoken of rewards, only a few nights before but what felt like a lifetime ago. 'You have assured me that you will accept no rewards, and I do not seek to force one upon you, but I can promise you, in gratitude from the people of the Eastern Dominion for all that you have risked for their lives, I will do everything I can to discretely secure your mother's safety and direct passage to Regenbogen when this whole affair is behind us. What is her name?'

'Lorraine,' said Lionel with a wide smile and slightly damp eyes as he evidently thought on his mother's face with love and longing. 'I miss her. Thank you for caring, Your Majesty, I will gladly accept that very kind offer – it makes my heart lighter.' He sighed and wiped his eyes on his sleeve before continuing ahead, leading the party for the first time since they had begun their journey.

Their path took them through a glade of chestnut trees on the outer extent of the estate. Early-morning mist wreathed the trunks and blanketed the forest floor with a living veil. The air was damp and cool, and Alene guessed that the day ahead would be another wet and stormy one. She was silently glad that they would be safely underground and would avoid the worst of the inclement weather. After they had walked so far that they were in danger of leaving the estate and re-entering open prairie land, Roan jogged up alongside her and drew her attention to a low stone wall, almost hidden by moss and low-growing bushes. As they approached it, Alene realised that Roan must have already known where to look, as even her sharp eyes had not been able to discern its presence without prior knowledge.

Kneeling beside it, Alene thought it looked almost like a well, although one with no water or bucket. Instead, a set of narrow stone steps spiralled down and into the darkness, disappearing from view. They appeared worn, regu-

larly used in ages past but no more. Astonishingly, the staircase appeared unobstructed by centuries of falling leaves
or branches, and no wild animals seemed to call it home.
Alene took this as further confirmation: the magic of the
emperor's gift extended to this ancient secret avenue, deep
beneath the surface of the earth.

Torches lit, they descended in single file. Alene was
leading, with Roan close behind. He seemed different to
Alene in some way, but she could not work out how. Nobody spoke as they made their way down, winding further
and further into the depths. Finally, she reached the bottom and her feet touched down on compact, damp earth.
A stone-lined arched tunnel led off in a direction which
Alene hoped was south – she was thoroughly disoriented
from travelling downwards in a tight spiral – and she set
off down it, pleasantly surprised that there was no need to
stoop as she did so.

It was warmer down here, and Alene soon removed her
travelling cloak and slung it over her pack. She could hear
Roan behind her and, after an uncertain amount of uninterrupted walking, he spoke.

'So, what do you make of our recent discovery?' he asked
her. She knew what he meant without having to ask.

'It makes sense that Frederick would know more about
the phantasms than we did,' she answered. 'Max told me
that they have a...library...of sorts at Woodrow which con-
tains all sorts of information on the history of The Empire.
It stands to reason that this would include the phantasms.'
She felt odd voicing what she had thought so much of since
seeing it: the Sanctum Praeterita. She hoped Roan had not
noticed.

'How much of it did you already know?' asked Roan
shrewdly.

Alene could honestly say that she had not known any of
the details and told him so earnestly. She conceded that
she had known some of the basics from what Gerecht had

told her, many years before, but that had been all. If she had known the full truth, she would never have kept it from her friends. Regardless, the whole story was out in the open now, and all involved were fully informed.

According to Frederick, there was an ancient relic, older than the infancy of The Empire and sung of in ancient voices of the past, thought by some to be more myth than history. This relic, rendered unknown and vague by the shadows of legend, was told to possess great and terrifying power, enough to – again, the stories were murky and clouded – break down the barriers between worlds and allow the bearer to walk as a god between plains.

Some stories even said that it was created by Cobalus, Unus' daughter who also created goblins at the beginning of time. If this had been some attempt by Cobalus to bestow her children with a form of magic similar to that which the elves received from Arcano and Eclaire, she had been unsuccessful. The stories also said that the unknown relic was considered too powerful for any one person and it was hidden far away from the greed of humans, elves or goblins. To ensure that it remained in its secure sanctuary, the Cardinal Phantasm of the age manipulated the future, as only they can, and crafted a prophecy. This prophecy had stated (and still does, Alene reminded herself) that anybody who attempted to remove this all-powerful relic from its resting place or to use it would face the immediate fate that all mortals must eventually accept: death.

'And so, our theory goes that this ancient treasure actually exists,' finished Roan as they recapped their conversation from the previous night. Despite being weak with fatigue at the time from her fruitless magic training, Alene could remember all of this part clearly.

'Yes,' she answered. 'And that is why Rowena wants the Cardinal – only the Cardinal Phantasm can rewrite a prophecy made by a previous Cardinal. All of that about breaking barriers of worlds and crossing to other plains...I think that's rubbish mostly. The world was a lot more religious then and it would be considered the ultimate power to stand amongst the gods. They said the phantasms came from between the worlds as well...maybe the legends got mixed up.' She and Roan were a slight way ahead of the others, and Alene often found that she could speak more openly and honestly when she was with him alone. It was freeing to speak her mind.

'Correct,' concluded Roan. 'At least, that's what I'd bet. Rowena will simply want this relic thing to attack Regenbogen – that kind of raw power could obliterate the painted wall in moments and freeze the Meander and the Rushing in a frigid gale. The armies of the Northern Realm would take the castle in no time. And, if what we suspect is right, she would not stop there. The world would be forever changed by that power.'

'And we mustn't forget the Republic of Caterva,' she reminded him seriously. 'They want us all gone: me, you, Gerecht, Rowena, Frederick...anyone who holds any sort of power, it seems, however slight or insignificant.'

It was certainly a lot to think about. Alene wondered again if Gerecht had known this amount of detail. Surely he would have told her, or did he mean to shield her from the troubles of the world? As much as she loved him, she reflected that this had not been his decision to make. She could look after herself.

She wondered where he was now. He must certainly now know that she was no longer at Regenbogen; news would have reached him by now. It had been a whole week since their departure and she missed him terribly. She wondered what Saggion would have to say about her actions. No doubt he would scold her when he saw her, call her out for her foolhardiness before quietly telling her he was proud when nobody else was listening. This made her smile and chuckle to herself. Roan asked her what was so funny, but she did not answer, choosing to keep this warm little joke to herself. It gave her something to turn over in her head as she continued along the tunnel.

Again, Alene noted the impeccable condition of the path and stones overhead, maintaining the arched shape of the ceiling. Not a loose stone or wayward root in sight. She thought about their initial approach to Woodrow, two days prior, and recalled that the wide avenue they had traversed from the Prairie Road had at first seemed poorly maintained. It had only become neater and more in keeping with the rest of the estate once they had neared the house. Was this also part of the glamour of Woodrow? Was this intentional to confuse or potentially discourage unwanted guests? Alene was unsure how this would work, but she reminded herself that it had been Roan who had led them to the gates, and he already knew where he was going. Roan had by now slowed down and begun an amusingly one-sided conversation with Lionel, so Alene made a note to quiz him on this later.

Her thoughts turned to Nox. Once they were out of the tunnel, she would find her moment to corner her oldest friend, to set things right. She was not going to lose one of her most valued relationships over this, she was determined. Once they were out in the open again, she would find a way.

CHAPTER FOURTEEN

Adelaide and the rest of the company rose well before dawn.

The Maelstrom had proven to be adequately
comfortable, and they had breakfasted on fresh fish by the
light of a few flickering oil lamps in the small bar down in
the cellar. As they exited the inn, still before any light had
crept over the distant horizon over the sea, Adelaide was
struck by how bitter the pre-dawn gust was. The scent of
saltwater was strong in the air and she drew the cape she
wore over her cloak around her tightly, shivering slightly.

The oil lamps had been extinguished some time after
she retired the previous night, and so now the only light
came from the lighthouse behind them. In its flickering
illumination, Adelaide could see Simeon already busy,
supervising the preparations of the horses whilst the ostler worked beside him, yawning deeply as he did. Rita was
also busy, coupling Betty to the rolling cage and smoothing out her mane lovingly as she did so. Rita's long blonde
hair shone in the glow of the lighthouse which gave her the
appearance of having a gleaming halo atop her head. She
smiled at Adelaide as she approached and struck up an easy
conversation. This had been the way for the previous days
of their journey and Adelaide knew that Rita appreciated
the company of another woman. Sometimes, these things
made a difference.

'Morning,' she called softly in the gloom. 'Did you sleep
well? I almost wish that I had opted for a feather bed in
the inn, but you know what the captain's like! He would

never have left anyone else in charge of this,' she tapped the cage beside her lightly, 'and I would never leave him outside alone all night. It's my curse for being a loving wife and a faithful soldier.' She smiled as she spoke, and Adelaide knew that she was merely teasing her husband whilst he was not there to hear. Adelaide smiled back. The previous night's stroll had cast a new light on Simeon Castello, and she was beginning to understand what someone as kind and gentle as Rita saw in him. He, for his part, was lucky to have her.

Despite this gentle exterior, Adelaide forcefully reminded herself that here stood a warrior to be reckoned with. She had seen her thrust the point of her spear through the back of a man's skull and observed as it erupted in a plume of blood and brain between his eyes, still alive for a fraction of a second longer before they glassed over with the fog of death. She had performed this all whilst in midair, vaulting from horseback to join the fray.

From that moment, Adelaide knew that she would like her. The following days had seen Adelaide move forwards from the rear of the company, away from Matteus and Thomas and to alongside Rita as she pulled the wagon astride gentle Betty. Adelaide was quietly amused by how perfect Rita and Betty were together: they were both peaceful, sometimes shy, souls with an inner strength to be ignited when required. This friendship with another member of the party almost made her regret what she must do in order to complete her mission. What would be the punishment they would face from Rowena for failure?

With controlled and regimented haste, the company proceeded down the winding trail to the harbour. Since the previous evening, the main dock had become occupied by a gargantuan wooden vessel. It towered above the tiny harbour-side buildings and was visible only by the light of the crescent moon, slowly disappearing behind the cliffs to their rear. From this vantage point, Adelaide could tell that this was no mere sailing ship – indeed, there were no sails to be seen – and it appeared, in fact, to be steam-powered. Colossal paddle wheels adorned each side and Adelaide was astounded by the ingenuity involved in designing such a marvel. She had never seen such a thing before.

'I would expect oil,' whispered Rita, coming alongside her and correctly guessing her confusion by her perplexed expression. 'It would seem that all the various wonders of this small town stem from oil: the lighthouse, the street lighting, even the tar they use to make their fishing vessels far superior to those of any other villages on the northern shore. It all comes back to the oil. If they can burn it to create light, they must surely be able to burn it to create heat and steam to power those vast paddle wheels.'

Adelaide smiled at her with raised eyebrows. 'Lord Fischer is certainly a man of business, isn't he? It seems there is no stone left unturned in his quest to make as much money as possible from his discovery.'

Rita returned the smile and added her own contribution to the speculation. 'I would bet that this is the very reason why Landsbyfjord is the northern terminus of the Sudhaven Ferry – Lord O'Hare would have to pay dearly for the technology and the means to construct such a mammoth and advanced vessel. I'm sure it's worth it though.'

'Hmm,' murmured Adelaide, her mind beginning to wander to something else. She had just remembered that the captain was not keen on seafaring. She looked again at Rita.

'How do you feel about the journey?' she asked lightly. 'I'm a little apprehensive myself, I'll be happier when we're safely in Sudhaven.'

'I'm not too worried,' she replied, reaching out and taking Adelaide's hand. She squeezed it reassuringly and continued, 'I'm hoping that Betty will cope well with it, she's a timid creature really. Do you think Enchantress will be okay?'

'Oh, I'm sure of that. I've not encountered anything which Enchantress can't handle in the many years I have been fortunate enough to be partnered with her.'

'That's so lovely!' exclaimed Rita, smiling brightly and suddenly at this. 'I suppose they are our partners, aren't they? Even friends. I often think I'm being silly, caring for Betty as I do, after such a short time. But now I feel much better, knowing you think of Enchantress as your partner. You've made me feel so much better, Adelaide. Thank you!'

'Does Captain Castello see Titan as a partner?' Adelaide asked after a moment.

'Oh yes, they've been together forever! Titan came with the office, as did his weapon, but it's been years since they met and they've built a very strong bond.' She suddenly looked around her quickly and added guiltily, 'I suppose Simeon...erm...the captain...would be embarrassed if he knew I had told you that. Maybe let us keep that between us.'

She smiled again and made to move away, but Simeon wandered over before she had moved. Adelaide could immediately tell by the look on his face that he had not heard a word of their conversation: he was not annoyed or embarrassed. He merely looked strained, apprehensive. Rita saw it too and reached out to stroke his face affectionately. He looked as though he wanted it too, but then he seemed to recall that they were not alone and, with a sideways glance at Adelaide, he pulled away and out of her reach. Rita's hand was left hanging awkwardly in the air between them. Simeon glanced conspiratorially around at the rest of his company, busy exchanging opinions on the newest leg of their journey a short distance away. He quickly took her hand, still outstretched, and kissed it briefly before turning and stalking away.

'He tries so hard to seem tough and strong,' she whispered as he retreated, almost to herself. She looked up at Adelaide. 'And he is, he really is. He just doesn't need to make such an effort all the time. Love is not a weakness.'

Rita dismounted and led Betty forward, the inhibitite cage following and creaking loudly in protest. It was to be stored in the hold throughout their journey and retrieved at the other side. Adelaide dismounted also and led Enchantress across the wooden gangplank, into the onboard stables where horses would be cared for by servants for the next three days. She stroked her goodbye and left to find her quarters.

By mid-morning, the northern shore was a distant haze on the horizon behind them and Landsbyfjord could no longer be seen at all. Adelaide supposed that, should it be evening time, she would be able to see the beams of the lighthouse guiding wayward vessels, but not in the full light of morning.

She stood on deck, quite alone and deeply breathing lungs full of clean, salty sea air. She felt as if she were flying, gliding across the deep, crystal-clear waters of the open sea. This feeling appealed to her and terrified her at the same time.

She longed to remove her stiflingly hot cloak – the chilly morning air of the dockside seemed an age ago. Despite feeling exceedingly uncomfortable, Adelaide dared not remove her layers. She was alone for now, but for how long?

She was proven right almost instantly. No sooner had she thought it, a door to the lower levels swung open and Simeon emerged, blinking in the dazzling light reflecting off the shining sea. He looked around and saw her looking his way. At first he looked surprised, then mildly alarmed. Eventually he smiled and walked her way, making sure not to go too close to the railings.

'I cannot help but keep feeling as though the open sea is no place for men. Fish belong in the sea; so do other creatures of the deep. Men belong in the field or the town, hard at work for their family and their kingdom.' He stood a short distance away as he spoke, not quite meeting her gaze and quickly looking away when their eyes chanced a meet.

'And what, Captain,' she replied, suppressing a smile as she did so, 'is the place where women belong? You have not spoken of them.'

He did meet her eyes this time. He hesitated, a comical flicker of inner turmoil as a myriad of thoughts raced across his face. Eventually, after some deliberation, he spoke – and it was with an air of formality and pompousness which Adelaide saw through with immediate clarity. A façade, a forced persona. She smirked inwardly, wondering if Simeon had even been able to deceive himself over the years that this was his true self. She saw more and more each moment she spent with him why Rita was so devoted a wife.

'A woman's place is at the hearth,' he said, in this forced and stunted caricature.

'She must put her family's needs before her own and be a loyal and obedient wife.'

Adelaide was not prepared to let this go unchallenged, so it was with another inward eye roll that she replied, 'But what of your wife? What of your queen? These women do not serve obediently in the home, awaiting their husband's return. Do you have any less respect for these women?' She was mildly enjoying teasing Simeon but could not put her finger on why. She very much wanted him to be true to himself, to have the courage to confront the much more tolerant and gentle man inside him and embrace him as a worthy facet of his own person. He deserved to know himself as few privileged others did.

'Both Rita and Her Majesty are strong women with insurmountable strength and courage. But still, they both serve:

my wife serves me as a soldier in my company, even if I do not ask her to serve me as a wife. The Queen serves the realm, as all monarchs do. But I suppose when you really consider the nature of servitude, we are all serving someone, both men and woman.' He paused for a moment, and Adelaide noticed that he had inched a little closer to the railing overlooking the sea. Then he spoke again.

'You forgot yourself.' It was short, and it seemed to escape his lips before he could stem it. Involuntary, but apparently not regrettable, for he looked her in the eye again and smiled – a warm and bashful smile, a natural smile which was quite unlike any she had seen from him so far, and a glimmer of what lay beneath the mask he hid behind. He clarified, 'You…soldier, erm… Miss Adelaide…you too are a formidable woman, and you should not forget to mention yourself when you list courageous and brave females.'

Adelaide was speechless, but for a moment only. The conversation had turned: she was no longer enjoying her mild teasing, and she was instead anxious and flustered, and slightly annoyed. He had no right to refer to her as he did. The look on her face must have reflected this change and his smile faltered, uncertain again.

'I think we both forget ourselves,' she whispered, her turn to retreat into a forced, formal veneer. 'I am a soldier and you are my captain – it is improper for me to not afford you the correct formality and respect. I will take my leave now if it pleases you.'

She turned to leave, whipping around and sending her long, black hair rippling out in sheets behind her. The silver in it caught the sunlight and it shone with a pearlescent sheen. She felt many different things, simultaneously, and especially felt a deep desire to be alone, away from the captain. A burning knot of humiliation and fear throbbed in her stomach and tears of confusion stung in her eyes.

Suddenly, Simeon leapt across the space between them and grasped her arm in his grip: firm but not forceful, assured and yet shaking. Her gasp caught in her throat, a painful lump, as she blinked away her tears to look at him – she would not let him see what he had done to her! He looked unsure, desperate to understand.

'I've offended you. I must apologise, I meant nothing by what I said – only that I have come to respect you. I have to admit, it was a somewhat begrudging respect, as I never expected a woman to conduct herself in such a dignified and regimented way. The little that I have seen of your fighting prowess is incomparable to the rest of my men – even Rita, whom until recently I had believed to be the most gifted warrior in the Northern Realm. But you outstrip her. And what is more...'

He stopped abruptly. Adelaide turned, in spite of herself, to look at him. He was stood at the railings, one hand still on her arm. He looked straight into her eyes, a wild look of desperation on his pale face. He did not know what he was saying – that much was clear – and he had yet to realise that he had reached the edge of the railing, overlooking the open sea. She felt confusion, bewilderment. He was professing an admiration and pride in her as a member of his team, so what had made him so very different from his usually stoic self? And why did it make her feel sick with anxiety? Was it because she was destined to betray him eventually, in the end, by killing his quarry and dooming his mission to ruin? She had wanted acceptance her entire life. And yet, if he knew the truth, he would not respect her any more. He would fear and reject her. As others had done, and many more would still before her end.

'Yes?' she said, prompting him to finish his sentence.

'And what is more...'

He let go of her arm and turned away. He suddenly realised how close he was to the edge of the ship and backed away hastily, so that it may have been comical in any other circumstance. Adelaide's heart continued to beat feverishly. She took three deep, quavering breaths to steady it and walked away without another word.

As she opened the door to slip below deck, she glanced back to see him staring out blankly to sea. She sighed and closed the door behind her.

Below deck was a warren of corridors leading in all directions. There were many other passengers aboard the Sudhaven Ferry besides their party, but most remained in their cabins except for at mealtimes. Adelaide wanted nothing more than to be alone: she was a churning melting-pot of emotions which she knew must be sifted through before she could continue on her mission. On her way, however, she passed the door to the ship's common quarters, where passengers could socialise and drink as they wished.

'Adelaide!'

It was Rita. She sat alone, just inside the doorway and was beckoning her in. Adelaide sighed and entered.

'The first mate says there is to be a storm!' whispered Rita dramatically as she sat down beside her. She seemed positively thrilled, and Adelaide gave her a quizzical look. She continued.

'I grew up in the north – these southern squalls are nothing compared to the freezing tempests I have endured in my youth. Don't worry though – these storms are common over the Mer Nuage at this time of year and they have never led to any deaths on board.' She said all of this with such enthusiasm and vivacity that Adelaide was taken quite by surprise.

'But will that not delay us? Will we not need to drop anchor and wait out the storm?'

'No, I shouldn't think so,' she replied casually. 'Besides, it's not the storm you should be worried about.' She had a mischievous grin on her face now, which Adelaide still found she could not earnestly return, but Rita seemed not to notice. 'There is a great creature, a leviathan of the deep, which lurks in the chilling depths and preys upon wayward travellers who find themselves unable to escape the vice-like grip of the frigid waves.' This time, when she looked at her friend, Rita realised that something was not altogether right, for she reassured her, 'Don't worry though, Adelaide - I'm just being silly! The storm will be over before it's even begun and I'm sure that the tales of anything lurking in the depths are simply that – tales! I'm just letting myself get carried away. I'm actually rather enjoying myself, being a part of my love's company and getting away from Ville Fleurie, for the first real time in years! We have two days of rest whilst we make the crossing, and I intend to spend it with my husband if he'll let himself relax enough to be with me as a husband.' She sighed suddenly and Adelaide thought she understood. She wanted Simeon to be himself – the man she herself had met the previous evening and had begun to like, very much indeed...

There was movement in the corridor outside and more passengers entered the common quarters. They were not members of their party and largely ignored them, one of them removing a stained pack of playing cards from an inside pocket as they crossed the room and sat down at a wooden table in the opposite corner. Adelaide took this as an opportunity to excuse herself and left. Two minutes later, she was laid on her bed, dark cloak hung on a hook beside the door, secrets and shame exposed.

As she lay there, afternoon became evening and her candle burned low. Eventually, it guttered out and she was plunged into darkness. Still, she did not move. In fact, she found the darkness a comfort: she felt hidden and protected within its embrace. The wind was picking up outside and she could hear its whistle beyond the hull. The ferry was rocking more than it had been. This must be the storm Rita had declared earlier.

As Adelaide finally fell into a fitful slumber in the safety of her darkened quarters, there were two pieces of crucial information that eluded her. The first was something which she would soon discover when she awoke: this storm was to last for several days, and the captain of the Sudhaven Ferry would make the difficult decision to drop anchor in the night and wait out the storm. This was to be a long and eventful wait.

The second piece of crucial information was something which Adelaide already knew in the depth of her heart, but had buried deep down, so much so that she was unable to recognise it when it flared and blossomed in her chest: she had taken the first lingering, uncertain steps to falling in love with Captain Simeon Castello.

CHAPTER FIFTEEN

After nearly two days of walking in darkness, the travelling party which had departed Regenbogen over a week before finally ascended the final stretch of a steep incline of the tunnel floor and emerged into the refreshing breeze of a balmy twilight. Nox could smell the fresh remains of a recent storm on the air and, glancing at the sky to the west, could see menacing clouds retreating over the horizon. She was thankful that they had avoided it: storms at this time of year were unpredictable, often amounting to nothing but sometimes catastrophic.

The ground beneath their feet was similarly damp and boggy, and they would need to find dry shelter before they could rest. Nox did briefly consider the safety of the tunnel as a possible shelter but reflected that Alene would surely wish to make more progress before they ceased travel for the night. Nox begrudgingly accepted that this was wise and glanced over at their leader as she surveyed their surroundings. They were currently standing in hilly grassland, the beginning of misty moors evident to the west and south, with a small copse obstructing their view of the north. The tunnel from which they had just emerged was so well hidden between two small knolls that it would have been quite impossible to find, save for those who already knew where it was or those who accidentally fell down it.

Alene glanced around at the party and smiled wearily at each of them in turn. The smile she gave to Nox was uncertain, apologetic almost. Nox sighed and nodded back. She could no longer find the strength to be outright angry with her, but neither could she smile at her with genuine warmth – and Nox was certainly not one to pretend to be genuine when she did not feel it in her heart!

Somewhere, deep in the fogs of her mind, Nox knew that Alene had not truly done anything wrong. This frightening new power which she had allowed to spill out from within her was not her design or plan, it had been there all along, throughout the many years she had known her. And besides, had she not known she was of elven descent from the moment they met? Mere girls, an age ago it seemed. She knew then that there would be a possibility of magic, and she had never given it a second thought. Nox herself was living proof that people did not need to be the same as their parents. And yet, to see it erupt from her oldest friend before her eyes had shocked and scared her. She did not trust those who practiced magic.

Alene knew where they were going it seemed, and she led the way towards the small copse to their right. It was dark beneath the trees, the last rays of twilight unable to penetrate the leaves above them. Alene walked ahead with Roan. A small, distant part of her wished that she could rush ahead and walk alongside them, but she continued to hold herself back. Instead, she fell in step with Griffin.

Griffin was altogether different from anyone else she had ever met. He instinctively knew her: her interests, her preferences, what she was thinking and even what she herself did not realise she was thinking. He had not pressed her to discuss her problems with Alene, and she was thankful for this. She had spent more time with him over the last few days and spoken with him on all manner of topics, more so than she could remember doing with anybody over such a short amount of time, except for Alene of course. She did not normally let people in, but Griffin felt different. He was warm.

Even her rare visits home to O'Hare Hall at Sudhaven on the Mer Nuage were silent affairs. She came, she went.

She thought of her father, Lord Drake, and how he always smiled so warmly at her return. But she could not forget the past. She would not forget that.

Griffin spoke quietly in the gloom and brought her back to the present. 'Thank you for being here with me,' he whispered, turning his head and smiling softly at her. 'I'm not one for conversation, but you have brought me out of myself, it must be said. I do hope...after all of this is over... and if we survive, that is...that you'll wish us to see more of each other.'

Nox blinked in surprise, then smiled back. She looked away and blushed slightly, but in the low light she hoped he would not notice. It was true he was not a natural talker – that first, stunted conversation they had stumbled through in the hillside cave on their first morning seemed a century ago – but he had improved considerably since then. She was beginning to carry real affection for him, and butterflies flickered in her stomach when she thought of spending more time with him. It was a genuine delight in these troubled days.

'I'll warn you now,' she replied, 'I don't tend to stay in one place for long. But perhaps we shall see each other when I visit Regenbogen from time to time.' That thought made her heart sink: in truth, she very rarely found herself in Regenbogen.

'You know,' said Griffin after a few moment's thought, 'I have spent my entire life within sight of the city frescos – up until now. The world beyond the Painted Wall is full of wonders and holds a powerful attraction for me. I find myself wanting to see more and more of this world: the Eastern Dominion, the Northern Realm, the wilds beyond and the Hinterworld beyond that. I don't even know if I would be capable of such journeys, but I would regret not asking you if you were interested also.'

He sounded suddenly shy, and Nox looked his way. In the gathering darkness, she could not make out his expression but she smiled nonetheless. Then she did something which shocked even herself: she reached out to where his arm hung limply at his side and gently squeezed his hand within her own. Then she let go. A mere moment, but which spoke more than a thousand words. Indeed, there were no more words between them as they walked on in silence, following the silhouettes of their companions ahead.

Nox's mind was racing. To journey with a new companion, no longer alone, would be a monumental change to her life of solitude, but a welcome one. Her heart leapt again as she considered the thought. It made her smile again.

She was still turning this over in her head when the group unexpectedly emerged from the dense trees and were confronted with a truly mammoth sight. Towering over them, built in the shadow of the moorland behind it, was the skeleton of Clagcowl Abbey.

Wreathed in thick fog which drifted ethereally down the slopes from the moors, the decaying ruin stood tall, proud, and yet mouldering, ancient and tired. Large sections of the walls had crumbled and fallen in ages past, the wooden roof rotted and collapsed centuries before so that the immense space within was open to the elements and had been reclaimed by nature. A towering beech tree could be seen from their vantage point outside, reaching skyward with outstretched branches that grew taller than the walls. The walls at either end of the hall were still standing, almost in their entirety, and the empty vaulted holes could still be seen where stunning windows of stained glass would have once been.

The moorlands behind it was where their journey would take them next. Known as the Sleeping Giants due to their rolling, humpbacked shape, they were well-known to Nox from her travels over them in the past. The abbey itself, however, was less familiar to her, never having a need to enter it before now. The moors would provide little shelter once they ascended their foggy slopes so they headed in the direction of the main gate to the abbey grounds to seek shelter before continuing in the light of day.

The outer yard was surrounded by a low dry-stone wall, each stone slab placed perfectly atop the ones beneath it to balance in situ for hundreds of years since its construction. Nox knew that its original purpose would not have been simply to surround the abbey yard, but would also have been to prevent the wolves and wild cats which called these chilly slopes home from entering the burial site where monks of the abbey were laid to rest in years gone by. This was evidently no longer effective, as Nox saw the silhouette of a large dog slink silently out of the gateway ahead which had lost its iron gates and was rendered an old archway. The party passed beneath this archway, the keystone above their heads bearing a carving of a large circle surrounding a smaller square: the symbol which all knew to be for Unus and his four godly children.

Clagcowl Abbey had, in its day, been a centre for learning and pilgrimage for all men who followed the word of Unus. Monks who lived and worked here were known for their authorship of great tomes of knowledge on all features of The Empire: geography, history, flora and fauna among many other subjects. They prayed day and night to all the gods, but especially to Consilii, the father of all humans. After the fall of The Empire, many ways of the old world had come to an end, but Clagcowl Abbey had survived.

For a time.

Eventually, however, the once-grand building could no longer resist the march of time and the monks had moved on. Rumours of a church in Cogburn had circulated for years now, but Nox knew very little of that.

What she did know though, she shared now with her companions.

'We need to be careful here,' she said, loud enough to be heard by all but in a hushed, anxious voice. Alene and Roan stopped ahead and turned to listen; Lionel was trailing behind and she waited for him to catch up before continuing. A chilly breeze blew through the yard, rustling the overgrown grass between the cracked gravestones.

Eventually, Nox spoke again.

'In the past, the monks who called this place home were thought to have powers of their own – bestowed upon them by Consilii. How much of that is true, I don't pretend to know, although the last monks to leave the abbey were said to have re-entered secular society and married. Men who can trace their ancestry back to these monks have demonstrated diluted magical ability since then, such as glamours, illusions and manipulations, so again I say that I do not know the truth behind the rumours. Despite this, I feel it prudent to mention it. There may be...remnants...of this magic remaining in this old place.'

She glanced once more around, then walked past the others towards the doors to the inner abbey. She did not truly want to be here – anything associated with even a hint of magic was not welcome to her – but she knew that the presence of wolves and panthers in the wilds surrounding them would not allow them a safe night's rest otherwise. These wolves were not as savage and threatening as the Rücken wolves but were more numerous and roamed the entire area by night. No, this was a necessary stop, whether Nox liked it or not.

The doors were rotten but remarkably well preserved. One of the double doors was perfectly positioned in place, just as it would have been when the monks closed it one last time. The other had fared less well, hanging at an angle on one hinge, although still in one piece. The resulting gap created between the doors was large enough for each of the travellers to squeeze through one at a time, Nox leading the way despite her own trepidations.

The inside of the abbey was cavernous, one ancient room where echoes of the past resonated from every wall as they stood inside the door and looked around them, mouths slightly agape. The roof was long-since gone, but Nox knew that the sight of it soaring above them to a pointed vault swathed in shadows would have been dizzying. Rubble and debris littered the flagged stone floor, the remains of splintered pews scattered here and there. The hulking carcass of a huge pipe organ, rusted and decaying, could be seen by the light of the emerging stars and Nox could easily imagine its notes filling the hall and overflowing to the surrounding countryside, inspiring awe and even fear in the supreme majesty of the gods to whoever might hear it on a summer evening, long ago and forgotten to history.

The group split up, looking here and there by the light afforded to them by the stars and moon for a place to sleep for the night. Nox wandered away from the others. Where would they be the safest? Where could they pass the night and resume their journey? Nox was not one to praise herself, but she considered her ability to keep herself and her companions safe one of her best qualities: it was not for nothing that she had thrived in the wild and survived through untold horrors, even if some of them did scar her to this day. One thing was certain – they were just as exposed in here as they were outside, with sections of wall crumbled completely to mounds of masonry which would be little defence from the local wildlife.

She was nearing the old stone alter when she heard a short whistle from across the hall.

She whipped her head around to see Lionel in a distant corner, beckoning them over impatiently. She joined him with the others and saw the source of his enthusiasm: a wooden trapdoor, set in the stone floor in the corner.

'That'll be the cellar door,' surmised Roan, bending down to grasp the metal ring which protruded from it. 'We'll be safe down there, surely! We can light a fire and keep warm and cosy until morning arrives. I don't much like this chilly wreck.' He motioned around him at the hall and pulled the ring upwards. The hinges of the trapdoor groaned in painful protest but it swung upwards and over without too much resistance. Nox had the sudden ridiculous urge to slam it back down, hard, and usher her friends away before they could descend. But the feeling was irrational, she told herself, and so Roan became the first of the party to step down onto the creaking flight of wooden steps. As his head disappeared, Alene followed without hesitation. Lionel was next, tailed closely by Griffin. He had nearly vanished from view when he looked around, meeting her gaze in the now near-total darkness. She nodded once to him and he continued. With a deep sigh and one last glance around her, she followed and swung the trapdoor shut above her.

They were now in total blackness. She felt her way down the remaining steps and her feet came to rest on another stone floor. They were not too deep, but deep enough so that any sounds from outside were completely shut out when she closed the trapdoor. She could hear movement ahead of her as someone rummaged blindly through their pack and removed some small items. Suddenly, sparks flashed into life, searing themselves to her vision in the otherwise dark expanse. She blinked furiously, but then she heard the unmistakable sound of stone on metal and she knew what was happening.

A few moments was all it took. The sparks became a warm flicker of flame and the room was illuminated. Roan was bent low in the centre of another large room, although nowhere near as expansive as the one above. He held in one hand his old hunting knife, in the other a flat, jagged piece of flint. He replaced them in his pack and instead removed small sticks and dry leaves, which he expertly placed around his flame which had been initially ignited on a scrap of oil-soaked wool. Nox was surprised and slightly envious that it had been Roan who had done this for the group and not her. Until now, she had fulfilled the role of providing shelter and fire. Tonight, she had accomplished neither.

She marvelled that Roan – the pampered son of a captain, accustomed to luxurious apartments and playing rogue in familiar, unthreatening corners of a friendly castle and knowing all that he knew of the world simply from reading about them in books – had collected this assortment of items for just such a necessity. Had he learned how to survive, out in the wilds of The Empire, in these last few days? Did she even pride herself to consider that he may have learned it from watching her?

Removing her own pack and moving towards the warmth of the fire, she looked around her and took in her surroundings. The room was mostly barren, save for some large jars against the wall and some dusty shelves which held little of note. Nox surmised that the monks must have taken most of the riches of Clagcowl Abbey with them when they departed, and she crossed the room to inspect the jars. Inside each was a large quantity of sweet-smelling oil. Oil was a precious luxury across The Empire, everywhere except for around the Mer Nuage where it was harvested in abundance and had made the area rich in trade and travel. This oil was different though. It had a curious aroma, surely intended to be burned to release its perfumes in ceremonies of celebration to Consilii.

She returned her attention to the fire in the centre of the room, which was now blazing and crackling merrily as her companions settled around it on rolls and huddled in blankets. She laid out her own roll and nestled in her blankets, contemplating the woman opposite her. Not long ago, but what may as well have been an age, Nox had surveyed Alene Idir across another fire, in the Grand Hall of Regenbogen on the night of their departure. She had been her oldest friend. She had been prepared to risk her life to aid her in her cause. What had changed?

As Nox reflected on this question, she found herself laying down on her roll and becoming drowsier in the delicious warmth of the fire. The crackling was soothing and she was soon asleep.

Seconds later, or so it seemed to Nox, her eyes opened suddenly and she was wide awake, although still lying flat in her blankets. It took her a moment to work out what had woken her so abruptly. The fire had nearly died out, so it must have been many hours since she had fallen asleep, despite the fogs of sleep rendering this mere moments.

From the corners of her eyes, Nox could tell that most of the room was now in darkness. Only their circle of light persisted and she turned her head to survey her companions, all of whom were still sound asleep. Griffin was closest to her, his face calm, carefree and relaxed in sleep. She sighed and sat up, intent on discovering what had awoken her. She stretched and yawned, the chill of the room hitting her as her blankets fell away.

She looked into the darkness, and what she saw caused her scream to catch in her throat.

On the very edges of the light, melding and bleeding into the darkness so that they were one and the same, were countless figures. Hooded, dark and silent, they must have been there for some time, watching her stir. Nox knew immediately that it had been this which had awoken her and she tried to move, to spring into action. She was shaking uncontrollably as she stumbled up, eyes darting around her to confirm that they were, indeed, surrounded. The shock was subsiding, her heart was beginning to beat again, only to go into complete overdrive as her adrenaline began to take over.

Not quite able to find her voice, and spinning around in a circle to keep all of the hooded forms within sight, she prodded Griffin awake with a gentle yet insistent kick to the back as she made her way around the fire, stooping to arm herself with Near and Far as she did.

Griffin rose slowly, appearing to take the situation more calmly than she had. After a moment's thought, he crouched down on his haunches and looked directly ahead at the nearest figure, right into where its eyes should have been.

Except there were no eyes. Only blackness was beneath the hood.

Nox was on the verge of bending slowly again to wake Alene, Near and Far held ready, when Griffin raised his voice and made the act unnecessary.

'Speak now!' he shouted into the darkness. 'Who are you and what business do you have with us?'

A cold current ran around the entire circle of onlookers. Nox noticed that they lingered on the very edge of the pool of light and wondered if that was why they had not approached sooner. Had they been waiting for the fire to die down? Alene, Roan and Lionel rose slowly, taking in the situation. Roan already had Reaper in both hands, readied as twin scythes for close combat. Alene had Dawn raised before her and Dusk held backhand for rear defence. They were taking no chances. Nox had no idea what was occurring, but she was at least glad that they were prepared to put up a fight. Even Lionel had his knife out, although for once it seemed that his courage would not be enough to sustain him, and he appeared close to collapse on the other side of the flickering embers.

Despite this, he was stood beside his friends.

The fire guttered, and in that moment the figures took another step forward. One of them, across the fire and nearer to Roan, raised a long, robed arm and pointed straight at Nox.

The room disappeared. Nox was somewhere else, somewhere she did not recognise but instinctively knew. She was surrounded still, but this time by women in long robes of red velvet. Their faces were not clear though. They were hazy, concealed by some manipulation. She tried to raise her arms, to feel the reassuring weight of Near and Far within her grip but found that her wrists were shackled, chained to a brick wall behind her.

One of the women approached. She drew a dagger of sharp, black metal and plunged it deep into Nox's breast before she had time to realise what was happening. Her gasp of shock transformed to a blood-curdling scream as the dagger burned in her flesh, twisting sadistically.

And then, quite suddenly, Nox was back in the cold cellar. Only now the room echoed with grunts and shouts as her friends dashed in all directions, weapons out and desperately attempting to push back their attackers.

Nox was on the floor, gasping for breath, clammy sweat on her forehead. She gave herself one second more to steady herself and then rose, swaying slightly as she did. She felt as though she had a mild fever and had run up a mountain, all in one!

She looked around her desperately, looking for someone to assist. Roan was fighting two hooded figures at once, Alene was slashing wildly with both falchion at her opponent and Griffin was darting everywhere at once, striking anyone he could reach with backward flips and spinning kicks.

The problem, Nox realised, was that none of them seemed to be gaining the upper hand.

Everyone was moving so fast and the room was so quickly returning to full darkness that Nox could not understand what was going wrong. Then, from across the room, she heard Lionel's voice, high and scared, yet determined and assured.

'Nox! Normal attacks don't work! They're just going through them!'

In that instant, Lionel's words and her own instincts ignited a spark of comprehension in her sluggish brain. She had to be sure, so she raised Far and threw it as hard as she could at the hooded head of the nearest aggressor.

It passed straight through and embedded itself deep in the side of an ancient wooden shelf behind it.

These were no living men, they were geiste. Which

meant only one thing!

The others seemed to have realised that, no matter how hard they tried, their weapons would have no effect on their enemy. They were reconverging on the embers of the fire, which even now flickered with its dying glow. They all stood, back to back in a circle, as the figures came nearer still. It was almost impossible to see them now, and it seemed that they gathered strength from this. As one, they lifted their arms to their faces and lowered their hoods.

A circle of monks surrounded them, but spectral, wispy, not quite there. Beneath their robes, they appeared to be formed from a cloudy green haze, although clearly still humanoid with a face, ears, nose. Their mouths were ripped wide, a maw of cruelty and spite as they began to shout and spit curses in unknown languages so that their horrifying voices bounced off the walls and ceiling, echoing in a cacophony of disgust.

It was their eyes which were the most chilling, however. They simply were not there. The heads watched them, but no eyes existed on their faces. A shiver of dread possessed Nox's entire body as she spoke, remarkably calmly, to the group.

'They're geiste,' she told them. 'We're not going to defeat them like this!'

She heard Roan groan in understanding behind her as he uttered, 'Of course!' Then he added, 'Alene, there's only one thing for it: you have to use your black fire! Magic can touch a geiste, even when no physical weapon can!'

Nox whipped her head around to look at Alene, momentarily forgetting their predicament. Magic? Was that really the right choice?

'But – but I can't use this magic!' spluttered Alene, eyes wide in panic. 'I've only done it once, and I don't even know how I did it then!'

'You have to try!' pleaded Lionel, trying to look in every direction at once. 'That might be all that can save us! I don't want to go to that room again!'

That room? Had Lionel been sent to the room with the women too? Had he been stabbed by that black dagger that seared her breast?

'Okay, okay, give me space!' snapped Alene. Nox knew that her friend must be under immense anxiety: she very rarely snapped unless provoked. Then Nox realised that, in the heart of danger, she had thought on Alene as a friend.

In spite of herself, she turned slightly so that she could see Alene out of one eye. She had dropped Dawn and Dusk at her feet and had stretched both hands out in front of her, palms up.

One second, then two. Then more.

For ten whole seconds, nothing happened. Then, quite unexpectedly, an orb of black flame roared into life in the queen's outstretched palms. It let off only the slightest amount of discernible light but nevertheless created a halo around them, so that the geiste took a faltering step backward as one, seeming to fear the new source of power before them.

It lasted only a moment though. Almost as fast as it had appeared, it began to flicker and shrink.

'Come on, Your Majesty, you're doing so well!' called Griffin beside her.

'Keep trying, Alene - you're doing fantastic! Just a little more,' encouraged Roan.

But the black flame guttered again and the halo of light around them began to retreat to its source. Nox gripped Near tightly, prepared for the resuming onslaught. Her heart beating wildly, she realised with genuine shock that she was willing Alene to succeed. Whether it was simply to save their lives or a deeper acceptance of her oldest friend, she did not care. She took a deep breath and, at last, encouraged Alene as she should have done all along.

'Come on and save our skins, Alene! Just be yourself and be proud of who you are! I know you can do it, just feel deep inside and remember – you are who you make yourself, not what others make you! We both have family who have chased us away, but you are the family I have found instead! Now hurry up and save us!'

The effect was immediate. The dying black flame blossomed and erupted in a blaze of light which radiated out and forced the geiste back. This time, however, it was not simply a halo of light but an actual ring of flames which pulsed out from Alene's hands and encircled them. As it passed through Nox, it felt warm – but not uncomfortably so. The geiste did not like it though and retreated further back than ever. One was struck by the wheel of fire and burst into flames, fading away into shadow and leaving behind no trace save for an echoing scream. Eventually, the ring stopped expanding and the geiste circled the outside, prowling just beyond the reach of the light.

Then something else happened. Alene slowly and purposefully sank to her knees and began to whisper quietly to herself. As Nox watched, the black flames which made their circle of protection began to change. They were no longer black; they were gradually turning a dark shade of indigo. Still they continued to change, transitioning through violet and settling finally as a light amethyst colour. What this meant, Nox was not sure, but she was enraptured by the change and could see the effect it continued to have on the geiste.

'We need more fire!' shouted Nox over the now-roaring inferno. Alene appeared to have reached her limit and the flames were expanding no further. They gave them room to manoeuvre though, and Roan readjusted Reaper into a bow as Lionel and Griffin hurriedly gathered together the assortment of packs and blankets, preparing to retreat.

Nox grabbed Dawn and Dusk from Alene's feet and prepared to help Alene herself when the time came. Beside her, Roan grabbed an arrow, wrapped another oiled cloth around its head and plunged it into the amethyst flames.

The end ignited instantly and Roan wasted no time. He notched the arrow and let it loose. It sailed over the fire, over the geiste in an elegant, precise arch, landing on target in a jar of sweet-scented oil.

The large jar exploded in a fireball, sending sheets of burning oil in all directions. Many geiste dissolved into darkness on impact, others steamed for a second before disappearing with a high-pitched scream. Alene's eyes snapped open and the ring of purple flames disappeared instantly. The room was now lit by pools of burning oil, and the small party of travelling companions used the ensuing commotion to flee the scene.

Nox grabbed Alene and dragged her to her feet, wrenching Far free from the wooden shelves in the process as she passed. Lionel, Roan and Griffin were ahead and they threw open the trapdoor at the top of the stairs, flooding the cellar with morning light as a dazzling beam cut through the darkness. As Nox and Alene neared the top of the steps and made to climb out of the cellar, they turned to look back on the scene.

Only one geiste remained, and it stood central amidst the smouldering pools of oil. It looked directly up at them, eyeless but unmistakably staring. Then it opened its mouth and spoke. For the first time, Nox understood what it said. From the look on Alene's face, she did too.

'Queen of this kingdom, hear this now before all is lost! Those who seek the power of the Cardinal will rip the divide between worlds. They must be stopped. They are known to you. They follow you wherever you go. The master and the servant come together and go together. Stop them – they are known to you.'

The figure finished speaking but did not disappear, and eventually Nox had to pull Alene away and out into the sunlight, slamming the trapdoor shut behind them.

The group took only minutes to recover from their narrow escape, choosing instead to put as much distance between them and Clagcowl Abbey as possible. As they left the overgrown graveyard and walked beneath the engraved archway out into the open wilds again, Nox estimated it to be no later than a few hours after sunrise. Nox walked now alongside Alene, thankful that her apology could be a wordless squeeze of the hand and a smile.

She heard a noise behind them and darted quickly, only to see that they were being followed. It was not as she had expected, however, as she saw that they were being followed by a medium-sized dog: shaggy, sandy hair with streaks of black and a long, bushy tail. When it saw her looking, its tail waved excitedly from side to side and its muzzle opened in what she would have sworn to be a smile. Nox shook her head and turned, continuing up the grassy slope which was already craggy in places and bore the unmistakable signs that they were heading up onto moorland. She had no idea where this dog had come from but was sure it would lose interest soon enough.

The afternoon wore on, and Nox found herself walking alongside Griffin again. Alene was a little way ahead, attempting to make flames dance across her palm once more. She was having moderate success, more and more with each attempt. They were remaining black, however, and Nox had not seen any sign of the amethyst flames since their near-miss in the cellar.

'You did a good thing, you know,' whispered Griffin beside her so that only she could hear. She looked at him and smiled: she knew what he was referring to.

'I said what was in my heart,' she answered honestly. 'It took a very long time for me to reach that realisation – more time than it should have – but I think I get it now. Magic is not evil, simply because some people who choose to use it that way are not as pure as they could be.'

'Who?' One word, but once again Nox knew what he meant.

'My mother, the Lady of Sudhaven' she replied, looking

away, out over the moors.

These lands were used for sheep farming and were dotted with remote farmsteads and crisscrossed with more dry-stone walls, similar to those of the abbey yard. The Sleeping Giants normally had a drizzly, damp climate but today was sunny and warm – it seemed as though any hints of rain had drifted westwards with the storm she had spotted the previous night. She saw that Griffin continued to watch her patiently for more information, so she continued.

'Lady Felicity O'Hare has the honour of being the host to a phantasm. Oh – not the Cardinal, of course, but a phantasm nonetheless. She received it at birth, as all hosts do, and it manifested its first distinctive signs on her eleventh birthday when she had grown sufficiently to control it. My entire childhood, I had this unnatural burden to bear, and really it should not have been my burden. She did not have the natural mothering instinct, it would be fair to say, and she did not want me around.

'I left home on my eleventh birthday – if Lady Felicity was old enough at that age to host a supreme, magical being, then I was old enough to make my own decisions and make my own way in the world. I had to share my mother with her magic and, unfortunately for me, her magic always won. She often had time for my brother, Thaniel – he was younger and demanded more of her – but I somehow ended up an outcast in my own home.

'Since then, magic has always hurt me. I don't know anymore if it's my own prejudice or simply bad luck, but magic has left a bitter taste in my mouth whenever I have been unfortunate enough to experience it. Personally, I could go my entire life and never be exposed to it again. Until today, I would have stuck to that view. But now I am beginning to see that I was being narrow-minded. Alene is my best friend. I don't like magic – I never will – but I love Alene and magic will not destroy any relationship I have with another person ever again!'

Nox realised how much she had been talking and stopped. She never spoke this much to anyone. Griffin was different though. She looked into his eyes as they walked and he reached over, taking her hand and clasping it tightly in his own.

'For what it's worth, I'm proud of you! Like you told Queen Alene, we can't choose our families. I never knew my parents. And, if I may be so bold, I would like to make you a promise: I will promise to protect you, as long as we are in each other's company – which I hope to be for a long time yet – from any magic which may find you. You have followed your heart with Queen Alene – she would never hurt you.'

Nox blushed and smiled. She was still holding his hand and made no effort to let go. Griffin appeared to be blushing as well. They were both speaking more than they ever did. What a strange effect to have on each other. Griffin was plainly casting around for a different subject to change the mood, as he next said, 'So what were those creatures this morning? Geiste?'

Nox felt that Roan could probably give a perfect answer to this question, straight out of a book, but Nox was determined to outdo him. She liked Roan very much but why should he be the only one to know things? She cleared her throat and answered.

'Like I said last night, the monks of Clagcowl Abbey had mild magical ability – supposedly from Consilii but that is up for debate in my opinion. Either way, when a magical being dies, they leave a much more defined imprint on this world than a regular human. Instead of simply dying, they create a shade, a spectral entity to walk in their place. I don't think it's intentional, they simply do. That shade is called a geiste, and often it will possess magic similar in nature to that of its living counterpart. Over centuries, geiste normally fade away, but those ones in that cellar had lingered and stagnated, becoming vile and twisted beyond recognition from the wise and learned men they had been in life.'

Griffin was silent for a while, thinking on this. Finally, he spoke again.

'You screamed and fell,' he said softly, intensifying the grip on her hand. 'What did it do to you when it pointed your way?'

Despite the warm sunshine, Nox felt suddenly cold.

'Did they do it to anyone else?' she asked.

'Only to the boy,' he said, indicating Lionel a short way ahead, 'and he looked as bad as you after he rose again. He was shaking all over.'

I don't want to go to that room again! That was what he had said. Nox wondered again if he had seen the women in red, the women with no faces who had stabbed her with a searing black dagger. She shuddered again. She was not ready to talk about that room.

She did not know where it was but felt as though she knew it at the same time.

Nox looked over her shoulder. The dog was still following them, tail wagging, chasing rabbits. She wished she could be so happy. Then she felt the reassuring pressure of a hand inside her own and looked into a pair of caring and slightly shy eyes.

Maybe she could be that happy.

The party travelled across the Sleeping Giants for three days. They were very much as Nox remembered them, and they encountered little in the way of hindrance.

Then, a few hours before sunset on the third day, Nox crested a hill and looked down into the sudden lowlands below. The moorland had come to an end, and ahead of them beyond the valley – closer than they had been since they had left the prairie over a week ago – towered the mighty Rücken. Alene came up alongside her and crossed her arms. Her gaze fell far down, to a narrow vale between two sheer cliffs of the range. This was the Vale of Screams and was the only reliable route they had into the Northern Realm. Nestled in the vale, on the very eastern end of it where it was its most narrow, was the Schloss Stieg: an imposing husk of a fortress, left to rot.

This was where they had been heading towards.

This was their entrance into the Northern Realm.

They had arrived.

CHAPTER SIXTEEN

The storm which had ravaged the Mer Nuage for four continuous days had yet to relent in its pledge to wreak havoc on anyone who may be so unlucky as to be at sea in such merciless weather. Incessant rumbling and menacing crashes of thunder overhead could be heard at all hours. The mournful wail of the vengeful and unceasing wind was like screams of fury, out over the tempestuous waves. Time no longer mattered aboard the Sudhaven Ferry: daylight had failed to penetrate the storm from its inception and night reigned on the Mer Nuage.

This was quite unlike any natural night though, Adelaide thought to herself one pitch-black afternoon. A night of any other sort would provide moonlight or starlight. Not this night though. All that was provided here were howling gales, bone-chilling torrents and thunder which seemed to split the very skies apart and rip gaping holes into the next world. Even the flashes of forked lightning which constantly punctured the calamitous skies failed to truly shed light on the scene.

Every day, Adelaide would ascend the wooden stairs to the strong, iron-banded door which led onto the deck. It was oaken, treated with tar on its exterior and was designed specifically for weather such as this, when the Mer Nuage wished nothing more than to drag any vessel foolish enough to be astride her into her ghostly depths, never to be seen again. Adelaide was immensely thankful for the craftsmanship of this door, and of the Sudhaven Ferry in its entirety, but she still opened it, once a day, every day, to look out on the storm which thwarted their mission in hopes of spying a distant ray of light, an end to the waking nightmare.

Today was no different. Adelaide ascended the stairs, grasped the iron ring in her left hand and turned it forcefully clockwise. It clicked, and she pushed outwards to open the heavy door. After she had given her first push, however, she felt the door being ripped from her hand and begin to swing outwards at great speed: the terrible wind had gripped it and did not wish to relinquish it. Adelaide was prepared, however. It had been the same every day. She doubled her grip and maintained her control over the door, peering through the gap created with trepidation, intent on discovering some lull in the devastation. This was not to be today though. The storm raged on.

Adelaide looked out into a pitch-dark abyss. No life could be out there, could it? She thought of any other vessels unlucky enough to be caught out of port in this weather.

Would they be so lucky? The crew of the Sudhaven Ferry had made the decision to drop anchor and wait out the worst of the storm, but even they admitted that they had not known of one as vicious as this for many years, this storm far outstripping the usual squalls which characterised this time of year. Their transportation was designed to provide safe passage for all travellers, in all weathers. The same could not be said for every vessel. Adelaide found that she was squinting through salty spray and near-horizontal rain as waves overtopped the railings and she was soon soaked through, her sodden fringe clinging to her frigid face as she pulled the door shut again with considerable effort.

Four days. They had made no progress for nearly four whole days, and Adelaide found that the idleness, the darkness and the constant, never-ending roar of the gale were enough to drive her to distraction. She caught herself thinking more and more of her mission: to stop the Cardinal Phantasm from falling into the wrong hands. She wondered what other factions may even now be advancing on Mort Vivant, the putrid, decaying swamps in the south of the Northern Realm where the new Cardinal was reported to be.

She shuddered involuntarily as she thought on the old man who had intercepted them on the Sunken Road, Pyre, and how he had alluded to their goal. Did he represent another group who meant to seize the Cardinal? This 'Republic of Caterva' as he put it?

She had certainly never heard of such a place, although that barely mattered. If they had their own plans, plans which did not involve utilising some form of transportation across the Mer Nuage, then they could, at this very moment, be approaching their mutual prize.

Adelaide then thought on the other information which Lorraine had given her: that her son had delivered a plea for help to Regenbogen. Lorraine had plainly hoped that King Gerecht would offer some form of assistance, but Adelaide was unsure what he would be prepared to provide. Did he also move on the Cardinal, or a team of his own choosing? How did she know who to trust?

Adelaide reminded herself that she could not even trust her own company. She planned to betray them, and that was what was best, was it not? She was a woman of her word, she would complete the mission she had been paid for, to thwart the efforts of Captain Castello, and that was all. She would kill this young boy; she was not above that. It was the only way to ensure that he would not fall into the wrong hands – she certainly did not see herself as a protector, a babysitter. That would not be her path.

She did not need baggage in the form of a young charge. She did not need baggage in the form of friends, of companions or family. In truth, she did not deserve it. She was broken. She could be a shadow of herself, an illusion, to accomplish an end but she did not deserve companionship as other, normal people did. She did not deserve to fall in love.

She flinched as the knot of fear and anxiety in her stomach churned suddenly and her head spun. She felt bile rising in her throat and she could have been sick right there, on the stairs, if she had allowed herself. She would not though. She did not show weakness.

She had managed to completely avoid Captain Castello ever since the storm had begun on their first night out of Landsbyfjord. She dared not set eyes on him, not now, not alone. She simply did not trust herself to not jeopardise the entire mission. That, and she thought that her heart might break if she let him smile at her again.

Love was not something which Adelaide either sought, wished for or deserved. It simply was not to be a part of her existence. And yet she felt elated, lightheaded and absolutely devastated simultaneously whenever she thought of him, of Simeon. She was a fool. Why did she have to fall in love? He would never return her affection, as nobody ever would. And why would he? She was an abomination, and he was married.

Rita. She had avoided her also. She did not want to be around her, to see her smile with a happiness which should be her own. Jealousy was not the correct word: she had learned many years ago that coveting a life of somebody else did not fix her broken one.

No, she avoided Rita because she dreaded her discovering her shame, her secret lust. What truly hurt Adelaide though was that she had honestly begun to develop a true bond with Rita, something which she thought must surely resemble a friendship – the first of her life. And now she had lost it, tossed it aside by daring to wish for too much.

Dripping wet from the howling storm, she negotiated the labyrinthine corridors of below deck as she made to return to her quarters, where she had holed herself up for much of their journey. The oil lamps which lit the hallways periodically were set to their lowest setting: oil reserves were not designed to last this long of a journey and fuel had to be rationed. As such, the light they provided was dim and inadequate at illuminating the path. Pools of darkness swam in the corners and recesses and the quality of the glowing lamps caused Adelaide's eyes to itch with tiredness.

She ventured down another set of wooden steps and deeper into the belly of the great ship. She traversed another corridor, flickering dimly in the half-light of a few lamps, and had almost reached her cabin when she stopped dead. *He* was approaching her, walking in the opposite direction and looking right at her.

'Miss Adelaide,' he said, stopping in front of her. Formal again. 'I am glad to have caught you at last. I have just been to your room, hoping to speak to you. Would you mind if we spoke together for a short while? I have things I would wish to gather your opinion on.'

She hesitated. She had avoided him for four days, specifically to avoid having to feel the churning, wrenching sensation she was experiencing at that very moment. She breathed, twice and deep – and hopefully surreptitiously enough to not look a fool in front of the captain – and replied.

'If you wish to speak to me, Captain, then I am yours to command. What did you wish to speak to me of?'

'Not here,' Simeon replied, suddenly in a hushed voice, and Adelaide was momentarily terrified that he wished to discuss their conversation on deck on their first day at sea. He continued, however, and Adelaide was saved from this notion, 'Our conversation concerns the mission, and we are not the only travellers aboard the Sudhaven Ferry at this time. Come.'

He led her down the corridor, away from her own quarters, and through a door into a different common room than the one she had encountered Rita in on their first day aboard. It was not vacant, however. Two other men whom she did not recognise were sitting on a low bench, smoking pipes and talking quietly to each other. They stopped abruptly when Simeon entered, followed closely by Adelaide, and they rose from their seats not long after and left the room, closing the door behind them. This was nothing unusual to Adelaide: travellers were often secretive and reserved the right to their privacy. Indeed, they were no different themselves in that respect.

They both took seats opposite each other. There was no fire, no warmth to speak of, and therefore the room could not be considered comfortable. Regardless, it sufficed as far as basics could, and they sat. Adelaide shivered in the chill which ruled the room: she had forgotten until this moment that she was soaked through from her venture above deck.

Simeon seemed to notice this too, for he said, 'Miss Adelaide, you are soaking wet,' and rose, walking behind her in a move to help her remove her sodden black cloak. A mark of gallantry, to be sure, but Adelaide jumped up as though struck and stared, stunned at him.

'Please do not touch my cloak,' she whispered, feeling both scared and maddened – altogether different from how she had felt the last time they had met. His look of complete confusion softened her anger though, and she added, 'I keep my cloak on at all times; I have...scars...which I would rather keep to myself.'

Simeon attempted a smile and sat back down. Adelaide sat as well. 'I understand,' he said, 'we all have parts of us we would rather hide. I apologise for being so presumptuous. But now, if you recall, I wished to speak to you.'

'If you don't mind me asking, Captain, why do you wish to discuss it with me? Why not Rita, or Matteus or Thomas?' Her heart beat wildly to think that he valued her opinion so greatly.

'I have already discussed this with each of them in turn,

some days ago. I would have spoken to you also, before now, if I could have found some time alone with you. That, however, has proven difficult.' He smiled again, and Adelaide scolded herself inwardly: she was stupid to have thought he wanted to speak to her above those he had known and loved for years.

'Eventually, we will escape this horrific storm and I do not mind telling you that this cannot happen soon enough for me. Not only for the mission, but I find myself being driven to distraction with this sense of helplessness crushing upon us. My fears of the sea are quite gone, however – I think there was only so much they could take before they abandoned me completely. A trial by fire, or water as it were.

'I'm rambling. What was I saying? Yes, when we finally slip from the clutches of the Mer Nuage, we will be able to resume our journey, and our mission.' He looked around him, including a surreptitious glance at the closed door, before continuing. 'I have never been one to discuss my plans with others, with underlings. Never. I do not mind saying that your influence seems to be changing me, hopefully for the better.'

Adelaide was taken aback, so much so that she was momentarily unable to make a sound. She simply stared at Simeon, eyes wide in shock. What did he mean, her influence?

He seemed to see her confusion. 'When we spoke last, and the time before that, you made me feel slightly ashamed of my prior conduct. You questioned me on my views of the world, of the role of women and men in particular, and I found that, long after you had left me, I was still too confused to fully process what I was experiencing. Had everything I had thought about myself been wrong? I maybe wouldn't go quite that far, but certainly I had been fooling myself with a fabricated persona for many years now. I found, when I thought deep on the subject, that I was a far more tolerant man than I had ever allowed myself to believe, in my obsession with being the ideal captain for Ville Fleurie. I have you to thank for exposing me. I do not know why you have had such a profound impact on me, you of all people. I feel some affinity for you, some attraction I cannot comprehend. It has taken me these days to realise this, but I feel you have changed me, hopefully – I say again – for the better.'

Adelaide found herself speechless, something which was increasingly usual for her recently. Attraction? What did he mean by that?

'As a result of this,' he continued, but no longer smiling, 'I find myself at odds with what I am to do. The spell of Ville Fleurie has begun to lift, the scales of my past conduct have begun to fall from my eyes, and I am confused, uncertain by how to proceed. Is what has been asked of me right? Can I blindly follow orders which would assuredly lead to war and the incarceration of an innocent person? Do I have that right? Does anybody? Not long ago, I wished for war, for glory...now I'm not sure I do, or if I even ever did. Is the price worth it? Is the cause just? I received no support from Matt and Thom, they are still brainwashed by the fogs of honour, serving and following orders. Rita brought me back into myself – I really do love her – but she insisted that I needed to make a decision for myself. And so, Miss Adelaide, I am turning to you for advice, something which the old me would never have done. You know of the Cardinal, of course, and I know that you are loyal to Rowena above me, but even so, I find myself craving your advice, your council. Tell me what you would do, and I will consider it with my heart and soul.'

Adelaide subconsciously rose and paced the room, acutely aware that Simeon was watching her every move. She had changed him? Had that been her intention? No.

She had often been aware of this effect she had on people, a bewitching influence which she had absolutely no control over. It came in very useful on some missions, but she had not intended to affect Simeon. Was this why he had complimented her, four days ago? This made her feel sick to her stomach.

Either way, could she play this to her advantage, for her mission? She was rather surprised to find that she would not do this. She would not abuse this man, as she had abused other men – and women – in the past. What did this mean for her mission though? She still intended to complete it, no doubt, but this changed things. She did, however, need to continue her role: the guise of an agent of Rowena, sent to join the team by her personal recommendation. Despite such uncertainty on how to proceed, she would be in danger if she were discovered. She was under no illusion that this man would treat her as a traitor if he discovered her truth.

She chose, in the end, to speak to him plainly, as plainly as she could. She would decide on her next move along the road.

'Do as your heart tells you. Despite serving her faithfully, I have a sense that Rowena will bring no good to the world with her acquisition of the Cardinal, but other than that, I cannot say. I feel that I must take my leave now, if it pleases you.' She smiled and turned to the door.

'One last thing,' Simeon said, causing her to turn around. 'I hope I have not made you uncomfortable at all over the past few days. I feel I may sometimes speak my mind a little too liberally with you, but I find that you help me to see things clearly, to see what really matters, a window into my truest and deepest self – a part of me I am rather unacquainted with, and yet a part which I fully feel to be earnest, sincere and genuine. It can sometimes be an uncomfortable experience, looking inwards beyond the rot to what is good and whole beneath, but I believe I have you to thank for prompting me to do so. I will not be the same again. Thank you.'

Adelaide smiled, warmly and radiantly, and left the room without a further word.

A sudden and somewhat abrupt change in her captain, but apparently one which had always been in there, waiting to be released. She had only just begun to realise recently that there was far more to Simeon than what people saw, and it appeared as though Simeon himself was now aware of this himself.

She felt elated. What Simeon was feeling was natural and pure. Did that mean he had truly meant every nice word he had said of her? She understood very little of who she really was, of her origins, nature and destiny. She did not understand this strange influence she sometimes had on others: how it happened, what she did, why it happened or how to stop it. However, despite all of this, all of this uncertainty, she saw a shining beacon of light in her future. She had helped Simeon realise his true self and confront his inner sincerity and, possibly, he could eventually help her to do the same.

Night fell, darker and heavier than the perpetual darkness had been so far. The oil lamps guttered as stray gusts forced their way in through distant cracks and crevices. Adelaide was surprised that the ship was still afloat.

She had always been told, years ago, that the storm would always be the most devastating immediately before the climax, and she prayed that this was so. Not to Unus or the other gods – Adelaide had never in her life experienced anything which could convince her of their value. She fully believed that they were there, pulling the strings behind the scenes for their own amusement, playing with humans, elves, goblins and whatever else there was in the world as children would play with marionettes, and this was precisely why she had no desire to ever be blessed by their presence. No, Adelaide prayed simply to all that was out there – hoping that somebody knew what they were doing, that they had a plan for her. She would not believe that she had been placed so brutally in this world without purpose.

Her wild and chaotic thoughts wandered to the horses below deck. They were being well cared for, she knew, but that had not stopped her from checking on them daily. Despite the tempest, they were coping very well indeed – possibly better than their human companions!

Her feet began guiding her subconsciously in the direction of the hold, where they and the inhibitite cage were being cared for. She would check on them before retiring for the night.

Ahead of her, a door swung open and Rita stepped out into the corridor. She looked at her and smiled, waiting before falling into step alongside her. Adelaide was uncertain: she had not seen Rita since her problematic and inconvenient feelings for the other woman's husband had begun to emerge. She swallowed and pushed this worry deep down: she was, after all, exceptionally fond of Rita as well.

'I think we've had the same thought,' said the other woman, indicating down the corridor where they were both now heading. 'My poor Betty and all the other brave steeds need our love and companionship now, more than ever. The least we can do is to check on them now and again, assure them that they will soon be riding across open grassland, out in the open fresh air. I think if I tell them this, I might also believe it myself.' She smiled and Adelaide could not help but smile back.

They descended more stairs and arrived at the entrance to the hold. This gargantuan room was half of the entire lower level of the ship, housing crates of spices, jars of precious perfumes and a myriad of other unknown treasures, on their way across the sea to a new lucky owner. The trade facilitated by the Sudhaven Ferry was what made Landsby-fjord and Sudhaven itself rich, and a spot of inhospitable weather was not enough to see it pause.

At the far end of the room were the stables. Enchantress tossed her head to and fro, her silver-grey mane whipping out in agitation as the gale roared outside. The horses had evidently become accustomed to the journey but were still not entirely at ease. Betty was of a similar nature, as was Titan.

The rolling cage remained against the far wall, undisturbed. Adelaide wandered over to it and gazed between its bars absentmindedly. In another week or so, the Cardinal Phantasm may very well be within these bars, being escorted back to Ville Fleurie, a prize for Rowena to aid in her designs of war. This was what she must avoid, but where did Simeon stand? Was he really having doubts?

Rita appeared beside her. 'It's awful, isn't it?'

Adelaide said nothing, so Rita continued. 'Is it really necessary that we chain up this young boy and treat him as a prisoner? That does not seem honourable and chivalrous to me.' She suddenly blushed and added, 'Not that I am questioning the orders of our queen, I simply wish there was a better way.'

They stood there in silence for a few moments more. Then, quite suddenly, Rita began fumbling with a fine chain of rose gold around her neck. She unclasped it and on its end was a small key. Slowly, but with an inexplicable air of certainty, she walked towards the cage and knelt down.

Beneath it, concealed in the shadows, was a long, heavy wooden case that Adelaide knew contained the weapons of their company, which they had been obliged to part with before boarding. Custom dictated that weapons must be relinquished upon entering a person's home if they so requested, and this ship was included. Only Captain Castello had been permitted to retain his claymore, in keeping with his status, but all other weapons had been locked away, with Simeon entrusting the key to Rita. Now, she bent low and placed the key in the sturdy lock.

Adelaide bent also, and as she did, she experienced a current like a bolt of lightning shoot up her spine, a chill in the air of which she knew immediately the cause: they were not alone in the darkness.

'Keep low!' hissed Rita, crouched beside her and bowing her head over the open box containing their weapons, including Adelaide's long, curved sword, *Father*. They remained bent, painfully still, ears straining for sounds of life behind them. Rita's hands inched, slowly, towards the oak handle of her battle spear. Taking her cue, Adelaide steadied her breathing into an almost trance-like calm and did the same, finding Father's hilt with her fingers.

Still, no sound came from behind them.

Were they imagining things?

No.

She had definitely sensed it.

Then:

'One,' breathed Rita, barely audible despite Adelaide being right beside her. She could not see her face behind the curtain of hanging blonde hair but imagined it taught with concentration.

'Two,' Adelaide prepared her legs for the pounce.

'Three!'

Both women twisted and propelled themselves into a roll, rising as one, weapons held high.

The hold was alive with silent menace.

From behind every possible hiding place – crates, sacks, wagons and jars – black-cloaked figures were emerging, melding with the darkness to vanish and reappear constantly. Their rusted swords were drawn and raised, but none made any movement towards them. Instead, they lurked beyond the light, faceless and menacing. Adelaide was not afraid. This was her true calling, where she truly belonged. She gripped Father tightly in both hands, poised for carnage.

Then, one of the figures, off to their left, spoke clearly. 'We meet again, my ladies. It will be the final time, I assure you!' The figure tossed his black hood back and revealed his face. Adelaide recognised him immediately: Pyre, the man who had accosted them on the Sunken Road.

In a bold and frightening voice, one ringing with authority, Rita shouted out, 'What is your purpose here? How did you come to be aboard the Sudhaven Ferry?'

Pyre held out his palm and, as he did so, a small blossom of black flames flickered into life there. They gave off almost no light at all, and yet Adelaide could see them clearly in the darkness.

'The Republic of Caterva will no longer accept the meddling of pretenders and fraudulent monarchs in the affairs of the common people,' he shouted clearly so that his voice echoed in the cavernous space. 'We will wipe out your kind, every last one. You will never acquire the Cardinal – you lack the honour!'

With that, shadows danced.

A number of figures broke off from the main group immediately and headed for the door which led to the upper levels. Adelaide and Rita, however, had much more pressing matters to contend with as swift men and women rained down on them, swords raised. Adelaide made short work of one man instantly by slashing once across his chest, horizontally from left to right, as he advanced. Dark crimson stained his tattered robes as he froze, mid-attack. His hood slipped and his face appeared, pale, shocked and scared, before he crumpled in a heap on the dusty floor. Who were these people?

Two more met a similar fate, as Adelaide leapt up high onto a stack of sturdy crates.

The high ground afforded her a good view of the hold and, as she forced Father down hard through the top of a cloaked woman's skull with a sickening crunch, she saw

Rita not too far away. She was spinning high, low and in every possible direction, her spear twirling in her nimble fingers with dexterous precision as it jabbed, parried and slashed with its claw-like tip. Three fell around her as she leapt out of sight.

Then Adelaide saw him: Pyre, not fighting or moving at all. He stared up at her with unblinking eyes, lips curled in an unsettling sneer.

She pounced. She thought of little more than ending him, of slashing him across his chest and seeing what came gushing out. Surely if he were to fall, the others would quickly surrender?

A simple, but costly, mistake.

Pyre continued to look up at her and, once only, he blinked.

Adelaide felt searing flames erupt around her and engulf her like a wreath. Black flames. His flames.

Mid-jump, she dropped like a stone, hitting the wooden floor with a crash. She writhed, she rolled, she screamed a blood-curdling note of desperation as she clawed at her thick black cloak, ripping it from her body to rid herself of the dark flames which threatened to consume her body.

Finally, she tore it free of her and tossed it aside, still burning. The commotion must have caused some of the robed enemy to pause, for she rose from the ground without confrontation and straightened up, looking around her.

Adelaide was aware of why she was being watched so closely. A sheer plunge of her heart confirmed what she already knew when she glanced to either side and saw them spread out wide on either side of her.

For Adelaide hid a secret. From the earliest day she could remember, she had been different. She had worn a thick black robe that covered her entire body every day for this very reason. Her shame was exposed.

On one side, sprouted from her right shoulder blade, spread a colossal wing, white as snow, gleaming feathers glossy and grand.

On the other side, sprouted from her left shoulder blade, spread a colossal wing, black as pitch, veined and ribbed with translucent bones and formed from an oily midnight leather.

For Adelaide was not a human.

Adelaide did not know what she was.

Nobody knew what Adelaide was.

Her shame. Exposed.

But this was not the time for that. The enemy marshalled, and so Adelaide rose – higher and higher on powerful wings – before crashing down upon her foes in a deadly whirlwind. She looked around wildly for Pyre, but he was nowhere to be found.

Adelaide turned and came face to face with Rita. Her jaw had fallen slightly open, her eyes were wide. But then something quite extraordinary happened: Rita shook her head, smiled, and turned away. She dispatched the last remaining enemy and sank to the floor, panting.

Adelaide approached her tentatively. Was it too much to hope that she was not disgusted or terrified by her? Rita rose with obvious effort and Adelaide saw that her leg was cut, blood running freely from the wound. Rita appeared to give it little worry though, and she instead removed her long cloak. Once she had ripped a long piece of material from the bottom of it, she tossed it with a smile to Adelaide. She then bent down once again, tying the long strip of material around her injured leg.

Adelaide willed her hidden limbs – the mismatched, secret wings which she kept concealed at all times – to fold inwards, tight against her back. This caused her considerable pain, as they were cramped and compressed far too much and were becoming weak from never being used. Despite this, it was preferable to the alternative of the entire Empire knowing what she kept a secret from everyone. She pulled Rita's cloak over them and felt herself relax at once:

hidden once more.

Suddenly, and with a lurch of the stomach, Adelaide recalled that their danger was not yet gone: a small number of the enemy had disappeared up the stairs towards the upper levels. Rita appeared to remember this as well, for she grabbed her spear and took off towards the door, Adelaide hot on her heels.

Up one flight of stairs, all was silent. The flickering lamps were as they always had been, the corridor deserted.

They heard a thud above them and they raced as one, up another flight of stairs, to meet a sight of carnage. Four of the cloaked figures stood over three tattered and bloody corpses. They whispered in the half-light and plotted their next move as Rita charged them with her spear held before her. She had penetrated the first of them before the others realised but this, unfortunately, was as far as she got. In the narrow corridor, a tall man with a heavy frame and thick arms lashed out at her in retaliation and struck her hard in the side of her head. Her spear was still buried deep in her first victim and she fell painfully to the floor, pulling a dead weight upon her.

Two of the remaining figures began to retreat in the opposite direction. Where to, Adelaide could not say. She advanced on the tall man, whose hood had been lowered to reveal filthy, matted hair to his shoulders and a multitude of cuts and scars across his sallow face, the eyes now staring at her were pits of madness.

She reflected too late that, in their cramped position in the narrow corridor, she was at a disadvantage: Father was designed for slashing and sweeping, and she simply did not have space for that here. Regardless, she advanced.

From his belt, the tall man withdrew a hammer: thick, black and deadly. He raised it and brought it crashing down with more speed than Adelaide would have thought possible from a man his size. She staggered back and it missed her, though she felt it pass inches from her nose. He raised it again and she took the chance, ducking beneath it to strike at his exposed chest with Father. It was not to be, however.

Somehow, despite seeing it happen to her friend mere moments before, she fell victim to a crushing blow by his free hand. She sailed backwards, crashing into the wall and sliding down it into a heap. Her eyes watered and her head was spinning. Her ear felt like it was burning where it had been struck and she fought the urge to be sick. Through her streaming eyes, she saw him advancing on her, hammer hanging limply at his side, for now.

He looked down on her, and the horrors which gleamed in his crazed eyes and flickered in his sudden leering smile sent a chilling wave of terror crashing over her as she opened her mouth to scream. No man had ever broken her soul like this, caused her to cry out in dread. But then no man had ever looked at her like this. No human heart could beat beneath his breast, his wheezing and irregular breaths were animalistic and carnal.

He stretched out his free hand – the one which had struck her with such ferocity – and clamped it forcefully over her mouth before she could make a sound. His hand stunk of dirt and blood, and the putrid stench would have made her gag if she had not been desperately fighting for air. He held her, pinned to the wall where she sat, colossal weight behind his grip. Her hand had lost Father as she fell but she clawed frantically at his exposed arm, raking his skin and drawing blood which bloomed and dripped to the wooden floor. He did not seem to notice, or care.

He smiled at her, an entirely disturbing smile that froze her in her efforts to escape as she gazed deep into the hollow recesses of his dark, haunting eyes. He dropped his hammer with a dull thud and he drew a short, curved knife – the sort you may use to skin a fish.

Adelaide began fighting again, shaking uncontrollably and yet still managing to fight. His crushing weight felt as though it would rip off her jaw, but it suddenly slackened slightly as though her attacker had been distracted by something. Adelaide took her chance and slipped to the side, successfully evading his grasp. She acted on instinct and did the first thing she thought of: she dove for his face, easily within striking distance, and plunged both thumbs deep into those unhinged eyes, those dark pits of insanity, so that he screamed like an animal as crimson fountains erupted and he stopped fighting her completely, instead staggering back and clawing at his face, shrieks of pain echoing around the barren corridor.

All of this was silenced, however, as the tip of a dark, smoky claymore burst from his chest. He fell to the floor, finally dead, to reveal Simeon stood behind him, Cumulonimbus drawn. Simeon did not speak, he simply dashed towards her and grabbed her still-outstretched hand – slick and red with hot blood. He grabbed it and pulled her up, and then he lowered his face to hers and kissed her.

And she raised her face to his and kissed him.

It lasted a second.

That was all it had needed to last for.

From the corner, where she still fought to disentangle herself from the corpse she had pulled down upon her as she fell, Rita had seen. She was unobserved by either her husband or her friend, but if they had been able to see her face, they would have seen a transformation as complete and as immediate as any imaginable. Her look of relief at her friend's safety and her husband's heroic appearance had gone. Now, in its place, was a look of shock, of betrayal, and of revulsion.

The kiss had broken. Adelaide began to smile but shook herself almost immediately. What was she doing? What was he doing? Then she remembered: there were still two more stowaways to be defeated, and there was no sign of Pyre either!

Adelaide grabbed Father and took off up the corridor, Simeon in close pursuit. There were few rooms off this corridor, and a quick glance through the doors of each one confirmed what Adelaide had already guessed. The last door at the end, at the top of a final flight of stairs, was her door. The one which she had returned to every day since their departure from Landsbyfjord. She raced up the steps and crashed through the door, out on to the deck and the freezing gale which engulfed it.

For a moment, Adelaide could see nothing. The darkness pushed in on her and obscured all of her senses. Then Simeon ran away, across the slick wooden decking to their right and towards the railing. She followed him and looked down into the churning waters of the sea. Down below, the final two members of the Republic of Caterva who had boarded the Sudhaven Ferry in secret were making their getaway aboard a small wooden lifeboat. Adelaide, in a moment of sheer lunacy, made to climb the rails and jump down upon them, but Simeon placed his hand on her shoulder. He spoke plainly to her, neither professionally nor personally. He seemed to have forgotten already that which had transpired mere moments prior, below deck.

'Don't,' he shouted above the gale. 'They won't get far in this weather. Their escape is foolhardy. Besides, Pyre is the real enemy to capture and I am sure he must still be somewhere on board.'

Adelaide did not say so, but she was certain beyond a shadow of a doubt that Pyre was no longer aboard their vessel. She was not sure how he would have made his escape from such a place, but she had been touched by his flames, and she instinctively knew that he was already many leagues away from their current location. She remembered that Simeon too had been burnt by Pyre, on their first meeting on the Sunken Road. Did he not too feel this certainty?

They stood and watched the tiny boat disappear into the night, and it was as it was soon to disappear completely into the edges of darkness, out in the violent grip of the storm, that a fork of lightning flashed across the deluged skies and illuminated the scene. In that split second, frozen in time as Adelaide and Simeon looked on from the deck of the Sudhaven Ferry, a black shadow rose from the depths of the waves and claimed the retreating boat and its fleeing occupants, the leviathan of the deep dragging down its prize to the calm and freezing depths of the sea.

CHAPTER SEVENTEEN

Night had fallen by the time Alene and her companions had made their way down the valley and were approaching the Schloss Stieg. The moon was bright tonight and Alene could see the gutted turrets and tattered flags whipping in the evening breeze. It was not a cold night, but the sound of the wind could help to mask their approach and passage. That would be for the better.

The Schloss Stieg had once been a grand palace, built for opulence in a time when the emperor would make grand tours around his lands. Situated in the only true convergence of the two halves of his cloven empire – not including, of course, the dangerous trek into territory to the north which had traditionally been goblin-held – this vale was a natural resting point as he passed from one distinct culture to another.

One emperor – which one was now forgotten to the annals of time – had been so enraptured by this place that he had made it his permanent seat, if only for a short time. He had commissioned a glorious rose garden beyond the eastern walls, where they would be better protected from the howling winds which funnelled down the vale to the west, and even changed the castle's name to reflect this new feature: the Schloss Stieg, the Rose Castle. Unfortunately, when the winter came and the harsh reality of the cruellest season was felt in its entirety, this fickle emperor abandoned the roses and returned to the Imperial City. The roses, however, had thrived to this day: no longer neat and trimmed but unruly, feral and so overgrown that they now created a dense thicket of perfumed flowers and needle-like thorns.

They were the only part of the castle which had flourished. The rest of it had decayed over time, centuries of abandonment until it was a putrid wreck. Bandits occupied it infrequently, different clans – usually part of the Union of Thieves and Outlaws – but always securing the allegiance of the farmsteads along the Prairie Road and always flying their own flag from the flagpole on the central tower.

The small group travelled swiftly and silently through the rose gardens, crouching here and there to avoid low-hanging thorns and moving in single file along grassy paths which must have once been well-tended and cared for. The plan was simple: enter the main courtyard of the Schloss undetected, make their way around its perimeter and leave via the western portcullis, making their way down the Vale of Screams and into the Northern Realm.

The vale beyond the Schloss had earned this harrowing name in recent years for being the scene of various clashes between bandit clans. Different clans would periodically make a play to seize the castle and its strategic location, prompting a standoff in the lands around it. The success of these attempts varied, but a general pattern had emerged: if the attack came stealthily from the east, with the cover of the rose forest, then the aggressors stood a chance of success. Any attack which was expected or even suspected by the current holders of the castle walls was doomed to fail – the Schloss was simply too strong to take by force with any number of attackers unless they came as an army prepared to siege. The western approach was different. The Vale of Screams was a long, straight ravine with nowhere to hide and of which the Schloss' high tower commanded a perfect, uninterrupted view, from its lowest extent in the meadows of the Northern Realm to its highest point at the castle gates. Any attack from this direction would fail, even one conducted via stealth.

A retreat may be different though, Alene told herself. She hoped so: their mission depended on it. If they could pass through the castle courtyard without alerting the bandit sentries then they could theoretically make a downhill retreat on the other side, down the vale instead of up it, and be far enough away before they were spotted. In this manner, they could avoid the archers' arrows from the curtain walls which extended across the entire mouth of the vale and be safely away before riders could be marshalled to pursue them. It was their only chance. This had to work.

Alene was directly behind Nox, who was leading their approach. They slipped silently from shadow to shadow, utilising their thorny cover as much as possible. There appeared to be limited sentry patrolling the walls above. Did that mean that their approach had remained a secret, as they had hoped? If so, their entire detour via the Sleeping Giants would have been worth the time it took.

The main entrance to the castle was within sight. Nox stopped ahead and crouched low behind the roses. Their scent was mild and pleasant, reminding Alene of evening walks with Gerecht in the wooded cliffs of Regenbogen. She shook herself: this was not the time to lose her concentration!

Roan, Griffin and Lionel caught up with them and together they peered over the thorns, observing their goal. The gates from this direction had been destroyed many years before, replaced with a primitive barricade of wood and masonry. Once again, Alene could see no sign of guards or archers. Was she paranoid to expect a trap?

It was decided that Roan and Nox would go ahead and scout out their route. They were the most experienced at avoiding detection and Alene knew that a little more knowledge of the terrain would be beneficial. She remained behind with Griffin and Lionel, waiting impatiently for her friends to return.

'We know the plan, right?' She asked mostly for the benefit of Lionel, for whom she had concerns over his ability to keep up with them. They had already consolidated their belongings between them: smaller loads would mean smaller targets to spot and a less conspicuous journey through hostile territory. Nox knew of a place where they could restock, half a day's journey from here in the Northern Realm. With this in mind, they carried only weapons and essential items. Lionel carried nothing, save for his knife. He was in need of as much assistance as they were able to give him. He nodded grimly at her. He was ready.

They waited five minutes for Nox and Roan to return. Eventually, they slipped back into their shared hiding place and reported what they had seen.

'There's nobody there,' whispered Nox. She looked confused but certain.

'She's right,' added Roan, frowning. 'If it were an ambush, the bandits would almost certainly have at least some guards on patrol. You know, so as not to seem too obvious. Do you think the castle could simply be abandoned?'

'No.' said Alene immediately. Nox nodded in agreement. Griffin and Lionel looked unsure, so Alene elaborated. 'No bandit would abandon the Schloss Stieg! It would be akin to surrendering it to another clan. I don't know what's going on here, but we'd better tread carefully. Come on.'

Silently, she slipped from concealment and made a dash for the gates. She moved without a sound, as swift and as agile as an owl in the night. She felt the breeze whipping past her as she sped towards the shadows at the base of the castle walls and felt alive.

They could do this!

She panted in flushed triumph as she reached the safety

of the shadows. She jumped when she turned around and realised that Nox and Roan had arrived immediately behind her. They were so quiet that she had completely failed to notice them on her tail. Griffin was nearly as nimble, but he maintained a similar speed to Lionel in a sign of silent encouragement. A few seconds later, they slipped over the barricade of debris in the entrance gateway and fanned out.

It had been Roan's idea to separate once inside. More targets made them more difficult to surround, and it made the possibility of rescuing anyone who might get caught more likely, as they could simply hide and wait for their moment to assist their allies. Alene reflected that this was a wise plan: Roan could be relied upon to think strategically in a tight spot.

Once inside, Alene ducked left and hugged the outer wall, keeping to the shadows. She skirted along it, keeping as low as possible and maintaining a constant speed. Even with the shadows, she was too exposed here to remain stationary.

As she ran, she glanced to her right and saw Griffin taking a more central route. He could use his body in astounding ways, clear great distances and heights, roll into the smallest of hiding spaces. She watched briefly as he ran as fast as he could at the brick wall of a low building in the centre of the courtyard. Alene was not worried, and she was confirmed right a few seconds later when he jumped, using his momentum to push himself up the wall with his feet. He grasped the rim of the flat wooden roof with his fingertips and flipped skywards, landing elegantly on both feet atop the building.

Without missing a beat, he streaked off across the roof and out of sight.

She could not see any sign of Roan or Nox, but Alene was not surprised at that. What did concern her, however, was that she had not sighted Lionel since they parted ways at the barricade. She hoped he was safe, that he was making his own way to the other side. Had it been wise to leave him alone? She regretted not keeping him with her.

Alene slowed down and ducked into a dark doorway as she neared the location of another gateway. This gateway led into yet another courtyard, wherein was situated the central tower. She would be more exposed once she entered and surveyed what she could see of it through the archway. Nothing.

Carefully, inch by inch, she advanced.

There was less shadow in this courtyard: the space was more open and the moonlight could reach more spaces that Alene could otherwise conceal herself within. Regardless, she advanced.

She saw no sign of the others. She saw no sign of anyone. She was beginning to feel more and more uneasy about this. She should have come across a guard by now, a sentry or watchman. She continued hugging the outer wall, moving clockwise around the perimeter. She remained as silent as she could, sliding from shadow to shadow.

Alene was halfway around the second courtyard when she noticed a movement above her. She stopped and crouched low, looking to where the movement had come from. High up on the highest turret of the central tower, beyond the parapet, was where she had seen it. But there was nobody there now.

She looked around her cautiously, more aware than ever how vulnerable she was. She could see the western gateway ahead, their entrance to the Northern Realm. She took a deep breath and made to set off again.

She sensed it before she saw anything this time. She was lucky that she did.

It saved her life.

She threw herself backwards and rolled on her shoulder, returning to her feet as the shadow of a woman fell upon her, the glint of steel in her outstretched hand. Alene backed up, working to regain control of her momentum as she drew Dawn and Dusk, raising Dawn before her and Dusk behind. The woman jumped and flipped, arching over Alene's head and landing behind her. She moved to strike the back of her neck with a lightning-fast jab of her steel blade, but Alene parried it barely with Dusk and moved on the offensive, twirling fiercely so that both falchions cut and stung in equal measure.

This woman was good, though. She blocked every blow with twin vambraces of dull steel on each forearm, waiting for an opportunity to counter with her blades, of which Alene now saw there were two. They were short, but she was quick and precise and laughed maniacally and callously as she pressed her advantage.

The ringing of steel on steel clattered and echoed off the high walls of the open courtyard. It was past the time for stealth, Alene knew now. She thought only of reaching the far gateway and escaping down the Vale of Screams. That, and reuniting with her party – wherever they had got to.

Then another thought passed through her racing mind: a possible way of putting some distance between her and her opponent. She knew how to control it now. It had come to her, down in the cellar of Clagcowl Abbey. Max could use his magic with ease, and yet she could not. What difference was there between them? She had given it much thought, but the solution had eluded her until her moment of need in the dark of the abbey. Max believed, with every fibre of his being, that he had been born with the right to wield his gods-given magical abilities. Alene, in contrast, had been filled with doubt and fear of her magic since it had burst out of her at The Audacious Magpie and she had craved the acceptance of others in order to accept herself. As she had stood in the darkness surrounded by her desperate friends and Nox had called out to her, she had made two important discoveries: the purpose of her magic, the motivation and conduit through which to channel it, was to protect those things and people who were important to her, and that she did not need the permission of others to be herself, but that the support of those who loved her certainly made it easier. Knowing these two things had miraculously unlocked a window into her soul. She could see it now, when she looked within herself, churning inside like a tempest of enchantment.

And so, in the moonlit courtyard of the Schloss Stieg, Alene continued to parry, duck and dive, spin and dance in a deadly ballet with her opponent. She did all of this, but simultaneously she was unlocking her secret window, calling out her internal storm and willing it to manifest around her.

A spark of black flame flashed through the air between them. The woman opposite her staggered back, eyes wide in shock. This did not last long though, and she soon regained her arrogant smirk as she raised her blades again.

The spark reappeared. This time, it flared for a few seconds and expired in an explosion of black light. Alene took the opportunity. She turned and ran, her eyes set on the gateway ahead. Beyond that was a vale of shadows which she had to hope she could slip down before any more bandits spotted her. She was nearing the gate when she turned, scanning the courtyard for any sign of her pursuer when she saw something which made her stop dead.

Three separate skirmishes were occurring at different locations across the castle courtyard. She had been so absorbed by her own conflict that she had not even noticed that the others had all been targeted as well, seemingly simultaneously. So this *had* been a trap, and Alene had led them all into it!

Mere strides away from dashing through the western gate, Alene turned and instead bolted up a set of stone steps which led up to a long walkway along the top of the outer wall. Nox was halfway along it, locked in combat with two slim men who fought with short daggers, just as Alene's adversary had. Alene glanced behind her as she ran: there was still no sign of her. She could see Griffin below in the centre of the courtyard, flashing around his single opponent in quick bursts of movement, ducking below the slashes and stabs to land powerful blows with his hands and elbows. The silhouette of Roan was visible on the distant walkway on the other side of the yard, Reaper in hand and loosing arrow after arrow as figures fell before they could reach him.

Ahead of her, one of the men slashed across Nox's chest and she staggered back. His partner moved in to take advantage of this, leaping forwards with both blades raised, only to fall like a stone, crumpled in a heap on the parapet with an arrow buried in his shoulder. Alene reached Nox, replacing her bow on her back as she redrew her twin swords. Her elven eyes allowed her to shoot moving targets in the dark, even while running, but she felt more comfortable in close quarters. She glared at the remaining figure before her, raising her swords and preparing to charge.

'You alright?' she asked Nox.

'It was a close call, but I'm not hurt,' she replied.

She bent her knees, preparing to pounce. But this time she felt it too late.

A blunt blow, hard, to the side of her head.

She tried to turn, but the world was losing focus. She felt herself fall heavily to her knees, dropping her swords as she flung out her arms to catch herself. The last thing she heard was a callous, cruel laugh of triumph from behind her. Then it went black.

When she finally became aware of her surroundings again, the first thing she could do was hear. She lay motionless, eyes lightly shut and mouth agape, but she listened with all her might for any hints of where she was or what danger she may be in. She could hear laboured breathing on the ground beside her, and whispered conversations occurring above her.

'What now, Prija? We have them all, do we kill them?'

'Soon. We need to know exactly how much they know. How complicit are they, and who is that beast who tails them?' Alene knew, despite this being the first time she had heard her speak, that this second speaker was the woman whom she had fought. The same woman who had struck her and laughed as she had sunk into unconsciousness. She also appeared to be in charge.

'Besides,' continued Prija, the woman, 'Sandrine values the life of this one. It might be prudent to take hostages instead. And this one holds power - I've seen it. True, natural power which could prove very useful when we reach Mort Vivant. If, of course, we can persuade her of our cause.'

Mort Vivant? That was their destination also – the swamps in the south where the new Cardinal had surfaced. Alene thought this over, her head buzzing with what she was hearing, attempting to make some sense of it. She stopped and listened again as she heard hurried footsteps approaching.

'Prija, we were wrong! The scouts are back in and they report that there was one more with them. They must still be around here somewhere!'

So, one of her friends was still out there? For one moment she dared to hope for a rescue, but she quickly realised that what they must do – what she would have to do if she were in their situation – was to escape through the west gate and complete the mission alone.

'The gates are guarded, they won't get far,' was Prija's reply. 'She's awake.'

Alene realised that she was talking about her and prepared her legs to support her weight as she felt rough hands grasp her and stand her upright. She opened her eyes and blinked in the glare of torches which had been lit around them. A brazier roared nearby and Alene looked at the woman who was her captor.

Looking at her properly now, stationary and with illumination, Alene saw a tall woman with pale skin and long blonde hair looking at her. She had dark eyes which were merciless and harsh and she was presently smirking unpleasantly at her captive. Her black clothes hugged her body and she had two swords on her hips.

Alene's swords.

Alene groped suddenly at her belt and confirmed with a sinking gut that her weapons were indeed gone.

'I believe I am addressing Alene of Regenbogen?' asked Prija with yet another sneer.

Alene did not answer. She glared back, defiant.

'There is much you could tell us,' continued Prija as more men and women gathered around in the firelight. Alene knew that these people had been waiting for them. There were so many that it was no wonder they had been caught. She turned her attention back to Prija as she continued. 'The hooded rider with the silver breastplate and the black cloak has not been seen for many days now. He pursues you, this we know, but he could also pose a nuisance to our plans. Who is he?'

The question was simple, and Alene found that she had no problem in disappointing her.

'I have no idea,' she said coolly.

Prija scowled but recovered quickly.

'The Republic of Caterva will not suffer false leaders for much longer,' she said, raising her voice so that all around her could hear.

It was Alene's turn to smirk. This woman, for all her strength, was not quite able to hide her uncertainty. She was shouting to be heard because she felt the need to prove herself. Alene had learned, from years of being an outcast in addition to being a queen, that this desperate show of conviction was rarely convincing. But there it was again: The Republic of Caterva. Just who were these people? They were not bandits, that was certain.

She might have asked, but she heard movement from by her feet as one of her friends stirred into consciousness. A young man, who could not have been older than eighteen, stepped forward and dragged Griffin to his feet. He looked groggy and disoriented, but he saw Alene looking pointedly at him and did not fight as he was held steady.

'The other two are already awake also,' said Prija, glancing down. Seconds later, Roan and Nox were standing up, looking neither groggy nor confused. They had evidently been feigning sleep as well. Alene would have expected no less from either.

She allowed herself a look around at her friends and saw that none of them looked particularly hurt. Roan's arm was hanging limply at his side and he winced as he moved it, Reaper strewn on the floor nearby.

Lionel was nowhere to be seen, however. Alene hoped he was not hurt. If he died, it would be her fault. She had insisted that he accompany them on their journey.

'So,' called out Roan through slightly gritted teeth as he held his arm awkwardly. 'I believe I am addressing the Republic of Caterva? Is anybody ever going to actually tell us what that means?'

Alene smiled in spite of herself. Only Roan could muster sarcasm at a time like this. She decided that this was probably not the best way to enter negotiations, so she stood tall and spoke.

'Your name is Prija, yes?'

The woman nodded.

'I know you hold pertinent information on our mission. I do not know how, but if that is so then you also know how crucial our task is. I ask you: why would you wish to hinder us? What future does your *Republic of Caterva* work towards?'

Prija opened her mouth to speak, then frowned and stopped. After a moment, she opened her mouth again.

The words never came out.

The men and women around them fell, dead before they hit the ground. Alene looked in shock and saw that each had an arrow of black wood protruding from their chests where their hearts were. She glanced quickly at Prija, who gaped around her in disbelief and fear, though was apparently unhurt. Alene and Roan were the first to jump to their feet, Nox and Griffin less than a second behind them.

They had barely taken two steps though when a shower of arrows peppered the ground at their feet. They would not get far – to attempt it would be suicide. They were clearly warning shots, and Alene turned back around and knelt, waiting to discover who her new captor was. The others followed her lead, including Prija who had gone paler than usual and seemed to be struggling to comprehend what was happening. The smirk was gone and had been replaced by something else, though Alene could not quite tell what it was.

It was not fear but was something resembling denial.

A voice filled the courtyard. It was loud and authoritative. This voice was filled with true conviction and leadership, stronger by far than Prija had been. Prija seemed to notice this too, for Alene saw her wince slightly.

'We are successful, my men! We wove our web and waited patiently, and we now have two flies caught up in it!'

The speaker walked into view. He was short, middle-aged and muscular. His clothes were animal hides and leather armour. He wore a tarnished crown atop his long hair which he wore loose over one shoulder. This man was a bandit, Alene knew instantly.

Multiple other men were descending the walls into the courtyard. Where they had been hiding, Alene could not guess. Even Prija's people had not noticed they were here, it would seem. They had sat in ambush, waiting to catch not only one group of intruders but two. They had been incredibly efficient.

The leader approached, his crown glinting dully in the firelight. 'Prija: your reputation is known in our circles.

Your father will pay for your safe return, I am certain.' He looked now to Alene. 'Your Majesty,' he performed a mock bow as he addressed her in his gravelly voice. 'You may ascertain from my headwear that I have played host to royalty in the past. That time, it did not go so well for him. Let us hope that your husband is prepared to pay.'

He glanced at the other captives. He must not have recognised Nox, for if he had he would surely have seen ransom potential in her as well. Roan kept his head down, as did Griffin. That was wise, thought Alene. Defiance would be punished with execution, she was under no delusion.

'My name is Xander,' he said, taking hold of Prija's face in his scarred hand and forcing it upwards so she was looking at him. 'I defend my people and we claim the right to anything which crosses our doorstep, so I'll be having those fine weapons of yours, for a start.'

He suddenly flung Prija to the ground and stood over her, leering. He reached down and grasped the handle of Dawn, which was still tucked in her belt.

Alene acted on impulse. Ridiculously foolish impulse, but she acted nonetheless. She dove at Xander and tackled him, taking him by surprise so that he let go of her sword and staggered. She was not strong enough to topple him though, and he grabbed her wrists roughly as if to force her backwards. Seemingly instinctively, Alene's skin flared with black embers and Xander released her hastily as if stung.

Griffin took the distraction and fell to the ground, catching himself on his hands and pivoting around, using the momentum of his legs to sweep two men off balance. They toppled into one another and fell into a heap, where they were quickly dispatched by Nox who had retrieved Near from the ground and then flung Far across the courtyard, hitting an archer who had been taking aim.

Roan, thinking on his feet as always, filled a bucket with water from a nearby barrel and immediately extinguished the brazier. Prija saw this and did the same, thrusting the torches nearby into the dirt. The courtyard was plunged into darkness, but Alene knew that Roan would already be picking off archers on the high walkways, aided by the light of the moon. Alene's eyes allowed her to see relatively well, and she saw Prija beginning to slip away, clearly hoping to escape in the skirmish. She could not allow that, not whilst she still possessed Dawn and Dusk. She grabbed the back of Prija's tunic and pulled hard, sending her to the floor. She would have bent to retrieve her beloved swords, but Xander had recovered and was rounding on her, sword drawn.

Alene prepared for a fight, marshalling her magic as she had learned to do by now.

But then Xander howled in pain and dropped his sword in shock. Alene looked down and saw the silhouette of a shaggy dog, its jaw clamped tightly in a vice-grip around Xander's thigh. He shook his leg, screaming in rage and agony, but the dog held on. Alene knew it would be now or never: she closed her eyes, held out both hands and expelled her magic through them, thinking of nothing more than saving her friends.

Amethyst flames erupted, a column of purple fire that engulfed Xander where he stood. The dog jumped free in time, as Alene knew it would.

Then something else happened. A horse came galloping at full speed through the middle of the courtyard, pulling an old wooden cart behind it. It clattered and crashed as it went, much faster than it should. It bumped to a halt beside them and Lionel jumped down, hastily ushering them all into the cart.

'Come on, hurry!'

Nobody needed telling twice. Nox, Griffin, Alene and the shaggy dog jumped aboard immediately, followed almost instantly by Prija, who did not say a word and looked at no one. Evidently, she wished to take her chances with them rather than the bandits. Roan rushed over and hopped on and Lionel shook the reins, sending them racing back through into the first courtyard they had entered and towards the eastern gate.

'Wait!' shouted Alene desperately, wheeling around to look in the direction they had just come. 'We need to go west! Turn around!'

'It's impassable, My Queen!' Lionel shouted back over his shoulder. 'The west gate is so heavily guarded, we'd be dead instantly! I even considered continuing alone, forgive me, and completing our task, but those bandits knew what they were doing from the start! The Vale of Screams is no longer open to us, they were expecting us!'

Alene would have argued, but what would be the point? If what Lionel said was true, then the mission was lost. It was with a heavy heart that they made their escape from the Schloss Stieg, through the rose gardens and turned north, only half aware that they were being pursued. By daybreak they were many miles away and quite safe but, for the first time since departing Regenbogen, they were without a plan.

CHAPTER EIGHTEEN

E arly morning found Alene and her companions stopping at last for a much-needed, though very des-
pondent, breakfast. Their commandeered cart was
a short distance away, the exhausted horse who had facilitated their escape grazing leisurely nearby. Before they had
even left sight of the Schloss Stieg, Alene had ordered that
Prija's hands be bound and that Roan and Griffin remain
vigilant by her side. She had retrieved Dawn and Dusk from
their captive, who had seemed too dumbfounded to protest at the time but had by now recovered her arrogance
and derision. Alene was undecided about whether it was
the correct choice to keep Prija as their unwilling prisoner,
but that was what they were to do for now. They could not
risk her alerting their enemies to their location at this precarious time.

The dog remained in the cart with them through the
night, and when they finally stopped, she still remained.
Roan had given her the name 'Hündin' and she seemed to
like it. She was currently sniffing around on the ground,
having already devoured the roasted hare that Nox had prepared earlier.

It had been Nox who had chosen their stopping point.
She had slid into place beside Lionel and taken the reins
as soon as they were able to swap over, directing the now
calming horse in a northward direction, into the rolling
foothills of the Rücken. They had heard wolves in the distance but, mercifully, had not encountered any. They were
safe in the radiant sunshine, though Alene could not help

but scan the mountain ridges above them for signs of Argentavis, the colossal carnivorous bird which Roan had told her about on their second day out of Regenbogen. That seemed an age ago, and Alene hoped beyond hope that their journey was not over already, withered and ruined on the vine.

'But there simply is no other route!' she suddenly exploded in frustration, throwing up her arms where she sat in the long grass and making her companions jump in shock. The horse shook his head and whinnied loudly, then returned without further ado to the important task of breakfast.

'Are we quite sure of that?' asked Roan hesitantly, as though scared of provoking a further outburst. 'We could double back and take the northern route via Saxe, or even brave the pass below the Vater Berg – but I know what you'll say,' he added hastily as she opened her mouth to protest, 'I know, both of those routes would have us pass close by Ville Fleurie! But the southern extent of the Rücken is completely unexplored – deep jungles with all manner of unknown horrors – and there are no other passes. None that we would survive the climb and the descent of without succumbing to exposure and hypothermia. I'm sorry, Alene,' he finished apologetically, 'I simply don't think there is another way.'

'Even if we could avoid Ville Fleurie,' added Griffin dejectedly, 'both of those options would add weeks to our journey. By the time we would reach the Northern Realm, Rowena would have already secured the Cardinal Phantasm and have him securely returned to Ville Fleurie.'

Prija said nothing. She was sat between Griffin and Roan amongst the mountain flowers and looked silently from one to the other as they spoke. She smirked knowingly and rolled her eyes, but Alene knew that getting anything out of her would be futile, and she would not give her the satisfaction. Besides, Roan and Griffin were unfortunately correct: there was no other way.

Then, quietly, Nox spoke.

'There might be another way.'

Alene thought she had misheard her. 'What are you say-ing?' she asked slowly. 'That you know of a way we could still succeed?' Alene could barely bring herself to hope. Hesitantly, and with a significant air of reluctance, Nox answered.

'There is another way...the only other way, I believe, which exists without significant danger of us perishing in the freezing mountain passes. If you're still certain that doubling back and passing by Ville Fleurie is out of the question...and that the Schloss continues to hold com-mand of the Vale of Screams...then our only option is to take refuge somewhere after our ascent of the Rücken be-fore beginning our descent on the western slopes.'

The group was silent, collectively waiting to hear what this solution would be. Alene was sceptical: she had never seen or heard of such a haven on the mountain peaks which Nox could be referring to, and the caves at that altitude would provide little to no protection from the elements or provisions with which to refill their supply bags after what was sure to be a perilous journey upwards. Despite this, she trusted Nox's knowledge of the layout of The Empire above that of all others. Prija, however, was not so trusting and let out a snort of scepticism.

'You are all fools!' she mocked. 'No such pass exists in the Rücken that could provide safe passage. You will all freeze to death before reaching the other side and I will not allow you to drag me to destruction with you! Be my guest – make the climb and perish in the attempt but I refuse to be a part of it!'

Nox merely gave her a look of loathing and contempt. Hündin stopped sniffing around on the ground to growl at her. Alene watched her friend closely: Prija's words had obviously had an effect upon her and she looked as if an internal battle was waging in her heart. Could this mystery mountain pass really be the answer to all of their problems? And if so, why did Nox appear to be so conflicted?

Eventually, she spoke again. 'There is a city which I have never visited, only seen from afar. It sits high in the clouds, invisible from this level and secluded from even the most seasoned rangers. This city is carved from the very face of the sheerest and most treacherous cliffs and has a way of life which, I must admit, I find ominous and unnatural.'

She paused, looking as if she might turn and walk away from them. However, she continued.

'I stole a glance at it only once, some years ago, midway through the Golden Summer, when the snowy passes were blanketed in wildflowers and seas of green, lush grass. Never before had there been a year like it, and I doubt there will ever be another. The very height of this summer nor any other can compare to those long, lazy days and warm, balmy nights scented with honeysuckle. Most people, including you all, I imagine, sought and craved shelter and shade, unwilling or unable to stand the heat. Some had the luxury of doing nothing, save for lounging all day and drinking all night; most continued their daily lives with little choice of an alternative, too exhausted at the end of the day to do anything but sleep. I, on the other hand, took this rare opportunity to traverse virgin lands: the high reaches of the Rücken which, any other time of year, would deliver certain death if found to be impassable.'

She stopped again, and this time she did turn and walk a short distance away. Prija snorted in scepticism and impatience, whilst Griffin and Roan looked at each other uncomfortably. Lionel looked as though he wanted to follow Nox, but Alene placed a gentle hand on his shoulder, shaking her head at him with a reassuring smile. Nox needed a moment, she could tell, but she could not pretend to understand why. If this place which she was thinking of, this city in the side of the mountain, had this strange effect on Nox, the bravest and most adventurous woman she knew, then was it really even a viable option? Again, she did not dare to hope.

She turned and sat down, reclining her back and head until she was lying down amongst the poppies and cornflowers, taking in their scent in long, contemplative breaths. She closed her eyes and the glare of the sun above her became a gentle, red glow on the underside of her eyelids. She heard footsteps approaching her and then somebody sitting down to her left. Lionel spoke.

'That summer – the one Nox was talking about – I don't remember it. What was it like?'

He sounded almost wistful, full of wonder and intrigue. Alene considered this. That summer held feelings of love, gratitude and carefree belonging to her, being the first full summer which she had spent with her new husband after their wedding. The whole city had been new and exciting to her then, and she remembered with vivid clarity the many walks which she took together with her love in the evenings, down the shady woodland paths to the town below and revelling in the closeness and affection which flowed effortlessly between them. She had felt unequivocally and completely happy, finally beginning to feel at home. She still got stares and ill-concealed contempt from the nobility and gentry which often visited court or stayed there on a more permanent basis but the common people of Regenbogen adored her. They cared very little that her skin was foreign and that her blood was impure. To them, she was their new queen and they made her feel welcome in a way which she had never felt. She was accepted. It was with them, and Gerecht, that she had spent those golden days many years ago, and it made her smile a bittersweet, heart-wrenching smile to think about it. Was all of that gone forever?

'It was ten years ago,' she told him. 'You're probably too young to remember it.'

She opened her eyes and blinked in the sudden glare of the sun, still beginning its ascension. She raised her head and looked around. Roan had a careful watch on Prija, who was sitting sullenly on the ground, legs crossed. Alene hoped that she was no danger with her arms bound but having Roan and Griffin on the case was definitely reassuring. Nox was returning, strolling through the thigh-high grass, which was dancing merrily in the gentle breeze, and so she rose to hear the rest of her story.

Nox smiled apologetically, before continuing with a reluctant sigh. 'That summer, I saw it in the distance, and that was as far as I was willing to go! The whole city seemed cloaked in sorcery and the arcane. Only magic could have carved that city from granite, I am sure. It was inhabited: that was obvious because there were colossal buildings of glass with fields of wheat and barley inside, as large as the greatest temples I have ever seen. Three I counted, and they were well-tended.

'I wouldn't mention it, only that there is no other choice. We could make the climb, assuredly, and seek the shelter of that mysterious place, or we could admit defeat. I believe they are our only choices.'

Alene thought about this as Nox turned and walked away again, her head bowed. If they could make their way to this unknown city and convince them to offer them shelter and restock their food supplies, then be able to make the descent with the benefit of rest and nourishment, and only then without these strange, unfamiliar peoples becoming aware of their true purpose or else immediately arresting them and leaving them to rot in some forsaken dungeon cell, then this may work. It was risky, but Alene also knew that it was their only real path remaining.

By mid-afternoon, Alene and her companions had successfully traversed the lower hills and were hiking steadily up a steep incline. It transpired that, despite her misgivings on this route, Nox had predicted the necessity for such a journey and had brought them within hiking distance of the very pass they were to travel across when they had stopped to rest that morning. As such, they had asked their borrowed steed and cart to take them only a few more miles before releasing her: the terrain had become much too steep and uneven to continue and they could ask no more of her. Griffin had been pained to let her go, but he knew it was for the best. There were multiple farms and ranches on the prairie and Alene hoped she would find a safe home.

It was Nox's turn to guard their captive and she walked ahead of everyone else, Prija a few feet behind being led by a length of rope around her wrists. She did not go quietly and spat venomous words and withering glares at anyone who caught her attention. Twice she attempted an escape, and twice she was brought crashing to the ground as she ran: once by Roan, and once by Alene. She had not resisted since, though Alene knew it was only a matter of time before a fresh attempt was made.

Earlier in the afternoon, Alene had looked down onto the prairie road and spotted an unmistakable glint of silver making its way along the Prairie Road towards the Schloss. They had been too far up in the hills for any of the others to see, but Alene knew it was their pursuer with the silver breastplate, reappearing at last after a lengthy absence. It relieved her to see that he apparently had no idea where they had gone, and Alene wondered what reception he would receive when he rode into the Schloss Stieg's courtyard later that day.

Alene dashed ahead of the rest – earning a biting remark from Prija as she passed – and stopped beside Nox. They walked side by side in silence for an hour at least. The slopes became steeper and their breathing became more laboured as they struggled to maintain speed up the craggy hills. A few times they were forced to pause and work together to negotiate sheer inclines, finding firm footholds and boosting each other in turn. These were thankfully never too tall and always led to new plateaus which they could walk on without too much effort and use to continue their journey across the Rücken. Prija never posed too much of a problem during these moments, it appeared that even she would not risk falling to her death over a cliff!

Now that they were higher, Alene could see the pass ahead of them, higher than she had ever been in these mountains. It appeared to be a high plateau between two taller mountains which, Nox assured, could be used to reach the western slopes and which was also the location of Nox's mysterious city. Alene could see that it would be an inhospitable and treacherous passing: a storm of white hale could be seen blowing in the pass and she knew that some form of shelter halfway would indeed be necessary.

'I'm sorry for the way I've been,' Nox said suddenly beside her. She spoke quietly so Prija could not hear.

Alene was surprised. 'You've already said that,' she replied. 'There's no need to apologise again.'

'No, I mean in general. I've let my prejudice colour my view of the world for so long, I'm ashamed of myself. I judged you, I even judged the people of this city we are heading for, simply because I suspected magic. I don't like what I see when I look at myself, I never thought of myself as intolerant.'

She bowed her head but kept walking. Prija seemed to sense that something was wrong, and began listening intently, walking faster to see what she could hear. Alene turned and glared at her, replying to Nox in a whisper, 'I know your history better than most, Nox. Your mother certainly has a lot to answer for, and it can't be easy living with a phantasm. It's enough to scare anyone, and I know you – I have done for many years. I get it. We can't choose our family.'

'We can,' Nox whispered back, raising her head to smile at Alene. 'I chose you and you chose me. We've been each other's family, and we always will be.'

Alene smiled, nodded and looked away. The lump which had formed in her throat stopped her from replying, but her heart swelled with love for her oldest friend.

They kept walking. Hündin gambolled around them playfully, especially as they climbed higher and they found themselves trekking through the beginnings of snow. The last cliff climb was the worst, and Alene struggled to find a good grip on rocks slick with ice. Prija scaled the sheer face with ease and Alene half expected to find her long gone by the time she reached the top. She was wrong, however, and arrived on the final plateau to find Prija sat sulkily in the snow waiting for them, Hündin sat beside her, smiling with what Alene suspected was pride.

This final plateau was downright dangerous. The wind howled through the pass and whistled shrilly between standing boulders. Each step was a gamble which could end in the unlucky traveller falling to their death down a frigid ravine or concealed cave covered in snow. The freezing snowstorm made visibility appalling and the party had no other choice but to struggle after Nox, heads bent against the worst of the weather, pulling their hoods up and cloaks closer around them to fend off the bitter bite of the blizzard. Despite detesting her, Alene found herself sympathising with Prija who was visibly suffering in her thin clothing which was ill-suited for such temperatures. She wished she had a spare cloak to offer her but, as they had disposed of their extra supplies the previous day, she had nothing to spare.

Even Hündin had stopped running ahead and was walking slowly with Lionel, nudging his legs periodically to encourage him along. Alene squinted through the swirling snow at Nox, walking side by side with Prija, still holding the rope binding her but much slacker than before. After all, where could she run to in this weather? Every one of them was completely white and any inch of exposed skin was raw and red. They were soaking wet up to their knees and Alene wondered how much further they could possibly go before they dropped from exhaustion or exposure. Lionel and Prija in particular looked as though they were near collapse. Alene reminded herself that Lionel had made a similar journey to this once before, but that had been on a much lower pass. Nevertheless, this experience had definitely given her a renewed respect for their young companion.

Night was beginning to fall, and Alene was close to suggesting that they search for a cave to wait out the worst of the storm when she bumped into Roan, who had stopped ahead of her. They had all come to a halt and Alene hurried to the front of the group, squinting through the blizzard to where Nox stood.

'What's wrong?' she called above the wail of the wind. The fresh snow at their feet was being whipped up into a frenzy and her eyes stung with cold.

In reply, Nox raised one arm and pointed directly ahead.

Alene raised her head and looked where she was pointing. Her elven eyes could see through the snow better than most, but even she struggled to see what Nox was pointing at.

Then she saw it.

They had arrived.

CHAPTER NINETEEN

I t was exactly as she remembered it.

Squinting across the field of ice, Nox could see the outline of a tall, narrow spire against the backdrop of an inky sky. Just where she knew it would be.

As they drew closer, the lower elements of the impressive structure swam into view. Titanic crystalline glasshouses could be seen off to their right, though they were curiously devoid of snowfall. The main structure did indeed appear to be carved out of a sheer cliff face of the towering peak above them, just as she had remembered. Towers and spires branched off at unnatural angles and jutted beyond the scope of the cliff, creating a silhouette of a many-horned beast in the sky.

At least one hundred smaller buildings and houses littered the scene before it, appearing to be carved from the same stone but removed from the cliffside. Strange lights illuminated the windows of these buildings but Nox could see no sign of smoke rising from them to indicate a fire. Indeed, upon closer inspection, she realised that they did not even have a chimney.

Her initial impression was reinforced. There was no way that this place could stand without the presence of magic: the structure was simply too chaotic. Half of the towers would be pulled down by gravity and many others would surely be ripped away by the vicious wind and ice. And besides, Nox could feel it on the air. It made her chest contract with anxiety and she steadied her breathing, taking deep gasps of freezing air which made her head spin as it stabbed her lungs with jagged icicles. Sorcery.

Something told Nox that this was not the same branch of magic that Alene had come to practice in recent days. No, this felt different. Regardless, some of her companions were close to their limit and needed rest. Nox knew beyond a shadow of a doubt that they would never make it to the other side of the Rücken without stopping. Exposure would claim them in even the driest of caves up here.

As they made their way through the little city of smaller buildings, Nox could see strange symbols and shapes painted on the doors. She looked to Alene to see if she knew anything about them, but she had her hands full supporting Prija, who was close to collapse and had gone paler than usual. Her eyes were closed and her feet dragged clumsily. Nox hurried back to help and supported her at her other side. A glance behind her saw that Roan and Griffin were doing the same with Lionel.

They arrived at last at a set of granite steps which swept grandly upwards to a colossal set of wooden doors. Each door was carved intricately with the same symbols which had been daubed on the other buildings and was encrusted with lattices of icicles and powder snow. The steps themselves were deadly, slicked with ice so that each step was crucial. Nox dared not hold on to the iron rail for support: she suspected that the exposed skin of her palm and fingers would adhere to it and be torn from her by the cruel frost.

Alene stepped forward. Nox was not surprised, having quietly observed her friend becoming more sure of herself over the recent days. She knew that Alene had self-doubt – had always had self-doubt – but that she was learning more about herself, what she was capable of and who she truly was beneath the surface. Nox also knew that this reflective journey was far from over, that there was still much more for Alene to confront in her heart and mind, but she was fighting her fears and allowing her friends to help her in whatever way they could. Taking charge did not come naturally to her, but Alene had tried her best. She had never stopped trying.

Nox silently renewed her pledge to continue to be there for her, for as long as she needed her.

Looking around her for support – and receiving it in the form of smiles and nods of encouragement from most – Alene raised her fist to knock.

Before she could knock even once, however, the doors swung inwards to reveal a dimly lit passageway of bare stone. Whilst most windowless passages such as this would have been decorated by flaming torches on wall brackets out of necessity, this one was not. Despite this absence of a source of light, Nox found that she could see perfectly well for a short distance down the corridor. It was true, the far end of the passage terminated in darkness, but Nox found this curious illumination without any torches disturbing. Then she shook herself angrily: she had resolved to be more open-minded.

So strong were the collective desires of the party to escape the perishing weather, they barely paused to consider their actions as they scurried over the threshold. The chill from the storm persisted within, so Alene led the way down the passage, around a corner and out of sight from the doors.

It got progressively darker the further they ventured in until suddenly the entire room was thrown into bright light and Nox threw up her arms to shield her eyes from the sudden dazzle. As she blinked furiously, she realised that they had unknowingly made their way out of the corridor and into a lavishly decorated room. Scarlet hangings decorated the walls and elaborate pillars of chiselled marble held up a vaulted ceiling. Intricate paintings were hung on each facet of the octagonal room and another three passageways led off in other directions. It was a crossroads of sorts, Nox realised, and a raised dais in the middle of the room – octagonal again – took centre stage. Two seats of polished dark wood and scarlet velvet sat upon it, but the room was quite devoid of life.

Nox found herself uncertain despite herself. She blushed and looked apologetically to Alene but was shocked when Prija's words reflected her inner worries.

'Erm, I know that I plan on killing you all myself one day, and I know that this fact might disqualify me from having a vote, but does anybody else think this was a bad idea?'

'What's wrong, Prija?' asked Roan in a mocking tone and a smirk. 'I seem to recall you were quite desperate to get out of the cold, what changed?'

Prija scowled and turned away. Nox could not help but agree with her. This place was eerie.

'Welcome,' said a quiet voice from the centre of the room. The entire party jumped as one. Lionel let out a little whimper of fright and Prija lowered both hands to her belt, realised she was unarmed and instead whipped around to look towards the dais. Nox saw a flicker of panic in her cold eyes and turned to look at the dais herself. Where before there had been two empty chairs, now there were two women. One was tall and stately with shoulder-length black hair and impossibly pale skin, the other had hair which was a lot longer, a lot lighter and who looked a lot younger than the first. What was this? Where had these women come from and why could they not be seen initially?

Nox assumed that the quiet voice had been the younger woman – possibly even a girl – but she was shocked again when the tall woman spoke again in the same quiet voice.

'You are unexpected in Bealoscylf. That, in itself, is unusual. One or more of you possesses intense power, enough to shield you from our vision as you approached. You entice us, enough for us to permit you sanctuary from the mountain's wrath. I am Jacquetta. She beside me is Viktoria. To whom do we address, and what is the nature of your journey?'

Bealoscylf? Was that the name of this place? Nox looked to Alene, who looked directly ahead at their two hosts. She stepped forwards and, as she did, the now-familiar black flames licked around her in what Nox interpreted as a show of strength. Nox was impressed, her friend had changed so much.

'My name is Queen Alene Idir, Iontach of Regenbogen and Her Serene Highness of the Eastern Dominion. Our business is not of concern, but I travel with Lady Jardinia of House O'Hare, Sir Roan Felix, also of House Thounshende, Griffin of Regenbogen, Lionel of Ville Fleurie and Prija of The Republic of Caterva. We would request shelter, for a short time only, if that would be considered by you and your fine city.'

Nox knew what game Alene was playing. By flattering their hosts, and by being as forthcoming as possible on the nature of their identities – even so far as to associate themselves with Prija and The Republic, she was hoping that the purpose of their journey would not be insisted upon. A clever tactic. She looked over at Prija and saw a flash of shock at being worthy of a mention. She looked to her right and saw Griffin and Lionel looking similarly pleased: the memory of being overlooked at Woodrow must surely have been on their mind. Roan simply looked smug and Nox knew why: he had been introduced as 'Sir', despite never being knighted in his life.

Up on the dais, it was the turn of the younger woman to speak. Her voice was much louder and commanding, yet still high and childlike. She looked at Alene with curiosity.

'You are elven?'

Alene did not look away. 'Half-elven.'

'And what was the name of your father?' asked Jacquetta.

Nox looked to Alene. Would she answer?

'I...never knew my father.'

'But surely,' replied Viktoria, 'one of those fine swords you bear belonged to him.'

'I arrived too late,' answered Alene – truthfully, Nox knew. 'I retrieved Dawn from his tomb, some years after his passing.'

The two women looked at each other, silently conferring. At length, they turned back to the group.

'We recognise your ranks, Queen Alene,' said Viktoria, 'and I echo my esteemed colleague's kind words of welcome to you all. You represent an eclectic and diverse range of regions and cultures between you, and this is to our liking. Sir Roan, your heritage is of particular interest to us – we had the immense pleasure of dining with your forebear, Emperor Ludwig, at the Imperial City when last we ventured out.'

'But,' started Roan, looking unsure of how to proceed, 'forgive me, but Ludwig reigned over nine hundred years ago.'

Jacquetta merely smiled. 'We have long memories.'

'It is true we welcome you, and you are indeed permitted to rest here and continue your journey whenever you are ready, but it is impermissible that you withhold your purpose from us. You owe us a debt of gratitude, and when you have seen as much as we have, you come to appreciate the value of information not forthcoming. We would speak with you alone, Queen Alene, the remainder of you will be shown to suites which we trust will be to your liking. Male and female do not mingle at Bealoscylf and, as a result, you will be lodged in separate wings.'

Nox was not prepared to leave Alene alone with these people and was glad when she spoke up. 'I would wish to equalise proceedings by inviting one of mine to join us, Ladies Viktoria and Jacquetta. Two of yours, two of ours. I find that fair, don't you?'

'You are bold, Queen Alene, and we like that,' answered Jacquetta with a nod of approval. 'Agreed. Sir Roan will join us, as the highest-ranking from within your circle.'

Roan turned and smiled sheepishly at Nox. She did not

care about being shunned herself but knew that Roan hated being held up to his mother's name. She looked at Alene, who nodded encouragingly to her. Reluctantly, Nox turned and was greeted by a young man in a white robe. He did not speak but turned immediately and led them away from the octagonal room and down another one of the mysteriously lit corridors. Prija and Lionel walked ahead with Hündin, just behind their guide, but Nox hung back and walked with Griffin.

'What do you think?' she whispered to him as they walked.

'Queen Alene has it under control,' answered Griffin with a reassuring squeeze of her arm. 'She and Roan may need to divulge more information than we wanted to, but we can be gone tomorrow. Realistically, one night's rest will be enough for us to continue at full strength.' He paused and held her arm so that she stopped walking and looked into his eyes. He smiled and whispered, 'We're nearly there. We'll acquire new mounts in the western foothills and be in Mort Vivant within a few days. It's nearly over!'

Nox was not sure if he was saying this for her sake, or if he were truly naïve enough to think that reaching the Cardinal would be the end of their endeavour. She appreciated his words regardless. He smiled once more and had let go of her arm to continue walking when Nox did something which surprised even herself: she took his hand, leaned in and kissed him gently on the cheek. He looked flustered and surprised but pleased as she moved away and walked on. Her heart swelled and, despite her surroundings, she could not help but beam with joy.

Alene returned to their lodgings after about an hour and

Roan returned, Nox assumed, to the men's' lodgings in the east wing of the palace. Nox could not quite decide if this place was a palace or not. Was 'temple' a more fitting description? She had spent the previous hour laying on her bed, flitting from anxiety at awaiting Alene's return to bliss upon thinking of her kiss with Griffin. Prija was her only company and since she did nothing except sigh deeply and dramatically from time to time on a bed in the corner, she was not too much bother.

When Alene finally returned, Nox immediately began asking her questions. What had she told them? What were they like? Were they still permitted to stay? Prija raised her head to listen as Alene reassured Nox.

'They wanted to see a demonstration of my magic,' she explained. 'They are mages, humans who harness external magic, so they were curious to learn more about my own internal source. They did insist on me divulging the nature of our journey though,' she admitted, somewhat apologetically. 'They could not see the truth before I said it, but I know that if I had lied then they would have sensed it immediately. I told them the basics of what they needed to know: that we travel to acquire the Cardinal Phantasm in order to stop others from doing so who would use it for catastrophic designs.'

This caused Prija to tut and snort in disbelief from the corner. Alene and Nox both turned to look at her, eyebrows raised. Prija was not forthcoming however, so they turned away again.

'Please don't worry, Nox,' assured Alene with a smile, 'I am certain we can trust these women. Now, we should get plenty of sleep if we are to rise early enough in the morning to reach Le Bois in the Northern Realm by sundown.'

Nox lay in the darkness, head spinning dizzily with information, too much to sleep. Alene fell asleep almost immediately, and Nox was not surprised. It had been over a day since any of them had rested, a few meagre hours on their descent from the Sleeping Giants. Prija was securely restrained on her own bed by both wrists – neither Nox nor Alene trusted her not to kill them and flee – and it was hours before Nox finally heard deep, rhythmic breathing from her corner. Nox could not sleep. She would not feel at ease until they were safely down the mountain into Le Bois, the forested region of the Realm where the people were kind and hospitable. They rarely communed with other parts of the Realm and were part of it in name only. They were sure to help them with supplies and not ask too many questions. Yes, she would feel better then.

Nox's mind wandered further and she settled on the small, hut-like structures which they had walked amongst upon their approach to the main entrance to this place. There had definitely been life in them, she held known it, and yet these cavernous halls and passageways seemed deserted.

Nox could not sleep. Almost absent-mindedly, she swung her legs down from her bed and slipped on her boots. She replaced Near and Far at her belt and walked to the door, opening it slowly so as not to create too much of a creak as it swung open. No request had been made for any of them to relinquish their weapons upon arrival, so Nox did not feel too guilty for carrying them now in a place where she was a guest. Inns were the only usual exception to this courtesy, so why had it been waived here? Was it a show of good faith, to help them feel comfortable and trusted? Or was it simply that these mages did not value their physical weapons enough to part them from their owners?

Through the silent corridors, Nox crept. She did not know what she was looking for, she just wanted to know more. After uncounted minutes retracing her steps, Nox slipped back into the octagonal room they had first arrived in. It was deserted.

A quick examination of the dais and the chairs upon it turned up nothing. So, it really had been magic by which they had appeared. Nox frowned. Was it her paranoia of magic which had drawn her out tonight? She thought on this as she advanced down another corridor, away from the octagonal room. She hoped that was not the only reason. She had resolved to be more supportive of Alene, and this would not be a good way of showing that. No, there was more to it than that. She needed to know more.

The air around her was becoming warmer, more humid and damp. She stepped out into a room which was a lot darker than the corridor, but hot and steamy. Nox felt as though she had entered a dense, wet forest with all manner of plant life growing in every direction which she could see. Tall, unfamiliar trees which soared into the darkness above and sweet-smelling flowers with large, jagged leaves. Upon closer inspection of the walls which retreated in a curve in every direction from the entrance, Nox realised that they were constructed from latticed glass. So, she was in one of the colossal glasshouses they had seen on their approach. Nox guessed that this was how the inhabitants of this town fed themselves but could not begin to guess how they produced so much heat without any fires. Magic? Maybe, but she suspected not.

She retraced her steps and this time turned left when she returned to the octagonal room. This corridor was longer than the last one and terminated at the top of a tight spiral staircase of stone. Nox crept down, not daring to go too fast for fear that she would be overheard and discovered. Should she be doing this? Was she spying? She did not know if it was right, but an irresistible urge to continue pulled her downwards. When she reached the bottom, she was shocked to hear voices nearby, and instinctively flattened herself against the wall in panic. When she clarified that the voices were not moving however, she bent low and crept on, intent on discovering more.

She crept as far as she could before arriving at an opening which led into another room. The voices were coming from inside, and Nox dared not glance around the door to take a look for fear she would be seen. Instead, she crouched low beside the doorway and listened.

'Have you sent word to Cogburn?' asked a voice, high and excited.

'Yes,' came the quiet, calm voice of Jacquetta in reply. 'I have sent word through the usual channels. They will know by morning and can dispatch their best mages forthwith.'

'And what will it mean, practically, if we capture the Cardinal Phantasm for ourselves?' asked another voice, wheezy and older this time.

'It will mean, Diana, that we can bring him home!' said Jacquetta. 'I do not need to remind you that over the centuries we have often come into possession of the Cardinal, and each time it has led to greater glory and strength. We have used that power to usurp the old ways, to shape the very mountain. Tell me, Diana, would *you* want to return to having a male tell you what to do, what to be, what to believe?'

There was a great deal of murmuring at this. Nox guessed there were at least twenty people within. She had also become aware of a flickering sensation, as if of light but not quite perfect, coming from the room. It seemed vaguely familiar, but she was more intent on listening and did not pay it much attention.

'Just as we have strengthened ourselves in the past by building bridges with like-minded allies, we now face an opportunity to strengthen ourselves again, with the acquisition of a new Cardinal Phantasm!'

This time, Nox heard clapping and chanting from the room. She had heard enough: these people were not to be trusted. She had been right all along. She had decided to return immediately to her quarters and inform Alene when she heard more which left her rooted to the spot, listening intently.

'It must be decided what to do with our guests,' came Viktoria's high voice. 'A number of them are of noble houses and would be missed.

'That matters not to us,' insisted Jacquetta. 'They must not leave, lest they withhold the Cardinal. The three males can join the workers outside in the city – they are not fit to live in the sanctuary. Two of the women must die but I would council that we spare the queen. She holds magic of a rather unique variety, possessing an internal well to draw from but lacking the arrogance and prejudice which characterises the elven people and which forces them to remain in the shadows. She could be useful.'

'How so?' came the wheezy voice of Diana, who seemed to hold a good deal of sway with the others. The crowd muttered in curious agreement. It was Viktoria who answered, but she waited until everybody had stopped talking before beginning.

'We were fortunate, a millennium ago or more, to stumble upon a much greater repository of magical energy than most mages will ever know, and we have used this to extend our vitality, as you well know, Diana! We have done what not even the elves or emperors have been able to do because our magic will never expire. Never! We have the fire, and we alone know of this. It is our secret.'

'However,' continued Jacquetta, seemingly continuing where Viktoria paused. 'We also know that our greatest weakness is that the fire cannot be moved. It was started here, in the safety of the mountain ice, and only here can we remain powerful. Quite the weakness, would you not agree, Diana?'

'And so, we reach our point,' concluded Viktoria. 'What if we could discover in her elven blood the trick to carrying magic with us, wherever we go? We could leave this place, take the fire within us and it would never run dry! Imagine that, Diana, imagine that.'

Nox turned, silently, to hurry back to Alene and mobilise an immediate evacuation from this terrible place when she felt somebody behind her. She had one hand already on Near when something hit her – a gust of warm, dry air – which sent her sprawling across the floor, clattering in panic and confusion and alerting all within to her presence. She looked over her shoulder and saw another woman stood where she had been, hands outstretched in the now-familiar gesture of magic.

Two women from the dark room approached her and forcefully dragged her to her feet, seizing her weapons and throwing them carelessly across the floor where they came to rest in a corner. Nox tried to fight, but she could barely breathe. She gasped and choked as a paralysis of fear enshrouded her. The first thing she saw was a large, golden brazier in the centre of the room, filled with a turquoise fire. As she was dragged past it, she saw that it was not wood or oil which burned inside, but large blue crystals. What did this mean?

Then she looked at the inhabitants of the room and her blood turned to ice. They were all standing around her, and they were all wearing long robes of scarlet velvet.

She was in the room from her dream, that horrific vision she had assaulted her during their encounter with the geiste in the abbey. The room which had haunted her waking nightmares, every moment since.

She was there.

Jacquetta and Viktoria were looking at her. They may have spoken. She did not know. She only knew what was going to happen. She must fight to stop it from happening!

Jacquetta smiled at her. Apologetically? Pityingly? Nox could not tell. Viktoria walked towards the roaring turquoise fire, never taking her eyes from Nox's terrified ones. Then, bafflingly, she thrust her hand deep into the flames. It appeared not to cause her any pain, and she withdrew it a second later to reveal that she was now holding a tiny spark of blue light.

The women holding Nox slammed her hard against a brick wall and Viktoria hurled the blue spark at her. It did not fly like a spark ought to, or flicker or float. It shot like a spear, through the air and pierced Nox's shoulder. Immediately, iron manacles materialised around her wrists and shackled her to the wall. The women left her side and joined their fellows.

Jacquetta approached her, and as she did she withdrew a dagger of sharp black metal. The women around her began to chant: the horrific words in tongues Nox had never heard, nor would ever hear again, filled the room and echoed from the walls and ceiling. Nox gritted her teeth and waited for the blow she knew would come.

It came, and it burned with a white-hot intensity so severe and fierce that her scream caught in her throat. She gasped and cried and tears ran down her face, her heart beat faster than Nox ever knew possible, as though it knew it would soon never be able to beat again. Finally, she cried out, and it was a guttural howl, a scream of a wounded beast. The dagger twisted in her breast and ripped her flesh, hot blood flowing down her body into a pool at her feet. Her legs could no longer support her, but she hung suspended on the wall. Nox wanted to die, the burning was too much, each shuddering breath felt like breathing poison. She coughed violently and blood drained from her mouth, each spasm agony.

The dagger came out. The shackles disappeared. Jardinia O'Hare fell in a heap on the ground. She was beyond speech, beyond questions. Beyond fear. Magic had got her in the end, as she had always known it would, ever since she was a little girl who was afraid of her mother.

But was this it? No, the same fate awaited her friends. Slavery, experimentation, and eventually, possibly, the release of death. No, Nox would not allow that.

She rose. The effort was killing her, but that was by now a foregone conclusion. She moved – staggered at first, then slowly trotting on legs that no longer obeyed her – across the room and towards the brazier of flaming turquoise. The mages realised too late what she was doing and moved to intercept her. She felt the tug of magic pulling her away, but she fought it with a scream of fury and anger and threw another woman away from her. It was her dying strength. Her last reserves. She must reach the fire.

She did. Exhausted and broken, Nox plunged both fists into the fire and, for the first time, at the very end of her life, Nox embraced magic.

She fell. Her legs had finally given up and Nox knew that her last breath was a moment away. She could no longer feel her hands, so she did not know what the magic felt like.

The very instant before her death, Nox reflected that she could have used that fistful of magic to save her life.

She would not have done so though. The thought had not even crossed her mind until that instant.

No. She had stolen this pure magic for one reason only. To save those she loved.

One last tear leaked from her eyes as they went blind. Griffin. She would not be showing him the world now. At least she had shared a moment of sunshine with him. One last ray.

And with that, she willed the magic of the turquoise fire into her last breath and it exploded from her lungs in a scream of warning, a scream which would reach her friends and save their lives.

Nox knew this to be true as her light went out.

CHAPTER TWENTY

The final cry, amplified by stolen magic, rushed down the deserted corridors and flooded through keyholes, echoing off walls and ceilings with an intensity and urgency so fierce that it had soon run out of control. The last breath of a living soul is a powerful magical element in itself – often being used by black alchemists in the past as a potent ingredient in arcane rituals – but when it is imbued with raw, undiluted magic as this one had been, its destructive capabilities were virtually immeasurable. Nox had not known this of course. She had hoped it would be enough to warn her friends – perhaps on some subconscious level – that they were in danger. She had no way of knowing that her call of warning would literally tear the building apart in its bid to reach them. It was a tsunami of grief, an inferno of pain and sorrow and a toxic cloud of agony and trauma, all fused into one entity that ripped her tormentors from the ground where they stood and hurled them back, some landing broken and lifeless on the cold stone floor. Far away, through passageways and tunnels which shook and quaked and cracked under the pressure of so much pain, it finally found its target as it hurled its way into the room of Alene Idir, throwing the door off its hinges and bursting through in a harrowing cry of despair.

Alene shot bolt upright, wide awake and sweating in panic. She touched her cheek with a shaking hand and found tears mingled with the perspiration: the sound she was experiencing was ripping her soul and breaking her heart. There was no doubt what it was, and an obsolete glance at her oldest friend's empty bed confirmed her anguish.

Nox had gone.

Prija was awake, and Alene looked at her across the room. She was white and clammy, her eyes wide in fear. Despite being enemies, both women felt in that moment a sense of fellowship, a shared desperation that eclipsed personal divisions. They both knew what this meant.

They had to move.

Alene jumped up without any further delay and yanked on her boots. She had flung her cloak around her shoulders, secured her weapons and had reached the splintered door frame before she heard the panicked shouting behind her.

'What are you doing? You can't leave me here, come back!'

Alene turned around in shock. She had been so distracted that she had forgotten that Prija was still a prisoner and was secured to the bed. How had she not even heard her calls for help? She shook her head and crossed the room at a run, fumbling with the ropes around her wrists before finally giving up and severing them with a cut of her knife. Prija jumped to her feet, rubbing her sore wrists as she pulled on her boots. She stood and looked Alene straight in the eye, the panic not quite gone but overshadowed by a steely plea for truce. The words did not come, but Alene felt a catch in her throat as she nodded once and handed the other woman her dagger. They were both on the same side now. For the moment.

Alene's mind was running too fast for her consciousness to keep up with. Her heart ached for Nox, but she could mourn her later when they were safe. For that was what had awoken her, Alene instinctively knew. Nox had warned them of something that Alene had no way of divining but she knew the purpose of this warning was to order them to flee. Alene has every intention of following that order.

Once outside the room, Alene and Prija found themselves in darkness. The unnatural light which had illuminated the passageways the previous evening had been extinguished but the scent of magic lingered in the air, as though the light had been ripped, its tattered remains scattered to the wind. Alene made to go left out of the door, drawing Dawn and Dusk as she went, but Prija placed an urgent hand on her shoulder and hissed, 'We should go this way! It leads back to the octagonal room where we entered, we can escape that way!'

Alene shook her head vehemently. 'We can assume that the others have woken up as well, but we need to make our way towards each other before we escape. They may be in danger, we're all in this together, we can't leave them!'

Prija looked as though she would argue. Alene half-expected her to turn and flee in the opposite direction, but she instead nodded and made to follow her. Alene was surprised but pleased. She had already begrudgingly accepted that Prija was a formidable fighter, and now that they shared a common goal she could truly begin to appreciate that.

They did not get far. They had barely turned the first corner when they encountered four women in red striding in their direction down the otherwise deserted corridor. An aura of light surrounded them and they continued their march towards them before stopping a short distance away.

'Queen Alene, we must request that you return to your chambers immediately. We have a slight issue in the crypts but we would ask that you leave the matter to us. Return to your chambers.' The request was frosty, urgent. Even if Alene had not been prepared, it would have aroused her suspicions. She heard a slight tremor, an echo behind the last sentence spoken which Alene did not recognise but guessed was another subtle layer of magic. She knew she was right when Prija moved behind her, turned and began walking away in the direction they had come.

'Prija!' shouted Alene.

Her voice must have cut through the glamour, for Prija shook her head and turned back, scowling at the woman who had spoken.

'Thanks,' she muttered quietly.

One of the women stepped forward, her hands held up in apparent surrender. 'Queen Alene, I bring you sad news: your husband the king believes you dead, slain at the Schloss Stieg. He now moves on the phantasm himself, intent on finishing your mission. If you come with us now, we could contact him without delay and reassure him that you yet survive. Come with us now, and you could save Gerecht from putting himself in danger.'

Alene was speechless. Her mind raced as she struggled to comprehend what she had just heard. Gerecht thought she was dead? Could that be true? Yes, she decided, it could certainly be true. She had known for a while now that her husband would have been working closely with Saggion to track her whereabouts, ever since he heard of her flight from Regenbogen. If they had learned of their encounter with bandits and the Republic at the Schloss, it would be perfectly reasonable to assume that she had perished in the chaos. So now he was making a move for himself? Alene knew that her husband was brave and would always put the safety of his people before the safety of himself, but Alene also knew that he was not a warrior, not a fighter. What dangers had he opened himself up to? And Saggion, well past his prime! He would never let Gerecht make such a perilous journey without being by his side. All of this raced through her mind as she heard the woman speak again.

'Those who seek the phantasm will use its awesome power to smash the barrier between worlds and march across the divide to conquer all! You have opened our eyes to the situation, and now we see much. Together we could stop this – you have much to learn in the ways of sorcery, but we can offer you so much more! Come with us, Alene. Lower your weapons.'

Alene blinked furiously. This was too much, she reeled with the overload of what she was hearing. Prija's voice cut through her foggy stupor like a whip, scepticism and mistrust clear as she spoke. 'Where is the other member of our party?'

Alene snapped back to attention as she added, 'Yes, where is Nox?'

The women made no obvious motion to answer, and Alene suddenly saw them for what they were. Even if what they said were true, and Gerecht did indeed believe her dead, these people could not be trusted. Nox was gone, she knew that beyond a shadow of a doubt. She readied her weapons and spoke in a clear and authoritative voice. 'Back off! We are collecting our companions and then we are leaving. If you attempt to stop us, we will use force!'

The response was immediate. The aura of light extinguished and the corridor plunged into darkness. Alene heard footsteps rushing away in the opposite direction before they suddenly stopped abruptly. Focusing her eyes in an attempt to see anything at all, she saw the shadows of the four women ahead. They turned and knelt, raising their hands before them.

'Get down!' shouted Alene. She grabbed Prija's arm and dragged her down to the stone floor as their black surroundings suddenly flashed and she felt the searing heat of magical flame soar over their heads.

'You...you saved me!' gasped Prija, coughing in surprise as she recovered her composure and stumbled to her feet.

'Just return the favour!' shouted back Alene, thrusting Dawn and Dusk into Prija's astonished hands as she raised her palms and let loose a furious stream of amethyst fire which lit up their surroundings with an eerie purple light. The torrent blazed down the corridor, licking the walls with a burning fury, but it faltered and died as it reached its target. Alene strained her eyes, squinting to see what had happened, and saw that two of the women were sat opposite each other with their backs against each wall. They were chanting quietly, perfectly in unison and Alene realised that they must be creating some sort of protection, some shield or barrier. They would need to go down first!

'Round here!' she shouted at Prija as she dove for cover around the corner behind them. Prija followed hastily and ducked beside her, poking her head around to see as Alene sent another fire column blazing down the passage towards their adversaries. It guttered out again upon hitting the protective shield. They needed a new plan. Should they retreat, and hope to meet the others once they were safe?

Then it all changed. A different form of magic hurtled down the corridor towards them and Alene saw it soar in a wide arc around the corner, golden and glittering, before it rushed her. She instinctively raised her hand to protect her face and it latched on to her wrist, enveloping it in golden light and burning so aggressively that she cried out in pain, sinking to her knees. Prija gasped and reached out her own hand towards Alene's wrist, supposedly to help.

'No!' Alene shouted in alarm, but it was too late: she felt an electrical volt pass between her wrist and Prija's, attracting them together with such force that Prija was nearly pulled off her feet. They met with a flashing spark and would not release, no matter how hard Prija tried.

They looked at each other, neither sure what to do. One thing was certain though: they were fighting for their lives! Then Prija surprised Alene by smirking suddenly and handing her Dusk. Alene took it in her free hand and Prija held up Dawn in hers. Alene knew what she was saying and smirked back in spite of herself.

They heard hurried footsteps behind them and turned to see more robed women hurrying towards them from the other direction. Alene and Prija looked at each other one last time and charged in.

Each woman was unarmed, but as the two unlikely allies rushed towards them, they raised clenched fists which began to spark as if charged with blue lightning. It was as though each woman wore gloves enshrouded in flickering light which zapped and leapt from one to the other in agitation and impatience.

The two groups clashed, and Alene and Prija dove, dodged and ducked in and out of reach, manoeuvring under and beyond lightning swipes and punches which crackled with static as they sailed past their faces, barely avoided. They swung their swords in return, turning together in a dance of battle, harmonising their movements so that their efforts not only attacked their opponents but also defended each other. More than once did Alene prevent what could have been a fatal blow to her comrade and she noted more than once that Prija was doing the same for her. Then Alene realised: this was effortless, this felt natural. Both women had quite forgotten their animosity and were fighting together for self-preservation and the effect was astounding. Their deadly dance continued, cutting down more and more of their enemy. Alene was elated.

And then an attack made contact. A punch of explosive blue power struck her in the chest and she froze, eyes bulging as she gasped for breath and doubled over. Prija noticed too late and dispatched her attacker, but the damage was done.

For a minute at least, Alene knew of nothing save for the constant fight to take a breath. Each one caught in her chest and burned, yet her heart screamed and it almost burst from her chest, beating faster than ever. Her hands tingled and itched terribly and she never felt Dusk slip from her weakened grasp. The pain in her stomach was so debilitating that she could not stand, but eventually she forced herself to straighten up, standing back to back with Prija amid a scene of fallen opponents and a few still standing, though weary.

'Thanks,' she gasped at Prija. Alene realised that without the other woman, she would now be dead.

'I returned the favour,' she heard Prija reply behind her, not unkindly but reluctantly. 'Can't you do that fire thing? The purple flames?'

'Not effectively with only one hand!' she replied. 'That was certainly their aim with this spell,' she raised their joined arms to indicate what she meant, 'to stop me returning fire with magic of my own.'

'Well, we keep it up then!' said Prija, and Alene could positively hear the smirk on her face. They dove forward but the final few women did not put up much of a fight.

'We work well together,' admitted Alene.

'Disturbingly so,' replied Prija.

They heard yet more footsteps coming from around the corner and raised their swords, expecting the first four women they had encountered to have advanced, but instead Alene nearly cried in relief as Roan, Griffin, Lionel and Hündin ran into sight and stopped in front of them. All looked dishevelled and wildly disoriented but none appeared hurt.

'We've been lucky,' said Roan, seeming to read Alene's thoughts. 'We made it out of our room before anyone arrived and these ones never saw us coming,' he gestured over his shoulder, where Alene knew she would see the four women who had thrown fire, injured or worse on the corridor floor.

Alene looked at them apprehensively and whispered, 'Did you hear it?'

They knew what she meant immediately. Lionel nodded sadly. Roan bowed his head solemnly. Only Griffin spoke.

'We knew it must be some sort of trick, so we headed this way as soon as we could to check on you all. Where is Nox? I'll feel better when I've seen she's safe.'

Alene did not know what to say. She looked at Roan for support who simply shook his head.

It was Prija who answered. 'I think we can be sure that Nox is dead.' She did not say it unkindly, and actually sounded saddened. Griffin looked at her and scowled, darker and crueller than Alene had ever seen him look before.

'You don't know what you're talking about!' he spat, his voice rising. His fists clenched and trembled and his knuckles were turning white. Alene was alarmed. This was not the Griffin she knew.

'Griffin...she's right. Nox...' Alene's voice cracked as she tried to say the words she had been dreading saying since she had awoken to find that her oldest friend's bed was empty. Griffin rounded on her, his face brick-red and twisted in a vile fusion of madness and grief. He looked as though he was going to punch her, but then he began shaking his head, eyes closed tight. He raised his trembling hands to his face and let out a bellow like a wounded animal.

Alarmingly fast, however, he was taking deep breaths and looking from one person to another. 'There needs to be something we can do!' he was saying, but almost to himself. 'Who did it? We need to make them pay, I'll kill them!'

'Griffin!' shouted Alene in desperation. 'This isn't you! You don't kill! Nox is...gone, and we can mourn her, but this is not the time for revenge! We need to be gone from here. Now!'

Griffin looked at her. For a moment, he seemed to be contemplating arguing. He was torn; he was seconds away from either fighting them all or turning and fleeing down the corridor, intent on finding Nox's murderer. But then all of the fight seemed to leave him and he nodded, shrinking before their eyes into himself until he was almost a shell, a husk.

Alene wanted to comfort Griffin, as he had done many times for her, but now was not the time. As one, they turned and fled. They met no opposition as they ran through the octagonal room and down the final corridor, throwing open the heavy double doors and diving out into the sunlight.

The mountainside was bathed in morning light, the storm a distant memory. They barrelled through the city of small stone houses, barely aware that dozens of men in green robes were emerging all around them to watch their retreat. They ran, not stopping when they tired but continuing, wishing nothing more than to put as much distance between them and Bealoscylf.

After they had gone so far, Alene felt her wrist relinquish its attraction to Prija's and they could run more comfortably. But Alene did not retie Prija's wrist, for she was no longer their prisoner. Even if Prija would not admit it, Alene knew that they had forged an unbreakable bond, fighting side by side and saving each other more than once. She wondered if Prija would go her own way when they descended the mountain, but Alene realised that she wanted her to stay.

There would come a time when she would stop running, but she could not let it be yet. As the snow disappeared and was replaced with sparse grass on rocky cliffs, and Alene's party finally entered the Northern Realm, she knew that when that time came, when she finally stopped running, she would be forced to accept that she had lost a part of herself. And when she did, she knew she would not be the same again.

So, for now, she kept running.

For now.

For Nox.

CHAPTER
TWENTY-ONE

The Sudhaven Ferry lurched its way into the sheltered harbour of Sudhaven a full week after its initial departure from Landsbyfjord. The southern shores of the Mer Nuage were of a much warmer climate than the northern fjords and Simeon watched them draw closer with impatience from his position on deck. They were so far behind target, and the ship felt as though it would give up at any moment and sink to the bottom of the sea. It had not been treated kindly by the storm, which had mercifully subsided two days prior and they had limped the remainder of their journey towards the haven of their destination.

The town bustled with activity but it was subdued, muffled. Life went on as usual, but Simeon could tell that something was different.

When they finally made port, and Simeon became the first passenger to cross the gangplank, he immediately felt his heartbeat soften. He had learned to cope with life on board but he did not realise just how much he had craved dry land until he felt it beneath his feet. His men would ready the horses and the supplies, so Simeon took a moment to breathe in deep, taking in his surroundings as he calmed, smiling in spite of himself at such a glorious afternoon.

It was market day, and Simeon experienced all the

sights, sounds and smells around him. Traders plied their wares with colourful calls and shouts of encouragement at passing locals; a stall nearby was littered with jewels of a hundred different colours, each differing in size and every one of them a very convincing fake. And everywhere, permeating the market and beyond, was the fresh smell of citrus – the famous lemon and lime trees of Sudhaven were hanging heavy with fruit at this time of year and every terrace and balcony proudly boasted at least one.

But as Simeon had sensed, not everything was as it seemed. The lamps and windows were hung with black silk and another look up the hill towards the impressive villa of O'Hare Hall told Simeon that its gates were uncharacteristically shut. Lord Drake was known throughout the Realm for being open-handed and warm with his subjects, allowing the use of his lower halls to the common folk for shelter or to seek his justice. Not today though.

'The people mourn,' said Rita quietly beside him. Simeon had not heard her approach but nodded silently in response. In any other circumstances he would climb the hill and offer his support, or condolences, but today was not any usual day. They had lingered at sea for too long, and Mort Vivant awaited them.

He turned and began walking back towards the dock. Rita walked alongside him but said nothing. She had been exceptionally quiet since the storm subsided, not at all her usual self. He worried about her.

But he could not truly look her in the eye. He loved his wife – more than his heart could take – but another had emerged who had made him question everything from his emotions to his very values and ethics, and he knew that he unequivocally loved her too.

That kiss. What had come over him? What madness had seized him to make such a rash mistake?

He had thought this many times over the last two days, but every time he did it was immediately followed by another thought: *was* it a mistake?

Matteus was making his way across the gangplank, leading the last of the horses. The inhibitite cage was already safely ashore and Thomas and Rolf were backing Betty towards it, hitching her into place.

Simeon surveyed the scene, his eyes raking the familiar faces, his heart inexplicably feverish, anxiety threatening to engulf him. Then he saw her, making her way through the crowd towards him and he breathed again. She had not gone. She was there.

He sensed eyes on him and turned to look at Rita. She was staring blankly ahead of her, but Simeon would have sworn that she had been looking at him mere moments before.

Finally, after what felt like an endless age, Adelaide reached him.

'Captain, we're ready for departure.' A clear, professional report, but one which made his stomach flutter and flip. He smiled at her, felt himself blush and turned away, grunting affirmatively in acknowledgment. She hurried off and he looked at Rita, who this time made no attempt to conceal that she had been watching him. He reached out and took her hand.

'I love you,' he said plainly. He smiled at her and she smiled back, but it was a begrudging smile, one shadowed by sadness, which he received from his love.

'Do you promise?' she whispered back, looking deep into his eyes, almost pleadingly. Simeon saw the sparkle of an unshed tear in the corner of her eye as he brushed a strand of blonde hair from her dark cheek.

'I promise to you, I swear it by everything I know, I love you and I will always love you!'

But I love somebody else as well.

Unspoken, but he could not stop the words from forming in his mind.

Rita smiled and blinked, a single tear escaping and flowing from her brimming eyes. She turned without another word and walked away. He saw her fuss Betty's mane affectionately and pull herself into the saddle. Within the hour, Simeon's team had left Sudhaven far behind, making their way south through the last reaches of civilised countryside before the wilds of Mort Vivant began.

◆ ◆ ◆

The inhibitite cage continued to prove a severe handicap as they travelled. As had been the case on the Sunken Road, they moved at a much slower pace than Simeon would have liked and sunset on their second day out of Sudhaven saw the team making camp beside a lazy river of clear, sparkling water. The horses grazed happily beside the bank and Simeon could barely imagine that such terrible things were going on in the world to necessitate such a mission as theirs.

He needed to be alone. He strolled away, barely looking where he was going, along the winding river until he was out of sight of anybody. He settled down in a meadow of long grass and fragrant wildflowers which swayed in the sunset breeze. He laid back and lost track of how long he had been there.

As each day had passed, Simeon had found himself thinking deeply on the nature of their mission. He had not been lying when he had spoken with Adelaide on board the ferry, he had begun to experience feelings of intense guilt and hesitation around what he had been asked to do. Up until now he had been following orders, and was that not right? He was Rowena's captain of the guard, after all. Recently however he had begun to think more of what was actually being asked of him. Was it right to deliver a young boy from his home into a life of slavery and abuse? Simeon knew the answer, but at what cost could he do anything to stop it?

Adelaide would know.

He sat up. The meadow had darkened around him and a chilly breeze had replaced the pleasant afternoon sun. He heaved himself to his feet and made his way back towards the camp.

Otters on the riverbank rolled around together and slid elegantly into the clear waters as Simeon passed by. Cranes wading in the shallows took off and flew low over the grassy hills into the distance. These animals were free to go where they wanted, and was that not worth protecting? Adelaide had encouraged him to look deep inside himself to what he really felt – his truest self. Without her, Simeon shuddered to think what he would be doing right now. Probably contemplating how to commit atrocities and spiral two kingdoms into a war that nobody needed. He was ashamed to recall what he had thought when he had heard about the Cardinal, only two weeks before. He had seen it as an instrument of destruction. He thought about the moment when he had first laid eyes on Adelaide as she rode towards him along the Sunken Road. To him, she had merely been a useless woman, sent to cause chaos amongst his team. He had seen her as inferior, purely because of her gender. He still did not know what he believed – a lot of that was still murky – but he knew what was right and what kind of person he wanted to be, and he had Adelaide to thank for that.

However, he also knew what he must do to become a better person.

Far away and years ago, he had made a lifelong commitment to his wife. Rita was even now awaiting him, probably grooming Betty and preparing for a night's rest. He did not know yet what his heart wanted, but he knew what the right thing to do would be. A commitment which he must honour.

Simeon began walking up the gentle slope which led the

way back to their camp, committing to his decision when he heard shouting and yelling over the brow ahead of him. Panicking, he took the remainder of the hill at a run and dashed over the crest to meet a catastrophic sight.

The camp was in turmoil. Horses reared and bucked in a frenzy with nobody attempting to calm them. The camp-fire had grown out of control and flared up, threatening to catch the dry grass and ignite its surroundings. Every member of the party was gathered around the hulking silhouette of the inhibitite cage and Simeon rushed towards the crowd who jeered and screeched in a triumph of hatred. Pure spite and malice were clear in every scream as Simeon reached them and looked over their heads to the shadow hunched over behind the bars.

A human, or so it seemed. Large mismatched wings stuck out from its back at unnatural angles like a bird that had lost a fight with a fox. Shuddering gasps of pain and fear emanated from the quaking wreck which had been imprisoned in the cage and Simeon immediately had two thoughts fighting for dominance in the bewilderment he had run in on: *what is that?* and *what has happened to it?* The beast was unlike anything Simeon had ever seen, but who had caged it and subjected it to such pain and humiliation? The fact that this was the fate the old Simeon would have forced upon the Cardinal was not lost on him and it made him feel physically sick.

Rita was stood at the front of the group, her spear held in one hand and the cage key in the other. A look of grim triumph was etched on her face as Matteus clapped her shoulder, seemingly in congratulation. Simeon rushed alongside her and tried to comprehend what must have occurred in his absence.

'What is this? What have you done?' he asked them both urgently. He desperately needed to understand.

'Rita found something out about one of our own, Sim,' said Matteus with a smirk which Simeon suddenly found revolting. 'But don't worry, we took care of it.'

Simeon approached the bars and looked into the darkness within. One white wing, one dark wing. Long, black hair with curious streaks of starlight shot through.

It took Simeon a second more before he put this information together with a glance around the group, it suddenly dawning on him who was not there amongst them.

'Miss Adelaide?' he whispered, his voice cracking in sorrow and disbelief.

Slowly, reluctantly, the huddled figure looked up, staring deep into his eyes with a haunted terror. Her face was bruised and bloodied and she flinched away as he reached through the bars to stroke her hair.

'What have they done to you?' he muttered so that only she could hear, his heart breaking as he struggled to take it all in. She looked broken, weak and frail, dying.

'Captain, the freak is under lock and key!' screamed one of the men from behind him. He turned to Rita and asked her one word.

'Why?'

She had the same look of grim victory on her face as before. She looked into his eyes and smirked. 'Why would I not? She is an abomination! You should be relieved I exposed her before we finished our mission – she was surely sent to sabotage us. She has had you under a vile enchantment, causing you to think unnatural things, but don't you worry my love. She's behind bars now!'

'Yes,' added Matteus, 'and inhibitite, as you know, Captain, strangles magic out of a soul and renders it powerless. You can rest assured now that any spell this atrocity had placed on you is lifted. All we need to decide now is what to do with her.'

Simeon did not know how to reply. He gazed in at the captive woman, looking but not truly seeing. What was she? She was surely no human: no human could have those monstrous wings growing from its back. What was her purpose? Did she genuinely intend to sabotage their mission? And the biggest question of them all: did this revelation change his feelings for her? Was she a caged freak, or a person struggling to find their place in the world, as he himself had experienced of late?

'I...I need time to consider this,' he told Matteus as he walked away. 'Nothing is to happen until I say so. Nobody is to go near her – she deserves peace, that is to be understood! Provide her with food and water.'

His head spun. Feelings of sorrow, foolishness and indecision fought for dominance, creating an echoing din inside his sluggish mind. He could not believe that he had felt so serene, barely ten minutes earlier.

He heard hurried footsteps behind him but did not turn. Rita caught up, flushed with triumph which made Simeon sick.

'The cause was nearly lost, but we stopped the brute before she could do any damage! We should be proud, my love – all in the name of our queen and for the glory of the Northern Realm!'

Simeon could not listen to this. This was not the Rita he knew, whom he loved. The Rita he loved could not stand by and revel in the misery of another living creature. She was formidable, but it was her mercy and compassion which he loved. This was another thing he had come to realise recently. But he did not love what he saw now – not now, and he hoped that he never could have. What had happened to his wife?

'I don't recognise you.' He said it quietly, but plainly. 'You are not my wife – it is you, and not Miss Adelaide, who has given me the true shock tonight! What happened? You liked her – you told me so! When did Rita Castello become the sort of woman to turn on a friend and condemn them to the mercy of a brutal mob? I would expect it of Matteus and the others – Ville Fleurie born and bred – but not of you!'

They had stopped walking. The camp was behind them,

they were surrounded by darkness. Rita looked up at him, her eyes glinting, but she remained silent.

He waited for her to speak, to explain herself, but no explanation came. He found himself getting madder and madder, his heartbeat racing. His breathing came in harsh pants as he struggled to remain calm. His world had begun to fall apart, and he did not know why. He needed answers, and he needed them now.

'Speak!' he bellowed. Birds took off in alarm from a nearby tree, but Rita did not flinch. She looked at him, as before. Then she spoke, quietly and calmly.

'I saw you,' she said. Simeon did not know what she meant, but she continued. 'I saw my husband kiss another woman. A freak. Yes, she was my friend – do you think that made it any easier to endure? I knew about her abnormalities, and yet I kept her secret. After all, it was one kiss. Right? I could live with that; the gods know that women are used to surviving with broken hearts. But that wasn't all, was it Simeon? I watched you. Closely. And what I saw was different. You had fallen in love with her. I recognise the looks – they used to be saved for me, the secret part of you which only I knew! But now you see her for what she really is, and the fantasy stops right here. She has bewitched you beyond recognition, you fool! Have the courage to end her pitiful existence and the whole affair can finish there. I'm very good at forgiving – we can go back to normal. You'll see.'

She looked away and began to turn. Then her arm jerked, as though she had moved to take his hand but then thought better of it. Instead, she turned away and walked back towards the glow of the camp.

Simeon turned and walked away in the opposite direction. He would have loved nothing more than to keep walking forever, away from all of his worries and pains behind him. That was not an option though.

He did not sit, but he paced. Up and down the river for

what felt like hours.

She has bewitched you beyond recognition. Was that true? He could not deny feeling a change, and had even attributed it to Adelaide, but he had never thought of it as a malevolent force. Had their kiss meant nothing to her? Had she been manipulating him all along? Were his feelings for her even true, or were they false emotions she had planted and grown in his heart?

For hours he thought on this. He did not hate the person he was becoming. There was still a way to go, but Simeon knew that he was a better human being than he had been before meeting her. And it was not wholly artificial – even Rita had said for years that it was the man inside him she had fallen in love with, and that she saw him every day. Adelaide had merely coaxed him out, and was that a terrible thing? He felt a poisonous toxin of intolerance, greed and lust for power being drawn out of him, had felt this way ever since he met her.

Inhibitite, as you know, Captain, strangles magic out of a soul and renders it powerless. You can rest assured now that any spell this atrocity had placed on you is lifted.

This particular phrase kept returning to him on a haze of other jumbled thoughts and conversations in his head. Matteus had said that, and Simeon trusted him to be correct on all matters relating to magical theory. He, after all, had read more books than Simeon had even seen. But if what he had said were true, would that not mean that any manipulations or enchantments would now be gone? And Simeon knew assuredly that his love for Adelaide was no weaker now than it had been the moment they kissed. She was different, to be sure. Did that change his love for her?

No.

The answer came to him immediately. Where every other thought took an age to surface from the fathoms of his mind, this answer was as clear, as crisp and as penetrating as a nightingale singing in his ear.

He loved her.
Simeon knew what he must do.

The camp was silent. He slipped in and crept past the dying fire where the party slept. Nobody remained awake on guard. Arrogance, Simeon knew.

There were two keys that could unlock the inhibitite cage. Simeon held one of them at all times. It hung on a thin leather cord around his neck and he slipped it off, inserting the key into the heavy lock as quietly as he could. The cage was newly crafted, but the padlock was old, rusted and encrusted in grime. It screeched in protest as he turned the key and a dull clunk echoed through the camp as the mechanism inside shifted, releasing the bolt and he swung the door open. Every sound was magnified a thousandfold in his desperation, but nobody stirred.

Simeon pulled himself up into the cage and shuffled over to the sleeping form of Adelaide. The second he entered it, he was overcome with a sensation of oppression and constriction which made every breath a battle and which seemed to forcibly draw out his essence and vitality until even lifting an arm felt like sinking in quicksand. They had locked her in here, against her will, scared and alone. His resolve strengthened.

He placed an urgent hand on her shoulder and shook her gently but with haste. She was lying on her side and the wing facing upwards was curled over her, shielding her from the hatred she had been forced to endure. It was leathery and black, cold but tough under his fingers as he reached out a curious hand to touch it. The one beneath her was different, white and feathery. He shook her again and she rolled over, eyes sleepy and red, meeting his in the darkness and widening in confusion. He pressed one finger to her lip and motioned for her to follow him.

Silently, they hopped down from the cage and across the camp to the horses. Titan and Enchantress were already prepared, as were Cumulonimbus and Father. No words were said, not until they stopped riding, many hours later in the cold light of dawn. Only then did Simeon reflect on what he had done. He had abandoned his wife, his men, his mission. And he knew he had done the right thing.

Adelaide smiled at him as they sat on the damp grass watching the sun rise. Then she kissed him. Her mismatched wings spread out on either side of them, no longer bound. Simeon smiled back. She was free.

CHAPTER TWENTY-TWO

They kept travelling, never stopping for long over the next few days. Simeon knew they had committed treason by abandoning the team; he also knew that they still had enemies out there – the Republic of Caterva would not have lost their trail so easily! Nevertheless, he knew what their next move must be.

As they rode, Simeon and Adelaide discussed all manner of topics. Simeon had never been so candid with another person – ever! They spoke of hopes, dreams, nightmares and passions. Simeon's love for Adelaide grew day by day, but he reflected often on his last moments with Rita. He would regret hurting her for the rest of his life. He wondered what she was doing now. Did she understand why he had done it? His fury and outrage at her inexplicable hatred towards Adelaide had abated slightly since he had seen her last and he wished he could be face to face with her, to explain why he had made the choice – for the first time in his life – to put himself first. As they continued southwards, he even began to consider that Rita's actions had maybe not been so irrational. It pained his heart to think of the agony and betrayal he had inflicted on her by turning to another woman after so many years of love and happiness but his love for Adelaide was equally strong. And the cowardly shame of it was that, away from Rita and removed from the unyielding insistence upon him to make a choice, he was much more at ease with his decision.

On the third day of travelling, Simeon saw dense trees on the skyline. They were almost there. Mort Vivant. He sighed and motioned for Adelaide to slow to a trot and he came alongside her.

'I've been thinking – a lot! We both agree...that is...neither of us think it's right...we're not going to turn this child over to Rowena, right?'

It took a moment for Adelaide to answer. At length, she did. 'I have now been honest with you, you know I never answered to Rowena, as I had previously lied - I'm glad we can be open with each other now.' She smiled at him, slightly apologetically. Simeon smiled back: he knew everything regarding Adelaide's true purpose, including her intended work against himself and his former team. After what they had been through, honesty came easily. He would have been lying if he said that it was not a difficult and bitter truth to hear, but he felt it impossible to hold any acrimony for this woman whom he had come to love. Was he a lovesick fool? He did not have a ready answer for this, and that filled him with a creeping anxiety and disorder which was difficult to dismiss.

'Once upon a time,' she continued, 'I was alone in the world and wanted it so. If people paid, I obeyed. I would have slaughtered this phantasm child we ride towards to keep him from you and your team – that was my mission, after all – but I have changed, just like you.'

Simeon was taken aback by this admission. He had not known her to be so bloodthirsty, but he could feel it in the warmth of her voice, the sincerity of her smile: she had changed, just as he had. If it were possible for him, why not her? Despite this, it prompted him to voice something he had been thinking all day.

'Are we making a mistake? Throwing our lives away for each other?'

She looked back at him. 'Do *you* think so?'

He considered it. 'All I know is that, since I met you, I have been unable to stop thinking about you. Two weeks, it barely seems possible, like a dream. Every chance I have had to be alone with you, since that night in Landsbyfjord when we spoke, I have seized and cherished. I would walk through flames and thunder to keep waking up beside you, but my world will not let that happen. We would never be free in that world, and besides – I no longer belong there. You have changed me, and I know it is for the better.'

'And you're not just throwing it all away for me, because I'm different and your people will not accept me?' She bit her lip anxiously, waiting for his answer.

'I'm not sure it's true that *nobody* would accept you, but Ville Fleurie is not a tolerant place. Bad blood with the elves of Marrowmarsh has soured their taste for anybody different, at least amongst the guards and sycophants of Rowena. But, to answer my own question: no, I don't think we're making a mistake. We deserve to be happy, by any means. But we will do the right thing – Rowena will still crave the Cardinal and we will not let that happen!'

She smiled again and turned away, but doubt had settled in his heart. Had he spoken the truth? *Did* he think they were making a mistake? He genuinely felt that this was his greatest opportunity for happiness, and his only chance to right the wrongs he had committed in his life by thwarting Rowena's plans for the Cardinal, but did this justify the pain he had inflicted on Rita? Could he put his own happiness before his duty, and was it really wrong to do so?

They reached the edges of Mort Vivant by late afternoon and Simeon surveyed it with trepidation. This was further south than he had been in many years and he was unfamiliar with this place. Dense trees, dripping with ivy and moss, crowded together and stinking quagmires of squelching ground gave way beneath the horses' hooves as they advanced. The stale air under the canopy of lush thick greenery was heavy with the scent of decay and age so that

the life and the death of the place came together in a dishar-
mony which should have been jarring, but instead simply
was.

They penetrated deeper. The small communities which
were dotted here and there through this strange world
were quiet and primitive. Anxious faces peered through
windows and from shadowy porches to watch them pass
by throughout the afternoon but offered no resistance
or communication. Simeon knew that these people were
different and peculiar in their ways: they were small in
number, worshipped different gods and had altogether
different customs than the rest of The Empire. For this
reason, they had been largely left alone and had never truly
been amalgamated into the Northern Realm. Each small
village was distinct, disjointed and removed from each
other. Simeon and Adelaide knew which of these settle-
ments was their destination and continued without stopping, although they found it necessary to dismount their
horses as the undergrowth became thicker and more ram-
pant, cutting the sunlight out almost completely so that
they made their final approach in a twilight gloom.

This grey and uninviting cluster of houses was silent.
The entire community had been built beneath the canopy
and thus no natural light penetrated the fog. Compact dirt
tracks wove like brown snakes towards the central square
where an ancient stone statue of a strange and unfamiliar
creature stood, hunched and gnarled. Thick green moss-
covered most of it, but the exposed sections which Simeon
could determine filled him with a dreadful foreboding that
he was being watched.

They looked around, and Simeon sensed it before he saw
it. An electric chill on the air made his skin tingle and his
stomach contract in apprehension. An aura of distress and
suspicion hung heavy in the air as they tethered Titan and
Enchantress to a sickly-looking tree in the centre of this
forgotten hamlet. Something was not natural here. Some-

thing abnormal was at work.

They were definitely in the right place.

Adelaide sensed it too, but whilst Simeon was gradually overcome with a dizzying breathlessness and an overwhelming urge to flee, Adelaide did not seem to be affected in the same way. Indeed, she appeared concerned at Simeon's reaction and held his arm affectionately. Her own magical nature protecting her, perhaps?

Simeon noted that there were no anxious faces peering at them from these houses. The entire village seemed deserted and he guessed with confidence that this unsettling atmosphere was the cause of their absence. All around them they could see evidence of recent habitation, and all around them they could also see evidence of a swift exodus as the small population had fled. To where, Simeon could not guess. He only knew that he too wished nothing more than to remount Titan and ride as fast as he could from this place of disease and rot. He would not though. He had a job to do.

Adelaide suddenly tugged urgently at Simeon's sleeve and pointed silently ahead of them. A small house of rough wood stood beyond another small clump of trees, and Adelaide's attention had been caught by something which immediately drew Simeon's curiosity as well: a faint, flickering light – as if emanated by a candle – was shining from within through an open window.

The two remained silent. Simeon was aware that they may not be the only ones here for the Cardinal, and he reflected too late that it may have been more prudent to have approached more inconspicuously, but he was sure that what they sought was within that hut.

They crossed the small central square and paused at the door. They looked at each other, deep into one another's eyes. This was what they had been working towards, all this time. Simeon's breath caught in his throat as he looked into Adelaide's eyes and saw his own fears and uncertainties reflected back at him. Then Adelaide placed her hand on the wooden handle and turned it. They entered.

Inside, the house was barren and cold. There was little in the way of furniture, but a small bed was situated at the far end with what appeared to be someone laying beneath a woollen patchwork quilt. Adelaide approached slowly, making no sound, and leant over the bed. She turned immediately and beckoned Simeon forward and he joined her, looking down into the face of a pale woman with what appeared to be a severe fever. Her forehead was beaded with sweat and her breathing came shallow and raspy. She was not conscious, but she shivered involuntarily from within the folds of the quilt. She did not seem old – perhaps thirty years of age – but was haggard and frail in spite of this.

Simeon looked at Adelaide, who shrugged at him in confusion. Why would she stay when all others had fled? One thing was certain: this was not the Cardinal Phantasm.

Then they heard a voice behind them, causing them both to jump in shock. They had seen nobody else upon entering.

'She won't wake. You need to go unless you want to end up the same.'

They turned and saw a boy. Young, probably no more than twelve or thirteen. He had thick blond hair that framed his face, but which was shaggy and unkempt, and deep turquoise eyes which stared at them in fear and uncertainty from across the small room. Simeon looked uncertainly at him. Yes, he was young, but he had an ancient soul, that was clear. His eyes held fear, but also knowledge, wisdom, tragedy, the horrors of millennia and the atrocities of generations of despicable men. What had this boy seen? Who was he? Where had he come from?

'Go!'

It was a command. Simeon suddenly felt his stomach lurch, his heart race and he was nearly sick where he stood. He needed to get out, this aura was killing him from the inside out and he felt sweat spring up on his face as he began shivering uncontrollably. In his haze, he looked up at the boy and realised with a jolt: *he* was doing this!

He was a fool to not have realised it immediately. They had come this far, and their goal sat mere feet away. The Cardinal Phantasm. And yet, he found it entirely impossible to take another step forwards. The room began to spin and his vision blurred further as he sank to his knees, a pain swelling behind his temple, threatening to cleave his skull in two. Why was this happening?

Adelaide walked slowly across the room, holding her hands up above her head in a sign of peace. She appeared unaffected by the swell of nausea which was afflicting Simeon and the boy flinched away from her as though he expected her to strike him. An aura of scarlet light licked around him as he stared fearfully at her, but he did not move. He simply watched her draw nearer and when she finally knelt beside him and placed a gentle hand on his shoulder, he sobbed and collapsed into her shoulder.

The awful sensations plaguing Simeon disappeared instantly. He panted in the dark, regaining his composure, as the young boy shuddered in Adelaide's arms and heartwrenching sobs racked through his entire body.

Then Simeon felt something completely different. A wave of fear, pure and cold, rushed over him and he felt tears well up in his eyes. Hateful voices echoed around the small room and screamed sadistic abuse at him. He could not make out any individual words, but they terrified him as he realised they would kill him when they got the chance. Why did they hate him so much?

It's because you're different from them.

He heard this voice clearly above the din of the others. It was spiteful, mean and full of poison and malice. Where would he go? He wanted to be safe. Why would they not let him be happy with his mother?

Simeon opened his eyes and found that he was flat on

his back in the dark room. The shadows of the rafters were above him and as he sat up he felt warmth re-enter his body. What had that been?

He crawled over to Adelaide and sat beside her. She still cradled the boy who wept silently in her arms.

'I've...I've never felt anything like that before in my life!' Simeon panted.

Adelaide looked at him and he saw that she was crying too.

'I have,' she whispered. Pain and sorrow filled her eyes, but Simeon still did not understand.

'For whatever reason, I did not feel the sickness which engulfed you,' she said. 'Why? I don't pretend to understand that, but I did have the honour of experiencing what you felt just now. Oh yes,' she continued as he opened his mouth to argue, 'it was an honour for us to feel what he has felt. He shared with us his pain and his anguish. He trusts us. I imagine it was a shock for you, but there was a chilling familiarity to it for me – it is the worst fear of anyone who is secretly different, and the tragic reality for many who are discovered.'

At length, the boy calmed down and looked at them both, eyes red with sorrow.

'You're the first person who I haven't made sick!' he whispered at Adelaide, the hint of hope in his hollow voice. 'Mother stayed with me – everyone else is gone – but she's sick and I can't wake her up!'

'Don't worry – we're not going to leave you! If you stay calm and happy, you'll never make anyone sick again. She'll get better now, I promise.'

She spoke softly, motherly, a gentle embrace to a scared child. Simeon did not know how she knew all of this, but he knew instinctively that she was right. She looked at Simeon and smiled, shrugging. She had no idea how she knew this either, but she also knew it was true. She would not lie to this boy.

'They left us both here,' he continued. 'They called me a freak, they said that evil would follow me, that I needed cleansing. They tried to take me away, but mother stopped them.' His voice cracked again and he dissolved into renewed sobs. 'Now I've killed her!'

'Listen,' insisted Adelaide, cupping his chin and raising his face so that he could see hers, 'I can't promise that everything will be fine now, but I can promise that Simeon and I will protect you and keep you as safe as we can. You have our word on that, you're not alone anymore!'

'I was never alone!' the boy insisted, suddenly sitting up. 'Mother has never left me, and I will not leave her!'

Simeon looked at Adelaide with concern. She shook her head surreptitiously at him. She would deal with this.

'What's your name?' she asked him.

'Tristan,' he replied. He hugged Adelaide again, then got to his feet and held out a pale, bony hand to Simeon. 'Nice to meet you.'

Simeon took the hand without hesitation and shook it. It was surprisingly hot. Simeon regarded Tristan with interest. Yes, he was undoubtedly the Cardinal Phantasm, but he was also a boy, caught between clinging to the comfort of a mother's embrace and the desire to be a man. What had this poor child been through? Unfortunately, Simeon knew exactly what he had been through and resolved more than ever to ensure that it never happened again.

'It's a pleasure to meet you, young man,' replied Simeon, smiling reassuringly at him. 'But, if you don't mind me asking, do you fully understand what has been happening to you over the last few weeks? Do you know what is causing this change in you?' he asked.

Adelaide scowled at him and pulled a face. Simeon realised too late that he may have been too blunt and was proven correct when Tristan turned and walked away again. He was not crying anymore at least: the shock of their arrival seemed to have finally worn off.

Eventually he answered. 'Yes...I mean...mostly. The Cardinal speaks to me, but it is so weak. I need to be strong, but it burns inside of me! It doesn't hurt me, you understand – I don't think it would ever hurt me – but the power inside me strains to be released. I think I've known it's been inside me for my entire life, simmering beneath the surface. It can't control the power coming out of me, so I need to do it until the Cardinal gets stronger.

'I know things now. Things that happened so long ago, secrets which nobody living remembers. I see frescos of the past, painted over my eyes when I least expect it, but I don't see them move. Not yet at least. Snatches of the future come to me too, but they are like echoes and shadows, I haven't seen them properly yet. He promises that I will though. When I'm stronger. I'm...I'm scared.'

His last sentence seemed to take all of his strength to utter. He was young and he was ashamed. Simeon could not begin to appreciate how much it must mean to him to find Adelaide – someone who he could be close to without hurting or scaring away. He was only a child, after all.

'We're here now,' said Adelaide, 'and we'll protect you.'

'Promise?' He looked at them from across the room where he stood, an overwhelming desire to trust them on his face but an inescapable fear and doubt still in his eyes.

'I promise. But we need to leave – people are coming who mean you harm. We must get far away from here!' Simeon knew that Adelaide was right: they had lingered here for far too long already. Their current location was the intended nexus for all those who sought the power of the Cardinal, whether for good or nefarious purposes, and they needed to put as much distance between here and themselves as possible before any other interested parties arrived.

'But mother...' he began hurriedly, glancing nervously over at the corner where the bed was situated.

'She's too weak to travel right now, but I promise we will come back for her one day. She is in more danger if you stay, don't you see that? Now come. Time is of the essence – we need to leave. Now!'

Tristan gasped at Adelaide's urgency and he looked for a moment as though he would simply refuse, but then a steely resolve appeared in his eyes and he nodded once. Simeon closed the shutters at the window as Adelaide searched through the cupboards for any food they could salvage. Tristan knelt at his mother's bedside, saying a tearful goodbye. Simeon could not hear the words he used but he would not have listened even if he could. The boy was saying goodbye to the person he loved most. He deserved privacy.

Then they heard it. Horse's hooves galloping closer outside, growing louder each second as they approached along the dirt track through the trees.

'We need to go!' hissed Simeon to Adelaide and Tristan. 'Is there a back way out of here?'

'There's a cellar we can escape through,' whispered Tristan, fear catching his voice as he moved with significant reluctance from his mother's bedside and took Adelaide's hand instead. He led her towards a dusky corner and Simeon followed hastily, but Tristan had barely had time to bend and grasp the edges of an old trapdoor hidden in the floorboards before the door to the hut flew open and somebody entered.

Rita.

Simeon merely stared at her, blinking stupidly. She stood in the doorway, spear raised and bitter resentment etched on her face. Eyes empty with contempt stared at Adelaide in the corner and she jumped, diving across the room towards the other woman.

'No!' shouted Simeon, drawing his own weapon and knocking Rita back in mid-leap. She landed elegantly on the dusty floor, crouched and deadly, but then she straightened up and looked at her husband instead.

'I see you're committed to your folly.'

What was she doing here? She must have followed them, Simeon realised. But this was not the time for this – they needed to be gone!

'Rita, I'm sorry!' he cried. 'I do love you, I really do! Part of me will always love you and I am so sorry for what I've done to you. One day, I hope you understand but I don't expect you to ever forgive me. You've changed, Rita! I saw it in your eyes that night! I'm sorry but it's true!'

Rita looked as though she had been slapped in the face. A thousand thoughts were shadows on her face and she looked at him again, eyes flashing with betrayal. 'I've only changed because of what you've done to me!' she screamed, spit flying and face red.

'You've made me like this – you and *her*! Don't you dare blame me for what's happened here, Simeon Castello! Have the guts to tell me to my face that this is *your* fault – that you alone have broken our marriage for a flight of fancy!' And with that she leaped again, barrelling into Simeon with an unexpected force which sent him tumbling backwards as she raised her spear again, bearing down on Adelaide.

Adelaide was too fast though. She pushed Tristan away, sending him too sailing across the room as she drew Father, parrying the spear blow and twirling into a counter. Simeon watched from the floor as steel clashed against steel, both women swirling around each other, quite evenly matched. They rebounded from walls and rolled across the floor, Adelaide's wings buffeting the air to stay upright as Rita's attacks became more and more frenzied, spear jabbing here and there, only to be deflected. Simeon did not dare try and intervene: the dance was too erratic to know whether he would simply cause more harm. He watched on powerlessly as they clashed.

At great length, they both began to slow. Exhaustion was causing both women to make mistakes and it was at that moment when Adelaide landed a blow, slicing a deep cut into Rita's forearm which flowed with crimson blood as she howled in anger. She looked at Adelaide with pure hatred and thrust her spear one last time with all her might, straight for the leathery black wing stretched out to Adelaide's left.

'No!' shouted Simeon and Tristan together.

Rita faltered. She shuddered, gasped, then dropped her spear with a cry of despair. She sunk to her knees, panting breathlessly as Adelaide staggered away to the other side of the room.

Simeon crawled over to Rita and tentatively put one arm around her heaving shoulders.

'You did this to me!' she coughed, looking at him with streaming eyes as she struggled to catch her breath. 'Don't ever think any different! I don't even blame *her* – I blame you! I love you, but I hate you! I can't bear to have you near me, and yet I can't even bring myself to push you away! I followed you here. Why? Because I was stupid enough to expect that you'd change your mind when you saw me. That was my mistake, obviously!'

She stood up and retrieved her spear from the floor. Simeon tensed, but she did nothing with it. 'I love you,' she repeated, 'but I see now that there is no spell. This is love.' One last tear fell from her eye as she sighed and turned to walk away.

'Rita, I'm sorry...' began Adelaide, but Rita turned suddenly and cut across her immediately.

'Don't presume to speak to me! Not after what you've done! I might blame him more than you, but this would never have happened if you had not come along! You were my friend...' her voice faltered as she turned away again, but her eyes wandered to the corner and rested on Tristan.

'Is that...' she asked. She looked to Simeon and he nodded silently.

'I...I didn't expect it to be a child. I mean, I knew it was young but seeing him here...it's a 'he', not an 'it'. To think what we were going to do to him…'

'You've reached the same conclusion as us then,' said Adelaide softly. Rita glared at her but did not say anything.

'Rita, we really need to go. You know as well as us that he will never be safe here! I love you, and I am so sorry for what I've - we've – done to you, but there is no solution which will make every one of us happy. Believe me, if there was then I'd do it, but there isn't. I'm sorry.'

Rita looked from Simeon, to Adelaide, to Tristan. She sighed, tired and defeated. 'You really do love each other?'

Adelaide said nothing. Simeon nodded.

'Then go. Save him. I won't say anything of this to anyone. You're right – he will never be safe unless you go. Of this, at least, we can agree. I only ask one thing in return: if you ever come to your senses, and realise what a mistake you've made, please never come looking for me. I don't think I could survive the heartbreak of losing you a second time.'

Simeon tried to speak, to say some words of thanks, but she turned and walked out of the open door. A small part of him wished he could call her back, to end on happier terms, but he knew in his heart that he had hurt her beyond recognition. She would never be his Rita again, and there could never be a happy ending for their story, but maybe they could find one apart. Two separate stories. Simeon knew he had found his already. He crossed the room to help Adelaide to her feet and embraced her tightly. They separated slightly and then he leant in to kiss her. This kiss did not feel stolen or sordid, it felt pure and true.

'I love you,' he whispered in her ear.

'And I love you back,' she replied with a playful smile.

This calm was short-lived, however. They barely had minutes to recover and open the trapdoor to the cellar before Rita was back, slipping in through the door and urgently shutting and bolting it behind her.

'Someone's here!' she hissed at them in alarm. As she

said it, Simeon's stomach lurched as he heard more galloping approaching them up the dirt track and Tristan gasped softly as it came to an abrupt halt in the square outside.

They froze, holding a collective breath as they heard a heavy thud and knew that someone had dismounted. There was only one reason why somebody would be this far out in the wilderness. The four looked at each other from their various positions in the room. Adelaide reached over and took Tristan's hand. Rita stood beside the door, looking thoroughly uncomfortable at finding herself back here and yet committed to the cause. Simeon had a thousand thoughts racing through his head. Who was this? Friend or foe? Could they escape? *How* would they escape?

There was silence outside for several long minutes, then Simeon gasped as the doorknob began to turn. This quickly devolved into rough shoves on the door as the mysterious newcomer realised that it was bolted and began attempting to force it in. This then progressed to brutal thrashing as the entire weight of a body was thrown against it and the door shook on its hinges, groaning in protest.

Simeon leaped into action.

'You need to go now!' he stammered at Adelaide, rushing silently over to her. 'Take Tristan and go! Get him as far from here as possible. I'll catch up somehow, but you won't make it far unless I stay to buy you time!'

'We'll all stay!' she insisted.

'Don't be silly, we can't put him at risk,' he shot back, gesturing at Tristan. 'He trusts you, he needs you! Get him to safety, as far from here as you can! Rita, please go with them.'

Rita balked. 'Don't be so stupid! I'm not going with *her*; I'll stay here and fight alongside you!'

'They need your help more than I do. Adelaide can't fight if she's looking after the boy, there's nobody I'd trust them with more than you! Please, Rita, you say you don't wish to see the boy hurt and abused as we planned, this is your chance to do something about it! Please, do this for me, as one last gesture that our love was real!'

She hesitated, then turned and headed for the trapdoor without another word.

Simeon took one last look at his wife. He did truly love her. He always would.

Adelaide embraced him and quaked in his arms as tears fell freely down her cheeks. He felt himself begin to weep as his lips met hers. He did not know if he would ever see her again, but a righteous fire blazed in him and he reflected that he knew he was doing the right thing.

He felt his love being wrenched from his arms as the pounding on the door became a deafening crash after crash. Rita grabbed Adelaide and dragged her down the trapdoor. He saw the top of her black hair streaked with silver disappear through the hole as he raised Cumulonimbus, planting his feet and prepared to fight. His tears flowed freely but he blinked them away as the door suddenly splintered into pieces, swinging off its rusty hinges and crashing to the floorboards.

A black cloak, a shining sword, a shadow-filled hood.

And a gleaming silver chest plate.

The newcomer saw the open trapdoor and charged towards it, howling like a wounded beast. Simeon launched himself in his path, bringing the colossal Cumulonimbus swinging around to meet him. The cloaked figure ducked, pivoted and parried with his silver sword, striking back with an animalistic force that sent Simeon staggering back, barely holding on to his weapon. The figure made another move on the trapdoor but Simeon rallied his strength and pounced again, grabbing his cloak and swinging him around, raising his sword to attack as he staggered. He swung with all his might and, as he did, the figure ducked and lost balance. His hood slipped and his face was revealed.

A man to be sure, but older than Simeon had expected

and certainly older than his strength and speed belied. His long greying hair was tangled and matted, as though he had given up on caring for it, but his complexion was full and healthy and spoke of wealth. His face contorted in rage as he lunged at Simeon again and dove beneath his swing, tackling him to the ground.

Simeon felt all the air thrust from his lungs; he gasped for breath and choked in pain. His attacker rose and reclaimed his sword, raising it for the killing blow. Simeon could do nothing to stop him.

And then he heard footsteps in the doorway. The cloaked man turned to meet the newcomers and the room exploded into pandemonium.

CHAPTER TWENTY-THREE

Into the old house in the swamps rushed five travelling companions and a dog.

After an unyielding journey across the Northern Realm, plagued by haste and grief, Alene Idir and her party had finally reached their destination of Mort Vivant and had rushed towards the unmistakable sound of trouble as swords clashed and howls of rage pierced the evening. Sounds of that sort meant one thing to Alene: they were in the right place!

Alene thundered through the remains of the shattered door, Prija and Roan at her side, to be confronted by the hulking silhouette of a tall figure.

A figure with a silver breastplate.

'You!' she gasped, drawing both swords as Prija and Roan armed themselves beside her.

She glared through the shadows at the man who had pursued them across the entire Eastern Dominion. As her sharp eyes grew accustomed to the darkness faster than the others however, her jaw dropped open and her eyes opened wide in shock.

'It can't be!' she whispered. 'It's not possible!'

He moved into the candlelight and Roan gasped too. 'Saggion?'

Chief Minister Saggion stood before them, silver sword raised. Gerecht's most trusted councillor, the man who had been a father figure to him his entire life – and to Alene since she had joined the royal court all those years ago – was someone she was simply not prepared to see here tonight. Her brain struggled to catch up, to comprehend what she was seeing.

'Your Majesty,' he panted. 'This man was attempting to arrest the Cardinal Phantasm!'

Alene lowered her swords, but Roan and Prija did not. Griffin remained tensed behind her and Hündin growled low and fierce.

'His Majesty will be so pleased to hear of your safety!' Saggion said, panting still but not, Alene noted suddenly, lowering his sword.

Alene felt her suspicion rising, the longer she looked at him. Why was Saggion here? If he and Gerecht had taken over from Alene and her companions in their task of protecting the Cardinal Phantasm when they assumed them dead at the Schloss Stieg then why had he been following them since the day after their departure from Regenbogen? And she recalled the words of the geiste as they fled Clagcowl Abbey: *Those who seek the power of the Cardinal will rip the divide between worlds. They must be stopped. They are known to you. They follow you wherever you go. The master and the servant come together and go together. Stop them – they are known to you.*

None of this added up, no matter how many different ways Alene attempted to justify it. This man, a man whom she loved and trusted as a father, had terrorised her from a distance as she had attempted to undertake an impossible task for the good of all, risking her life. And, if Saggion were the servant, where was the master? Alene did not think she could stomach the answer – she had already begun to dread in her soul what she knew to be the truth – but she heard herself asking the question anyway.

'Saggion, where is Gerecht?'

He looked at her but did not answer.

'You've been following us for so long – why did you not reveal yourself to us?'

'Your Majesty, this man must be apprehended!' he insisted, pointing at the man whom Alene did not recognise, climbing up from the floor and regaining his sword.

Why was he not answering her? She was asking simple questions. Where was her love, her husband, her king? The Saggion she knew would not leave his master – he had never done so, as long as she had known him.

'You came here for the Cardinal…but not to protect him, did you Saggion?'

Saggion took a step towards her, his sword still raised, but Prija and Roan both took a step forward too.

'Come quietly, Saggion,' said Roan slowly, Reaper in each hand. 'We're escorting you back to King Gerecht under charge of treason!'

He laughed. A cold, callous laugh that Alene had never heard from the wise old councillor. 'You have no idea what you are talking about! I will find the young Cardinal and present him to my king, and I shall march proudly by his side into the next world!'

Alene did not take in what she was hearing, she only knew that Saggion must be stopped. She dove at him, as did the others. She raised Dawn to deliver a swipe to his shoulder – and her attack never made contact. It passed through him as if he were mist and she stumbled forward. The form of the chief minister faded and died. A glamour.

The sudden sound of hooves retreating told Alene everything she needed to know. She did not know what it was, whether her suspicions had finally caught up with her conscious thought or whether it was the sound of him retreating which caused her to fly into a maddening frenzy, but Alene tore across the room and was out in the square before anyone could stop her. A crazed haze of betrayal and humiliation had descended upon her and she would not let him get away – not without answers!

There! At the far end of the open square, cape whipping out of sight into the shadows of the dense trees, she saw him. Alene did not think – she merely felt all of her rage channelled into a black fireball in her outstretched hands and she hurled it with all of her might. It streaked across the square, past the diseased tree, past the gnarled statue and struck its target in a fiery black explosion. She had never stopped sprinting and reached the tree line to see a white horse, rearing in fear as magical flames caught the dry trees. There was no sign of her quarry though and she charged on, intent on catching him. Anger burned in her soul as she realised he must have been thrown from the saddle by her attack and she ran faster than ever. She heard splashing to her left and changed course, ducking and thrusting her way through the undergrowth.

She reached a foul-smelling bog amidst the trees and paused for breath. The air in her lungs burned with each breath and she was panting heavily. Her eyes raked the tree line, penetrating the gloom for any sign of her prey.

Suddenly, Alene saw it: a glint of silver in the blackness. She felt her humiliation and heartbreak swell as she barrelled through vines and thick grass, avoiding low branches as she saw him ahead, leaning on one knee and panting laboriously. He saw her and tried to rise, turning his back to her as he fled, but he was too tired and Alene was merciless. One more black fireball hit him between his shoulder blades and he fell forward onto the marshy ground, groaning in pain and defeat.

Alene stood over him, breathing deeply yet triumphantly. Slowly, with apparent difficulty, he stood and turned to face her. She scowled at the face which she had so often smiled at with love and warmth. Now she saw only the betrayal and hurt he had inflicted upon her. She could still not comprehend what had occurred over the last few minutes, but she knew that she needed to find out.

'Saggion! As your queen I demand that you tell me what

your purpose here is!' she snarled at him. He looked at her without expression and her anger reared inside her. 'Tell me the truth, Saggion! Who did you come here to capture the Phantasm for: yourself or our king?'

He smirked. 'Oh, young Alene, I am so proud to see your slumbering potential finally awaken! I have watched you for so many years and waited. I must admit, His Majesty and I had begun to worry that your arcane skills would not manifest on schedule, but I am satisfied to see that we were wrong to be anxious.'

This made even less sense to Alene. Gerecht and Saggion had known about her magic all along? No, that simply could not be true!

Saggion seemed to read her mind and he smirked again. 'Oh yes indeed, we knew! It's been quite the long game, you see – King Gerecht's acquisition of the Cardinal Phantasm. You won't have seen of course, but a new Cardinal is always and without exception in a very fragile state of mind when they manifest. That has the potential to rip people apart who come too close, so an individual with strong magical ability – internal, mind you, not human like mine – would be needed to make first contact and secure their cooperation.'

Alene gaped at him. What was he saying? 'And that...that was...?'

'To be your role? Yes,' finished Saggion with another smile, although this one seemed more pitying than any other. 'I valued the direct approach, I must tell you. I felt that, with the right incentive, you would come to value our plan as much as we did, I advised that we indoctrinate you as early as possible after the wedding, but Gerecht always believed that your unusually strong morality would prevent this, so he kept you in the dark. Believe me, we never believed that you – a strong half breed with powerful magic and a human need to interfere with the world which, quite frankly, pure elves simply lack – would fail the task and necessitate that I step forward to finish it! I was to observe you on your mission, nothing more. Keep a check on your progress. I admit that we were foolish not to anticipate interference from third parties – the so-called Republic of Caterva has been a particular thorn in our side! But it will be no matter in the end.'

Saggion paused. Alene could hear no sounds behind her: she supposed that she must have run further than she had realised and got lost amongst the dense foliage. Alene was still struggling to comprehend everything she was hearing. 'Hang on,' she said, furrowing her brow and forcing herself to concentrate through the raw emotions pumping through her body, 'Are you telling me that you *selected* me? My heritage – what, you considered me a perfect breed? But I saved Gerecht – and you – that day on the road from the bandits! Gerecht invited me to Regenbogen and we fell in love! No, you didn't select me! We fell in love!' She was crying now, tears of anguish flowing down her mottled face as she began to fear something which she had never feared before: had everything she had felt for him been false?

'It is true, indeed, that the king came to feel a fondness for you in recent years,' said Saggion, emotionless again, 'but not from the beginning I'm afraid. You were hand-selected, my dear, and you walked into our trap on that day with the bandits. We played a risky game, I admit, using ourselves as bait, but I assure you that we were never in any real danger. And besides, we caught you, did we not, my queen?'

Alene felt sick. And yet there was a thin sliver of doubt in her heart – a hope she held on to feverishly. What if Saggion was lying? Gerecht might not be involved at all! He might need her, be in danger!

'Don't feel a fool, my queen,' he continued, beginning to take slow steps backwards, towards the trees. 'You are not the only one to have been deceived. Only Rowena, the Rose Queen, has ever truly suspected His Majesty – and she has done everything in her power to thwart us for years!

'Now, Your Majesty, I fear I must be gone – those friends of yours will simply not understand. But it's not the end for you, Alene! It is true, Gerecht began your relationship with impure intentions, but he cares deeply for you! Come with me, you have great power which I could help to nurture. This world is dying Alene, and our plan will not fail! Join us and help us break through to the next world, where even more power awaits us! You could be glorious – resplendent in your power and might!'

Alene took one step back – how could he possibly think she would listen to him after all he had told her? But then she thought of Gerecht: she could see him again, after all these weeks, and force him to tell her it was all a bad dream – that he still loved her and that they could return to Regenbogen as king and queen, husband and wife. He would love her. She would be loved.

She took a step forward.

'Alene, my love!'

The voice came from the darkness to her left. She did not dare believe her ears and so she slowly – slowly – took her gaze from Saggion and looked into the deep shadows which came with nightfall. It was him, her love, her whole world, Gerecht. He had come to save her, to make everything alright again. She could barely believe what she was seeing and all urgency and sadness at the world left her shoulders in an instant. She wanted to rush at him and let him envelop her in his warm embrace, wipe all the evils of the world away, but something held her where she stood. She beamed at him, tears of joy flowing and her heart feeling lighter than it had in weeks.

'Go with him, my love. Go with Saggion and we can be together again! We will rule together, just as we did, as we will forever!' His voice was warm, affectionate and caring. But it also felt distant, indistinct as though Alene were hearing it echoing down a long tunnel. She furrowed her brow: that did not seem right.

Then she looked closer. The king was tall, regal and strong. His hair was long and full, thick waves of chestnut flowing down his back and his face radiated with a flush of health. No, this was not right. She loved Gerecht, she saw him this way every day in her mind's eye, saw the man he was on the inside, but this was not the true likeness of the King of the Eastern Dominion. In reality, Gerecht was weak, sickly and frail.

'It's not you…is it?' she asked quietly. What was she saying? Was she throwing away her chance to rejoin her love?

He stood, still and silent. He smiled, but it was hollow and empty.

'Alene?'

Alene jumped and spun around to her right. Another figure was emerging from the darkness and Alene held her breath, recognising the voice but not prepared for what she was about to see.

'Alene, I've been looking for you for so long!'

Nox stood at the tree line on the very edge of Alene's vision. She looked as she always had: travelling cloak long and worn, emerald eyes which shone with adventure. Her hair was long and chestnut, just like Gerecht's, but hers hung around her face and framed her playful smile.

'Nox – I'm so sorry!' sobbed Alene, wanting again to approach but not quite managing it. 'I'm so sorry we went to that awful place! I'm sorry you died – it's my fault, you came to help me!'

Her oldest friend stood there, feet from her. Her heart swelled with sadness and she cried in sharp, painful gasps as she grieved for her. 'Who will I have now? I miss you Nox! Why did you have to leave me? I loved you as a sister – I need you to know that! We were the family we chose together, right?'

'I'm here now, and I don't need to go away,' Nox replied, smiling sadly at her. She reached out from across the clearing and Alene would have sworn that she felt a warm hand stroke her cheek, but Nox was much too far away to do that. 'You need to go with him,' she continued. 'Together you can use your magic for new purposes! You can bring me back, then we can be a family again! Go with Saggion, Alene – go with him.'

Alene smiled and turned back to Saggion, standing opposite her, flanked now by her husband and her friend. She took another step forward.

Then she stopped.

This was not right. Nox would not embrace magic for such a purpose. She had begun to accept Alene's magic towards the end, true enough, but she would rather remain dead than have herself wrenched back from death by arcane spells or black magic. Alene knew this as a certainty!

'Nox...you're not really here, are you?'

Nox's expression suddenly twisted grotesquely. 'It's your fault I'm dead!' she spat maliciously. 'Come with us now! We will not stop until we have the power to put right all the wrongs that our Empire is plagued with, and all the other worlds as well!'

'Come with us,' repeated Gerecht, 'I was vulnerable once – I won't ever let that happen again, no matter the cost! Help us!'

Alene looked from one face to the next. Three faces, all so painfully familiar. And yet, each one a mask, a distorted and twisted imitation. She took a strangled breath. She was drowning, fighting to reach the surface as the fog choked and restrained her frantic mind.

'None of you...none of you are real!' she choked. She looked at Saggion, face racked with concentration, and she suddenly understood.

This was him. All him. She saw it back in the hut – a glamour, a deception. How was he doing this?

He dared to mock her with Nox's shade? Everything which had happened – her pain, her death, this was his fault!

Her husband was not here…he did not even love her. She had been used…manipulated. The two people she loved most in the world were gone…taken from her…an iron fist had punched a hole in her chest and was slowly but sadistically gripping her heart, squeezing it tight in a vice of ice.

The fog grew thicker, her stomach heaved. Her tears scalded her cheeks as they cut rivers down her grey face. She was alone again. Alene felt herself spiral, into a darkness of grief and despair. The clearing dimmed, blurred and span maniacally and her broken vision came to rest on Saggion, still staring at her with a grim expression. She hated him. He had done this to her.

'Come with me,' he said one more time.

'No!'

The word exploded from her mouth and, in that instant, Alene Idir was gone. In her place was a beast of rage, a creature of darkness and sorcery. The fury and savagery of her wrath seized control of her body and she twisted in bizarre and abnormal shapes, raising her arms high above her head. She heard chanting: a strange and foreign tongue which she did not recognise but which she knew was coming from her own mouth.

Her feet left the wet ground. She rose higher, slowly, her boots hovering only inches from the ground but it was enough to make Saggion freeze, fear creeping into his eyes for the first time. The illusions beside him flickered and died.

Alene's skin began to smoke. Black, monstrous tendrils of putrid black mist oozed out from every pore and encircled her, licking the ground and causing the grass at her feet to wither and die, yellow and dry. It wreathed her, smooth and ghostly, and as she opened her eyes – completely crimson now and glowing with cruelty – the dark fog crept forwards towards her hated prey. It slid silently across the ground, strangling all life as it closed in.

Suddenly, it appeared to change and instead moved swiftly and with menacing crackles. It shot toward Saggion, tentacles of smoke thrashing and brutal. They weaved around him, poised to deliver death.

But he merely laughed. His composure regained, he stood amidst the deadly fog, surveying Alene. 'Did you wonder why I chose to wear such conspicuous protection? This armour, My Queen, will not allow your darkness to approach or infect me. There is nothing you can do!'

But then he fell. As the fog dispersed to nothing and Alene fell with a crash to the ground, her legs giving way beneath her, she shook her head groggily and looked at Saggion from where she lay in the mud. He was already staggering to his feet, an arrow protruding from his right shoulder. His face was a grimace of pain and as white as death.

Alene could not find the strength to stand. She cried out as every joint flared and her limbs trembled as she tried to put weight on them. She heard running behind her and Roan flung himself to the ground beside her. A quick glance and a hand on her shoulder were all he had time for however, as he raised Reaper and let loose another arrow. This one did not make contact though, it sailed through Saggion as he faded into darkness. Alene groaned and lay back down in bitter defeat. The true Saggion was gone. He had escaped.

Alene had barely looked up into Roan's concerned face when she felt exhaustion blurring the edges of her vision and she slipped into unconsciousness.

CHAPTER TWENTY-FOUR

I t was the following midday before Alene stirred this time. She lay groggily, staring up at the ceiling of the dusty, threadbare hut for a long time before anybody noticed she had awoken. She could hear voices not too far off but they were disconnected, as though multiple unrelated conversations were occurring at once. She forced her addled brain to concentrate but it throbbed in protest.

What had happened? Over the next few minutes, it began to come back to her. First in irregular drips, then a steady stream as memories of the previous night seeped back into the nausea of her consciousness, eventually becoming a raging torrent as inescapable waves of heartache and anguish washed over Alene and threatened to engulf her forever.

She gasped lightly and raised a hand to brush the tears away which had escaped her dark, almond eyes. Her husband was not the man she thought he was. Had he ever been? She felt used, abused and manipulated. Had he ever grown to love her truly? She did not know the truth; she did not even know if she cared anymore. But still, amid the murky quagmire of her uncertainty and grief, a shining pool of crystal-clear hope existed – tiny but undeniably pure and untainted – which held on to the lingering possibility that Saggion might be wrong, that Gerecht was not involved in this at all, that her love was real.

She had slept for a long time. Why? She thought back, forcing the grinding in her head to subside as she turned back the clock in her memory. She saw a horrifying fog, a deadly cloud emanating from her and gliding across the swampy ground like an ethereal black cloak. She had done that, but she had no idea how. She did not even know she had been capable of such abominable arts, for this was clearly magic of the blackest nature. How had this burst from her? Where had it come from? Why? She would not think of that now – it was simply a step further than she was willing to go at present. However, she knew that a day would come soon when she would have to answer these questions. Not now though. Please not now.

She sat up. The small room looked completely different in the light of day. The sunlight was dappled and green but still bright enough at this hour to light up the whole room, and Alene used it to survey her surroundings. The bed in the corner was still occupied by a fair young woman, but she dozed upright now, propped up on a pillow with her patchwork quilt draped loosely over her lap. Roan, Prija and the stranger whom they had encountered the previous night were sat at a scrubbed wooden table in the corner but were so deep in conversation that they did not notice her sit up.

Unlike Roan and Prija, the stranger was wearing a thick travelling cloak and appeared tired and grimy. Alene listened without making a sound.

'I searched all night,' she heard him say mournfully to Roan and Prija, 'but I couldn't find any sign of Adelaide, Rita or Tristan beyond the edge of the swamps. They've taken Betty and Enchantress but Rita grew up in the north - she's uncannily skilled at avoiding detection and will be doing everything she can to stop our enemy from following her and capturing the Phantasm. I need to trust that they can look after each other, but I've nowhere to go now, my path is as unclear as it has ever been.'

These names meant nothing to Alene, but the mention of the Cardinal caught her attention. She rose slowly, holding her head, and as she did, she heard excited barking behind her. She turned to see Hündin running through the open door and she jumped up at her happily, licking every part of her she could reach. This made the others turn.

'Alene!' exclaimed Roan, rising immediately and helping her over to a vacant seat at the table. Griffin and Lionel entered from outside and joined them, Griffin looking as angry and inconsolable as he had done ever since they had left the mountains.

Alene looked around at the anxious faces, all turned towards her. How much did they know? Then Prija spoke.

'I've filled them in, Alene.'

Alene did not understand what she meant. 'What? How do you...?'

'I've known all along,' she answered in a rush, looking away from Alene as she did.

'I'm...I'm sorry, Alene! I know you don't want to hear this, but it's all true. When we first met, I assumed you were involved – the Republic has known what Gerecht has had planned for a while, we have spies everywhere! By the time I knew I could trust you, you'd just lost your oldest friend. You weren't ready to lose your husband too! This was not the way I wished to repay my debt to you for saving my life, countless times – I promise! I can see now that I've caused more trouble by shielding you from the truth, but you've shown me more tolerance and acceptance than anyone else I've ever met, and I won't forget that! My allegiance is with you all, please accept my apology.'

Prija turned away, blushing, and stood up to leave the table. Alene reached out a hand and grasped her wrist, stopping her and making her sit down. The unlikely friendship had begun in unusual circumstances but had grown, somewhat reluctantly and hesitantly, over the previous days. Prija eyed Alene uncertainly, searching her face for a flicker of understanding. Alene thought she understood and smiled uncertainly at her. They were all together now, that was what mattered. It had to be, otherwise Alene did not think she could cope.

'My husband...the king...Gerecht...it appears that he is our true enemy,' sighed Alene, looking down at her fingers as she wrung them apprehensively. She could feel all eyes on her again, but still dared to hope that she was wrong – so desperately wrong. '*The master and the servant come together and go together.* That's what the geiste told me. It makes sense I suppose. I feel like such a fool!'

'So now we've got King Gerecht *and* Queen Rowena to worry about?' asked Lionel, his brow furrowed as he considered the implications of what he was hearing.

'It would appear so,' said the newcomer. He turned to Alene and spoke directly to her. 'Your Majesty, my name is Simeon Castello, formerly the Captain of Ville Fleurie. My people and I were sent to acquire the Cardinal for Queen Rowena, but through a series of circumstances...more now than I can even make sense of...I realised that what I was being asked to do was not right or moral. We planned to leave The Empire with the Cardinal Phantasm and take him far from here, to keep him away from Rowena and whatever she had planned for him – he was only a child! We couldn't just let her take him!'

There were understanding nods from the others at this, but something stirred in the recesses of Alene's memory and she shook her head. 'No, I think you're wrong. Last night, Saggion told me that Rowena had suspected Gerecht for years, that everything she did was to prevent his success. I don't think he had any reason to lie about that, could it be true that she is actually not our enemy after all?'

Simeon looked at her, ashen-faced, as though the earth was being pulled out from beneath his feet. Alene turned to Prija who looked at her again and shrugged. 'The Republic have long suspected Rowena – they even have a spy within her most trusted council – but I suppose it is possible...'

Simeon shot her a mistrusting look. 'The Republic of Caterva have a spy in Ville Fleurie? Who?'

Prija smirked and shook her head. 'That's definitely not need-to-know at present and, considering it would ensure decisive retribution for me which would almost certainly result in my eventual assassination, I will keep that secret to myself for now. Rest assured though,' she added, looking to Alene, 'that anything I can divulge which *will* help us in any way, I will do so immediately and without question. I know how to earn loyalty.'

Alene acknowledged this with a nod and voiced the question she had been forming in her head. 'If all of this is true, then Gerecht must mean to eventually amass an army. If it is true that he wishes to march into the next world – whatever that even means! – and that an army which marches with the power he craves at its head is rendered unbeatable, then he must first gather men to create one. I know the people of the Eastern Dominion – they would never join this lunacy! This is one part amidst all of this insanity which I can't rationalise away with a ridiculous answer.'

'There is a suspicion,' Prija said slowly, 'that he has recruited the Wærloga.'

Nobody spoke. The Wærloga were warlocks who practiced black magic but were traditionally enemies of Regenbogen. It seemed beyond possibility that Gerecht would ally with them, but she was beginning to realise with dawning numbness that she did not really know her husband at all.

'So, what now?' asked Roan to the room at large.

Nobody had an answer to this, and a silence loomed. Finally, it was Lionel who answered.

'We need to fight!' he said from his position on the floor. Hündin lay on him with her head in his lap and her tail flopped from side to side as he scratched her ears, but his face was deadly serious. 'We can't let Gerecht or Saggion get their hands on the Cardinal! We need to do everything we can to stop that from happening.'

'As I've already said,' said Simeon, 'Adelaide and Rita have him safe! They'll never leave his side, and I know it will be impossible to trace them!'

'Well that's great,' drawled Prija sarcastically, 'but since we've only just met you, you won't be offended if we've got trust issues!'

'Oh, you should *not* be talking!' shot back Griffin, speaking for the first time. 'You knew all along what was truly at play and you said nothing!'

Prija looked like she was ready to fire back, but Alene stood up, taking charge at last.

'Listen, we will not fight amongst ourselves!' She turned to Simeon. 'Can we trust your people to keep the Cardinal safe?'

Simeon nodded. Alene trusted him. She did not know why, but she felt it emanating strongly from within him.

'Right. In that case, we need to make plans. Prija, do you still wish to join our cause? Now is your chance to leave otherwise.'

'I do. We began our alliance – our...friendship – in a slightly unorthodox manner, but I am more than a little shocked to realise that I do truly consider you allies... friends...acquaintances. It appears now that the goals of the Republic and your own are aligned anyway but regardless, I'm here for you Alene.' She smiled. Alene wished she would smile more often.

'We need to know where Saggion has gone.' she told her. 'I am in no doubt that he will eventually lead us back to Gerecht. I need people I trust to find out what is going on - I'll believe nothing until we have hard proof! Griffin, will you go with her?'

Griffin looked as though he may argue but he did not. He nodded and disappeared outside without a word.

'This talk of breaking barriers between worlds is beyond my knowledge, but I need to know more,' she continued to the room at large. 'Roan, we need information.'

He shrugged and shook his head. 'No books in the Regenbogen library ever spoke of such barriers, I'm afraid.' He looked dejected: the library at Regenbogen had never failed him before.

'The Shadow Archives!' said Simeon in excitement. 'They're in Ville Fleurie and contain all the magical knowledge of the Realm, although no one would be seen dead in it – Ville Fleurie is not particularly tolerant of magic.'

'Ooh, you're making us all so eager to go to your amazing city!' said Prija in a stage whisper which every one of them heard clearly.

Alene ignored her. 'I want to avoid Ville Fleurie for now, Simeon, at least until we know Rowena's true allegiance for certain.'

'We could try Woodrow,' suggested Lionel.

'I definitely plan on sending a pigeon to Woodrow as soon as we are able,' answered Alene, 'but we would never make it back over the mountains. Max will assist us, I am sure, but that might be all he can do for now.'

Roan suddenly spoke up. 'I've read of these Shadow Archives. They're a repository of magical knowledge?' he asked Simeon, who nodded. 'Then we need to travel to the source of that knowledge!' He looked at them all, waiting for a response. When none came, he rolled his eyes and continued, perturbed that they had obviously spoiled his dramatic flair. 'Marrowmarsh!'

Alene had been afraid he would say that. She had not been back to Marrowmarsh since her expulsion and she had no desire to return. She heaved a great sigh and nodded. There was wisdom in his words. Besides, if they learned of some way to stop the barriers between worlds being broken, or some way to strengthen them, she would need to learn how to use her magic to do this. What better teachers than the elves themselves?

'If I'm going to Marrowmarsh, you're coming with me!' she said to Roan. 'You're going to be invaluable at finding a solution to our problem, and I doubt that the elves will be forthcoming with their knowledge. There might be lots of reading!'

Roan smirked. 'I think I can manage that.'

'I would like you to accompany us too,' she said to Simeon. 'We need to be as diplomatic as possible with the elves, so it will be beneficial to have representatives from both Regenbogen and Ville Fleurie.'

Simeon nodded. 'I'll do whatever it takes. My wife and my love are both risking their lives to protect the Cardinal Phantasm – I am ready to do my part too!'

Alene was slightly baffled by this response, but was pleased nonetheless. She wished Nox were here – she would have known exactly what to do. She was gone though; they would have to manage without her.

'What about me?' asked Lionel. Hündin barked loudly. They had become very close lately. An inseparable team!

'Lionel, I know you won't like this, but I want you to stay here.' She said softly. He opened his mouth to argue and she raised a hand to stop him. 'No, no, I'll hear nothing against it! We need someone here in case the Cardinal returns with Simeon's people. We've no way to contact them and we need to know if they return!' Alene did not say so, but she also knew that she had asked a lot of the boy already – he had earned this, the end of his journey. He did not look happy though and rose to exit the hut with Hündin at his heels.

They all left the table soon after this. Alene still did not know how to feel, but she had surprised herself by taking charge, finally and assuredly. She had known all along that there would come a time when she could no longer lean on her friends and expect them to help her make every decision, and she supposed that this time had finally come.

They all had a journey ahead of them, possibly longer and more arduous than the one they had just completed, but Alene took solace that somewhere down the road of that journey would be answers – and that was what Alene needed more than any other comfort at this time. She would find her answers, and she would find Gerecht! The silver pool of hope was still shining clear and pure inside her and she held on to that solace with everything she had. She would find him, and she would bring him home.

Their evening meal was a very quiet affair. Considering that they would soon splinter into their separate groups, there was not much in the way of conversation. Alene knew what everyone was thinking – she was thinking it too: would this be the last meal they took together?

Alene sat close by Roan. As he ate, she watched his face and smiled. He truly was her closest and most trusted friend. She may have known Nox the longest, but Roan had been there for her through so much of her more recent past – and she had been there for him in return. She was glad that they could continue to be there for each other on this next stage of their journey; Alene did not think she could bear returning to her ancestral home of Marrowmarsh without Roan by her side. She knew he was anxious for his father, Captain Felix, and what Gerecht's actions could mean for him and their city, and she took his hand in hers, smiling at him. No words were needed.

Roan had not told any of the others about what he had seen in the clearing the previous night: the black fog which she had somehow conjured. He had not mentioned it to her either and she was glad of that. She was sure that she would encounter this nature inside her again and she hoped that Roan would be there for her then too.

And so, the party spent one last night together. This was to be the beginning of a new stage of their adventure, which had suddenly swelled in importance and significance. They had a new adversary, or rather they now actually knew who their adversaries were, although Alene still refused to believe it could be so simple. One thing she was certain of though, was that the consequences of failure were even greater than ever.

At dawn, the small group of travellers broke for the last time. They rode silently away from the house of the Cardinal Phantasm, Lionel waving sadly from the doorway with Hündin sprawled morosely at his feet. They continued in single file until they reached the edge of the swamp and overlooked open fields. Prija and Griffin bade a quiet farewell to Alene and the others – neither being predisposed to shows of emotion – and rode away into the morning mist.

Alene turned her gaze north, Roan and Simeon beside her. The Cardinal Phantasm was out there somewhere, but her mission now pointed her to her past, to Marrowmarsh and, eventually, to her husband. She would come face to face with Gerecht sometime soon, and when she did there would be answers, but until then she had duties to fulfil, people to lead.

Yes, she was a leader but she was a friend as well. She would lead, but it was not a weakness to rely on her friends when she needed them. Indeed, Alene reflected with a smile on her mottled face, she considered it her greatest strength.

She was the Queen of Regenbogen.

But she was more than that.

She was Alene.

EPILOGUE

The Weeping Widow was known throughout The Empire. Not because it was a particularly tall peak of the Rücken – it was in fact only half the height of the Vater Berg – but for its breathtaking waterfall which dove from the crest of a sheer overhanging cliff halfway up its western flank. For nearly three thousand feet it would fall in one sheer drop before plunging into the churning waters of the crystalline pool below. The vapours enveloped the base of the Widow and created a shroud of concealment around it. It truly was a sight to behold.

What was not known throughout The Empire was this: a sprawling warren of caves burrowed their way beyond the falls and into the very roots of the mountain. These caves were encrusted with crystals – the same crystals in fact which dusted the sediment of the river which flowed away from the falls and which were also to be found near the source of the river on the mountainside. The crystals of the cave, however, were not dust or shard but colossal formations of faceted mineral. These crystals had a deep turquoise hue and glowed in the darkness, creating a perpetual half-light. These crystals made this the ideal home for Samael.

The land itself is stitched and held together by magic, and a dedicated few could draw small amounts of this out and mould it to their own ends. Samael was one of those few. All magic came from the ground, and returned to the ground when it was spent, thus maintaining a natural equilibrium. The greatest concentration of magic, however, could be found trapped within these crystals, and it was for this reason why Samael called the Crystal Caves his home.

Every day he would rise and practise his craft. It took considerably less effort to extract magic from this location than anywhere else and thus Samael could practise more without tiring and thus continued to grow in strength and prowess, although he was beginning to slow with age and time. He had heard stories of witches in the mountain passes – far, far above his subterranean dwelling – who crushed and burned the crystals to release a constant stream of magic which could be harnessed with little skill at all. This was considered positively abhorrent by Samael, who believed two things above all else: that the balance of magic in the world must be maintained for all eternity, and that only those who dedicated their lives to the never-ending pursuit and constant exploration of magecraft were worthy enough to reap its rewards.

On this particular morning, Samael had not been practising for long at all. It was a new skill he was attempting; one which Samael was eager to refine. He was so intent on sculpting his intention within him – critical for any spell – that he did not sense the intruders until they had already dismounted outside the entrance and were making their way along the treacherously slick stone ledge around the edge of the pool. He paused; curiosity piqued.

At length, three men entered. Samael frowned: he had only sensed two. All three were soaked from the waterfall's drenching mist but they paid no heed and instead walked directly to Samael who walked forward in kind to receive them.

'Greetings, Lord Samael, I bring communion from Her Majesty, Queen Rowena. I hope we find you well?'

Samael grunted. 'Well enough, but I am no lord – not any more at least, as you well know! I am sceptical that anything you bring from your queen could bring me happiness. What do you have to say? Say it now, quickly, and leave me in peace!'

Samael was no favourite of the Queen of Ville Fleurie, and she was no favourite of his.

'I trust you remember me,' the newcomer continued. 'My name is Sir Augustin Fidèle, Premier of the Saffron Guard, Her Majesty's personal protectors and defence.'

Samael scowled in spite of himself. 'How could I forget, Premier Fidèle? It was, after all, you who escorted me to the palace gate all those years ago upon my banishment, never to return.'

Fidèle had the insolence to blush at this but he continued nonetheless. 'Yes, I remember it well. But regardless, the queen has sent me personally to collect you and return you forthwith to Ville Fleurie. You are needed on a matter of the utmost urgency and discretion.'

It was Samael's turn to blush this time, but not from humility. He could not believe what he was hearing. 'I was banished!' he hissed through gritted teeth. 'Humiliated before the entire court, after devoting my entire life to your city! I concede, the path I wished to take with my craft did not match the vision your queen had for her city after the death of the king – a king, I remind you, who was a great patron of mine for many years! And because of that: banishment!'

Fidèle waited patiently for Samael to finish ranting before taking a deep breath and continuing. 'The Cardinal Phantasm has emerged.'

Samael rolled his eyes. 'Do you think that escaped me? I sensed that had happened weeks ago!'

'But did you also know,' continued Fidèle with considerable patience, 'that King Gerecht of Regenbogen has made clear his intentions to capture the Cardinal, use him to change the prophecy, seize the *Corbeau Cœur* and use it to penetrate the divide?'

This, Samael did not know. He was momentarily speechless, which was a rarity for him, as Samael always had something to say. He recovered and said smoothly, 'How do you know about all of this? You are merely a glorified bodyguard.'

'I am trusted above all others by Her Majesty, and it was necessary that I stress the severity of the situation to you, as I am sure you appreciate that it would be quite impossible for the queen to make this journey to beseech you herself. As to how Queen Rowena knows, rest assured that there is very little which goes on in either Realm or Dominion which does not pass by the ear of my lady. Can we count you as an ally, in agreement at least that this horrific declaration must never come to pass?'

Samael nodded begrudgingly, turning the information over in his head. 'He'll never achieve this! It's a fantasy of a deranged man!' he muttered, almost to himself.

'I would not be so sure,' said Fidèle quietly. 'The rumour which has reached us is that he has enlisted the support of the Wærloga.'

The Wærloga? That did change things.

'Regardless, I shall never set foot in Ville Fleurie again as long as I breathe!' insisted Samael defiantly. 'Banishment has left a bitter taste in my mouth. I hate to think of what has become of the Shadow Archives in my absence!'

'The queen did anticipate this response,' sighed Fidèle, finally showing signs of impatience. 'She acknowledges you as the only person whom she trusts to help her and her people and asks that you put aside your past differences with her for the greater good. In return, she is prepared to reinstate you as the Prime Mage of Ville Fleurie.'

Samael considered this for a moment. Did he want this?

'She also gives me leave to inform you that you need not return to the City of Blossoms immediately, as your purpose lies elsewhere, to the west.'

It did not take long for Samael to deduce what he meant. 'Marrowmarsh? Rowena wants me to visit the elves?'

'There are ways to strengthen the divide, My Queen believes – ways which are only known to those most adept weavers of magic, and she wishes you to discover these and use them to fortify this world, in case King Gerecht does indeed succeed in capturing the Cardinal and retrieving the Corbeau Cœur. Will you accept?'

There it was, the final question. Would he indeed?

'It must be a dark prospect if Rowena is turning to magic,' he said to the head of the Saffron Guard with a bitter grimace. 'Your queen truly is an odious woman, but it would appear it's no longer about her or me, is it? And besides, I want one thing clear – if I am to do this then I want my *pet* back, immediately.'

'That...can be arranged,' replied Fidèle with a look of revulsion.

'Well then,' cried Samael with a sour laugh which echoed around the sparkling cave, 'let it begin.'

Printed in Great Britain
by Amazon